SANTA FE

A Piece of 'Mi Vida'

SANTA FE
A Piece of 'Mi Vida'

A Spaniards Legacy

ERIC SANTIAGO MARTINEZ

Columbus, Ohio

SANTA FE: A PIECE OF 'MI VIDA'
A Spaniards Legacy

Published by **James Martinez**

Copyright © 2023 by **James Martinez**

Library of Congress Control Number: 2022933283

ISBN (hardcover): 9781662939037
ISBN (paperback): 9781662939044
eISBN: 9781662939051

—————————

Santiago's family is multi-generational Spanish who in the late 1500's settled in the Española Valley in Northern New Mexico. Santiago is surrounded by violence and heartbreak. Santiago is caught up in a world defined by a cultural continuum that is driven by Spain's military expansion through Europe into the Americas over several centuries. As a young boy, he lives in two worlds, one during the day, and the other in a dream world at night. Santiago has little or no control in either. The essence of who he is seeks understanding. His sleep world makes him a passenger on a ghost train taking him back in time where he becomes part of the continuum that has defined his life. What will he find? Will he understand before it is too late? Is it more than a young mind can bear?

—————————

CONTENTS

Chapter | 1

ALL ABOARD

"W hy is it so cold?" The morning was extremely cold. I was awakened by my brother Billy who was silently getting out of bed. I often wondered where he went early in the morning. It wasn't every morning, but it was often enough that I wondered. Calling it morning was strange, it was still dark and cold outside. Where did the night end and the morning begin? I had the habit of over thinking things. It got me an ass whooping sometimes. I didn't know when to shut up. Billy and I slept in the apple cellar. Our two-room adobe house was not big enough for our parents and their six children, so here we were with the apples, the pears, the chile', the rats, and the spiders.

Our orchards were healthy and mature. They had been planted by my grandfather and his father. We were multigenerational Northern New Mexican. We were descendants of the early Spanish Conquistadores who settled in the Southwestern United States. A few years before Jamestown the first settlers arrived in what is now Northern New Mexico, and it is reflected in the unique culture that evolved from the interaction between the Spanish Settlers and their new environment. We lived off the land and grew, bartered, or bought what we needed to survive. Today, I shivered in the cold. I wonder why I volunteered to sleep with Billy in the damp room.

I was 6 years younger than my oldest brother and I followed him around like a puppy, desperate for his love and attention. I often got it, although not in the way I intended. His response to me was often the same, "Santiago, get out of here and stop asking so many questions!" As I got out of bed, the cold seeping in from outside quickly woke me up. The familiar smell of ripe fruit fully woke my senses. It was the pungent smell of the fruit and vegetables mixed with the aroma of the century old building that greeted me every morning. The smell changed as the contents of the cellar aged. I had smelled these aromas from the earliest days of my existence.

Every morning I looked up to check for spiders. A few months back I woke up to light footsteps of a spider on my forehead. The spider had woken me up from a deep sleep. I could tell it was a big one. The fear froze me for an instant and then, "slap' the spider was dead. The wet remembrance was with me every time I went to bed looking up at the ancient, stained ceiling. Spider webs were a reminder that they were there. I was traumatized for a while after that. I would wake up feeling things crawling on me, squishy and wet. I could feel my heart racing with the apprehension that there were more, and they were coming for me.

"That ceiling gives me the creeps!" I often muttered to myself. Further adding to my discomfort was the multiple times I heard the pitter and patter of rats scurrying on the old wooden floor of our cellar and in the other two rooms of our home. The proof of their existence was evident in the small gnaw marks on some of the apples. The floor was ancient, the ceiling too. The ceiling panels bulged downward from years of moisture. "Is it going to fall on us?" I asked my brother on several occasions. He gave me a hard nudge and told me to stop asking stupid questions. The spiders, rats, and strong smell of fruit became normal to me, so did the bull-snakes my father caught and released under the floorboards. "The best mouse traps you can get," he declared. Now I was really scared!

This morning I made up my mind that I was going to follow Billy out into the darkness, my curiosity had finally outgrown my fear. If he caught me, there would be hell to pay but I was used to getting my ass kicked by Billy. I waited until he opened the door and slipped outside. I could see that the morning light was still trapped by the night's darkness. The moon lit up the landscape, majestic and spiritual, the light shrouded by the dark. The first thing I noticed was our water well, the silhouette was distinct. Our well was a hole in the ground, several feet deep. We would peer into its depths and see the cool darkness below. We were entranced by it and wondered why the water never changed within its deep and mysterious cavern. We swore we saw snakes and worms swimming in it. I am sure that the glittering light and our imagination got the better of our young minds. My grandfather and his father had dug it and built a small wooden structure around it. It resembled a small booth with a pulley at the top. The pulley was used with a rope to drop a bucket into the dark cool water. The water was purified as the earth filtered it. "Water is our life" my grandfather would say. All I knew was that its cool and soothing effect as it flowed down my parched throat was a joy. We used the water for all the family needs. It was used for drinking, cooking, and bathing. It was a privilege for us to be embraced by it every day.

The well had always been here. My grandfather often explained it to us. "For centuries, the descendants of the Spanish Conquistadores have survived in the fertile valley, Española." He was proud of his heritage and shared it with us every chance he got. "The Spaniard named Española when Don Juan de Onate y Salazar claimed the valley in the name of the King of Spain in the year 1598. As the Spaniards entered the fertile valley they were overcome with its beauty, exclaiming that it was as beautiful as a Spanish girl, an Española. Our family are the descendants of the Salazars."

The native blood moon dominated the night with its light penetrating into the narrow, perfect rows of our orchard. The fruit trees were casting their unnerving shadows of entangled branches as if they were reaching towards the heavens. The dark silhouette of the trees was beautiful and scary at the same time. I felt the excitement as I stepped away from the cold yet comforting shadow of our adobe house. Adobe, mud bricks built with our hands, our mud, our straw, and our sweat holding it all together.

I saw the dark shadow of my brother as he silently glided down the path through the alfalfa surrounded the fruit trees. I heard the pigs grunt as he walked by. I was silent and scared, comforted by the orchard and by the fact that Billy was in front of me, he would save me. We immersed ourselves in the orchard as the water flowing through the acequias twinkled in unison with the stars, both singing an ancient song of life. I was struck with memories that came flooding in as primal feelings from my soul overtook me. The five hundred years in North America had created a unique cultural blend of the indigenous people and the Spaniard. I felt it all as I followed my brother through the trees wondering where he was taking me. We stepped out of the orchard's shadow into the full moon's glow through the field planted with corn, chile', cucumbers, melons, and sweet peas. Like our forefathers, our livelihood was planted and tended to by all of us. It was present in my life through the natural love of my grandfather, my parents, my siblings, and by me. I really loved the juicy taste of our sweet peas. There was never enough, the sweet goodness gone too quickly.

I was lost in thought as if floating through space. I was startled by a loud crack. I stepped on a pruning twig! I froze in my tracks, ducking from view just in time. I could see my brother stop and turn to survey the night. Why did I have to follow him? The moonlight gave his face a strange countenance. I wondered what it meant. I realized that as the air got colder the moonlight dimmed like a candle reaching the end of its life. I could feel the old in the air. My thoughts grew sharper as the air got thicker.

We neared the indentation in the earth that had always puzzled me. It was the only place where the cattails grew. I would learn that it was like a footprint left by an early steel machine. It marked where the old train had walked a century before, loaded with humanities finest and worst, part of the Anglo migration to the south and west. I learned that this was where the Chile' Express used to run. The Chile' Express was completed in the late 1800's, connecting Denver to Santa Fe. Originally the plan had been to connect Denver with Mexico City, but it only made it to Santa Fe. The rail houses still stood in Santa Fe as a testimonial to a time long gone.

As I followed, a mist began to rise from the train's earthen memory. A shiver ran over my skin, top to bottom. A strange smell overtook my consciousness. I recognized the strong odor, but I struggled to identify it. My body was overtaken by a strange aura, an out of body experience I had never felt before. I could feel my body shiver and start to shake. What did it all mean? Through the fog I could see a small light in the distance approaching very slowly, partnered with a strange low wail that sounded like a wolf, a Devil Dog. I looked for my brother, but he had disappeared into the fog. I found myself trying to speak to Billy. "Be careful, don't go in there. I don't like it. Wait for me!" I knew I was talking but I wasn't making any noise. I yelled out, "Billy, where are you going? Billy, where are you going?" Again, I was yelling but it was silent. I was afraid. Should I go into the fog? What was in there that my brother wanted to see?

I knew my brother was brave. I had seen it time and time again in response to my father's demands, violent responses, and actions. He always protected us at great injury to himself. "Stop it, leave her alone, dad, stop it!" I heard it over, and over again. This young boy stood in front of a huge man with red eyes that bore holes in your soul, in a futile attempt to protect mom and us. "So, you want to protect her, let's see." What came after that was always the same. I drove those thoughts from my mind. "What is that noise?" I whispered to myself.

The fog got thicker; the approaching light got brighter, like an eye penetrating the black and gray. I wondered why this part of our little farm was covered in a dark gray fog. I had never seen this before. A shiver ran through my body. Was this real? The fog was speaking to me in whispers, inviting me to a strange realm. Then I saw it, the warm glow as it approached like an orb. I somehow knew that the totality of my life was coming at me not as the past but as a simultaneous manifestation of past, present, and future. I knew in the essence of my being that I had to board this beautiful and scary Ghost Train. How could a six-year-old boy understand this? I had to find Billy! I saw a smile appear from the depth of the iron beast.

The conductor was a ghastly apparition with the biggest smile I had ever seen. The teeth and the mouth that held it together were bigger than the rest of his face. It drew me forward, enticing yet frightening to behold. The mouth was surrounded by a heart shaped face with inset eyes, black and shiny. His body was contorted, flowing like cream in coffee, white on black, bone and flesh. It appeared as if the bones were a cage, holding something in, a spiritual whispering calling me in to be absorbed, contained within it. I felt a pull. In the depth of my soul, I felt a warmth from an ancient place. It was soothing in its quiet silence, and it was at odds with the creature on the train.

Chapter | 2

EL GUACHE

"Wake up, the skunks got into the corn!" My brother tapped me on the head. I hated when that happened, it would be a long day. I got up and put on my tattered clothes. I couldn't shake the journey of the night before and what I saw. "Was it a dream?" It didn't feel like a dream. The face and that menacing smile would come to haunt my nighttime and daytime hours, I just didn't know it yet. I shook off the eerie feeling. The morning was bright and clear. I couldn't wait to help my brother do our daily chores. "Hurry up we have to hoe the corn today and cut the alfalfa between the trees and don't forget about the mess the skunks made." Billy spoke as he walked towards the fields.

We always worked before we ate. My brother was anxious, I recognized the mood. I felt the beginning of a new day and hoped that it would be a good one. We were on our way to the fields, five brothers and one sister. My sister was the oldest and was often put in charge of us. She always paid the price, taking care of us was like herding cats, Bobcats. "Dad wants us to start with the corn and start hoeing until we are done. Each of us will take a row all the way down. When you're done, start the next one and work your way back up." Annette was on her way leading us to where the work was. "You don't have to tell us what to do, we already know." Billy's response was always negative

SANTA FE: A PIECE OF 'MI VIDA'

when it came to my sister. "Just shut up and do it! I'm tired of getting in trouble every day because you guys do whatever you want." My sister Annette glared at Billy and went to work.

Billy seemed to be alone in his thoughts. His spirit was focused on how his entire life was one of extreme love, extreme terror, and extreme hatred. The older he got the stronger the transition was from fear to anger. All of this was part of the essence of who he was becoming. Right now, he was walking with a single-minded purpose, his destiny was calling out to him. "Why is it that our mom or my sister are the ones to lead the brigade of child labor into the fields?" Billy muttered to himself. He had noticed that dad didn't spend too much time with us, he came at the end of the day and checked our work. We spent many a night out in the fields because our dad didn't like the amount or the quality of the work. Billy knew that mom was tough as nails, but his fear was driven by his father.

We started working the fields first thing in the morning and kept at it until the heat became unbearable. Normally we went through our daily routine of drawing water with our bucket from the well before we went out to work in the orchard and the field. Then the call from Billy. "Come on, we have to feed the pigs!" Billy would yell as we walked. There was always some other chore added to the list. Today was different, the skunks were out. The area around the corn plants had to be cleared. We would be out late to drive the skunks away. We had to be able to see them. He looked back and saw his brothers following behind him with corn fed smiles and a true joy. My sister was the only one that did not look happy. The day ended without any turmoil.

It was the weekend, and we got some time to play. "I'm the king of the mountain. I dare you to attack my castle." Arthur was standing on top of a pyramid made of chopped and blocked wood. He was wielding a sword made from a river willow. Arthur was fair skinned and had wavy hair that he combed to the side. Sometimes the adults around us would call him 'Chato' because he had a slight pug nose. My dad was rough on all of us, but he seemed to be harder on Arthur. Arthur was different than us. He liked to read and was a bit of a loner when he could get away from it all. My dad wanted us to be together as often as we could. Annette was the oldest and when she wasn't outside with us, she was inside helping my mom. Billy was the oldest son and ran the show when my parents weren't around. Juan was next. Juan was the guitarist as he took to it more than the rest of us. Arthur was next he was the reader. I came next, and Michael was the baby of our family. I often resented him. He was treated better than me, at least that is what I thought. We were only a year apart and competed constantly.

"I'll attack it!" I always challenged Arthur who never failed to educate me and put me in my place. I tried to get to the top of the wood pile only to have my sword swatted out of my hands by the quicker and stronger Arthur. I grabbed a piece of wood and threw it at him, it was a direct hit. Arthur doubled over and I saw the look on his face. I knew I would pay, sooner or later I would pay. "You little punk, when I get you, I am going to beat the shit out of you!" I was off and running towards Michael. "Look over here guys!" Michael was chasing something with his stick. I rushed over and saw that he was chasing a bull snake. "Let's kill it!" Arthur was there in an instant. "If you do and dad finds out, we'll be sorry. The bull snake eats the rats that eat our fruit and vegetables." By now Arthur had recovered from the direct hit. "Let me see it. I bet you I can catch it." Arthur approached the serpent and got down on one knee. The snake was fat and was hidden in the alfalfa. "He is going to bite you. Just leave it alone. Let's go make some bows and arrows." As I said this, I saw Arthur reach down and slowly approach the snake from the back.

The serpent was dark brown and black turning to a yellowish color as it thinned towards the tail. We had always been taught to look at the tail and make sure it wasn't a rattlesnake. As soon as his hands got near the back of the snake's head the snake turned and lifted its head up looked at us as if it knew us. Its black tongue was flickering out and we knew it was ready to strike. Its head was thick at the top and narrowed to a point. Its tongue was dark black and split into two at the end, like the fork at the confluence of the Chama River and the San Juan River. "Give me your stick, I can use it to catch it." Michael gave up his sword, but he didn't like it.

We walked the bosque every day looking for willow branches that formed a 'Y'. These were perfect for sling shots on one side and swords on the other. We would cut old tire tubes into strips and connect them to the stick and use them to have wars with small rocks. "Why mine? It's perfect for a sword and later I'll use it for a sling shot." Michael had found the perfect branch. Arthur took the stick and broke both ends off and made a smaller 'Y'. He used the stick to prod the snake. The Bull Snake responded by lunging forward attacking the stick. Michael and I let out a fear filled yell as we moved back. "Leave it alone or I'll tell dad!" "Go ahead you little chicken! I'll tell him you're lying." To this Michael got quiet and him and I got closer together and moved back. Arthur prodded the snake again and this time it slithered away into the alfalfa field with Arthur on its tail. He made several attempts to catch the snake by trapping the head of the snake with the stick.

"I got it!" Arthur triumphantly proclaimed. Michael and I approached as Arthur was sliding his hand under the stick and grabbing the snake by the neck at the base of the head. Arthur walked towards us with a big grin on his face. The snake had wrapped itself on Arthur's arm. "Man, this thing is strong!" I was awestruck! I wondered how he could do that? We were young children but here he was with a snake wrapped around his arm. "Do you want to hold it?" He asked as he grabbed the tail and unwrapped it from his arm. "I don't want to!" Michael replied as he moved back ready to run.

I was unsure, I wanted to, but I was scared. "Can I touch it?" "I saw a smile cross my brothers face, sure go ahead." As I approached, he stretched it out from both sides and flung it at me. My instant fear was so overwhelming I couldn't move or breathe. In my head I was sure it was going to bite me and that I was going to die. "You better not tell!" It was all I heard as I flew away from the scene. "I'll tell them that you hit me with that piece of wood!" By the time I got to the door I knew he was right. I went into my cellar bedroom and sat down and cried. He had scared me so badly that for a few days I was afraid to walk in the alfalfa. I knew that Bull Snake was waiting for me.

It was Sunday morning, and it was beautiful outside. The Martinez/ Baca clan was on their way to a new day. Billy was walking towards the pig pen, and I knew it was feeding time. I raced behind him trying to keep up. "I hope he rides El Gordo today!" I spoke out loud as we walked. My brother had known that pig from infancy. As a family, we raised hogs, chickens, and rabbits and ultimately, they ended up on our table. Too many times we fell in love with some of them just to watch my parents butcher them. We had just finished feeding the pigs when my mom came out and called out to us. "Annette, Billie let's go!" My mom ordered as she walked out of our kitchen with a knife and a small hatchet.

Annette and Billy knew where they were going and why. Like usual, we approached this task by birth order, oldest to youngest. As if on cue, Annette and Billy started driving the chickens into the coop. "The brown one, that's the one you have to get." It was comical, and as spectators, we enjoyed the show. "That way!" My sister Annette yelled. "You go to the left I'll go to the right." It was as if the chicken knew it was D-Day, dinner time. It flew around zigzagging away, with Annette and Billy hot on her trail. The chicken was clucking and digging as its talons tore through the dirt as it ran for its life. "You guys stop laughing and form a circle over there towards the ditch and don't let her get through!" My mom was on a mission. After a few attempts we were all mumbling, that chicken was driving us crazy. It ran towards every opening in our line and just would not go into the chicken coop. "Okay, stop for a while!" My mom was deep in thought as we caught our breath.

"Billy, go get some chicken feed." Normally we didn't use the feed during the spring and summer. The chickens ate what they could catch, the insects were plentiful. "Here chickee, chickee, chickee." Billy was putting chicken feed at the door and inside the chicken coop. All the hens and the roster recognized that a feast was being laid before them and started entering the coop except for the one we wanted. "Here chickee, chickee, chickee." Billy moved slowly towards the hen and started dropping a few granules in front of her. As Billy backed up towards the coop the hen followed pecking for the pellets heading into the coop. The other chickens were busy eating and finally, our dinner walked into the coop. Billy walked in and closed the door behind the hen. Billy approached the hen and in an instant the coop looked like a tempest. There were hens clucking, running, and flying in all directions. The debris of the chase was everywhere. In a desperate last-ditch effort Billy took a dive and got the hen and wrapped it up across his chest. I felt bad for the chicken, it was as if the chicken knew its time in the coop was over.

My mom had moved a stump from the woodpile setting it upright. "Bring it over here and hold it." Billy's face was contorting as the hen was still trying to get away. We all watched in anticipation. All we could hear was the noise coming from the chicken coop. "They're saying goodbye to it." Michael spoke with a note of sadness in his voice. "You won't complain tonight when we are eating fried chicken." Juan was closer to the stump than we were. "I can hardly wait. I love fried chicken. I don't care if we kill it, that's what they're for. What are you worried about? We do this all the time!" Billy walked slowly toward the

Cottonwood stump with the squirming chicken in his hands. My mom reached over and snapped its neck, it was dead. "Put its head down and hold it against the stump." Billy held it down and in an instant the axe came down shimmering in the sun. Billy released our headless dinner. My mom began the process of plucking and gutting our meal.

That evening we sat down to eat. The chicken was served with potatoes and red chile'. As usual my dad got the lion's share leaving the rest of us to salivate and consume small portions of the bird. When the serving was done my mom got to enjoy the neck and other small leftovers. "All right mom, you get to eat your favorite pieces." Michael was grinning as he exclaimed, truly happy for mom. We all cracked up laughing. We knew she ate what was left to ensure that her family ate. I looked over to my father who was gorging on the prime white meat. He was oblivious and uncaring that his wife and kids were eating small pieces of meat and lots of potatoes while he sat there smacking his lips. I was upset and he knew it. Going forward, it would become a tension between us. I was reminded of his selfish cruelty every time I opened the refrigerator. The top shelf was off limits to us. The top shelf held the bologna, hot dogs, whole milk, and any other fine food products in the house. We did get to share on some occasions, but we ate the beans, chile', tortillas, and potatoes on the lower shelf. Looking back, we got the better end of the deal. Our mom always made sure we ate.

The day after the adventure with the chicken, I caught sight of Billy petting his pig. El Gordo seemed to know who had fed him and loved him since birth. Now he was the king of the pigsty. "Are you going to ride El Gordo?" I asked with enthusiasm. My brother responded with agitation that had been stirred by my insistence in shadowing his every move. "Why do you ask me that every time we come down here? If you ask me that again I'll throw your little ass in there, so you can ride him." Billy's comment made all my brothers snicker. They hoped that he would. I felt the fear rush over me, I was afraid of that pig. I had watched him time and time again as he threw my brother into the slime. I had watched as he chased all of us out when we went in to upright the bowl and bring it closer to the end of the pig pen so we could feed them and give them water. I was always put off by the aroma created by the muck. No way would I ever go in there. The smell and my fear shamed me. I wanted to be brave like my brother.

The first time my brother rode El Gordo excitement filled the air. Our cousins had come over to visit and, as usual, the dads' beer drinking, and bravado resulted in an adventure of some kind for us kids. Most of the time it was a boxing match that resulted in a lopsided ass whooping for our cousins. My father worked at the New Mexico State Prison and raised us as convicts, our cousins never stood a chance. I wondered why my uncles let it happen, knowing what the results would be. I didn't want to do it. I could see the fear in my cousins' eyes. I knew I had to do it, or I would be the one to get it. However, that day the adventure would be different, exciting. My dad had seen Billy in the pen with El Gordo and saw how the pig acted. My dad was always bragging about El Gordo and his son.

Today my uncles' admiration for the hog was the kindle that ignited the hog riding, and all the hog riding events that followed. "Mira no mas el tamaño de ese puerco, que tantas libras pesa? Look at the size of El Gordo! When are you going to butcher that one?" My uncle asked with pork chops on his mind. "Quien sabe, who knows?" My father responded, obviously very proud of his pig. "I don't know how much he weighs but look how big he is. Look at all the little ones he has sired for me. I sell most of them." My father boasted, "Why would I get rid of the goose that lays the golden egg?" he asked. "Better to butcher the rest and keep my Gordo".

El Gordo was huge. He looked like a big branch that been cut off an ancient sequoia tree, a huge trunk with a tail and head attached. His coat was ashen white when it was not covered in grime. You could see black dots underneath the hair on his skin. His snout looked like an octopus tentacle that had been severed in the middle. I imagined being sucked in by that snout if I got too close. I was really scared of that pig. His tail was strange in that it was curled and small. It reminded me of the game Pin the Tail on the Donkey. The tail was much too small for El Gordo.

His demeanor was scary and intimidating. His grunts were low and deep, more like a rumbling. He ruled the pigsty, and he knew it. His eyes were the color of his fur, and you got the feeling that he was looking at you, almost daring you to get into the pen. "That pig is almost as big as a horse." My uncle exaggerated as he drank. "No way anyone could ride him. How would they hold on?" As soon as we heard my uncle and my father start up the man talk, us kids started trying to sneak away, we were getting that funny feeling. Our fathers continued debating whether anybody could ride El Gordo. My dad boasted proudly. "Billy can ride him!" And with his next breath he was yelling, "Billy, get over here. Your uncle is saying that you can't ride El Gordo. Get in there and show him how it's done." We all turned around to see the show. We were all glad that we were not my father's favorite son.

Chapter | 3

RODEO

As Billy got into the pen, the hogs snorted and scattered in all directions. The chaos they created added to the intensity. Now it was just Billy and El Gordo alone in the center of the pen. To everyone's surprise Billy did not approach El Gordo but instead began talking to him in a low voice. Everyone leaned forward listening, but we were unable to hear what he was saying. As my brother spoke to the hog the animal stood taller and began making a low grunting noise. Billy lowered himself into a half stance and scanned the area. It appeared as if he was ensuring a way out if he needed to escape from the pen. Billy did not show fear and exhibited pride in his ability to enter a place no one else could or would.

Billy was of medium height with brown hair, hazel eyes, and light brown skin. Billy was known for his athleticism. He loved to fight and helped our father make us fighters as well. His hazel eyes changed colors and were penetrating as if they were looking inside of you. As he continued speaking to El Gordo, the hog began to calm down as his grunts became quieter and fewer. Slowly, Billy approached the hog and reached out to touch him. El Gordo let out such a bellowing grunt that we all gasped in fear and apprehension. By now the crowd had grown. Our moms, aunts, and our cousins and friends had joined the group.

I could see the fear bordering on terror on my mom's face. My sister, the eldest, stood next to her. Billy did not move as El Gordo took a step forward.

During all the drama we had barely noticed the clouds encircling us. The wind started to blow; we could feel the temperature drop. Billy and El Gordo continued their dance. My brother stepped forward and started scratching the hog on his snout, head, and his thick fat rolled neck. El Gordo relaxed and closed his eyes as you could see him relax and appear to smile. My brother slowly moved his scratching operation to the back of the no-neck. He started rubbing him down from top to bottom like he did when he was a piglet. It seemed strange now, El Gordo appeared large next to my brother. All of us were entranced as we watched. Now Billy began to scratch him behind both ears and in a slow, fluid motion he mounted the animal. In an instant, El Gordo bolted through the slim with my brother pasted to his back. We all broke out into laughter as my brother was carried from one end of the 50-foot pen to the other. "I told you Billy would ride him!" My father squealed with joy, beaming as he moved and slapped my uncle on the back. You would have thought he was riding El Gordo. "Este vato se avienta! This guy gets it done!"

In an instant El Gordo reached the fence and pivoted right. Billy slipped off and landed in a fresh pile of pig pen muck. The small crowd went wild. "That was crazy!" Billy laughed out loud. El Gordo walked back and with his snout dug into the muck and flung it hitting Billy straight in the face. We could smell the impact. He stayed there in the muck laughing as he looked at the sky and watched the raindrops start to fall. El Gordo ran around the pen as if he were playing. The group went hysterical slapping each other on the back until their stomachs hurt.

Billy got up and went to El Gordo who now remembered his friend. Billy hugged the hog and started talking to him as the hog relaxed. Billy slipped a leg over him as he talked and stroked the large animal without sitting on him. He slowly lowered himself onto El Gordo as the hog grunted and looked back. The hog walked slowly with my brother on his back. To the amazement of us all, my brother was riding El Gordo. This time they strolled around the pig pen like if they were in a parade. I yelled out in excitement. "I knew you would do it Billy." In an instant the startled pig's ears lifted, and he bolted. Billy's legs flew back almost kicking himself in the head as he flew backwards and landed in the muck. The roar of the laughter continued. The rain arrived and flowed down Billy's face. He felt good as a calm peace came washing over him. His short life passed in front of his eyes. He just laid there, letting the thoughts of his late-night trips run through his being. They were becoming a powerful urge. He remembered his midnight journeys with a sensation of joy and dread.

It was a storm like few others, violent, wet, and powerful. The Sangre de Cristo Mountains were in full bloom, the lightning strikes were getting close, the booming of the thunder was deafening. The cloud covered mountains had been named by the Spanish settlers. The sun shining on these mountains during dusk and dawn gave them a dark red tint from a combination of light, soil, and atmospheric conditions. They named them Sangre de Cristo, Blood of Christ. First came the winds, both refreshing and foreboding, hinting that the much-needed rain was on its way. The clouds started slowly releasing raindrops on the Earth's sweet flower bouquets. The rain picked up in volume and velocity making music as it danced on the grass, bouncing off the tin in the pen, and became a percussionist using the firewood as its drums. Then the missiles started to fly, quarter size hail. The family crowd dispersed running up the short hill that led up to the two-room mud brick house to continue the reverie, all except Billy and his shadow, me.

Billy lay in the muck enjoying the bombardment of rain, hail, and the magic of the heavens sweet cadence. I watched in silence, wondering why Billy was laying in the muck and what he was going to do to me if he caught me spying on him. El Gordo had retreated into the small hut-like structure, content to be out of the rain. I felt a chill rush over me. Billy got up and went up the hill. He knew better than to go in the house with pig mix all over his body. He did what he always did when life on the Spanish farm left its strong scent on his body, he climbed into the irrigation ditch and rinsed off. He knew I was there. I could feel that he felt a compassion for me, his younger brother. He was always there loving me and in his own way watching over me. Love was a powerful force. Time would tell if it was enough. Billy climbed out of the 'Acequia', the irrigation ditch and went inside to a dry towel, pats on the back, and the consumption of vast amounts of alcohol. He knew it was going to be a long night. My dad called his son over. "You did good, I am proud of you son. Your uncle ate his words. You rode El Gordo! You are becoming a man!" Then he handed Billy a beer. "Here drink this, you've earned it." Billy walked away a little bit taller and a whole lot prouder. He was drinking his first beer, from his father no less. In our world a man proved his strength and virility by how much he drank. I knew that it would be a long night. I watched in silence and felt sad. I felt like I was losing my brother.

Chapter | 4

FALLING

I feel myself dreaming, but am I awake? I drift through the darkness. "Help me, stop me!" I yell into the void. I keep falling. I recognize the fall. I have had these dreams for as long as I can remember. As a young child I know that they are part of my life, a piece of 'mi vida'. My spirit is trying to understand how I came to be. My past is calling out to me as if it wants to explain. What I don't realize is the vastness of this past. I try to wake up, but I can't. A powerful force is trying to show me something. My fall begins to slowdown, and I see the face I saw that night, the first night I followed Billy.

I recognize the grin flowing like liquid mercury as it grins through me. I recognize that I am back on the old train track with the fog so thick that I can feel water droplets forming on my face. I hear a loud screeching, metal on metal as it pierces the night. Then it appears, he appears. The grin is morphing again and is now walking on all fours reminding me of a Silverback that is not walking but flowing as it moves. Before I know exactly what is happening a hand is pulling me to the ground and my brother whispers harshly in my ear. I can feel spit land on the back of my neck as Billy asks, "What the hell are you doing? I don't want you here! Why does your dumb ass have to do this?" I feel fear and sadness at the same time. My brother's heart is pounding against my back and his hand is covering my mouth. I look up and see what appears to be a train moving through the fog again. There is a distinct orb separating the world I live in and the train that has emerged. The floating grin looks back and shifts into that world and stands in front of a tall slim man wearing a uniform. The uniform is void of a face. It is frightening to see the black void where the face should be. The soldier is standing proud. It reminds me of the people in my life. We stand like that.

The uniform is gold and red with a crest on the center of the torso. I am transfixed on the image. The crest has a helmet with plumes in the top center, a green tree on a gold background inside a shield with eight circular stars surrounding it. I wonder what it all means. I have seen this on my grandpa's wall, a small plaque mounted on the wall in his small one room home. The first time I saw it I asked him what it meant. "It's a Coat of Arms," he replied. "It's the history of our name and our family." My grandpa turned and walked outside and left me wondering what it meant. I feel my brother as he twitches and rises upwards. I feel a power pulling him, wanting to take me along! I know that the pull on me is through my brother. As I lay with my face pressing into the alfalfa, I can smell and feel the work of my life. I can taste the alfalfa in my mouth and feel its coolness on my skin. I visualize my family.

This moment reaches into my core. It's deeper than I can understand. I see my grandfather who loves the land and its life sustaining growth from the earth. I am always amazed at his ability to pick fruit, hoe fields, irrigate and tend livestock, and the myriad of other activities that it takes to survive off this land. My thoughts are shattered as I feel my brother poised on his elbows, he has a strange look on his face. His hazel eyes have changed colors to match his environment, he is staring longingly at something. As I lay there, I move my hand and feel something cold and smooth. I'm alerted to my surrounding as it rains in both worlds, and it feels clear and older somehow. I feel a medal in my hand, it has a chain attached.

As I grasp the medal, I feel the length of the chain that is attached to it and look down at it curiously. I see it is shiny and I grasp it tightly, I want it. In an instant my chain of thought is shattered as Billy is on his feet running towards the fog. I'm trying to get on my feet and go after him, but I can't get up. "I don't want you to go!" I weep as a sadness overcomes me. I remember the medal and look down at it. The medal shows a military cloak and a wreath bordering the edges of its oval shape. In the middle it has the image of a man on a horse dressed in armor. The name St. Martin illuminates the medal. I have seen images like this before.

I recognize them, images of Conquistadores; Cortez, Oñate, Coronado, Don Diego De Vargas and many more, but this is much older, ancient. The man has a sword in his right hand and what appears to be a cloak in the other. It's strange because the only light I have is the full moon, yet the image is crystal clear. The metal comes alive as I see a man sitting at the feet of the soldier riding the horse. His face is lifted towards the heavens in the cold winter rain. I can see that the man is poor. I don't know why he is looking up at the soldier and why the soldier is looking down at him. The vision is clear, the beggar is sitting at the gate to a large fortress with the sounds and movement of military soldiers all around. The hoofs of the horses splashing in the mud reverberates out of the walls of the fortress. The roads are muddied with dirt and horse droppings. There is a stench in the air of rotten waste and cold mud as the darkness shrouds the Earth and everything in it.

In my vision, it's the middle of the day yet it feels dark, and it is very cold. I know that the beggar is freezing and being ignored by all who enter and exit the fortress. He reminds me of some of the poor people in my world. I feel bad for the beggar and glad for the Soldier. Suddenly, the Soldier removes his cloak and draws his sword. I look intently. Billy's image has filled the void where the soldiers face is. I know it's not him, but I see a part of him in that face. I flinch as it appears that the soldier is going to kill the beggar. As I watch, I see a look of compassion on the soldier's face, and I realize that he is cutting his cloak in half. "Here, take this and cover yourself, our heavenly father wants this for you." As he speaks the beggar reaches up and takes the cloak. The poor man's body is racked with violent shivers from the cold and speaks in a low raspy tone. "Who are you and why do you imperil yourself by cutting your military cloak?"

The beggar knows that a Calvary Officer for the King is bound to protect his honor, cloak, and sword. Only through death is it to be removed from his body. The soldier is bound by honor to fight till the death to keep it. The beggar continues, "Your eminence how will your men gather to protect and follow you as their leader in battle if they notice half your cloak is gone? How will you explain it to them?" The beggar asks in bewilderment. He knows by the Coat-of-Arms that this man is a high-ranking Imperial Horse Guard. The soldier's reply is simple yet telling. "I am a man who has seen enough death." The man on the horse is Martin de Tours. Martin knew in his heart that his days as a Cavalry Officer were coming to an end. His spirit and mind returned to the catalyzing event that punctured his soul so that the old could seep out and the new flow in.

As the images from the train continue, I gather myself and scream into the dark, "Where are you, Billy?" I feel a cloud as it consumes me. I am suddenly moving slightly backwards, or is it forward, I cannot tell. I hear the cracking of metal on metal, my fear puts me into a deep sleep like state, yet I am awake. I can see the same soldier upon his horse, cold and foreboding, as he gathers the wind. "Rome needs you!" Martin roars to the Soldiers of the Imperial Horse Guard. "Julian, our fearless Roman General will drive the Francs out of Gaul and establish the Rhine as part of Rome's Empire. We must lead the charge on the enemy of the Roman Empire as our fathers have done before us." Martin was the son of a high-ranking Imperial Horse Guard Officer and as such, was expected to follow in his footsteps. The Persecution of Christians had recently come to an end with the Roman Emperors decree making Christianity legal. Martin's parents both believed in Paganism, but Martin had converted to Christianity at the age of 10 and began his lengthy and difficult path on the road to salvation. He kept his conversion to himself as there were many, if not most, who continued to persecute Christians in violation of the Emperor's Decree.

I continue with these images and then I realize that I am laying on the floor inside of a boxcar and that the train has brought me to this place. I can still feel and hear it lurching forward as it sways back and forth. As I sit up, I look out into sheer darkness. I remember the strange images that began floating as I traveled back. I am truly afraid and curious. I remember the outside of the train as if the train was moving backward and forward at the same time, bringing me to this place of strange people, activities, and surroundings. I am baffled as to why cars turn to wagons, wagons to carts, carts to horses. I recognize all of them but know none of them.

I know I am in a tunnel and the train is being pulled into it, down, down, down it rolls. I am falling, and falling, and falling and a spiritual essence is doing the same. "I want to go home! I want my mom!" I scream as a gentle hand touches my shoulder. "Be quiet little one! You are but a guest on this quest." The voice calms me, but I am still scared. "What am I doing here? How did I get here? Where is Billy? I want to go home!" I can't breathe and sweat is pouring down my face. The calming voice continues. "This is but one journey of many that have molded and defined the journey that is your life. The answer to your questions will come soon enough. I am here to prevent you from getting lost in the abyss of time. Do not fret, ride the Ghost Train and you will see!" The voice is silenced. "Who are you? Come back! I need you to help me find my brother so we can go home." I am overwhelmed by the silence as the voice is gone.

I look up and see the sky, the dawn is approaching. I feel that it's almost time to wake up. I notice from the edge of my consciousness that this military officer is changing in front of my eyes. There is a group of people in front of him. He is wearing a different cloak, not a cloak, but a robe. Martin is speaking. "It has been said that this new religion is not a true religion. It's been 361 years since the man Jesus revealed that he was the son of God by dying for our sins. My family has served Kings and Emperors on this Earth for time immemorial. I have been called to trade my military cloak for this robe of faith in the belief that all earthly Kings will kneel at the seat of the one true God."

The story continues as I learn that his last military campaigns had been hard on Martin. One image stood clear in his mind and troubled him to the very core of his being. During a bloody and highly contested battle, his forces retreated from the battlefield due to overwhelming enemy forces. As they retreated, many were being killed as the enemy pursued the King's forces. Once Martin and his soldiers were at a safe distance, he turned to assess the damage and caught sight of a young man's body, a man who died a noble death. That sight shook him. Martin had watched him die.

Martin had met him the night before as he went from campfire to campfire sharing his faith and thankfulness to the new messiah. Converts were spreading his message to the entire known world. At one of the fireside huddles, he stopped to talk to a young man, much younger than the rest. "What path brings you to this place? It is a true wonder that a young man such as yourself is willing to die for our King." The young man replied, in a clear and resolute tone. "I come from La Villa De El Gauche, my lord. My village has suffered from the ravages of the Francs and my family has suffered much hardship." "What is your name young man?" Martin asked with true interest. "My name is Guillermo." "You will join me in my tent tonight, we have much to discuss."

Later that night Guillermo approached the tent with trepidation. "What does the great leader Martin want to discuss with me? Why me?" He is startled by a voice coming from the interior of the tent. "Ah, there you are, come in, come in, make yourself comfortable." Guillermo fidgets as he sits with a high-ranking officer of the Soldiers of the Imperial Horse Guard. Guillermo is out of breath. "Good evening, Sire, it is an honor to sit with you tonight." "The privilege is mine. It is not often I witness bravery such as yours from a such a young man." "It is my duty and I take it very seriously. I will fight with you until the enemy is vanquished or until I lose my life." Guillermo spoke with pride. Martin nodded his head with a deeper appreciation of the price that was being paid by all for the sake of kingdoms and the glory of Kings.

Martin and Guillermo spoke deep into the night, sharing tales of their lives. Martin spent most of this time with Guillermo explaining to Guillermo the new faith sweeping the land and his conversion to it. When Guillermo left, he looked up at the sky and felt the rain wash over his face. He saw the stars so clear they brought tears to his eyes. Guillermo cried for his family. Somehow, he knew he would never see them again. His mom's tears brought sadness to his heart. Guillermo had gotten into a dangerous situation when he stole food from one of the landlords to feed his family. Now here he was fighting for the powerful that exploited his family.

I feel the waves of sleep washing over me and my visions turn to that fateful battle. During retreat, Martin saw that one of the soldiers was not fleeing. He recognized the young man, Guillermo, who was attacking the Gaul's with his sword shimmering in the light as it struck down enemy after enemy. "Guillermo, fallback, we will avenge this day!" Martin yelled as he rode towards Guillermo, warding off enemy soldiers as he rode. "Guillermo, let's go! Guillermo, look behind you! I fear that you are going to be killed!" Guillermo reared his horse to the left and fatally cut down a Gaul. Guillermo's battle cries could be heard over the agony and thrill of the battle. Guillermo maneuvered his horse in such a way that the dead warriors of Gaul protected him from those wanting to kill him. Martin had never seen such a display of bravery and finesse.

During the battle Guillermo fell from his horse landing on his back. Martin arrived and dismounted falling to his knees at Guillermo's head. Instantly, a fine misty rain fell from the heavens. Martin felt a tug at his heart. His soul merged with a spirit that frightened him and assured him that his path would take him to a new battlefield. As he looked down on the face of Guillermo he spoke. "My dear young friend, I pray that I will have the courage to serve my new master in the battle for the souls of his flock as you have shown me today. I believe that our lord put you in my life to show me the value of each person's life on this earth. Please forgive me if I motivated you to this tragic end." As Martin spoke, he saw a look of peace and conviction as Guillermo's life slipped away. Martin wept as he never had before. He vowed that his role in leading the young into battle was over. He was awakened by the approach of enemy combatants, and he mounted his steed and followed his men into the woods, not in fear but in conviction to live and fight the fight of his life.

I saw Martin standing in front of a tribunal. The members were very serious and scary. "Sir Martin, we have reviewed your petition to be released from military service to our King. We are amazed at your belief that you can leave the service of the King by merely asking to do so. What demon has possessed you that you would ponder such a thing? Never have we seen anyone in front of this tribunal requesting such a thing. After careful deliberation, we view this as an act of treason and cowardice. We hereby order that you be cast into the dungeons of Mount Leon. The fact that you are requesting this action in the name of this new religion, based on the false belief that a single God is all that exists, leads us to believe that it is actually fear of battle and not this so-called faith that drives your request." The tribunal magistrate was stern in his pronouncements. "What say you?" He continued, "We are all curious to hear your tale." The tribunal members looked at each other with shared derision towards Calvary Captain Martin. Martin had been praying the whole time secure in his belief that his lord and savior Jesus the Christ would protect him.

Martin started to speak choosing his words carefully, speaking slowly ensuring that he did not say or do anything that would further inflame the tribunal. "I stand before you as a loyal subject who has served the King with honor and loyalty. I do not request to be released from military service out of cowardice or selfishness." Martin continued, "As a boy of 10 my spirit was consumed by the one true God introducing me to his son Jesus Christ. I was called to serve him but hesitated because as the son of a long line of the Royal Guards it was expected that l would follow in my father's footsteps, which I have done. Of late my soul has been troubled as I watch the slaughtering of many men, some of them barely old enough to ride and yet are urged to do battle and often lose their lives to a savage rival." The image of Guillermo still consumed his mind and his heart. "I have been called to serve God, but I can still serve the King. I will go into battle, but I will not kill." The tribunal sent him back to the dungeon and discussed the matter. The overriding concern was to ensure that they did not set a precedent allowing others to come forward and claim allegiance to a God to avoid battle.

As these images flowed through me, the train started to lurch taking me back to my life in El Gauche. I saw Martin's life accelerate as the train did. Martin was released out of prison when the battle being used to label him a coward did not happen, adding to the credibility that Martin was destined to serve his God who had intervened on his behalf. Martin pursued his quest becoming an Archbishop and would come to be known as the Patron Saint of Soldiers, and as the Patron Saint of Conscientious Objectors. He was the first known to be granted an exemption from battle due to religious beliefs against the killing of another. I wondered how I understood these images and how Martin could be both. As the images faded, I grasped the medal that I found in the mist. It hung around my neck. I felt the strength of the medal. "I know that I am on a journey and that something or someone is taking me on it. But why am I dreaming? I want to know why...." In my heart I knew that it was Billy in that battle. I didn't understand.

Chapter | 5

'MATANZA'

T he following day I awoke to find Billy sitting at the foot of the bed. "You were dreaming again last night. I'm curious what do you see in your dreams, am I in them?" A shiver ran down my back and into my body like a fire moving on and through a Piñon log when it's set ablaze. I did not know what to say. I remembered that through the fog of the train ride I could see my brother with a beautiful woman doing things that I did not understand. The lady smiled at me, and I saw the image of the train conductor mocking me. I knew Billy was in trouble I just did not understand how and why. He was doing things with that woman that he knew were wrong, but I saw the euphoric look emanating from his countenance.

"I don't remember the whole thing. I only remember that I am on a train rolling backwards to olden times. That's all I remember." I was afraid to discuss the rest. "Don't tell anyone about your dreams. I want you to find a way to stop dreaming, make yourself wake up. I am worried about you." I did not tell him that in a funny way it felt like I was dreaming inside a dream. "I found this yesterday in the corn, do you want it?" Billy reached out and took the medal from my hand. Billy had tears flowing down his face as he walked away. I never saw him take it off after that. Billy would wear The St. Martin metal for the rest of his life.

It had been a long summer since the rodeo with El Gordo. There had been a few more rides but the shine wore off and my dad moved the party out of our farm and into the bars and roadways. The summer had come to an end with a huge Matanza, a cultural social gathering centered around the slaughtering and butchering of an animal, in our case a hog. My father had applied to the Department of Corrections for subsidized housing next to the prison and it was approved. The house would be available in a few weeks, so we started getting rid of the rabbits, chickens, and pigs. We sold or gave most of the animals away. We all felt the impending gloom around El Gordo. I did not understand exactly what they were going to do about El Gordo, but I heard jokes about Rocky Mountain Oysters.

We separated El Gordo and started feeding him corn. As the summer turned to fall, we prepared for the big move. "Today's the day." I heard my dad speaking to my mom. My mom replied, "We have everything ready. My sisters will be here by noon. My aunt and mom and some of their friends are coming as well. They are all excited. It's been a while since we did this. I think it will be good for us. The boys are worried about moving to Santa Fe. Annette not so much. She is actually looking forward to it." My dad replied with a strong threatening voice. "I'll have a talk with the boys, what is their problem? They will do what I tell them and not complain about it!" My mother replied. "Leave them alone, they're kids!" "Haven't I told you, don't tell me what to do! Worry about the Matanza, the food has to last us a bit. Don't give it all away!" My dad walked away; he had spoken.

My uncle was the first to arrive. He's my dad's older half-brother. Story had it that on her death bed, my grandpas first wife had shared her concern about her best friend. I heard my mom talk about it to her sisters and anyone who would listen. The story was both sad and funny. "Billy's mom was crazy. Agapita was an old maid and good friends with Abelino's first wife. I guess Abelino's wife told him to marry her so that she wouldn't be alone." My mom would then proceed to tell a joke. "You know that men are well behaved and follow instructions, so Abelino, who didn't want to, married her obeying his first wife's orders!" Hearing this all the women would laugh. They knew better. "Her family is from Santa Cruz and the whole family is crazy.

"We visited once for Christmas. When we walked in the house, it was in shambles, and they were cursing and fighting. I never went there again. My husband was raised in a way that would make him crazy too. I guess Agapita didn't get along with the neighbors and would have my husband call them names and throw rocks at them when he was but a young boy. Adding to the insanity, his half-brothers would tie him up and whip him. Billy was the son of that 'other' woman, they detested him and showed it." My aunt always responded the same way. "That explains why he's so crazy. I guess they put him through hell. You need to take your children and get the hell out of here before he kills one of you." Each of my aunts and their husbands always discussed this, though never in the presence of my dad. They feared him and after a few years they were hesitant to visit. My mom returned to reality and got ready for the festivities. She was hopeful that the drinking during the day would not turn into hell late into the night.

My brothers and I were told to haul wood and stack it. My dad was busy ordering us around when Alex War showed up in an old Chevrolet pickup truck with sun-stained paint and multiple dents. There were three other men in the back along with several big pots and basins. They got out of the truck and a whirlwind of activity was immediate. "Buenos Dias! And what does my friend Alex War have to say this morning?" As my dad shook hands with Alex, they both walked towards the fire pit, Alex checked to ensure it was burning hot. They talked about the recent happenings, murders, fights, drunken events, divorces, parties, etc.

SANTA FE: A PIECE OF 'MI VIDA'

"Remember, you have to keep the water extremely hot the whole time or we won't be able to peel the hair off the pig." All the discussion was in Spanish. "We are going to need another tub, that's not enough." War continued his discussion with anyone who would listen. "I got lucky this year. I got a tag to hunt elk in Tierra Amarilla. Let's go with me Billy. You know I get one every year whether I get a license or not. The meat is great, better than deer meat. The Forest Rangers try to keep us from hunting without a license. To hell with them, they stole that land from us." My father beamed as he spoke. "I can't go but Billy will. He is a hell of a shot.

By now the fire was raging and the water was bubbling. "Andale bro, let us kill a pig. You are going to love it. We are going to get some good cuts of pork." War spoke with a chicharron eating grin. His name was Alex Guerra, but everyone called him War because his last name literally translated to War in English. War scared me a bit, he had a look that most kids would be afraid of, especially his mouth. When he laughed his lips pursed like a catfish fighting the hook, being pulled out of the murky Rio Grande. This morning he was in a good mood. Him and his buddies were drinking beer and passing around a bottle of liquor. His face was red, his eyes appeared as if they were bulging out of his head. They were red with a base of white with jagged lines radiating from the front and center to the back. His face eerily looked like the face on the train.

Alex War smiled at me, and I felt a cold shiver run down my back all the way down to my feet. I could feel the medal that I had found lying against my chest even though I had given it to Billy. "How can I have this, I found it in a dream?" "Santiago, wake up and move your ass, what's wrong with you?" I recognized Billy 's voice. It was different, full of sadness, fear, and pain. The feeling I got was the same as when I followed Billy to the train tracks in my dreams, or whatever they were. "If dad catches you daydreaming, he will beat your ass." Billy gave me a swift kick in the ass and walked away.

My father was barking orders. "We have to keep that fire burning. The water has to be extremely hot, so we can peel the hair off nice and clean, so we can make chicharrones." We all loved chicharrones, the thin layer of fat surrounding the body of the pig with a small layer of meat that was deep fried to a crispy delight. I loved them when they were fresh, not too much when they were cold. My sister and my mom were setting up a makeshift table and placing knifes, buckets of water, and lots of other supplies. I focused in on the knives. Suddenly everything came to a halt. I could feel the tense excitement in the air. We could hear the fire crackling and could feel the heat flowing towards us. I heard the sharpening of knives, the water boiling, the people shuffling about.

One of Billy's friends threw him a rope. "Here you go bro, time to rock and roll." All eyes were on him as he walked towards the pig pen. It took him a while to come out of the pen with El Gordo in tow. The hog was walking gently along, unaware of what awaited him. My brother was walking tall and emotionless. "We will have some chicharrones in a few!" Alex War whistled while he walked towards El Gordo who was starting to get fidgety. "Where is the rifle? Billy, stop bro, don't spook him. The meat is more tender if he's relaxed." War walked over to El Gordo. "Talk to him bro, keep him calm." In an instant a shot rang out splitting the silence. I knew my life had just taken a big turn. I was curious and a bit scared as to where it would take me. I looked for Billy and saw him helping War and his friends tie a rope to the hind legs of the huge hog. The other end of the rope went over a strong limb of the ancient pear tree. The tree was older than me, older than my father. That tree had always been there. Man, those pears were good. The Era of El Gordo was over. The silence was deafening for a bit, then the hooping and the hollering of the Matanza took over.

As I watched, hot water was poured over the pig and the three began to peel the hair off El Gordo, who was now hanging lifeless. They were working quickly, all the time talking and teaching anyone who wanted to learn. "Keep the water hot, if not it becomes a bitch to remove the hair. We can't make chicharrones if the hair is not completely removed and the skin scraped clean." I heard one of them say that it was a mistake a lot of people made. Before I knew it the outer layer of fat and meat had been cut into thin strips and cubed. Now they were in a pot, deep frying in their own fat. The rich aroma filled the air. Thoughts of the living El Gordo began to disappear. As the matanza continued, the belly was opened from the rear end of the hog to the head making sure not to tear the bladder. "It will ruin the meat." Once the insides were removed, War raised up his hand motioning for everyone to listen up. Everyone became silent and the air stood still. The only thing that could be heard was the local Spanish music playing on the radio in the background.

The music was primarily Spanish ballads about love gone bad, families divided by violence, hero's dying sad deaths, poor people suffering at the hands of the rich, and other tragic events. The ballads serve as a cultural transference, much like the verbal passing of history and culture by the Tewa Indians. The Tewa Indian's passed their legacy from one generation to the next, verbally, it was part of the continuum. These songs became an oral history of the Hispanic experience in the Americas starting with the Spanish settlers and evolving to include the Mestizo, who were the offspring of the Spaniard and the Native American. They were the foundation of the Spanish Southwest.

War continued his presentation, relishing every minute. "No matanza is complete without taking a part of the life that we just sacrificed." I could hear my father explaining to us and anyone who could hear him. "Now is when they will pass the heart and the other organs around to be consumed bite by bite until it is gone." As he talked,

I saw that the insides were piled on the ground. The pile had a mixture of blood, entrails, and organs all heaped together. As I watched, I heard a gasp from the women and children as War dug through the pile and cut out pieces that were different. "Who wants the first bite?" War was glowing with pride and bravado as he held a solid ball of meat. "What's that?" I asked. "El Corazon, the heart of El Gordo!" I heard Billy speak loudly as he stepped forward with his hands outstretched. War handed it to Billy with a smile. "Right on hermano, your pig, your heart. It's only right that you take the first bite."

As War handed it over, the blood covered both of their hands. My brother looked at it with apprehension and it felt like hours as we all waited for the 'mordida', the bite. Everyone knew how much Billy cared for El Gordo. Suddenly the heart was in his mouth with El Gordo's blood dripping down his chin and onto his T-shirt. The heart was then passed around to anyone who had the courage to take a bite. When it was almost gone, I heard Billy, "Give it to my brothers." Juan shook his head, "No way bro!" The laughter was jolly, the party had started. Arthur and Michael stepped back simultaneously.

I was so involved in the spectacle that I hadn't realized that everyone had stepped back from the center except me. As I looked around it looked as if I had stepped forward. "He won't do it!" War spoke to the crowd, mocking them, and me. "Oh yeah he will 'pendejo' dumb ass. That's my 'carnalito', my little brother. That 'vatito', little dude, has balls bro." Billy responded as he walked over and took what was left of the heart and walked it over to me. I saw it in his eyes, he knew I could do it. It's as if time came to a halt. I could see the leaves twinkling in the soft wind blowing through the valley, shimmering, dancing with the sun. My life was standing all around me, the people I loved, the place I loved, the only life I had ever known.

I got the familiar feeling that I got every time Billy made me do things that I was afraid to do. These things were always things that

I used to watch older boys do. I remembered the carnival earlier that summer during the Fiestas. I was so excited to go to the carnival. Even though it came every year for the Fiestas, this was my first time. I was entranced by it all; the lights, the Ferris Wheel, the rides, the sound of the bells, song of the machines, the voice of the vendors and entertainers, the crowds of people separated by age, family, and village. It was magical to me. I watched as families walked by together laughing as they ate cotton candy, hot dogs, funnel cakes, and a wide assortment of carnival food. I could smell the sweetness of the cotton candy as it was being swirled around the cardboard handle. I wanted some but we didn't have any money, or if we did none was offered up. It was all strange to me. I wondered if I would ever come to the carnival with my whole family. I knew in my heart that I wouldn't.

"Santiago, see that boy over there with the candied apple? Go over and kick his ass." Billy pointed at a kid that was older than me. I could tell by his size and the way he looked. His clothes were nice and new, I could tell by how bright they were. What I really liked were his boots. His cowboy boots were shiny black and matched his belt. "What?" I was hoping he was kidding. "I said, go kick that boy's ass! Don't make me tell you again." "He's too big for me. He didn't do anything to me!" I stuttered as I spoke. I recognized the knot in my stomach. I got it every time my brother made me do scary things, like jump in the river before I knew how to swim. He always pulled me out right before I went under until I learned how to stay afloat. "I don't care!" He spoke as his face got next to mine. "Either you go over there and kick his ass, or I'll kick yours."

His hand was on my shoulder, not in a nice way. I knew he meant it. I mumbled as I began to walk towards him. "Remember what I taught you." My brother was a Golden Gloves boxer. My dad used to take him to the Boys Club in Santa Fe. It was situated in the toughest, most dangerous part of the city, Alto Street. The Boy's Club was across the street from the projects on Alameda Street. You did not want to walk in that neighborhood at night. It was known for its gang activity. Many of its residents ended up dead, maimed or in prison. Most of them went to the Boys Club to escape or to hang out. This was one of the places where my brother learned the art of street fighting.

I walked up to the finely dressed boy and punched him in the face. I was surprised when I saw that I knocked him down. As with my dad's friends and their sons when they came to visit, I didn't want to fight or hurt him. Instead of getting on top of him the way my brother Billy had taught me to finish it, I yelled at him to get up. I saw the look on his face. "You're a coward, hitting me when I wasn't looking." He spoke as he got up and he came at me, rushing me. I slid to the side and grabbed his arm and pulled hard, his momentum sent him to the ground. I saw a figure rushing me from the side and before he got to me, I saw Billy step between us and move swiftly as he quickly beat up the intruder.

Suddenly, I felt strength and excitement rush through me, and I went ahead and practiced my skills on the older boy. Billy grabbed me and we started running. I looked back as a crowd started gathering, pointing, and chasing after us. They stopped their pursuit as two Rio Arriba County Sheriffs walked into the vicinity. I would find out later that the boy and his brother were from Cordova, a small village north of Española. They were known for stabbing during fights. "Watch it with them, they all jump in and will stab you." I had heard my brother and his friends talk about them with anger and trepidation. I knew this was not over. I heard later that my brother had known who the boy was all along and had planned the whole thing. My brother and his crew were from El Guache and neighboring Hernandez and had a long running feud with the families from Cordova.

"Here, take a bite. Show everyone that you're not afraid." I was back in the present and images of Alex War taking his bite and the blood dripping down the sides of his chin made me cringe. The blood was thick and red, almost black. "Bite it and swallow it, don't think about it just do it." I closed my eyes for what felt like hours. The aroma of the flesh was overpowering. It smelled like the meat I had eaten before, but it was much stronger. Billy nudged me on the shoulder. "Open your eyes 'pendejo', stupid one, it's time for you to grow some 'lluevos', balls." I felt the coldness of the thick powerful red blob of meat and took a bite. The taste was strong, and the flesh was hard to chew. It felt like chewing rope, stringy and tough. I felt my body convulse wanting to remove it from my mouth. I could feel El Gordo sliding down my throat. I saw him as I swallowed, he was now a part of me. I got sad. I knew I would never see a hog rodeo again. I knew my life would never be the same. I was awakened by a cheer and several men laughing. They were all patting me on the back, some were calling me a man. I wondered how a young boy could be a man.

The party really got going now. Inside the house the women had been preparing food for the feast and were heading back inside to finish it. I followed my mom and sister Annette into the kitchen, hoping to cleanse the lingering taste from my mouth and throat. I felt it lingering all the way down into my stomach. As I walked into the kitchen, I was careful to be quiet and stay out of the way. I knew that the women would kick me out if they thought I was intruding into their world. They had lots to do and lots to talk about. It was a different world in the kitchen with the women. I was mesmerized by the discussions they had. The secrets were here, sheltered in the collective memories of the women who held it all together. The kitchen was a beehive of activity with work being shared at a rapid-fire rate. The wood stove stood in the corner, it looked old as it released heat into the small kitchen. The cabinets were white underneath years of decay and use. The floor was covered with white linoleum that was worn and frayed exposing the

ERIC SANTIAGO MARTINEZ

wooden floor underneath. The table was made of metal and had a slide
out that we pulled out only when we needed more table space.

The women continued with their discourse, mostly about the
men. The men were not talked about so nicely. According to most of
the women, men were terrible. They cheated, they drank, and they
detested most of their other manly habits and behaviors. My aunt,
unlike the others had mostly good things to say about her husband.
"Henry took me to Santa Fe yesterday, we ate at the Pantry. I love the
food there and he knows it." "My cheapskate husband seldom takes me
out, he spends his money in the bars buying drinks for cheap women
who will screw anybody if they buy enough drinks." I wondered how
all of them could be talking at the same time and yet they heard all the
conversations and remarked on them.

Teofila and Gabriela were preparing blood sausage. "Santiago, go
bring the intestines, we need them to make our delicacy." Both women
laughed as they continued to prepare the blood. They added lard and
'chile pequin' to it and simmered it till they became one. Chile' pequin
was the dark red ripened chile' that came from the chile' pods that
were woven together, 'ristras', they resembled a bunch of grapes. They
were then tied up high and allowed to dry in the hot New Mexico sun
to the point where the texture was stronger than the normal red chile
pods. These were then cut and cleaned by hand. This chile' flavor was
fuller and more robust than the regular red chile'.

I ran out to get the intestines, the tripe, and found them in
a small bucket. I ran to take them back. "You have to clean those! Get
into the ditch and wash them. Don't worry about how they smell or
feel, menudo here we come." By this time my brothers were on the
bank of the acequia laughing at me. The acequia was running strong
this year. The current was strong, I had to fight to stay upright. My
younger brother was laughing. "Be careful or you'll drown. That would
be funny, who would stop you?" Arthur joined the chorus. "I wouldn't.

It'd be funny to watch." "You two can get in there and help him, if not, shut up." Juan was always there protecting me, mostly from Billy. He had taken many a beating on my behalf, but it didn't stop him. Later in my life I would realize what a blessing he was to me. "Let me see them. Okay, that's good. Hurry up take them to mom; they are waiting for them."

Teofila and Gabriela were talking about our cousin. Jose had gone to a dance last night and as usual got drunk and started talking to all the women, including the married ones. "Ese garañion, al fin pago por su modo de desrespetar al las mujeres." Teofila was ranting. "That's what the dog gets. He was always disrespecting women and acting like they were all there for his pleasure." Gabriela responded as she continued to work on the blood sausage. "Maybe that's true but they didn't have to kill him, everybody knew how he was." "I've been on the receiving end of the disrespectful and filthy advances by Jose. I wanted to slap his dirty face." There was no holding Gabriela back. "That pig did it to all of us at one time or another. My old man had to straighten him out last year at the Fiestas. He gave him a good one." My mother broke the discussion. "How is that sausage going? The men will be here soon, drunk, and impatient. I don't want to hear about it later tonight."

All the women fell silent knowing the danger lurking for her if Billy Sr. drank too much. The rumors of the abuse were well known. Sometimes the bruises could not be hidden. The silence was broken as Aurelia and Lupita continued arguing about how best to cook the red chile' and if Jose deserved to die for disrespecting women and screwing any woman that would have him. All the women claimed to make the best red chile' in the valley.

During all of this I was enjoying the chicharrones that were killing the taste of El Gordo's heart in my mouth. The whole time I was thinking about the fact that I was eating him with every bite. I was waiting for the fajitas to be done. The fajitas were made from the meat that held the belly together. It was sliced thin like a belt thus the name fajitas, belts. I found my sister Annette helping with the rest of the tortillas, the aroma filled the air. Annette was quiet as she struggled with her fear of what the night would bring. "Mom is it okay if I go spend the night with auntie tonight? She reads a lot and shares a lot of stories with me. I can help clean up all of this before I go. She said she will bring me back tomorrow on her way to Albuquerque. She promised to help me go to college when the time comes."

My mom was silent as the sound of the men outside continued to grow as they drank, bragged, and argued. When my dad got like this, everyone kind of stayed away and humored him. "No, bro, look at how good the food is. Let's eat, drink, and be merry because tomorrow we die. Isn't that a saying from somewhere?" Our dad took the lead as the beer and whiskey continued to flow. His life as a prison guard had made him tough and mean, his upbringing probably set the stage. "Which one of you wants to find out how much of a man I am? I'll take on any of you." The others continued to party making sure not to antagonize him.

"We are almost done, let's put the food out and call the men in. What happened to Petra? She was supposed to bring the pies. I saw George outside and I wondered why she's not here. Did any of you ask George?" My mom continued. "Don't tell me George is still cheating on her with Margarita. I swear, if I ever have her to myself, I am going to smash her face in." My mom suspected that my dad had also taken pleasure in her arms. Margarita was known for her flings with all the married men and that she mocked the wife as she was having sex with the husband. All the women in the room shook their heads in unison. They all shared the same thoughts and hatred.

The discussions now turned to marriages, births, divorces, and to the war in Vietnam again. The war in Vietnam was very interesting to me as I watched every day on the news on our black and white TV. Everyone had a son there or at least knew someone who did. They had found my cousin Norman outside the bowling alley, dead with a rifle in his lap, he had shot himself in the head. He had come back from the war different. I remembered the last time I saw him.

I was walking home from Reggie's store and was surprised when he pulled over and backed up to where I was. "Do you want to go for a ride little cousin?" I jumped in with a smile on my face and my heart beating fast. Norman took me cruising to town and then back. On the way back I saw dead man's curve up ahead and I felt shivers run down my back. Many a car had approached the turn too fast and flown off, killing some and maiming others. As these thoughts raced through my brain, my cousin Norman down shifted, and I heard the small block Chevy groan as we entered the curve faster than I had ever gone and that was saying something since my father drove fast, especially when he drank. We surprisingly made it past the turn and my cousin dropped me off where he picked me up. "I'll be seeing you little cousin, take care." I saw him drive off and I never saw him alive again. I cried when my cousin died. I remembered how big he was and how he played the organ with the local bands who recorded songs mostly about love lost, friends going off to war, and the joy of cruising while listening to the radio.

The energy in the small kitchen was growing. I saw the calabacitas, the tender squash, corn, and cheese simmered to a perfect blend being pulled off the stove by Annette. The calabacitas were done. The women had it down to a science. "Go tell your father that the food is ready." I ran out and told dad and he ushered the men in, and we all had a huge meal. We were part of a rotation of matanzas between friends and families. Man, I loved these even if today it was El Gordo hot off the kill unto the grill.

The party was finally over, and my dad and Billy came inside. My mom and Annette were finishing up washing the dishes, sweeping, cleaning the floor, and putting all the food away. We would be eating this food for days as nothing was ever wasted. My brothers were talking about the festivities, making fun of the visitors as they laughed. "Be quiet and stop making all that noise." My dad told us to shut up and a silence fell over the household. "Bring me something to eat and hurry up!" I wondered how he could be hungry after eating all afternoon into the evening. "Hurry up I won't tell you again. Why do I always have to ask you so many times?" My mom and my sister looked at each other and the rest of us moved away like magnets when they repel. My mom gave her a sad smile and gently nodded to her. I could see the fear in both of them, especially my sister. My mom and my sister moved towards the stove and the refrigerator to warm up some of the day's pork driven feast. "I don't want any of that! I've had enough meat for today! Make me some enchiladas!"

"The beans and chili are gone. We had more people eat then we planned for. War invited all his friends over. I don't know why you had to give them all that beer. They came in here like they were starving, harassing Annette. My Annette is a child, and those pigs came in talking to her the way you and your friends talk to your whores at the bars." The look on my mom's face was a look I had seen before. The anger and the fear created a demeanor that usually ended in violence towards her. We all wondered which one of my father's responses we would see tonight. Based on the amount of alcohol consumed and the collective bravado of the day we all suspected it would be the violent one. "You guys go outside, now! Don't come back in until I tell you!" My father spoke in that scary voice that we hoped we would never have to hear. When my father turned to face us his monster eyes were red and shiny and could pierce through your soul. We all rushed outside except my brother Billy who moved closer to my mom and Annette. We went and stood outside my grandpa's single room home.

The night sky was brilliant. It was pitch black and the stars were twinkling. I could feel the wind on my face. All the old spooky stories came out on nights like this, the real scary part was inside. "I'm scared!" Michael started to cry as the four of us stood outside my grandfather's hoping he would let us in. I had noticed that he had not stuck around for long. Once the Matanza was over and the food was prepped he had left with a look of disgust on his face. It was obvious he wanted to be as far away from the drunkenness as possible. We all peered inside but it was dark.

My grandfather's house was a single room with a bed, wood stove, and a pantry covered by an old blanket that served as a curtain. He was in his late seventies and still very active. His one room house was simple. The most prominent item was the large crucifix hanging on the wall over his bed. The Cross looked old and heavy, sometimes the corners of the cross had spider webs on them making it look eerie. His bed pan had always confused me. I wondered why he just didn't go to the outhouse like us. I was squeamish around the white bed pan with a lid on it. I knew what was in there and wanted nothing to do with it.

Our fear grew as we were all hoping he would help us and stop my dad. He had stopped my dad a few times but the last time he had intervened it had not gone well for him. I remembered that night as I stood in the dark, my dad had yelled at him. "Mind your own business old man?" My grandpa had not wavered. "You're drunk again! Why do you keep drinking and abusing your family?" My grandpa had always been there for us but as we got older, and my dad got meaner we saw less of him. "I told you to mind your own business." My father had knocked my grandpa down and warned him not to interfere ever again. I guess it worked because we were alone, huddled together outside. "Stop crying! Do you want him to come out here?"

My dad's voice pierced the night. "Shut up I told you! It's none of your business what I do! I told you to make me something to eat, now do it." My mom responded and her reply was not good. "Why do you always get this way when you are with your friends? We are your 'familia', not them! They come over here and you pay for the beer and we're here wondering what we're going to eat." "I told you to shut up!" My father responded in the voice, and we all knew it was the calm before the storm. We heard the scratch of the old wooden chair as it moved away from the table and the loud bang of a fist slamming the tabletop. I started to shake, and a dark fear and pain swept over me. The three of us started crying.

Juan spoke with a sound of dread in his voice. "Move to the side of the house he can't see us there." It was almost completely dark now. The silhouette of the orchard was foreboding as if demons were lurking in the shadows. The glittering star filled sky was not magical tonight, it seemed to illuminate a spirit of darkness. There was a group of clouds to the side that the moon was glowing through. As the clouds morphed, I could see images, strange and evil. My father's voice broke through the night. "Annette, bring that plate over here and put butter on that tortilla! Hurry up!" "Leave her alone, she's a little girl. Why don't you talk to those drunks that way?"

The plate smashing against the wall echoed in the small kitchen. "Dad, let's go for a walk. Remember you told me you would take me night fishing down at the river. The moon is perfect for that. We can catch us some fish for breakfast tomorrow." Billy pleaded with his father. "Be quiet and go outside with your brothers. You know what will happen to you if you open your mouth again, you little punk." We waited for Billy to exit the house, but he didn't. "Annette, why is it taking you so long to get that butter on that tortilla! I told you to hurry up?"

I could hear my sister crying. "I am daddy, I'm almost done." Annette was 14 years old and had the features of both Spanish and Native American women, she had an exquisite and beautiful exotic look. Annette had wavy hair that flowed like the waves on the Rio Grande. Her brown eyes were deer-like, alert, and primal, her upbringing required it. Annette was smart, more times than not she led her class in academic performance. She was quick witted and agile like a cat. She was always busy chasing her brothers around just like cats chased mice.

"Didn't I tell you to hurry up? Who do you think you are?" We stood frozen as we heard the wailing of my sister. We knew she had been hit and that it was bad! The sound of the slap was like a bolt of lightning in the kitchen. We all felt it. For my part, it hurt more when I heard it coming from a family member than when I was on the receiving end. I was helpless to do anything to prevent it. The sound of the table crashing brought us to the door. Juan was the first one through. As we approached the door we heard and saw a scene we had experienced before. "Stop it dad, you're going to hurt her?" We saw my dad turn around and face Billy.

"You little punk, you think you can stop me from running this family?" We saw our dad push Billy off his feet. We all rushed in and started yelling for him to stop. Billy was yelling at my dad. The hatred in Billy's voice filled the room. Annette was shaking and sobbing in the corner. "Stop it dad, stop it!" My dad pushed us all out of the way and walked towards his car and as fast as the thrashing started, it ended. He was gone into the night. It was a long night for us, our life and our love and been shattered again. I knew that all families were not like ours. I had seen families together, the mom, dad, and the kids. They would be laughing, holding hands, and enjoying each other. I wanted that, but my life was here.

Chapter | 6

FIREFLY

I feel a hot dream cascade through my body. The train is moving along the track. I feel it moving swaying back and forth. I don't want it to move! I'm afraid of where it is taking me. I feel the sweat rolling down my face and back. I know that it is taking me back in time. I feel the presence of a warmth inside of me keeping me calm. I think I've heard a voice, a calming voice but I can't figure out what it is saying. I no longer see the Roman Armies, but I do see the face of the conductor as he walks towards me. He is greeting passengers as he walks down the aisle. I notice that the passengers are dressed differently. The clothes they are wearing are not like I normally see but it's like they are at a costume party like the ones I see on TV.

I shudder as I remember Billy's words to me about not sharing my dreams with anyone. I see that there are people on the train from all walks of life. Some are laughing with each other, some are cowering against the walls of the train, and others are walking and stalking, like lobos preying on the weak. The ghost train is floating through sceneries that are changing from the past to the present. The train is flowing forward again as if a trip has been taken to the source of the river and has now begun its flow back through time. The people seem the same as us. It's as if some of them are in my family. The images in the windows appear to be alive, all of them. I know they are not from my time. Why am I seeing all of this? I do not understand! It reminds me of history class from school but it's nothing like what the books and teachers say. The faces are all looking at me but can't see me, except for the conductor.

Suddenly, the train screeches to a halt. As soon as it comes to a full stop, I feel a hand on my back and a voice in my head, it is soft but urgent. "You will hear the doors open. As soon as you do, get out and run as fast as you can." A female voice is talking behind me, and I trust what she is saying. I get up and start to run out when I notice someone moving in the adjacent car. "Billy, is that you? Let's run, we have to get out of here! The lady told me to run for my life, let's go!" I see the figure that I swear is my brother as he looks at me. His face is swirling like the clouds before a storm. He seems to be sad as he reaches out a hand to me. I see the face of the conductor floating towards me with hunger flowing from his entire body. I start running as fast as I can. I look back and see the conductor chasing me. I feel his eyes on my back as I run, and I run, and I run! I know in my heart that he is too fast and that I cannot get away. I start to panic!

I don't want to become part of that train riding its ghostly track for eternity. I see the heavens in front of me, stars twinkling like angels, with the sky calling out to me. The night air is old and cold, and the evil is still chasing me. The faster I run the closer he gets. I see two moons in the distance, one in the sky and one reflecting on the surface of the river, shimmering as its light permeate and reflect the movement of the water. The moon seems to become one with the water, it's alive! The moon is alive! It is blending with the living creatures beneath the surface. I can see through the water that there is life in it. Even now, I see life from the past transitioning to the present. I see fish that are big, almost too big. They seem to be crawling out of the water headed towards me.

ERIC SANTIAGO MARTINEZ

As I look back over my shoulder, I see that the conductor is gaining on me. His grin is forever there as if he knows something I don't. Does he have a plan that I can't know about? I feel my legs try to move faster but they can't. My breathing is becoming difficult. I am running out of air as I try to get back to my time. I get the feeling that the past is trying to catch me. In the distance, I can see my family through the kitchen window talking. They are all smiling. I want to be there with them. I cannot hear them but now I am running towards them. "Where is Billy?" I scream into the night. I see that they can't hear me, they are too far away. The train is not there. I am watching them the way I watch TV except I am not in my home but in the darkness running for my life. I hear strange noises squeezing around me from all sides. I have heard some of them by the river at home. I recognize the screeching of the owls at night, the crickets whistling at each other, the hawk as it dives to eat, and many more. Mixed in with those sounds are new ones, meaner ones, stronger ones. All of them seem to feel me and want me out of their world. The predators are out and the main one is after me. I see good intertwined with the bad. The predators and the prey, will I get away? Hard to say when it's all night and no day.

I feel heat crawling up my back as the conductor reaches out to grab me. I look back over my shoulder and I see black blood dripping from his mouth. He has a look of pure evil, the other predator creatures are surrounding me, they are helping him. I can feel scratching down my back. The scratch is tacky as if it wants to stick to me. As the panic sets in I see myself wanting to quit but in one last effort I turn left and jump into the river. I am underwater, looking up through its depths and I see the conductor looking for me. I am running out of breath, dreading what will happen when I surface and come face to face with the evil menace. The area around me starts to light up. It reminds me of the nights when my brothers and I went outside to drive the skunks from our fields and the fireflies were out. The light penetrated through the night.

Now the night surrounds the flashing light floating through the air. A warm glow fills the water. In what seems to take hours I flashback to the time my brothers and I were chasing the fireflies. It was a yearly adventure for us. We would see hundreds of them. We would get a Mason Jar and put holes in the lids. We ran into the alfalfa field to catch them. Our strategy was to swat them with our shirts and knock them down. Their light would go off and we would kneel and wait. The firefly would wake and light up then we would catch it and put into our jar. It was beautiful. They became our night light for a few nights until they died, or we let them go.

On one of our adventures, we spotted one that was larger than any we had ever seen. All of us wanted it! It was as if the firefly knew we wanted it, so it flew up into our large apricot tree and sat there. It was teasing us as it lit up. It was dark and I decided to climb up the tree and catch it. I put my jar down and grabbed a branch and lifted myself up into the tree. I had climbed many a tree and knew that the trunks grew in layers as it went up. At each layer the limbs got smaller and there was more of them. The higher I climbed the thinner the branches got. I neared the top and I could feel the branches sway. The firefly lit up and I maneuvered my body and reached out to catch it. As I reached to catch it, the tree limb I was on disappeared and I fell into the tree headfirst. I was falling and felt the blows as my head struck the branches. When I woke up, I was in bed. I was delirious and saw my mom through the fog as she checked on me. I was in bed for a couple of days unable to think. I would find out later that my parents should have taken me to the Emergency Room. The joke was that our Emergency Room was the room that our family slept in.

"Why is he chasing me, looking at me, all the time and what is Billy doing on that train? Who are all those people and why does the scenery change?" I am going over these questions in my mind as I'm under water. I feel me permeate the water. I am running out of air and

chars

my lungs are ready to burst. "Relax little one, you have nothing to fear as long as you stay clear." The voice belongs to the women who seems to be watching out for me. I have never seen her before, but I can tell that she knows me. "Who are you, please help me, I don't want to drown. Billy taught me how to swim but I can't hold my breath any longer." I take a deep breath and feel the water fill my lungs and the conductor is looking at me as I am forced to surface. The conductor reaches out for me, but I am just out of his reach.

"Don't move any closer no matter how badly you want to. The evil one will draw you in! Know that he can't have you if I am here. Remember, you are here to learn the lessons that history must teach. Look around you, do you know where you are?" I look around and see a huge boulder sitting on the side of the river. In an instant I see the river speed up. I watch as the river gets lower and lower, and the rock slowly slips into the water. Then I recognize it, it's our swimming hole rock. I am drifting towards the conductor. I see through him and in him. I get close enough and then in an instant I am being pulled into his mouth. The smell makes me gag and I throw up into his mouth as I enter the dark.

"Santiago, wake up, Santiago wake up!" I wake up, my mom is shaking me. "Santiago, are you sick? Look, you threw up in your bed!" I get up and stare at the mess. My mom touches my forehead with a worried look on her face. You don't have a fever." "I'm Okay." I reply as I get up and start getting dressed. "Here help me." My mom is already taking the hand sewn blankets and sheets of the bed and will take them out to wash them by hand. I put on my clothes and look down at my torn tennis shoes. I wonder every day why I can't have new ones. I rush and finish getting dressed.

We start walking and my mom stops and hugs me. "I love you my son, don't ever forget that. I always will. I know you're worried about moving, we all are. I am glad, you will go to better schools. You are very smart, and I want you to do good in school. I loved school when I was young, but your grandma didn't let me go. I was a good student and the teachers really liked me. Your grandma took me out of school and put me to work for rich people, cleaning their houses and babysitting their kids. Your aunts got to go to school but I didn't. I want you to go to school, do you understand?" "Okay mom, I will go to school and do good."

"Why did you have to work? Why didn't grandpa and grandma work?" "Your grandpa worked as a sheepherder in Colorado. He was gone for months and then he would come home and give money to your grandma, but I guess it wasn't enough. Anyway, my mom started sending me to Colorado to pick lettuce during the summers. It was hard work and I never got a penny from any of the jobs I did. I do not want that to happen to you. A good thing that came from that is you, your sister, and brothers. I met your dad at one of those jobs when I was cleaning house for your uncle. Your dad is what I got for being taken out of school and forced to do hard work!"

Chapter | 7

THE MOVE

"Santiago, let's get going, we don't have all day!" Billy yells at me to catch up. The walk towards the river is perfect, it's a beautiful day in New Mexico. The sun shines bright, a cool gentle breeze is shimmering through green growth all around us, and the temperature is perfect for a swim. "Billy, you be careful, keep an eye on your brothers! If you let one drown, I'll have to make another one, someone has to hoe the fields and pick the harvest!" My mom and Annette are laughing as they stand in front of our house. They have the wash tub and the scrubbing board ready. They are waiting for the water on the stove to come to a boil. They are getting ready to do laundry. My mom pats my sister on the back. "Let's get this done I won't take dirty clothes to our new home." My mom comes from a small town in Northern New Mexico and is used to doing hard work to take care of us. She hardly remembered her life there, except for the bad stuff and there was plenty of it. We all laughed at her joke as we continued our walk to the river.

We had always swam in the river since who knows when. I didn't know a time without the river being a part of my life. We were all impressed by the excitement of our swim. "I'm hoping that Billy will swim across!" My excitement was over the top. The river's current ran so fast and strong that I couldn't believe anyone could swim it.

I enjoyed it when he did, and I dreaded it at the same time. "You know he will, he always does." "No, he doesn't! Last time we came he didn't even get in, he stayed drinking with those guys in the truck, they were smoking too." Michael seemed to gather information just to argue with us about it. He was a spoiled brat. As the baby of the family he was always protected, and he used it. Billy yelled over his shoulder as we walked. "It's none of your business what I do. You better keep it to yourself if you know what's good for you!"

"I'm glad we woke up early to go swimming. What a beautiful morning! I'm going to miss this!" Juan was talking to Billy as we walked. "What's going on with Sammy? Randy told me that he was in jail." Juan was good friends with the younger brother of Billy's friend. Billy didn't answer, his mind was somewhere else. We continued walking down the small easement at the end of our property. My grandfather had given the easement to the Acequia Commission so that they could access the water gates by the river. I had asked why trucks with mean looking men and sometimes men on foot passed through our property. They scared me although my dad and Billy talked to them as they passed by. I often wondered why they drank and carried fishing rods if the purpose of the easement was to work on the gates to the overflow ditch. Oh well, I was told to shut up and stop asking stupid questions, again!

"Dad said we can come and swim every summer when we come back to help grandpa with the trees and stuff." Michael piped in. "You're not going to throw us in the deep part, are you?" I regretted the question as soon as I asked it. "Look at how much alfalfa I cut yesterday. One of these days you guys will be old enough to help." Juan was a good worker and sometimes he had to remind us. "What do you mean, we already help!" Arthur responded with a "how dare you?" We all wanted to talk at the same time. Juan and I played the guitar together. I envied how he played lead guitar like my dad. He got that look when I missed a chord or was out of step. His look was scary in a way, he had the look now. We walked in silence for a bit then the chatter started again. We were brothers on a journey. Our journey was to the river where our ancestors had gone swimming for centuries.

Billy was awe struck by the beauty of the morning as he walked past the orchards and the freshly cut alfalfa. He could smell the unique scent enhanced by the gurgling of the water running in the acequias. We could see the cottonwood trees that lined the river. The bosque was a tangle of wild, overgrown vegetation and was hard to get through. It reminded me of the jungle movies where the group had to use a machete to cut through the thick underbrush. We did not have a machete, so we endured the branch scrapes, pokes in the eyes, and mosquito swarms that attacked as if on que. We used to tease that the mosquitos flew in formation. I kept getting an eerie feeling as if we were being watched. The Conductor's face was embedded in my mind's eye. I shook it off. I loved the river. It was a place of peace for me, most of the time. The raging water in the Spring and the slow-moving water in the Fall, mirrored my life.

"Can we swim at the dam first? Let's see if the diving board will hold." Arthur was excited to use the diving board as he had been one of the main architects. We had built a diving board using an old piece of wood, a shovel, and a lot of muscle. The dam was one of many water-control valves that were built to manage water through the extensive centuries old acequia system. The water flowed through the gate into a small pond then out the other side into the river. The pond was surrounded by debris, old trees, empty beer bottles, and other items discarded by the water or the people using it. Many times, when we came down here, there were other people hanging out, usually men and teens. If they were swimming, we would jump in and join them. In our mind the pond belonged to us, it was at end of our property. If they were fishing, we were disappointed and carved our way to the river to swim as we didn't want to get hooked. Today was a good day, no one was at our pond.

"Let's go, just be careful, don't fall in the water, it's strong today." In an instant Billy was in the water and once again we all dived in by age. Michael and I were a bit hesitant, the water was flowing fast, and the pond was full. "Get in, what are you waiting for?" We stood there for a while looking in and had not paid attention to Juan getting out of the pool. I saw Billy's eyes following something, he was smiling. I felt a cold hand on my back, I was airborne into the water. Michael was right behind me. The water was cold, but it felt good. "Help me, I can't get out." Michael swam to the edge and was trying to get out, but the current was too strong. Juan reached down and pulled him up. "Stop crying or go home. We came to swim and if you can't, go home." As we got out of the water, we walked over to the makeshift diving board we had built. "Can I go first? I never get to go first! Why do you guys always go first? Santiago always wants to go first? It's not fair!" Michael went on as usual. He had this thing with me from the beginning of time.

We were always together. We played together, bathed together, and competed. Since we were only one year apart the competition between us was always there and it often ended up with him crying and blaming me to anyone who would listen. "Stop your bullshit or go home! We are tired of you always crying and running to mom and dad to tell on us. Santiago, you go first. The pool is nice and deep. Watch it with those dead branches on the other side." Billy was on my side most of the time and often, I paid a price for it. I looked around and took in the scenery. I regretted what I had asked for. The water was flowing fast, and the wind was moving the tree leaves back and forth, the shimmer was other-worldly.

I approached the diving board with trepidation. We had built it the day before but had to go home before we could try it out. "Hurry up, what's taking you all day?" My brothers were all complaining and waiting anxiously for their turn. I nervously stepped on the board and walked to the edge. It was scary up there as I watched the water rush through the pond on its way to the Rio Grande. It looked as if the distance between me and the water was at least a mile. Suddenly, I felt a hand on my back as Billy shoved me. I plunged into the pool. The water slapped me as I did a belly flop. The shove drove me forward. Man did it hurt! I immediately began to sink. I hit the bottom where I felt the rocks cut into my skin.

At that moment, I saw the image of the conductor and the face of the women that had pulled me out of the river when I ran from the conductor during my journey on the night train. As I broke the surface, the laughter of my brothers was boisterous as they doubled over in glee. "What's so funny you guys? Look at my chest! I hit the bottom, I thought I was going to drown!" I did not say anything to Billy as I knew better. According to his behavior towards me, the more he put me through the better. I guess that's the way he saw it. If I survived it was all good. I always did survive but I wondered why he gave me more attention than my brothers, this kind of attention. It seemed as if the more I cried the more he picked on me. I could feel that he loved me, it was just the way he showed it that troubled me. We all took turns diving and none of us noticed that the mud and rocks holding the diving board in place were coming loose. Juan got on it and was feeling good. Juan had done a back flip the last time he dove. He stepped to edge of the board and jumped up. The board fell out from under him, he and the board slid into the water. We laughed so hard we almost peed our pants.

Billy was already walking to the river as Juan climbed out of the pond. We had to run to keep up. As I ran, I forgot about the blood running down my chest all the way down to where the sun doesn't shine. Not to worry, river water would wash it clean. We fought through the bosque and eventually we got to the riverbank. The ducks taking flight scared me, yet there was something that thrilled me at the same time. The river was wild and ran strong. Even though I knew the small eddy where the ducks swam was there, the ducks taking flight always startled me. As we waded into the shallow end of the river I wondered if Billy would swim across it.

We grew up hearing about those that had tried, and their lifeless bodies had to be fished out of the water downstream. "Are you swimming across today? It's really running fast. Maybe we can come back when it's calmed down, then you can do it?" Juan was imploring Billy to stay on our side of the river. The other side, the pueblo side, was the deep end. You could see the river speeding by so fast that the debris it carried flashed by crashing into each other and into fallen cottonwoods protruding from the shore overhanging the river.

Billy looked across, he didn't say a word and walked right in. We followed him in, wading in as far as we dared. The water got deeper and got stronger the further out we went. We waded downstream to a place where you could barely see a ripple of a wave. When the water was high it looked normal but as the water level lowered during the summer months you could see the tip of a rock sticking out. The water had carved under a massive stone creating the perfect swimming hole. It protected us from the rivers current if we didn't swim too far out. We began to line up and wait our turn to climb up and dive into the water. It was hard to get up the slippery stone. Many times, we were assisted up with a not so friendly butt shove until Billy and Juan got tired and left us to our own devices.

We could hear Michael scream with joy as he leapt from the rock. "Wee! Wee!" Arthur was next as he dove and slipped through the surface of the water without a splash, smooth as a dolphin. I envied his athleticism. Like Billy he excelled. We were all good, we had to be, but he was better. Just as we were all smart, he was the smartest. Arthur read a lot which got him into trouble with our dad. As he splashed in, Billy through a stick into the water up stream. "Swim out and get it!" Arthur swam easily way out and got it. "Hand it to me." Billy threw it out again. "Santiago, go get it!" I swam out and could feel the current taking me. I couldn't quite get to it, and it sped by. "Here goes another one!" Billy threw the stick further upriver giving me more time to go get it. I swam up and got it. I felt good. I knew someday I would swim across the river like Billy. We were all good swimmers considering the way we had been taught.

My recollections were fuzzy. I remembered being shown how to move my hands and legs and then being tossed into the shallow water and told what I had to do and what not to do. "You have to lay flat on your stomach and move your arms and kick your legs!" Just before I lost control, I would feel two hands reach in and pull me out and we would start again. "Kick your legs, don't let your legs go down into the water." Billy, Juan, and sometimes Arthur continued. "Fill your lungs with air so you can float! Lay flat on your belly." The voices seemed to come from all sides. Eventually I was left alone to put into practice all the instructions delivered to me in rapid succession. What a beautiful day it was when I took off and swam.

As we were swimming, we were startled by voices coming up behind us. The Mares brothers, Felix and Rudy broke through the bosque and started yelling at us. The brothers were known and feared by most. I had seen them defer to my father at the bars while we sat in the corner and watched him get drunk. It bothered me as we sat there watching them get drunk on my dad's dime. I often wondered why my dad bought drinks for everyone at the bars, especially the women, while we sat in the corner hungry wanting to go home.

"Do you even know how to swim?" Felix yelled at us as Rudy pointed and laughed. It was hard to tell which one was which. Both Felix and Rudy were lanky and scary. They had jet black hair that was long and greasy. Their eyes were dark, and their teeth were crooked and had stuff on them. My dad said they were full of shit and some of it was stuck on their teeth. We laughed when he said it, but it was not funny now. We often saw them walking down the dirt road in front of our home, talking loudly, waving, and flailing their hands in the air as if they were talking to someone in the sky. When we saw them, we tried to make ourselves smaller, take up less space. They looked like monsters to us. We had been warned to stay away from them. We were glad to do so.

Billy had been watching from the middle of the river and quickly swam to shore. "Hey guys, what are you up to? Are you going to take a swim? The water is a bit dirty. It must have rained in Tierra Amarilla. My dad will be here in a while to swim with us." "We don't swim bro, we use the river to hide the dead!" Felix responded with an evil stare on his face. It had long been suspected that they had killed Benito and thrown his body into the river. Benito's family had gotten some money from a land sale, so Benito always had cash in his pocket and didn't hesitate to flash it around town. Six months prior the brothers were seen at Tito's, the local bar, with Benito getting drunk. The three of them left at the same time and Benito was never seen again. The State Police investigated talking to several witnesses. The State Police had determined that they in fact were the last to have been seen with him.

No charges were ever filed as the brothers claimed that Benito had driven himself home. A few months passed until one of the locals found Benito's car. The person that found the car stated that as he was fishing, his hook got caught on something in the water. Since he only had one hook left, he got in the water and followed the line and bumped into the car. He ducked into the water and recognized the car. There was no sign of Benito. The door was open and some believed that he had crashed into the river, managed to open the door and was washed away. The story told most often was that the brothers had killed him, stolen his money, and driven the car into the river. Either way, everyone knew the brothers were behind it.

"How's your dad doing these days? We haven't seen him at the Delta Bar lately. Is he still working at the Prison? My cousin Fermin is

in prison for killing that dude from Medenales. Fermin told us your dad
threw him down the stairs a couple of months back. Fermin said that
your dad then threw him in the hole to cover it up. Your dad needs to
be careful what he does in there. When they get out, they'll find him
and take care of it. Your dad is a tough hombre, but he's just a man."
Rudy was talking at all of us with a threatening look on his face. "My
dad will be here in a bit, so you can talk to him about it." Billy knew
that several ex-convicts had come looking for my dad to get pay back
only to get beat up out here as well. The brothers looked at each other
and continued walking down stream talking as they did. It was obvious
to me that it was about my dad, and it wasn't good. "If you ever see
those two, stay away from them. They are both crazy as hell and more
dangerous than crazy. I'll let dad know what they said. He'll make
them wish they hadn't talked to us." We continued swimming, but the
atmosphere had changed.

  After that confrontation, my brother seemed determined to
cross the river. "Be careful bro, the water is running deep and fast,
a bunch of logs are floating down." Billy seemed not to hear Juan as
he headed upriver on the shallow side. "I wish I could swim across!"
"You'd drown." Michael responded to me. "Look at the way he does
it. He goes upriver so that he can get to the other side before it hits
the dam downstream. He'll have to go a little higher today, the water
is running faster." Arthur had analyzed it and knew the mechanics of
it. "I hope he makes it! I'm scared, what if he drowns?" Michael was
obviously scared. I responded, "He won't drown, he's done it before.
Billy's stronger than anyone. I'll cross someday just like he does." We
waited for what seemed like an eternity. "There he is!" Juan shouted as
he pointed.

  I could barely see him; he was flying by on the other side of the
river near the bank. "How is he going to get out?" Arthur asked obviously

concerned. Juan responded in a determined voice. "There's branches around the bend that hang over; he'll have to grab on to one!" My heart was beating so hard that I could feel it wanting to pop out of my chest. I couldn't stand it anymore and started swimming down along the bank. I needed to see him get out. I started to get scared. "What if he doesn't get out? What if he misses and can't grab on to the fallen tree? Where will he end up?" My questions were spoken but I didn't wait for an answer from anyone. I wanted to save my brother, but I felt helpless. I got near the bend when I heard Juan yelling at me from behind, telling me to go back.

"The water around the bend is too deep!" He was yelling at me. In my agitated state I had forgotten the repeated warnings about not swimming to the bend as it was way too dangerous. I quickly stopped swimming and abandoned my rescue mission. I nervously waited for Billy to cross on his own. I often wondered why Billy did it. I noticed that Billy was on the bank on other side. "He made it! He made it!" I started moving upriver with him, he was on his side of the river, and I was on mine. The river in front of him raced past. I watched as he fought his way through the bosque. He would have to go upriver again. I watched until I couldn't see him anymore. In an instant we saw him swimming towards us. I watched in amazement as he got to us as if a magnet had pulled him in. "Let's go, time to go eat."

We walked up the small path to our home laughing and rough housing all the way. We had gathered willow branches and were having a sword fight with each other. I loved my brothers more than I could understand. Later that day I heard Billy telling our dad about the Mares brothers. I saw the look on my dad's face and knew something big was going to happen. I fell asleep quickly. Tomorrow was going to be a pivotal day in my life. I had a very restless night, images from the train rides flashed through my brain. They were images of people, mountains, oceans, animals, children, cities, all morphing into something I wanted to understand. Added to this was the events of the day. Our day had been perfect until the Mares brothers showed up. It felt as if something always showed up to shatter our happy moments.

When I woke-up I could hear a commotion outside. I rushed up, got dressed, and hurried outside. The baby blue Ford truck was loaded with so much stuff the truck looked small. Our stuff rose high above the roof. It looked strange, all our belongings heaped up and strapped on. The truck was a 1956 Ford, baby blue with dents in it. More times than I can recall, we used that truck to haul sand from the arroyos to make adobe bricks. It was hard work but was exciting as well. My dad and Billy would ride in the cab with the rest of us in the bed of the truck. The only safety feature was my dad yelling at us to sit down warning us that if we didn't, we would fall out.

We sat and enjoyed the open air most of the time. When it was cold or raining, not so much. The fact that we were young did not exempt us from shoveling the heavy sand. Billy and Juan did the bulk of the work. "Throw it to the back first." My dad ensured that the load was to the front center of the truck bed. "Put it towards the front so that we don't pop the leaf springs!" When we were done, we rode behind the sand or sat on it. "Arthur, you and Santiago take the shovels and do some work. Santiago, do ten shovels and let Michael do some." My dad made sure we worked. "Get up there and move some of that sand to the back." We all had to do our share.

As my dad and Billy climbed into the cab, I noticed that they looked like the El Guache version of the Beverly Hillbillies, like the sitcom we watched on TV. Only we were moving to the Penitentiary of New Mexico, not to a mansion in Beverly. It was very exciting but scary at the same time. I watched as Billy and my dad drove off. I wanted to go but the truck bed was loaded to the sky. We stayed to help my mom pack the next load. There wasn't that much left, we had very little to pack. That night we all shared beds made of metal frames that were banged up and multicolored due to years of use. The colors were brown, black, and rust, with history banged into the metal. My grandfather sat in silence as he watched his extended family in the process of leaving him behind.

My grandfather was light skinned with blue eyes. His family was one of the original Spanish settlers in Northern New Mexico. The land we worked was part of several land grants that the King of Spain bestowed on his subjects in the new world. Land grants were not private property but property that belonged to the community. These properties were appropriated by the carpetbaggers post Mexican American War. The stealing of our land led to the continued festering of animosity towards the "Gringos that stole our land." Out of the hundreds of thousands of acres that were originally owned by the original Spanish families, only a few thousand remained. Our culture was strong and refused to be assimilated and continued a subdued guerrilla warfare that picked away at the 'evil ones'.

We would often hear about people from both cultures always fighting with each other. In El Rito, my mom's family had lost most of their land. We didn't understand most of the talk around it. The highlight of our visits was the time we spent with our uncle Donald. He was the coolest dude you ever wanted to meet. I remember being happy and feeling proud every time I was with my uncle. He had jet black hair that he wore slicked back. He wore a leather jacket and drove a 50's Mercury with baby moon rims and dual exhaust. His car was the coolest and so was he. He had an attitude that excited all of us and worried our parents. At family gatherings he was often the center of discussions, usually revolving around him running around with the women of El Rito. Rumor had it that some of the women were married. "His good looks are going to get him in trouble." "He needs to be careful, 'que no lo capen'!" "He better be careful or they are going to castrate him."

"Hey 'primos', cousins, let's go throw a cruise." Cruising with Uncle Donald was the best. His car was fast, and he didn't hesitate to show us just how fast it was. The last time we went cruising with him he was drinking beer. As we drove, Billy and Juan were asking a lot of questions about the car. Most of it I didn't understand like what made it go faster, pipes, and other parts. "You are lucky uncle, I bet this cost a lot of money?" Billy was fascinated and it rubbed off on us. "Is this the fasted car in El Rito?" Juan asked excitedly. "It's one of them, there aren't too many cars here. The cool cars are in Española and Santa Fe." "Do you like Low Riders?" Juan was fascinated with Low Riders. "They look cool, but they are hard to drive on dirt roads, they scrape everywhere. Most of the guys that cruise them are crazy. Be careful not to get in with anyone if you don't know them or if you know they like to fight. You don't want to get caught up in that." Rumor had it that my uncle made money by selling stuff that was illegal. I didn't know what they were talking about and I didn't believe it. Donald was cool. "Here's your dad flashing his lights, let me pull over and see what he wants."

We all turned around and saw my dad get out of his car and meet Donald between the two cars. I couldn't hear what they were saying but I could tell that my dad was not happy. I saw my uncle step back putting his arms out in front of him. "Roll the windows down!" Billy told Juan and Arthur who were riding shotgun in the back. "I don't want you taking my boys out cruising. They're too young and I don't want them to see and learn the wrong things. It's your business what you do but I don't want them seeing you smoking that crap." "I'm just taking them for ride, that's all." My dad walked to the side of the car and he was not happy. "Who gave you permission to go cruising with your Uncle Donald?" "He asked us in front of mom, she didn't say anything, so we came." Billy always spoke up in a way to keep us out of dad's wrath. "This is a cool car huh dad? Can you make ours like this?"

Michael got away with asking questions at the wrong time. "Get out and get in my car, it's time go home." "Don't forget what I told you." My dad pointed at Uncle Donald and my uncle nodded his head. That was the last time any of us saw him alive.

On our many trips to visit my grandma Magdalena's home in El Rito we kept hearing stories at all the family gatherings, usually in the kitchen, about our uncle. "Donald is going to get his ass kicked if he doesn't cut his shit out, something bad is going to happen." Donald's mom sounded scared. "I tell him and tell him, but he laughs." His answer is always the same. "Let them try it, I'm not afraid of them. If they were men, their wives wouldn't be looking." "We are concerned about you going with that hippy girl. We don't want them here!" We heard it repeatedly, the community was up in arms. "How could this native son choose the hippies over his own?" Well, as predicted, a worse thing happened that would hurt us all very much. Everyone in El Rito knew about and talked about the Hippie commune in the mountains north of El Rito. We used to see the girls and a couple of men at Martin's General Store. The girls and women were dressed in long dresses with flowers and ribbons in their hair. The men had beards and long dirty brown hair.

I used to look at them in bewilderment. The women were beautiful to me more because of how nice they were. The men were kind of scary. I didn't like the way they looked at us. It was obvious that one of the men was the leader. The others all did what he said and were friendly with him even when he was mad at them. I would see him get close to the girls and whisper things to them. Sometimes they would laugh and other times they would gather their stuff and climb into the old bus with flowers and stars spray painted on. There were all sorts of happy images painted on the sides of that bus. My favorites were the words painted in flowers, 'make love not war'. They would often ask if we wanted to buy handmade necklaces and bracelets. Sometimes they would sell fruits and vegetables. The locals swore they were selling the fruit and vegetables to the same people they had stolen it from. I noticed that some of the women had hair on their underarms which I thought was strange. They had a smell that was different, herbs or something.

The story around El Rito was that one of the hippie girls, the prettiest one, had grown infatuated with my uncle. They began sneaking around and doing their thing. Many of the men were jealous and the women resented it. "What is Donald doing screwing that dirty gringa, what's wrong with our girls?" They continued, "Linda from down the road is much prettier and she let Donald know that she likes him and yet, he ignores her!" The talk and backstabbing became a daily event as the strange couple, hippie and local, eventually stopped trying to hide it.

The girl called herself Freedom and shared her concerns with a local girl that she met through Donald. She shared that the Commune leader 'Sycho' was not very happy with her. "He told me I belong to him and that I better get back in line with the rest of them. Sycho continues to put pressure on me! He keeps telling me and telling me. We're a family my sweet Freedom. Your sweet love must stay with us. I want you to stay away from the Spanish man. He is all about using you and then he will cast you aside. I explained to Sycho that Donald is good and that he believes a lot of what we do. I won't stop seeing Donald. If I must, I'll leave the commune. Donald says we can live together."

The man who called himself Sycho was from New York and had fled when his number came up on the Vietnam Draft Lottery. His family was poor so he couldn't run to Canada. Like many others, he learned that New Mexico was a good place to hide. Most Americans still thought that New Mexico was a foreign country. Before he came to El Rito he went to San Francisco, then to Santa Fe. He followed a pattern set by many predators and preyed on the young girls that had bought into the free love and peace movement. Once he had his following, he bought a bus and migrated to the Land of Enchantment. One night my uncle drove Freedom back to the commune to find Sycho waiting outside. He confronted my uncle. "You continue your relationship with Freedom with complete disregard on the negative impact it is having on my community. I want you to stop or it will be a huge mistake for both of us!" My uncle approached with a gleam in his eye and tried to explain that he and Freedom were in love and wanted to be together, even if it meant that she would leave the commune. He figured that either way there was no way that this gringo could beat him in a fight. In an instant, the hippie pulled out a shotgun that he was hiding behind his back in the dark of night and shot my uncle point blank almost cutting him in half. The commune fled never to be seen again. There would be no justice for my uncle. This further enflamed the hatred and mistrust towards all gringos! As some put it, "These hippies are the new batch of carpet-baggers only this time it won't happen!"

The community was outraged and gathered to avenge his death. When they got to their camp, the hippies were gone. One of them spoke with hatred. "Cowards, all of them." Another man followed with his anger. "Damn fly by nights! I knew they were no good!" Yet another spoke out. "I reported to the sheriff that they were stealing my eggs and chickens!" Fred Archuleta added to the cacophony. "I heard from Mac that they were paying him to go find those funny mushrooms. I guess they took them and got high with them. I know they were growing marijuana, some of Martin's sons were stealing the plants. I heard that whatever they couldn't sell they smoked!"

The locals had become a mob hell bent on revenge. The discussion continued through the night. As alcohol fueled the anger it fueled the resentment. I heard that many of the residents had gone looking for them in the surrounding towns and villages, but they were gone. They never found them. My uncle was killed, and the killer got away with it.

I was broken hearted. I found it hard to believe that a man that was as strong and cool could be killed by a hippie. I remember weeping for my uncle remembering how badly my dad had treated him. Why did he have to take us that day? Why couldn't he let us finish our ride with him? Maybe if he had let us, my uncle would still be alive! I wondered where the Conductor was.

Chapter | 8

ANOTHER STEP

I had dreamt last night but I was glad I had not boarded the Ghost Train. I was in a school in Santa Fe and strange faces and voices were all around me. I was walking around trying to find my way but every path I took was wrong. As I began to panic, I found myself in the mountains where my family went to pick Piñon every year. I saw the mountains spreading out as far as I could see. The mountains unfolded like a green carpet with different shades of green, black, and almost white. The sun and the terrain were linked together as they created a synergy that made them grander and more spectacular together. I felt free as I peered far away. I could feel the grass under my feet as the sky got dark with black cotton ball like clouds gathering to bring dark, brutal rain. I woke when a shadow touched me from behind. I had escaped something! I didn't know what. The sun was shining outside, the sound of my family brought me joy. I flew out of bed, today would change the rest of my life.

"Let's go, one more and we're done! Let's go look at our new house. Where's your grandfather at? We need to say goodbye." "He went to Reggie's. He should be back in a little while." Juan responded. He was always aware of where grandpa was. Reggie owned the small 'Tiendita', community store where he sold all the basics. He was a strange looking man. Reggie had long, jet black hair and a beard to

SANTA FE: A PIECE OF 'MI VIDA'

match. Reggie's beard was so long it hung down to the middle of his belly. During Halloween his store was the place to go. He had a big barrel filled with candy and nuts and he used a big scoop to fill our bags. He always made us Trick-for-a-Treat. During Christmas he did the same thing. It was in our culture to go out as kids and ask for 'Mis Chrismes' which meant, give me My Christmas. He gave us candy the same way.

My grandpa was a good man. He provided us with food and support when both were needed badly. My mom would forever be thankful to him. In her mind he had saved us more than once by putting himself between us and the alcohol driven monster that came home. We all turned as my grandfather walked up. It was 1964 and my grandfather had never owned or driven a car. Grandpa walked to Reggie's small store and bought the few items that he needed. It included a half pint of Tokay, a cheap wine, which he kept in his back pocket. I never saw him abuse anyone, except me, in my mind. He was always chasing me away so he could protect my little brother Michael.

My grandpa showed up and gave us each a piece of candy. "Are you ready to go? It won't be the same around here." He spoke to all of us but looked at my mom. He was both relieved that he would no longer have to deal with his son but worried about us. My mom walked up to him and gave him a hug. I could feel their sorrow and love for each other. "Let's go!" My father instructed us all. We piled into my dad's new car, the newly released Ford Mustang. We were like kids in a candy shop to be in his car. It had brown paint and black interior. Billy would follow us in the old truck. At age fourteen he did not have a valid driver license and I couldn't't help but notice how small he looked inside the truck. His head was slightly above the steering wheel as if he was stretching his neck to look out the windshield with a crack running down the middle of it. I watched as my dad walked over to grandpa and said goodbye. They shook hands and my dad got into his new car and we were off. The new car added to the euphoria and trepidation of moving to a big city, Santa Fe, the state capitol.

Our trip to Santa Fe was uneventful. This was the second time I could remember going to Santa Fe. The first time my Godmother had come for me to spend some time in the Capitol City with her family. My stay there was short. She had five children and they stuck together like the chicks in our farm did as they followed their hen. "Jimmy, why don't you and Santiago fight and see who wins?" The oldest sister was bent on watching us fight. My stay there started this way and ended this way. The oldest sister was the meanest one and encouraged her siblings to confront me every time we were outside. I seldom saw my Godmother and when I did her kids pretended that they were being nice to me. "You know you were born in Santa Fe. Your mom and dad lived here for a little while. They lived on Duran Street. My sister lived on the same street and that's how I met them. Your mom was pregnant with you, so I used to go over and help her."

"Your mom is a good woman. I wish your dad was nicer to her. Right after you were born your dad got a job in Los Alamos and you guys moved back to Española." My Godmother walked up to me and gave me a hug as she pulled me into her full bosom. I felt uncomfortable. It was as if my face was trapped between two pillows. I couldn't breathe and tried to pull away, but her love kept me pressed against the pillows. "I love you my handsome Godson." My visit was cut short after my second night. I started crying and nothing she did to comfort me worked. Her kids ridiculed me no matter how many times they were told to leave me alone. Finally, they got me in the car and drove me to El Guache, my reception was less than friendly.

As we drove out of Española and through the small communities, it was all new to me, like a fairy tale. I had heard of families that had moved to find jobs and always wondered how it felt. We passed several cars along the way. The Sangre de Cristo mountains were off in the distance, it was a brave new world for me. When we arrived in the city, I was overwhelmed by all the buildings, cars, and people. The first thing I noticed was the Veterans National Cemetery. The white headstones all in a row shadowed by the green grass and tall trees was surreal. "What is that?" Michael was leaning over me and was fascinated. "That's the place they bury soldiers." I felt uneasy as I looked at it. Even though I had never seen it I felt as if I had. Was it in my dreams? Something inside told me I would see it again, from the inside. I shook the thoughts as our journey continued. I noticed that there were more white people than I had ever seen. I found myself noticing their clothes and the way they interacted with each other. I also saw Spanish people interacting with them, this was foreign to me. All I had ever known were people from my own culture. There weren't any gringos in El Guache.

We drove through Santa Fe and onto a stretch of highway that took us to the State Prison. We arrived at what would become our home. As we drove into the prison property, we could see the Penitentiary looming in front of us. The building was a dull gray and was surrounded by a tall fence. There were houses to the left and houses to the right. The houses to the left were bigger. "That's where the Warden and his management team live. The Correctional Officers live over there." My dad pointed to the left. As dad spoke, we all looked over to see where our new home was. I noticed that there was a baseball backdrop in a weed infested field between our home and the highway.

Dad drove down the road and followed the road as it looped and went in a circle. Our house was the last one, number 13. We all got out of the car and ran to the front door. I looked back and saw Billy pull up into the driveway. Our furniture looked funny. The house was new to us, and the furniture was old, and it looked it. As my dad opened the door my mom was telling him that they really needed new furniture. "You better get a job. I'll need help paying for them." "The kids are going to need clothes for school, we can't send them to school looking like that. Did you notice how the kids were dressed as we drove through town? I can buy a couple of things for each and put some other stuff on lay-away." My mom was getting us ready for school.

We followed them inside. My dad did not respond as my mom talked about what they needed and how beautiful this home was going to be. What a surprise our new home was. It had running water, a toilet that flushed, three bedrooms, and a kitchen. We ran in and checked out every room, letting our fingers graze along the walls as we ran from room to room. There were new beds and a table in the kitchen. It dawned on me that the metal beds had been left behind. Through the windows in the living room, we could see that there were trees that had small grey berries. We came to call them monkey peanuts even after we found out they were Russian Olives. We would make a habit of having Monkey Peanut wars with each other. If they were thrown right up close, they delivered quite the wallop.

These wars often escalated into fights with our new neighbors. Of great joy to us, the front yard had a lawn. Michael and I played in it for the first time. I felt the coolness on my body and looked up at the dark blue sky. As I was getting up from rolling around in it, I heard a strange hissing and rattling. I looked over and saw a rope that was coiled up, but it was strange it had a head. I almost fell to my knees as the head was moving and grinning. It felt like the conductor was reminding me of something, but I didn't know what it was. I ran into the house, went into my room, and laid there for a while. Was I going to continue with my night journeys? I prayed that I wouldn't, but somehow, I knew I would. The soft voice of my dreams came back to me. "There is much you do not understand."

The back yard was blocked in with a high wall. We climbed up and we had a clear view of the prison yard. There were thirteen houses built in a circular block and ours was the last one in the circle. This would be our playground with the twelve other families that lived here. Most of the families were from Northern New Mexico. The fact that they were all from different places gave us more diversity than we had ever seen. This was a challenge as we tried to adjust. Four of the families had kids that were in our same age group, these would become our lifelong friends. I was caught off guard as I heard voices coming from behind our house. We ran to the back, and we saw the prisoners on the other side of the fence. I could not understand exactly what they were saying. "What happens if they escape?" Arthur was analyzing the situation. "You guys get over here, we have to unload the truck." My dad made sure we unloaded it quickly, he had somewhere he had to be.

The Penitentiary Houses were all built of cinder block and were built using prison labor. They were all square and tan in color. The only difference was that some of them were two bedrooms, and some were three. Our three-bedroom looked like a mansion to us even though it was slightly over 1000 square feet. Three bedrooms would prove to be a challenge for an eight-person family, one of which was a teenage girl. We soon found out that my mom had found a job making moccasins for Lazaar's on the outskirts of Santa Fe. One of her friends had referred her and she was hired on the spot. We would also find out that she opened an account at Montgomery Wards and had already started to furnish the home. My brother Michael and I shared bunkbeds in the same room as my brother Billy. Our brother Juan stayed in Espanola with our grandfather. Arthur was assigned the couch and my sister got the other bedroom. We started to hang out with the other guard's kids.

"Where are you from?" The group of kids asked us. When we explained where we were from, they shared where they were from. Arthur asked the two brothers leading the group, Sonny and Gilbert, where they were from. "We are from Truchas, have you ever been up there? We own property up there. My dad says when we get on our feet we are going back up. We don't like it here. Our cousins are tough, a lot tougher than all of you." "I don't know about that." I responded with a challenging voice. "We're from Spaña and we're pretty tough, I bet we could take them."

Jake stepped forward. His family was from Dixon. "What did you say? You want to try it with me? We live on the mountain, and we are tougher than all of you from the valley." We were unaware that each of us was repeating what our fathers had been teaching us since birth. Jake was older than me by a year or two. I didn't want to fight he was much bigger than me and I was regretting my response. This would not be the last time my big mouth got me into a fight. Sometimes when you got into a fight with one brother the other brothers, cousins, and sometimes dads and uncles would show up to protect the family reputation. Jake had extremely dark and shiny skin and was wide-bodied. His entire family was like that. His father was the same rank as my father and looked just as mean. Jake was a little shorter than me but stocky. Suddenly, he shoved me, and I fell backwards landing on the lawn. I got up and started to back away. I was unaware that Billy had been watching the whole time. Arthur stepped forward and was ready to pounce. "Arthur, let Santiago do it. Santiago, kick his ass. Just do it the way we do it, box him. You know the drill. You kick his ass, or I'll kick yours."

I was scared. I could feel my body tingling and my eyes were darting from face to face. The crowd of kids had grown, almost as if they had been called to witness the fisticuffs. "Come on, punk!" Jake spoke as he moved towards me. I could feel my heart pounding. It felt like it was going to pop out of my chest. I feared Jake, the crowd, and my brothers who would make me suffer mercilessly if I lost. As I stood up Jake rushed me. Jake took a swing at me, and I countered so fast that I surprised myself. I felt the bones in his nose as the blood gushed. I watched him as he fell to the ground. He lay there putting his hand to his nose looking at the blood on his fingers. You could hear a pin drop among the circle of kids. "Get up Jake, you can take him!"

The kids were egging him on. I felt sad and good at the same time. I watched as Jake got up. The other kids watched in awe as one of the leaders of the Pen kids got up off the ground holding his nose trying to stop the bleeding. "Do you want some more? I didn't want to fight you, but you asked for it." Jake looked around the crowd then at me with a look of surprise and sadness. He turned and walked away towards his home. I noticed then that the older kids in high school were watching the scene unfold. Billy and Arthur got close to each other with Michael standing to the side. I was certain that Juan would have joined, remembering he had stayed in El Guache. All of us were sizing each other up by age and size.

The feeling out process had just begun. Jake and I were friends after that although we did fight every now and then. We learned how to play as a team, but we still fought sometimes while playing football, basketball, or baseball through the years. All of us were very competitive and had been taught to fight out all our problems and disagreements. We were all a product of our Spanish culture modified by fathers that dealt with violent convicts. Jake came close but he was never able to take me in a fight. He tried a few times. After a while he accepted the fact that he could not match my speed, strength, or skills.

I became a daily fighter and I got better and better as a result. The more I fought and won the more I wanted to do it. It came natural to me from constant training and from the constant violence we endured from our father, his associates, and their children. We would fight together a lot after that. Unknown to most outsiders, gang activity ran strong in Santa Fe. Gang activity was driven by families. It was more like clans than gangs. If you messed with someone, their whole family became your enemy. Since all of us were from the outside, we became our own street clan, our surrogate family. What a tough family we would become.

ERIC SANTIAGO MARTINEZ

The prison compound was out in the middle of nowhere. You could walk for miles and get nowhere. It was hot outside and my mom kept reminding us that we would be going to school soon. We became familiar with our neighbors. We would go out and explore the empty fields around our community which were flat, grey, and shrubby. The summer was hot and stuffy, I missed our river. It got just as hot in El Guache as it did at the Pen, but we could escape to the river. Here, we had nowhere to hide from the heat. Our only refuge from the heat was the shade of the Monkey Peanut trees and the water hose.

Our walks became a lot more interesting. I remember the first time we saw a horned toad. I was entranced with the brown, spiked, oval shaped lizard that wobbled as it ran. At first, I was afraid of them, but Arthur started catching them. He had learned how from our new-found friends. I had my second encounter with a rattlesnake that was in our front yard. I started waking up early in the morning to listen to the voices coming from inside the fence of the Pen. I could hear the convicts yelling so I would try to hear the words. It was difficult due to the distance. The air was cool in the early morning. I liked being outside in the coolness and would lay down in the cool grass and look up at the sky and watch the lazy clouds float by.

As I got ready to lay down, I heard it... the same hissing and rattling as before. Danger was coming from the grass. I took one look and realized how close I was to laying on it. I ran inside. "Billy come and see, quick! I just saw a snake outside and it's lifting its head and making a funny noise!" He yelled at me. "Don't touch it or get near it! It will bite you and it has poison in its fangs! Let's go see!" I ran back outside as fast as I could being careful not to step on it. I would find out that the heat of the day made the snakes lethargic. The snakes showed up often in the morning while the sprinklers were on, and the air was cool. It wasn't always Rattlers. The Bull snakes did as well. This was my first experience with a rattlesnake, and I was both amazed and frightened by it. It was greyish in color with black markings on its back. When I got close to it, I was enthralled with how quickly it coiled into a circle with its head up in the air on one side of the coil and its rattling tail on the other. Its head was shaped like a scary heart and its tail wiggled its menacing rattles.

Billy was right behind me walking like a man on a mission. "Go get me the shovel from the garage and call Arthur and Michael out here. Tell them to hurry up. This is a big one!" I ran into the house excited. I wondered what Billy was going to do. "Billy wants you guys outside right now. Hurry, check out the rattlesnake on the lawn! Hurry up!" "Wow!" Arthur ran outside with Michael on his heels. "Is Billy going to kill it, I wanna see." Michael was happy. I ran to the garage and got the shovel. Billy took it from me. "You have to chop off the head if you want to kill it. If not, the part that's attached to the head lives on." I wondered how that could be. My thoughts were shattered as Billy aimed the shovel, and with a quick move severed the head. I felt bad for the snake as part of it continued to wiggle for a bit. "Look how it is still wiggling, that was cool!" retorted Michael.

Billy aimed the shovel again and cut off the rattles. "Dad puts these in his guitar, he says it brings good luck." I had heard them in the acoustic guitar when we played. We all had to play the guitar because our dad was good at playing the guitar. He used to play in bands before he got married. When he talked about it, he was bragging but seemed sad at the same time. I wondered if that was why he hated us sometimes. Maybe he wished he could play in a band instead of working at the State Penitentiary. That evening we gave him the rattles and with a smile on his face he dropped them inside the guitar.

One morning my father came into our rooms and told us to get ready, that we were going to Española. It was time to finish bringing in the harvest. We all got ready and ate breakfast before we left. I loved breakfast, my mom made fresh tortillas, chile', beans, and eggs. The aroma of the tortillas filled the house with a certain warmth and familiarity. The aroma was part of the fabric of my being. I had smelled it from the beginning. I always associated that smell with love and family even during the hard times. We always had beans, chile', and tortillas. My mom rolled the dough with a rolling pin that also served as a punishment tool when she needed to remind us that she ran the house when dad was not there.

I was always impressed with how perfectly she molded the dough into circles, each one the same size and thickness. The tortillas would cook on a 'comal', a flat cast iron skillet. She knew when to flip them over. She waited till they were perfectly cooked with black splotches on the white texture of the dough. They were slightly crispy on the outside, and perfectly soft on the inside. On a good day we could eat them straight from the stove with butter. As we ate breakfast, my dad explained to Billy what he wanted us to do. "Your grandpa needs help to pick the apples, pears, and peaches. Make sure that these guys help you. Juan is already there so all of you will pick. Put the fruit in the cellar and your mom will go this weekend so you can dry, can, and sort the fruit." "Okay dad, we will."

Billy liked being in charge and was tough on us. He knew that if we didn't do what was expected he would be the one to pay the price. He chose to make us pay the price with a swift kick in the pants or a slap upside the head, more if need be. It normally only took the threat. Many times, I had witnessed him literally getting beat to the point where my mom had to intercede and received the same thing. We were all fearful of my dad. His wrath and subsequent physical violence were a constant in our lives. We knew no one would defend us, they were afraid to.

After breakfast we all piled into the back of the old ford and got on the road. We drove slowly on Highway 14 for two miles and merged onto 285. It was exactly two miles on Highway 14 to Highway 285. This would become our challenging destination once we got bicycles.

The road went up and down and the round trip was 4 miles, but we did it. The road was desolate and very few cars traveled on Highway 14. If they weren't going to work at the Penitentiary, they were on their way to Cerrillos the next small community south, or to the ghost town Madrid.

Madrid had been a booming mining community where the workers were paid in script that they used to buy all their needs from the company store. The town had died, no one lived there anymore. The few times we traveled south was on Sundays, we went to Catholic Mass in Cerrillos. A couple of times my mom took us to Madrid to check it out. The buildings were run down, and you could hear and see the doors banging with the wind. On this day we were headed north through Santa Fe on our way to El Guache. When we got there, we saw the trees laden with fruit. It was time to go to work.

Chapter | 9

SINGING

The train comes to a stop. I'm dreaming again; I can feel it. I get out into a world I do not recognize. There are people walking around singing songs celebrating an event I know nothing about. I see men, women, and children moving past. Some of the families have a team of horses or mules pulling a cart with wooden wheels that appear to be oval instead of round. The wheels are different sizes and shapes as evidenced by the up and down and side-to-side movement of the cart. The carts are full of belongings, and for the most part, the people seem to be happy and eager in their movement. The people are speaking Spanish, the language I was born into. I find it interesting that it looks like they are moving the way we did. I wonder where they are headed. The men are dressed in pants with short leggings and have long socks covering the bottom of their legs. Some of the pants are different lengths. I can't help but notice that their clothing up top are loose with puffy sleeves, bright colors, and appear to be heavy with the load of all the bright colors.

A cart goes past and the young man with the reigns smiles at me as he passes by. His cart is overloaded and the mules that are pulling seem to be struggling. The load is twice as high as the cart. It looks like an ancient version of our old Ford truck loaded to the sky. There are children seated on a makeshift bench in front of the load. There are six siblings in all, four boys and a girl are on the bench and the oldest boy has the reins. Seated next to him is a short, older women. Riding in front of the cart is a man on a horse. His horse is brown and white and is carrying the man at a dignified pace and the horse is prancing. Both the man and the horse seem to be out of a movie. The man is dressed like a soldier.

The soldier is dressed like a Spanish Conquistador. His helmet is made of steel. It covers his head and has a visor in the front. I notice that there is a strip of metal running from the back to the front. It reminds me of a curved knife with the sharpened end pointed towards the sky. The soldier has a full beard, and his black hair sticks out of the back of the helmet. He wears a breastplate that looks like a vest. The metal matches the helmet in color. His arms are covered by a multi-colored shirt that puffs out on the shoulders then tapers tight at the forearm. The brilliance of the colors stands out. The sleeves are a light purple with a sky blue embedded into the purple at the top then it becomes solid purple. He is wearing a dark red cloak that flows backwards tied around his chest and neck with a rope woven of several strands. I notice that the same material flows from under the breastplate. The purple and blue flow down below his waist and they look like a flower that is upside down. I stand in awe as I look at him. I feel connected to him. I feel myself standing a bit taller as he passes by. A part of me wants to be him.

As I walk through the marketplace, I see men and women that look like royalty and many more that obviously are poor commoners. In a way they remind me of my family and neighbors. I know that some of our neighbors are rich compared to us. We are the poor ones. The richer people wear the same clothes as the working class, but I can see that their clothes are made of finer materials that shine in the sun. The rich men are cloaked with their family Coat-of-Arms exclusive to their family and to the king. The women are dressed in two basic styles with variations between the poor and the rich. The poorer women are dressed in a one-piece dress of poor quality. I can see that their clothing is old, they are dull and frazzled. I've seen these people before. The vendors are out hawking their wares. I can smell food drifting through the spectacle. It smells like our last mantanza. I recognize the smell of the chicharrones. I ache to be home, not our new home in Santa Fe, our old home in El Guache. I continue meandering through the fog of events and movement. I am seeing them, but they are not seeing me. I feel an evil warmth on my back. I look back but I don't see anything. I hear singing. A voice rising above everything else gets my attention. I pick up the pace until I see the face.

As I listen, it becomes apparent to me that Spain has just defeated the Moors and driven their leadership and armies out of Spain. The 800-year occupation would forever influence Spain as the Arabic culture was imbedded in all the social institutions. The magnificence of the Mosques bear testimony to the grandeur of Spain's golden age under the Moorish leadership. The Golden age resulted in the richest libraries in the known world. The greatest accumulation, up to this date and time, of art, music, architecture, and many other areas of human cultural evolution, numerous libraries, and institutions. Imbedded in this was the conflict between the Spaniards and the Moors. Two men beside me in the street begin to talk excitedly together. I recognize the Conquistador leading his family in the cart. "Where are you going Pedro?" The man in finer clothing replies with a smile. "I'm off to Granada. Many of the Moors have left their lands and my family has bought a fertile parcel for me and my family. You should investigate it. King Ferdinand and Queen Isabella are in dire need of money to expand Spain's holdings."

The other man replies with a hint of longing in his tone. "My family is poor my dear friend. Nothing would make me happier than to go to Granada with you." The clothing explained why one was going to Granada and the other had to stay. As I walk in front of a Catholic Cathedral, I hear singing from inside giving thanks to God. There is a group of men standing outside, one of them turns and stares at me with fire in his eyes as he sings. I recognize the voice, it's the voice I heard earlier. The other men in the group do not see me and I know the man. He is the Conductor! I wonder what he's telling or doing to all the people I see. My curiosity is getting the better of me. I am transfixed on the scene before me. I am slow to react, I notice the man with fire in his eyes leave the group and walk my way.

I realize that he's walking towards me. I can feel my body tremble! I do not move! As he gets closer, I see his true being under his borrowed skin and clothing. His bones are show white and are contorting like the reflections on the surface of a lake. As the Conductor nears me, I want to throw up. I see images of people coming from inside him. All of them are crying as the Conductor eats the young, the old, and their loved ones. The screams are loud. They contain sadness, pain, fear, and hopelessness. I feel their reality and feel as if I am being pulled into the muddy river of death. The closer he gets the stronger the stench.

I can hear their tortured pleas. "Save us, please save us! Walk to the priest and have him pray for us! You better run while you still can! Get off the train and stay off!" The voices of the dead are coming faster than I can listen. I see the face of a young mother come out of the conductor's belly. Her face is splotched with black and red shapes like lakes scattered in the mountain. Her lips are painted bright red, and her eyes are jet black. Her face contorts between pain, lust, and despair. She looks like the one I saw Billy with on the train doing things that I did not fully understand. I wondered if that was why she was here. Her face is sucked back in, and another face appears in her place. This face is one I have seen. He looks like me and is talking to me in a strange mix of languages. "Run Santiago!" He is gone in an instant as more faces twist in pain as they appear to flow out of the bowels of the conductor.

Then out of the blue I feel a pair of strong hands yank me away from the conductor and I find myself in a small room. The room is dark and smells like fish. The ceiling is low and there's a small mattress in the corner. The floor and the ceiling seem to be reaching for each other. There is a strange glow in the room. I see a black that is dark and clear at the same time. It looks like water deep in the ocean, almost like being in an aquarium. Am I floating in liquid black? The mattress cover is made from the same material as the poor women's dresses and is lumpy and uneven. It is stained from blood that drips from the ceiling. The floor is gritty, dirt with threshing is scattered throughout. I see spider webs in the corners. The webs are a lattice serving as a trap for whatever insects find their way into the quivering trap. They will soon find out that they are about to be served. I wonder, am I in a trap? I see the web vibrate and a spider is walking slowly to where a fly is trying to wiggle its way out. The fly has no clue as to what is headed its way. The spider turns towards me and smiles. I think of the one that I smashed on my forehead.

Man, I wish these dreams would end! I am still trying to figure out what they mean. The walls of the room are old and damp. I am in a room that reminds me of the cellar that Billy and I slept in minus the fruit. I can see where the ceiling was stained. I want to cry out but am afraid to. I start to pray when I hear creaking coming from a small hole in the wall. Something is being moved out of the way from the other side. I had not noticed the hole through the darkness of the room as it is small. I suddenly remember the rhyme my father spoke. "Welcome to my parlor, said the spider to the flea. Step into my parlor for some tea." I get the feeling that I am in the parlor now. "How about some tea?" Is the web vibrating, am I the flea?

I start crying. I am so tired of these night journeys. I try to wake up, but something is holding me in the dream, or nightmare. I start to shake. "Be quiet, pay attention to the events that are unfolding. The knowledge will serve you well as your life unfolds." The lady's voice is a comfort. I settle down, I know that I am not alone. "Why do I need to be here to learn, can't you just teach me? I do really good in school. If you explain it, I can learn it. Please, I don't want to be here anymore. Why is Billy here, I don't understand?" Her voice comforts me, "There are somethings in life that can only be learned by living them. This journey on the Ghost Train is one of them. You must be careful. The Conductor is very dangerous. You must not let him catch you."

Chapter | 10

ON MY WAY

No matter how hard I try, I can't wake up. I hear the small door open and people talking quietly on the other side. I watch as a man, a woman, and two children crawl into the room headfirst on their hands and knees. "You would think that Spain would treat all of its citizens with dignity, after all, it's 1593! We are not barbarians." The man has a black beard and a white patch of cloth on his head under a hat as if he were hiding it. The black hat looks like a triangle with a long point in the front. He gently urges his family into their hiding place. Standing behind the family are a couple who are gently urging them into the hidden room. "Hurry and get in we do not have a lot of time. The Crown's soldiers are looking for you." "Thank you so much for saving us! We are forever in your debt. How much longer do you think before we can buy passage to the new world?" The man in black is obviously animated. "It will take a few days. The Crown is cracking down on those that are helping the Jews escape, they call them traitors to the faith. Our people are being murdered by our own country!"

The man in the room with me is talking with someone on the other side of the wall. The family is now secure in the room. Bags of food are being pushed through the door along with a bed pan and a pail of water with a small ladle. "Don't worry, you will be safe here, please stay quiet, the soldiers are identifying all Jews deemed as heretics. They will arrest you and you will stand before the tribunal of the Inquisition for determination of your loyalty to Spain and the Catholic Church. I am sure you aware of this, as you are here in hiding. I mention this only to remind you of the peril you are facing."

The man continues, "As you know, they have classified Jews into three categories so you must use the knowledge to save yourself if you are captured. The one viewed the darkest are the 'Conversos Falsos', the false converts. The Conversos Falsos practice Judaism while pretending to be Christians, such as yourself. All Converts are being vetted to ensure that your conversion to Catholicism is sincere. They are aware that some converts are faking conversion and practicing Judaism in secret. The Inquisition is dealing harshly with them if the determination is that they are in fact, practicing their Judaic religion underground. The increase in hangings and burnings is of great concern to many of us. Many Spaniards are falsely testifying against all Jews so they can take your wealth. We will get you passage as soon as we can as there are several families fleeing to the new world. "

The discussion continued. "The Jews that practice their religion openly are being treated less harshly as the Crown doesn't have to worry about treason with them. In a way they are respected by the fact that they choose to practice their faith in the open instead of in secret. Don't for a minute think that taking off that hat and showing your true faith will save you. You are known in the barrio as a Converso Falso. Your neighbor's testimony will be used to convict you.

The third group are the true Conversos, the converts that are true in their conversion and loyal to the church. If you are apprehended, you must persuade the tribunal that you are one of these. Now that I think about it get rid of the Kippah, the skull cap will hurt you. This group is problematic in that it is very difficult to distinguish who is true and who is not. All three groups are being persecuted and some of the wealthiest are being executed. My source in the inner circle has told me that the Crown is in financial trouble created by the extended battle with the Moors and its aggressive expansion of the Kingdom here and in the New World."

The man on the other side of the wall continues his discourse. The family listens even though they understand what they are up against. "The death of many does not quell the egos of the few. The Inquisition is made up of the nobles loyal to King Ferdinand and Queen Isabela. A priest acts as an advisor to the tribunal but is unable to vote as it is forbidden by the church to kill. Of note is that it is a Royal Decree that any Jew brought in front of the tribunal will have all their properties and belongings seized by the Crown only to be returned if found innocent of the charges. It is no wonder that the wealthy Jews are the first to be accused and properties seized. Is it any wonder that few are found to be innocent of the charges? My contact informs me that seldom are the properties and wealth restored. They become part of the national treasury. I must go now but I will be back with some food in the morning."

The family sits in silence. I hear when the silence is disturbed by the crying of the youngest child, the daughter. "Why are they doing this to us? I'm scared daddy?" The girl is merely a child and wears a simple dress with a bodice, covered with a wrap that serves as a coat. Her shoes are different from what I am used to. They look solid as if they were carved out of wood. She appears to be close to my age. She reminds me of one of our cousins. She has long black hair that is wavy like the ripples on the eddies of the Rio Grande. Her skin is creamy with a hint of brown with full lips and dark round eyes under eyebrows that pull you into her face. The young boy is holding his sister calming her down. The mother steps forward and hugs her children. "Do not worry my children. Our God Jehovah will deliver us to a new promised land. Now go to sleep. The mattress in the corner will have to be used by us all."

Dark silence fills the room. I listen like a fly on the wall, seeing, hearing, feeling, and smelling everything. I feel the way I often feel when my father comes home after a night of drunkenness with his friends. It feels like the calm before the storm. First the winds begin to blow like my journey through the town square before arriving at this tomb like room. Now the mist has begun. I wonder, will the rainfall be gentle in its life sustaining flow or are we in for a thunderstorm? I know that I am getting ready to find out. If it's anything like my awake life, get ready for a storm! I often wonder why our dad does that to us when all we want is to love him and be loved by him. I understand how this family feels right now.

At home I disappear into my sleep as if I am having an out-of-body experience. My room turns dark, and the walls start to close in on me. I feel like that now. I feel that it is now morning in our dark holding cell. I hear movement behind the passageway, and I quietly move towards the opening. I have to get out of here and find my way back to the train. As scared as I am to get aboard, I prefer it to where I am. At least there I can flee. Here the darkness holds me in its liquid gel. I am fully immersed in a darkness that is starting to seep inside. I remember the gentle lady's voice. "You have to get on the train no matter what. If not, you will be stuck forever. You will be doomed to repeat the scenes before you." My fear of the conductor is as bad as the fear in this darkness, but I am trapped in this dream, and I want out. I wish Billy was here, he would take me home. I know I saw him or felt him on the train. Where is he?

As the door opens, I exit the room and enter a living space and there are soldiers in the room. They have the homeowner sitting in a brown chaise that is spotted with age. His face is bloodied, his wife is across the room with her back against the wall sobbing quietly. "Get in there and bring those Conversos Falsos out!" The soldier in charge is speaking to the youngest soldier of the contingent. All the soldiers are wearing armor with shiny swords at their sides and others with their lances at parade rest. "Si mi Capitan!" The young soldier responds. I can't help but notice that the young soldier looks like the young soldier dying on the battlefield so long ago. I wonder how I could see the same face in and out of myself. "Do they have any weapons?" The captain's voice pierces through the room. "No, they are but a scared family who have been good servants of the Crown who fear for their lives. Please Capitan, have mercy, for God's sake, think of the children." "My orders are clear. They must go before the Inquisition and if they are as you say, they have nothing to fear. Andale', hurry up we must deliver these and go forth and find the others!"

As the young soldier crawls into the secret chamber the smell of human waste startles him. He looks around and sees the family. The father is standing in front of them ready to protect them. "Let's go, you have been charged with treason and must stand in front of the tribunal to determine if the charges are well founded." The young soldier's voice is firm, but I detect a hint of compassion as if he does not want to do this. "We have done nothing wrong and have served his Majesties reign by providing financial assistance to his subjects when no one else would!" "Do not make me use force to remove you from this room in front of your wife and children. If what you say is true, I am certain the Tribunal will make that determination and you and your family will be released."

The soldier is pleading with him. He does not want to kill anyone. He is from a long family line that has served in the army of whoever was the eminence at the time. His family are descendants of the Martins, later to be Martinez. In his heart the young soldier knows that the young family is doomed, it breaks his heart. What happened to his beloved Spain? For centuries they had been united in their quest to rid their country of the Moors. They finally accomplished it and instead of uniting to make their country better, they had found a new enemy, the Jews.

"Please don't hurt my family! I beg of you in the name of God in Heaven." The young soldier moves forward with his sword in his hand. "You will move towards the door immediately! Do not force me to run you through in front of your family. Do it now!" The father steps to the side and tenderly moves his wife and children to the door. As he does, the soldier gets close to him and whispers. "Leave the boy behind. My wife and I will raise him as our own. You must instruct him quickly and quietly or all of you will be taken. Hurry before someone else enters, then it will be too late." The son is 14 years old and has been named Bernardo Ortiz, the family name has been changed to blend in with the Spanish.

The stories of the Jews who had stood in front of the tribunal, found guilty of heresy, and subsequently being hanged or jailed were plentiful and impactful. The ones who were found innocent were few. Several of their friends and neighbors had been taken and most of them had not come back. Señor Ortiz felt the love from the soldier and prayed that he really did care and was truly going to save his son. "Take that Kippah off your head! You are supposed to be a convert!" The father gingerly takes the Kippah off, kisses it, and tosses it under the bed. He knows what is coming and he knows that Jehovah God will deliver him and his family, and if death be the result, it is part of God's plan.

The father hugs the mother as she starts to kneel to leave the chamber. She weeps for her children. "Please 'mi amor', you must be strong." I watch as the man in black consoles his wife of many years. "If they know that you are weeping for a son that is hidden, we may not make it to the tribunal. This way we save him and give ourselves a chance to prevail. Better that one of us live to tell our story and help others then that all of us should perish. God has sent an angel to touch this soldier's heart and save our son, we must honor that." The mother starts out of the room with a pain so deep that she wails in a low voice to protect her son.

The father goes over and whispers in his son's ear. The son could be seen shaking his head and trying to walk forward and join his family. The father holds him, and I see the son's head bow and the father follows his wife and daughter out the small opening. "Get under that mattress and be quiet. I will be back to get you tonight." The young soldier exits the room hoping that he is not found out. It would be sudden death or a life in the dungeons for the rest of his life. Bernardo did as he was instructed and crawled under the bed. I saw as the soldiers led the family away. As the mother looks back over her shoulder, one of the soldiers asks. "Why are you looking back?" That soldier then looks at me and smiles. It is the conductor's smile. I realize that the conductor knows of the young man hiding under the bed. I feel a chill run down my back. I watch him walk towards the opening in the wall and stop. He turns and walks away. He knows but acts as if he has a plan and is saving a treasure for later.

Chapter | 11

FRUITS OF OUR LABOR

I wake up and my heart is troubled. I am back in El Guache. I hear my grandfather calling us to work. "Bueno 'Vamos a trabajar', time to pick fruit." My grandfather was 76 years old in 1964 and could still work us into the ground. He spoke to us in Spanish a lot. I don't remember him speaking English very much. "We will start with the peaches. We have to be done by lunch time. You two, no messing around like you know how." Michael and I look at each other. We did tend to watch the others work. "Billy, you and Juan get the ladders and the buckets out. The rest of us will get the bushels and the ropes. 'Apurale!' Hurry up! Let's go!" Grandpa was good at creating a sense of urgency when we worked. He was no nonsense, and we knew it.

My Grandfather Abelino had blue eyes and a head full of hair. His nose protruded out drawing you in to his face which was thin and strong. His hair was gray and dropped down like the hair on top of a head of corn when freshly picked. A self-confidence flowed from him as he went about his daily business. The huge cottonwoods that ran along the high-volume irrigation ditch were the product of his great grandfather, his father, his brothers, and himself. They had planted them by getting small offshoots from the river and planting them on the edge of the Acequia.

The Cottonwoods had thrived. Their long thick roots could be seen following the edge of the ditch like a huge serpent protecting the land south of the acequia. The beautiful farm and orchard were a testament to the pride they took in their heritage, and in their way of life. They took good care of their inheritance as our family's survival depended on it. My grandfather's face was very handsome but could become hard as a stone if upset. His mother came from the Salazar family, a very influential family in New Mexico. She was a direct descendant of Don Juan De Onate y Salazar and her and my grandfather's families were large landowners who had settled on the opposite side of the river from the San Juan Pueblo as evidenced by the large number of Martinez landowners on both sides of us.

The Spanish had renamed all the pueblos after Catholic Saints, and they were an integral part of our culture. There was conflict between the two cultures. The conflicts were usually over land, water, or religious beliefs. During the summer months we would see the young Indians on the opposite bank of the river. Unable to get in and swim across the river as it was too deep and ran too fast, we would shout obscenities at each other in a mix of broken English, Spanish, and Tewa. If we could have gotten across, there would have been a confrontation. As we grew up there were multiple fights.

Billy was on the move repeating the orders as he directed traffic. "Get the ladders, buckets, and bushels and let's go." "Billy, make sure your brothers get going. Let's pick as much as we can before it gets hot." "Okay grandpa, can we go swimming this afternoon to cool off?" "Yes, you can but only for a few hours. The water is running lower so watch out for branches and logs under the surface. Like we have always taught you, there have been people who have gotten trapped in them and couldn't get free. Anyone swimming and not paying attention ends up in trouble as the water pushes them against the logs and holds them in place." The discussion continued as we all worked. "Over the years several people have drowned. Keep an eye out for your brothers. Stay close to the swimming hole and you will be okay. As the oldest you have to protect your brothers. I know it's hard, don't lose sight of them or it may be too late."

The picking continued all morning. We used all kinds of methods to pick the fruit. My grandfather and Billy used ladders to pick the fruit filling the buckets with peaches, apples, and pears. When the buckets were full, they would pass the buckets down to us and we would pour them into the bushels. "Negrito, don't pour them so hard, you will bruise them!" I hated it when I was called that. My brown skin was treated as a negative. I didn't say a word I just passed the empty bucket back to him. Michael and I picked what we could reach from the ground. We also helped by climbing the trees and pitching the apples to a brother below who placed them in the bushel.

We went from tree to tree picking what was available to us based on our method of picking. We worked together. We were a fruit picking machine. Once we got started there was no stopping. The higher branches were hard to get to. The fruit couldn't be tossed down one at a time, they would hit the branches on the way down, this is where the ropes came in. Billy and Juan would climb up to the high branches with the ropes tied around their waist. When they positioned themselves in the apple grouping, they would pull the buckets up and place them on makeshift tables formed by tree branches. When the bucked was full they would lower them to the ground where we would pour them into the bushels. This process was repeated for the peaches and pears. "Make sure you keep the apples separated. The red delicious in one, the yellow in another, the Roman Beauties in one, and the Jonathon in another."

The process was very tedious. Picking and filling all the bushels took a lot of time and then we had to take all the bushels to the small road, the easement that ran the length of our property. From the side of that road, we would then load them into the truck and transport them up to the house where we would prepare them further. This is where we further separated them by type, size, and quality, nothing was lost. The damaged or those with worms and bird bites were used for pies, apple butter, jellies and sliced and dried for future use. The healthier were separated into the large storage bins in the cellar.

The compartments were made from a hodgepodge of plywood, old tin, boards and whatever else was available to make the separations. We had at least 50 apple trees, 20 peach, apricot, plums, and 'moras' (small black berries). It took us all week to pick all the fruit, haul it, and separate it. During this time, we also harvested all the corn, melons, cucumbers, and several other vegetables. Every afternoon we went swimming in the river. During the week it was interesting to watch my grandpa climb up on the ladder. It was obvious he had been doing it a long time. He scampered up the ladder and picked at a pace that was amazing while managing the entire harvest.

Our orchard consisted of trees lined up in perfect symmetry. The trees were evenly spaced making four rows that ran through the alfalfa. It was a sight to behold, the green trees surrounded by a field of green alfalfa. This time of year, it was beautiful. The fruit hanging from the trees gave the orchard a surreal ambience. When the sun was behind them, they looked like Christmas trees with fruit hanging as the decorations. The alfalfa was covered in blue and purple flowers bringing the hanging fruit to life.

The harvest was the anchor to the centuries old practice of growing sustenance in harmony with mother nature. The connection to the land was the venue from which the culture was shared and taught to the younger generations. The stories we heard during the entire process were interesting and funny, especially when the group of workers from the Acequia Association cleaned the Main Ditch every year. The 'mayordomo', the ditch boss, used a rod approximately 20 feet long to assign segments to the workers. The number of rods or Tares were assigned alphabetically by landowner and the number of rods was determined by the acreage of the landowner.

For as long as I can remember I wanted to be part of the crew. There were workers of all ages and sizes and the camaraderie was intoxicating. The stories about drinking, fighting, chasing women, and all the current events were shared. By the end of the day plans were made to go spend what they had earned, especially by the young bucks. Man, I wanted to be one of them! I would find out later that we represented our family and there was no money for us, just work. Several men worked for some of the landowners and got paid. Some of them made a lot of money as they took on the responsibly for more than one landowner. Nurturing our orchards and fields was a way of life and we were in harmony with it.

The part of harvesting I disliked the most was the process of slicing and cutting the damaged fruit. My mom and my sister oversaw this, and it literally was like being in jail. "Make sure you cut out all of the bad parts, I don't want to eat worm poop!" Annette was very assertive, she had to be. "I wonder what Soccoro is doing?" Annette's thoughts often centered around her cousin Socorro. They were the same age and were together every chance they got. "Mom, do you know that Uncle Eddie is in town?" "Yes, I talked to your auntie yesterday, she told me he was coming." "Can I go visit for a while before we go back to Santa Fe?" Annette really wanted to see Socorro. Soccoro was very pretty, and she was ahead of the other girls in her womanly development and always had boys chasing her. Annette on the other had was shy and would never think about having a boyfriend. Dad had seen her talking to a boy after school one day and she had paid dearly. Dad's words had hurt her, especially when he called her a dirty name. It had broken her heart. She didn't really understand. She just knew it was the worst thing you could call a woman.

Too many times Annette had heard dad accuse mom of being one when he came home drunk and often ended up hitting her when she defended herself. When the women around the table were talking bad about a woman they did not like, they called them those names. Never again would she do anything that would have her dad call her that. "You can go this evening if you help me get your brothers to work, we have a lot do." Annette was on a mission. She watched our every move. She was going to see Socorro! She was determined to go see her cousin, she just had to hear her stories about her boyfriends. Annette had never kissed a boy and Socorro had gone a bit further. The stories excited her in a strange way. Her brothers were going to get the job done one way or the other. Once the peeling, putting out to dry, and canning was done we celebrated with fried chicken and fresh apple pie. The picking was over, and the fruit and vegetables were put away for the winter. Annette didn't make it to Socorro's that night.

The following morning, we went with Annette to visit our uncle. Our uncle was Puerto Rican and he and my aunt lived in California. He had married Socorro's older sister, so he wasn't really our uncle, we just interacted with him as if he was. Once we got there Annette and Socorro disappeared into the house, and we stayed with our cousin Jito. Billy and Juan had gone off with some of their friends, so it was Arthur, Michael, and me. We were at our real uncle's house, my dad's older brother, Humberto. "Let's go inside." Jito was halfway through the doorway in an instant. "Hurry up we have some candy inside. My uncle always brings chocolate when he comes to visit." "You're lucky Jito!"

Michael was right behind him, and he couldn't wait to sink his teeth into the sweet chocolate. Arthur and I were following at a slower pace. "Hey there, long time no see. Man, you guys are getting big. How are your parents doing?" My uncle Eddy had a huge smile as he greeted us. "Good." Arthur responded as I stopped walking. My Uncle Eddie had a funny look on his face like if he had a secret. "Hey guys, I brought you guys some candy." Jito walked up and gave us each a Snickers Bar. "My mom said we could only have one." As we were unwrapping the candy bar our uncle reached into his pocket and pulled out a pocketknife. He had a menacing look on his face. "Okay, which one of you wants to go first?" We looked at each other with a quizzical look. I felt funny inside. My uncle had a scary smile on his face and was holding the knife in the air moving it back and forth. "You guys are eating my candy. I like to eat little boy balls, who goes first?" I stepped back right away and started running down the long driveway to our home. I found out later that he was just kidding. To me, it was real. I lost my candy bar as I ran. I never liked my uncle after that.

We spent the remainder of the summer doing odd jobs and roaming around the bosque. We would have wars shooting whatever projectiles were available to us. We made swords and spears from the willows that grew next to the river and fought with those. Too many times we would hurt each other. We never told on each other. We were afraid to tell our parents because they would really give us something to cry about. During most of this time our parents were in Santa Fe, so we were alone with our grandfather who paid us no mind. We used this time to do whatever we wanted. Normally it involved breaking something. I noticed that Billy's friends would come over in the evenings and he would disappear with them returning late into the night. The summer was at an end. I could feel it in the air. Normally after a long day we were tired and ready to call it a day.

We had built a campfire just for the heck of it. We pretended to be Indians as we danced around trying to sound convincing as we did war dances. All of us were tired and we started to settle down. We watched as the fire dwindled, it was time to call it a night. We got buckets of water and put out the fire. We slowly migrated into our house and got ready to sleep. I couldn't help but notice that Juan had changed. Juan looked wild in a way. We had only been gone a few weeks but his time alone in Española had changed him. He had been hanging with Gary who lived nearby. Gary's dad had been captured by the Japanese during World War II and was part of the Bataan Death March. I did not see his dad very often but when I did, he had this faraway look on his face and didn't talk much.

Juan had the freedom to do whatever he felt like doing. Grandpa provided minimal supervision. From what I heard, Juan and Gary were getting into trouble. I had heard my grandpa talking to my mom asking her to talk to him. He was afraid that if our dad found out he would let Juan have it. We all went to bed except Billy. As soon as we were done, he cleaned himself up and he went out with his friends. In no time at all we were all in a deep sleep. The hard work and hard play had worn us out and it was literally, lights out.

Suddenly, I hear a loud ruckus bellowing through our ancient home. The laughter is loud and continuous. My brother and his friends were coming back from a dance and the party effect was still very much alive and well. I could tell by the loud drunk discourse that they had gone to a dance featuring the local music sensations Tiny Morrie, Al Hurricane and Baby Gaby. The three brothers filled auditoriums everywhere they went. When they were in our area, they normally held the dance at the National Guard Armory with people coming from all the small towns in Northern New Mexico to enjoy their music. The dances were like a holiday and people came from all around to sing, dance, drink, and fight. I had been hearing stories my whole short life about these dances. Stories were told about how good the music was, how pretty the girls were, and all the excitement. With the growing popularity of Rock-n-Roll, all the local bands were mixing it in with the traditional Northern New Mexico Spanish music. Music by Elvis Presley, Richie Valens, Buddy Holly, the Beatles, the Rolling Stones, the Supremes, Chubby Checker, and many more were all the rage. I loved the new music.

It was obvious from the ruckus and horseplay that they had a great time. Their laughter was intoxicating, it made me laugh even though I didn't know what they were laughing about. By the sound of their flow of events, they had enjoyed all of it. Oh yeah, let's not leave out the heavy drinking. "Hey bro, I told you Priscilla would let me touch her!" I hear one of them speak, it sounded like Miguel. Miguel came from a large family of brothers and sisters. They lived a few miles north of us in Hernandez. "I don't think you did anything bro! Where did you get her alone?" Little Billy was harassing Miguel making him prove his story.

Little Billy was also Martinez, so they called him Little Billy to distinguish him from my brother. Little Billy was short and wiry and not afraid to tangle with anyone, especially when he was out partying with his friends. He was the one that they laughed at when they ran into someone looking for trouble. He would mock them to anger them. Little Billy believed they underestimated him because of his size and angering them put them at a disadvantage. He had brown dirty hair and old clothes, he had big teeth in relation to the rest of his face giving him a scary look, like an evil midget. I could see that his old Chuck Taylor tennis shoes were torn and that he was wearing ripped jeans and a plaid shirt that was too big for him. "I took her into the parking lot and found a car that was unlocked. I don't know who owned the car, but the back seat was comfortable. I should have left the owner a thank you note. Instead, I left him a wet spot in the back!"

The laughter erupted! Now my brothers and I were part of the party. Miguel had everyone in tears with laughter. Antonio was laughing and seemed to be enjoying himself. It was obvious that they had an exciting evening. "He did, I was with him!" He made her show it to me." My brother replied as he broke out in laughter, and he patted Miguel on the back. "Do you want me to show you what her pussy looks like?" Miguel had jumped on the bed without waiting for an answer and dropped to his knees. He pulled down his pants and underwear and laughed as he had everyone's attention. By now my brothers and I were wide awake and were laughing with Billy and his friends. Miguel got his penis and testicles and pulled them back between his legs until they were not visible. They caught on to the reenactment and were in stitches. "This is what her camel toe looked like." Miguel was triumphant and obviously proud of his bad boy accomplishment. Miguel was fair skinned and had brown hair and green eyes. Miguel's hair was wavy, and his dimples accentuated his smile. It was known that he had no problem with the young girls from the area. I was troubled with all of it. What is a camel toe?

"Santiago, get the guitar and play it for us! Last Kiss by Jay Frank Wilson is my favorite. You guys be quiet I want to listen to my little brother!" Rock and roll music was taking off, and we were being taught to play both. I got the guitar, sat down, and started playing. "Oh, where oh where can my baby be, the lord took her away from me. She's gone to heaven so I have to be good, so I can see my baby when I leave this world…" As I played and sang, the room got quiet, and everyone settled down. The friends started to sing along. I was on top of the world! In an instant I was part of their group. As long as I could remember I had wanted to hang out with my brother and his friends. I was young and they laughed at me when I asked. "You're too little and we don't baby sit." That was the nicest of several responses. I played a few songs and the rowdy bunch laid down on the bed in the wrong direction with their feet hanging over the edge. The rough housing and the excited reminiscing had lulled the young band of brothers to a hushed mumble. My brothers and I laid down the same way. We also had to sleep sideways so all of us could fit on the bed. It had been magical! My brother had passed a hat around and demanded they put money in it for me. They put in a few cents. It wasn't enough to buy a candy bar. It didn't matter. To me it was a fortune. For a moment in time, I felt as I was the most important person in the room.

Chapter | 12

ANOTHER DAY

arly in the morning I was the first one up. It was beautiful outside. The birds were out singing, the flowers were reaching up to the sky, and the water was flowing singing its magical song of life. I felt good, a peaceful feeling overwhelmed me. I felt that all was good in the world. But underneath it all I had a nagging feeling that was disturbing the beauty and serenity of the new day. Last night while I was singing, I could smell the alcohol on Billy and his friends. They were drunk, it was obvious. I couldn't help but wonder how they got the alcohol. We were poor and didn't have a lot of money. When my dad brought us and left us to manage the farm, he brought us enough food for the week. He gave my grandpa a few dollars for incidentals. Where had they gotten the money to consume so much alcohol? For just an instant last night, I saw the face of the Conductor amid my brother's crew. The Conductor looked content as if he was happy among them. The image was fleeting and soon disappeared. I attributed it to my dreams.

Before my brother's crew had arrived, I was in a deep sleep and thought that I heard a train's whistle coming from our farm down below. A shiver ran down my back. I could see the cold black steel emerge from the fog. The front of the train was massive. It had a large grill in the front like the ones I saw on some of the old cars. This grill was large and shaped like knives running from the top to just above the tracks. The train was like a black monster that would destroy everything in its path. At the time I didn't pay any attention to it. I shook it off as just another dream. I went back to sleep only to have the ruckus wake me up. But now here I was enjoying a beautiful morning as I pondered these two occurrences. What did it mean? "Good morning, Grandpa." As I was walking down towards the river taking it all in, my grandpa was walking up with some vegetables in his hands. Every year there was residual fruits from the main harvest. We would go down looking for the stragglers that were not mature to pick during the main harvest. "Good morning 'negrito', where are you headed so early? I take it from all the noise last night that you guys had a good time. Don't worry your dad will not find out. Be careful down there, the rains in the mountains have the river running higher than usual. Are you going swimming?" "No grandpa, I'm just out for a walk." My grandpa nodded his head, "Bueno, have a good day and be careful down there."

"What's going to become of these boys?" Abelino reflected on his way up to cook his calabacitas one of his favorite dishes. He took the squash, corn, green chili, and cheese and sautéed them creating a unique dish that watered the pallet. He was looking forward to his breakfast. Abelino's experience as a judge for the county of Rio Arriba had given him an insight into how much trouble was out there waiting on the young men and women of their community. The lack of recreational facilities and positive social organizations created a ripe environment for alcohol and drug addictions and all the social ills that came from that. He had seen too many lives ruined by the surge of addictions in the valley. Abelino was saddened by how many lives had been ruined and lost. Every family had a relative in prison in Santa Fe or in an early grave. He was especially worried about Billy and Juan.

He was hearing from all his friends and relatives about their exploits. Billy was out of control and Juan wasn't too far behind. When his first wife had died, Abelino had been heartbroken. She was the love of his life, and he of hers. In her death bed she had made him promise to marry and take care of her best friend Agapita. He had to admit that he had often looked at her in ways that were totally sexual. So, he married her, and they had one son together, Billy Sr. His son Billy had been a handful as his mom never let him out of her sight and protected him even when he deserved discipline. Abelino now regretted his failure to correct him. He was ashamed and angry about how his son treated his family and swore that next time he came home drunk and abusive he would call the cops. He swore he would use his influence to lock him up. He was tired of it!

The rest of the week was spent picking the residual fruit and vegetables. There wasn't much left but what was there was really good. Most of the time was spent doing what we normally did. We went swimming, exploring, climbing, playing, and fighting with each other. My brother continued to come in late with his crew in hand. Sometimes with beer but all the time with alcohol on their breath. No one seemed to question the fact that he was 14 years old, or maybe it's that we were alone with my grandfather, and he was hands off except when it came to work. Saturday morning my mom and Annette showed up with my dad. My dad gave some last-minute instructions and left my mom to tend to us.

My mom Adelida was born and raised in a small town in Northern New Mexico, El Rito, which means small river. The small, isolated village was nestled in a small river valley north of Española. The story she told was of a life filled with work, hurt, and disappointment. I did not like to go there. Every time we made the trip, we asked the same question and got the same answer. "Are we there yet?" "Be quiet, we'll be there soon." It was dry and arid country, and it was extremely cold in the winter. As kids we were afraid of our grandmother so during the winter we would stay outside for as long as we could until the cold drove us inside. My father seldom stayed with us there. He would drop us off and go to the small bar in the town.

Too many times we sat and waited for our drunken father to return, most of the time in a foul mood. The ride home was always an adventure listening to the ravings of a mad man. My mom always ended up on the wrong end of that and the payment was made when we got home, sometimes on the road. I had heard the women in our family talking about an event that happened when my brother Arthur was born. I guess he was to be baptized and my father was late due to a full night of drinking. He showed up late to pick up my mom, Annette, Billy, and Juan, and they left to the church in El Rito. In his anger and haste, he drove too fast and went off the road. The only person that was seriously hurt was my mom. The damage to her back would never completely heal due to its severity and the multiple traumas that were to follow.

My mom, as the oldest of six children had been thrust into the role of surrogate parent. My grandpa Jesus was a sheepherder who worked in Colorado for months at a time and my grandmother delegated it to my mom so she could go around the small community looking for work, and according to my mom, to socialize. To hear my mom describe it, my grandmother resented my grandpa for leaving her to take care of the household while he was away. When my grandfather came home for a few weeks my grandparents would fight over money and his drinking. The story validated the fear that I felt around my grandmother. My grandma, Selena, was to me a horrific family member. Most of this feeling was due to an overactive imagination as a young child. I felt the opposite about my Grandfather Jesus, who was one of the kindest most sincere people in my life. I didn't see him that often. He was my Godfather and he always made it a point to sit me down and have chats with me. I always felt good around him. I knew he loved me. My grandfather was a short man and walked as if he was always happy. He had a happy, hopping walk even when he was drunk. He had a thick beard most of the time. The few times that he shaved, there was a stubble that was always present.

The story told was about a night that my grandfather came home late and drunk. The story was one that was told repeatedly. The story whether told accurately or not was one that his children and close relations would never forget. The story spread quickly through the small Spanish village. My grandmother's version was much different. "Where have you been you worthless drunk? You're gone for months, and you go and drink and spend money you should give to me for your family. You should be ashamed of yourself. I should have married a real man!" My grandmother began to scold and batter the man although he had his boss send her money during the year. My mom and her siblings told this story in many ways mostly based on age. The older children spoke a bit more harshly about their mother. "I give you enough to take care of you and my kids until I come back. Leave me alone woman! Don't be using my money to support that bastard of yours living with the Montoya family because they won't support him. If you would have told me you already had a child, I would not have married you!"

The story my mom remembers is that as my grandpa walked to the stove to get something to eat my grandmother pushed him. He landed on the stove with his hands preventing his total body from falling on the hot stove. A scream rang through the house as my grandfather's hands were burnt. The smell of burning flesh quickly filled the air. "What have you done? How can I work now? You are truly an evil, evil, woman! God forgive you for what you have done because I won't. Tomorrow you can go back to roaming El Rito spending my money and ignoring my children." The next day my grandfather was gone! The next time I saw him was at the mortuary. My mom would always end her story the same way. "I never forgave my mom for what she did." I could see she really loved her dad. According to her, he was the only one that ever showed her compassion until she met my dad.

My mom carried a lot of pain and resentment from her childhood. As a teenager my mom worked for the wealthy families and to hear her tell it she never got paid. "I never got a penny! My mom kept it all. I really liked school and she made me quit so I could work. Even as a child she left me at home taking care of my brothers and sisters while she partied all over El Rito!" Her story continued with jaded memories of her childhood. She would tear up when she recounted the story of her youngest sister. The way I understood it, a newborn child died while my grandmother was out. The baby was left at home with my mom to watch her. My mom continued with her sad story.

"Mom would go off and be gone all day and leave us by ourselves at home. Sometimes we didn't have food and we ate whatever we could find. She did leave bottles for the baby. One day she left, and the baby started crying and would not stop. I wasn't a teen yet and I was scared. I didn't know what to do. Meanwhile my younger brothers and sisters started to cry. All of us were hungry and scared. I sent my sister to our aunt's house for help." My mother recounted stopping her narrative every now and then to issue instructions to one of us. "Billy, you and your sister go get the gunny sacks for the chili."

We grew our own chili and processed it the same way as the fruit with one significant difference. Every year we would take the ripest chile', just turning red and make ristras, which was chile' pods held together by yarn tied in a way that resembled grapes hanging from the vine. I was amazed at how the chile' was woven together using twine. I would watch as each four to six-inch chile' pod was tied and placed in an intricate pattern. The ristra when finished were four to six feet long and were hung, ripened, and dried. This would then be stored for future use.

My mom continued with her story. "My aunt came and got the baby and took her away. We never saw her again. For years we wondered what had happened to her. One day I overheard the grownups talking about how she had died. I had always believed it was my fault. I felt that since I was the last one to hold her, I had done something wrong." "Did someone tell you that you had killed her?" Juan asked in bewilderment. We had seen animals die when we killed them to eat them. The thought of someone killing a baby scared him. "You didn't kill her did you mom?" I asked the question knowing the answer I just needed to hear it. "Of course not, I just thought I had because no one ever talked to us about it. It was hard on me because I carried the guilt around for years. It wasn't until I was grown up that I wasn't afraid to ask about her. When I asked, I was told she died suddenly." "What does that mean mom." It means that the baby died while asleep at your aunt's house. I guess it just happens sometimes, no one knows why." "That's weird, how can somebody just die in their sleep?" Arthur looked perplexed. In his logical mind there was no explaining it.

"Mom, tell us the story about you going to school and my aunt having to hold your hand." Annette spoke up. Annette listened to this story repeatedly if mom was willing to tell it. She could relate to mom. Mom was the oldest child of her family as well and had gone through the same emotional roller coaster rides as Annette was currently on. The only difference was that the details were different. The challenge of managing her five younger brothers was more than she could stand. Her fear of answering to dad overrode any thoughts or desires of not doing it or doing it half-spirited. She dreaded having to deal with Billy. He told her where to go and seldom did what she told him to. It had gotten to the point where Annette ended up doing hers and his. There was a couple of instances where Billy had pushed her creating a deep, down fear, and hatred of her brother. Annette wondered why he never seemed to let up. Despite her making this known to her mom nothing ever changed. Annette felt as if she didn't matter and it hurt her to believe this, but she did.

Our mom began her story as we continued to work. "We used to walk to school every morning but to get there we would have to pass in front the Archuleta's house. Their dogs would come out barking and growling at us. Those dogs were scary. I talked to your grandma about it, but she just told us to throw rocks at them. Our aim wasn't very good and over time the dogs began to get closer knowing that they were in no real danger. One day the dogs came out and the big black one came so close to us I could see inside his eyes and mouth. His teeth looked like white knives to me, and his eyes were piercing through me. I saw his fur on his neck and back rising as if plants were springing from the ground in fast motion. I froze!" All of us stopped working. Even though our mom had told the story several times before, her body language was always the same as she relived it. After a few seconds that felt like hours, the story continued.

"I started crying and turned and ran home with your Aunt Josefina telling me to stop all the way there. Your Uncle Reynaldo and Aunt Juanita were hot on my heels, we were all scared out of our senses by that dog. Your aunt Josie was always the brave one. Right before we made it back to the house Josie caught me. "Let's go Adelida, you know what's going to happen if mom finds out we didn't go to school." Mom's story came to life. We could see mom walking down the dirt road. Mom continued with her story. "Reynaldo and Juanita were breathing hard and had a worried look on their faces. I explained to them that I was afraid of the dogs and could not make it past them. "Cover your eyes and hold my hand." You would have thought that Josie was the older sister instead of me! "I'll walk you passed the dogs, you two, walk in front of me and as far away from the driveway as you can."

My mom repeated herself often, obviously loving and bragging about her sister. "We were just kids." Mom returned to her story. "Anyway, I closed my eyes and your aunt walked us by the dogs yelling at them to go away and leave us alone. The owner heard her and went outside and called his dogs back into his yard. Your Aunt is the best to this day." I believed mom. She was my favorite aunt. Her kids, my cousins were my favorite cousins. There was as many of them as there were of us and we paired up with them pretty much by age. We all had a partner when they showed up, it was always a good time. We would eat, drink, and sing while my dad sang and played the guitar. Man, those were good days. Our home was filled with happiness. Too bad there weren't enough of those days.

After we were done for the day, we all sat and enjoyed fresh apple pies, the best I have ever tasted. The juicy sweet apples with spices would always warm my heart and the love for my mom and my family. My mom's pies were made from scratch and came out of the iron oven perfectly cooked. The crust was a uniform brown with a smattering of openings to release the pressure, and enough fruit to quench our hunger with a savory aromatic delight. Our dad was not home yet and a part of me was glad. When he was around it felt like the rest of us were not there. His presence was so strong it overshadowed the rest of us, what he said went or else. Too many times it was 'or else' for chores not done to his liking, behavior not deemed appropriate, or just because.

Chapter | 13

THE CRASH

It had been a good day! The together time was awesome! We had laughed and enjoyed the love of family. The absence of my dad hung over us like the dark clouds over the Sangre De Christo's. It didn't always rain but when it did it poured. Before we went to sleep my grandpa came over to talk to my mom. I recognized the look. Grandpa was concerned but I could not hear what he was saying. When my mom came back inside, she walked around our mud brick house hugging us and telling us that she loved us. When she hugged me, I cried and held her tight. It wasn't very often that this happened, I could feel her sadness. It was times like these that I hated my father as much as I feared him. I knew that he hurt her more than we saw. There were mornings when I saw bruises on her face that the makeup could not cover up. I felt guilty in the hate. I loved my dad and was sad because I felt and thought that he hated us and that was why he hit us so much. It felt hopeless. I knew there was no one that could stop him. Many complained and talked bad about him, but they walked away and left us on our own. Too many times I wished that I could leave with them. I couldn't, we were trapped.

We were all asleep in our makeshift beds and I was tossing and turning when I heard a ruckus coming from the kitchen. "I found your son out getting drunk with his friends, he's only 14! Why did you let him go out?" My dad was demanding an explanation from my mom. "Leave her alone dad, she didn't do anything wrong. She told me to come back early, and I didn't, it's not her fault!" Billy's voice was slurred and hesitant. You could hear that he was on the verge of saying something he would regret. "So what, you think you're a big man?" My father responded in the abusive tone we all recognized. "Leave him alone? He learned how to drink from you and your friends. I asked you not to take him cruising from bar to bar with you!" My mom was standing next to Billy. "What did you think was going to happen?" Billy blurted out a response. "Yeah dad, I learned this from you guys. I like it when I'm with you. My friends and I do the same as you guys." Billy was trying to take his father's attention from his mom.

Billy had been out with his friends, and they had partied all night. Billy was becoming more brazen. He was fighting every chance he got and doing whatever it took to fill his appetite for wine, women, and song. "He's living his life too fast, something bad is going to happen, you have to do something." My mom was sharing her sorrow with her husband. Our dad was hearing this from many of the people in his circle of friends. Tonight, he had gone out looking for his son. The problem was, him and his friends were drinking the whole time they were looking for him. As usual, he was buying the beer, driving his car, and paying for the gas. The drunker they got the faster he drove. They were on the back roads looking for a house that he was told Billy and his friends hung out at. He had driven this road a few times, he was not familiar with it. "Billy, man this car hauls ass, give it a little gas, let's see what this baby will do!"

Jody was our dads second cousin and his best friend and was always with him, never pitching in just egging my dad on, stoking his ego, and helping him spend his money. "Watch this!" The car lurched forward as our dad downshifted and accelerated around a turn. "Look out bro!"

It was too late as the Mustang slammed into a dog crossing the road. The dog was dead instantly and the car came to a sudden stop. "Son-of-a-bitch, look at my car! My insurance is already high, now it will go through the ceiling!" They continued to drive to the house looking for Billy, only now the front end on the Mustang was all banged up and leaking antifreeze. They found him and all the way home my father ranted and raved. "It's all your fault! You will get a job and pay for this." Billy was silent as he sat in the passenger seat taking the verbal abuse. He was used to it. A couple of times he almost spoke out, but he was not quite inebriated enough to do so. My father had crashed another car.

Now the events of the evening were unfolding in front of all of us. I could feel my brothers beside me and knew the fear and dread they were feeling. I was feeling the same way. Suddenly I heard the crash of the table and a scream from my mother as she went down to the floor. "Leave her alone, you son of a bitch!" Billy ran at my dad and pushed him from behind knocking him down. There was a moment of silence that seemed to last a lifetime. "Billy, you need to run son! Get out of here now! Juan, hurry, go get your grandpa! You three, go into the other room and stay there. Do not come out, do you understand, do not come out!!! Annette, you go with Juan and stay at your grandpa's house until I come to get you, hurry all of you!" We all did as we were told by mom except for Billy. "I'm not going to leave you alone mom! Don't ask me to do that!" "You need to get out of here, I'll hold him as long as I can!" Billy stepped over and helped my mom up. By this time my dad was stirring from where he had fallen. All of us were crying as we ran off to do what mom said.

I could hear my dad's movement as he got up off the floor and rushed my brother. We all could hear the striking blows as he pummeled my brother. "You want to hit me from behind you little pussy, I'll kill you!" "I'm sorry dad, I was scared for mom. I didn't mean it. Please dad, I'm sorry, please, I'm sorry." I was crying in agony. I could hear my brother, my hero, begging, crying, and being hit repeatedly. "You're going to kill him, stop!!!" My mom's voice was moving across the room. "Leave him alone, what is wrong with you, that's your son!" "Shut up, do you want me to go show you who's boss around here?" I recognized that voice. It was from another person, another thing. I could hear evil in it. I slowly got up and walked slowly to the door that led into the kitchen. "Santiago, Santiago, where are you going, don't leave me here." Michael was crying, cringing in the bed. "Be quiet, I have to help Billy." I did not know that Juan and my grandpa were entering through the outside door. I ran and stood behind them in the dark of night. The madness from inside was consumed by the dark of the night. I saw the stars and they added to the fear and helplessness. I was small and I felt it.

I stood in the dark shivering and listening to what sounded like choking rasps coming from Billy. "What the hell is going on in here?" My grandpa's voice echoed in the small room. "Let him go right now you coward!" "You better get out of here old man! Remember what happened to you last time you stuck your nose where it doesn't belong!" "May God damn you for the evil man you have become!" Juan quickly stepped into the kitchen and saw Billy red faced and glassy eyed. My mom was trying to pull my dad off Billy but was unable to. My dad was a big man, and my mom was petite, half his size. Juan ran to my mom's side and started trying to pull my dad away from Billy. We all rushed nearby and started screaming at him using the words mom was using. My dad turned around releasing his son.

I had never seen anyone look like that. It was strange the way Billy just melted, slipping down into the old wooden floor like water on a windowpane during a heavy rain. My father stormed out of the house yelling and shoving grandpa out of the way, ranting and raving but none of us were paying much attention to the words, we were focused on his location and on Billy's condition. We stood to the side watching mom and Juan as they rushed to Billy's side checking to make sure Billy was okay. "Billy, my son! Billy are you ok?" I saw that Billy was getting up. "I'm okay mom, is everybody okay? Where is dad?" Billy came out of his blackout. The smell of alcohol filled the air. Both Billy's were drunk, and the drunken patriarch had left the building.

Chapter | 14

FLOWING

I could feel myself shivering, I was starting to recognize when I was dreaming. The clanking of metal on metal is clanking in my body as if I am part of it. I am back on the train fearing the presence of the Conductor. I feel the train going through a storm. The passengers are in shock, and they wear it on their faces. I hear it in their voices. In my dream I have been following Billy as he climbs aboard. He does not look back to see if his little pest of a brother is following him. The train lets out a puff of smoke and I hear a loud horn blast through the mysterious fog. The smoke contorts as it swirls in and out. I can see images floating around inside. The Conductor, women and men of all ages are interacting with each other. Why aren't they running away. Billy is with them; he has a girl by the hand. She is smiling through him at the other passengers. The cloud goes back out of the train the same way it came in. I try to wake up, but I am awake in my dream as if a magnet is holding me in the dark. I slide down low in my seat hoping to make myself small not to be seen. I did not know how futile this was. I would find out soon enough.

The railroad car I'm in is dark and the benches are in a straight line. There is one on each side with a narrow aisle in between them. People are walking down the aisle having to adjust every time they run into someone going the other direction. Most of them can walk right through each other, their bodies blending and reappearing on the other side. I know I am dreaming but my dreams are becoming vivid and eerie. It is magical and menacing at the same time.

As the train rolls the blur crystalizes into moments of lucidity. I'm curious as to where the Conductor comes from when he appears walking down the narrow dark aisles. My curiosity was getting the best of me. I wonder if I can go see without him seeing me. What will he do if he does? I decide to move a little bit forward towards the caboose. I want to see what is powering the Ghost Train. The people in the cabin are in the middle of their activities. I recognize some from before and notice that they do the same thing every time as if they are stuck in that behavior. One couple catches my attention more than the others. I never make it to the caboose.

The man holds the woman by her arm, her reddish gown flowing down like the water falls in Nambe. It looks strange as if the water is exiting the bottom of the gown and coming back in at the top. The liquid fluidity is never ending. What does it mean? Where does it come from? Why does it keep flowing and flowing, and flowing? The gown is covered in rosettes and yellow flowers like some of the flowers that grow in the Picuris Pueblo near Peñasco. The colors ebb and flow as if they are part of a larger essence, continuous as if they are trapped. The man is dressed strangely. His trousers are black with the legs tucked into boots that look black as stone.

The boots are shiny as if they are made from a jewel. The boots are different, they have high heels and a long front. The boots seem to stretch out forever, yet I can see the end of the point coming back into the heel. The man and the woman are trapped in each other's arms as they continuously flow back into each other. The woman's face contorts. The man is running his hands up and down her body. I can feel the power of her passion. The woman's face then changes into a smile content with the man's hands wrapped around her as if she belongs to him. He seems to be guarding and protecting her. The woman's face then turns into agony. The man's hand is stuck on her face, stuck in a slap. The Conductor's face flashes in and out of the man peering out with a grin so powerful I can feel the heat. I can feel the woman's pain and fear and the man's anger and shame. At their feet there are babies crying reaching up to be held and others crouching down to get away. This scene repeats itself flowing like the train on its ancient tracks.

I hear a faint whisper, it's the lady that has been taking care of me. "You will soon understand what this means. You have seen this in your own life, yet you do not know what it means and where it leads. To understand where we are, we have to see where we have been." I recognize the voice. It was the voice that had pulled me into the lake so long ago to protect me from the Conductor. I look around but she is nowhere to be found. "If you decide to move forward and explore the journey and destination of the train you will need to be extremely careful and patient. You will not see it in one piece, but in many pieces. That is the nature of the phenomenon. Beware the Conductor! He is the only one that can see you, except for myself and one other." As soon as I hear her warning she is gone. "But I don't want to be on this train. Get me off, please get me off! I don't know how I got on, don't leave me." It's too late. The voice is gone, I'm left in the train. "So how am I choosing to ride the train?" Then it dawns on me. I'm following Billy. Even though I can't t see her, I see a shadow of her deep in my soul. This scares me and calms me at the same time.

I look forward and see a man dressed in plain trousers and a torn shirt. In his hands I see a rosary with most of it in his pocket and in the other a scroll wrapped and sealed. I can see the lines in his hands like my dad's when he shakes hands with another man and turns it into a bone crushing contest. The bones are sticking out of the skin. I know the scroll is very important to him. He opens it and starts praying. He looks at everyone inside the train and I see that he loves them and wants to get their attention. He looks through me and I can tell that he wants to stop the train and get people off, but the train keeps on going.

Another man sits down next to him, and he has a baby in his hands. He leans over close and whispers to the praying man. The two nod their heads in unison, they have agreed. The man is dressed in red, white, and blue is talking out loud. He is preaching like a priest. "The inquisition continues with more and more Jews being taken and property seized. How can people stand around and watch them hang knowing that the Crown is getting rid of them to steal their holdings?" The priest continues to finger the rosary, a voice answers from the back. "The Jews are greedy and take advantage of us. The Pope forbids us to lend money for interest as it is usury and is considered a sin. Their faith allows it, so we borrow money from them, they get rich, we get poor!" Comments continue to fly in the cabin getting louder and louder. I can hear weeping and gnashing of teeth coming from outside the train. Instantly voices inside are echoing, getting louder and louder. All are talking about the issues of their times and lives. They all talk but no one listens.

As the train rolls on, I can see people hanging, burning, and children crying. Standing next to all of them is the grinning Conductor, bloodied from head to toe. He looks at me with a smile that sends shivers through me, and I feel a coldness. I am cold and I feel as if I'm freezing like when it snows, and we wrestle in it until we can't stand the cold anymore. Only now it is darker and stronger. The Conductor's skeleton shows through, like the neon lights in the window at the bars my dad frequents. The light is flowing in his body, his bones are full. I see small pieces in his mouth. His teeth are red on white. I recognize that familiar smile on his face, then he is gone. The train keeps grinding, swaying forward, passing through the contorted images as we speed forward.

The train's passengers are riders from the past. The passenger faces appear to be the same, but different in a strange way. I see people I know, recognizing their faces yet it is not them, or at least not completely. The clothing and surroundings keep changing with bright colors and styling, but the people are linked. The buildings and people are changing, moving forward from the past, my past? Out of the darkness comes a loud screeching noise like an animal in pain. I look out the grimy window and notice that I am on the edge of a large body of water. I wonder if this is the ocean. I have heard about it from the lucky ones that go to Disneyland. The edge is surrounded with boats, their sails hanging limply at their sides. People are moving aimlessly around. They remind me of the movement of the ants when we disrupt their mounds, except these are brightly dressed people.

I exit the train and walk towards a ship that is weaving back and forth in the water. I look beyond the boat and see that the movement of the water is endless, reflecting the sun and the puffy white clouds with every ripple. The sea gulls are gliding in the sky. They look like kites in the sky without the string. Their wings are white with black. They move their wings up and down then hold them straight out and glide over the water. I want to fly like them and be free from this life.

As I approach the ship, I see that a line is forming, and people are boarding. The ship is strange to me. Its appearance resembles what we are shown in our history books. I remember the lines 'Columbus sailed the ocean blue in 1492'. I am stunned that it is true. At least the ships look like they are. Sticking out of the ship into the sky are poles, ropes, and sails. The sails are hanging loosely down the poles or masts, as our book had called them. There are ropes everywhere. The tangle of ropes reminds me of spider webs. I think of the spider webs in our outdoor bathrooms and how scared I am every time I must go. I shudder as I remember smashing one of the spiders on my forehead.

The ship itself is a dirty brown, shaped almost like a bathtub. The front tapers to a point that reaches upward towards the sky. On top of the masts the flags are blowing in the wind. Their bright colors of red, yellow, gold, and white flutter in unison. They have red crosses emblazoned on them; they look majestic. How beautiful and powerful they are. The walls of the ship are made of long boards that were somehow bent to wrap in from the bulge in the middle to the pointy front of the ship and backwards to the handrail wrapped deck. There are colorful people standing on the deck. Several of the people resemble the ones on the Ghost Train. There are six protrusions attached and centered at the top of the ship's edge starting in the center of the ship and are spaced evenly towards the front and back. I don't know what they are, but they look important. I can feel the excitement in the air. The dock is laden with crates, horses, soldiers, and to my surprise a few families and their children. I hear the people talking in Spanish. They are discussing how the discovery of the new world is creating excitement and opportunities for Spaniards willing to leave the safety of Spain. I look at their faces and I want them to see me. I want to be part of that journey.

I learn that Jews fearing the Spanish Inquisition are finding ways to circumvent the boarding requirements through false documents, bribes, and some desperate enough to go as stowaways. The result will be a large community of Jews in Northern New Mexico. I have heard my grandpa talking about it. The Spanish nobles realize that their way into the King and Queen's court and its many blessings is to excel at procuring gold, attaining glory, and by converting the Indians to Catholicism. The Jews joined the quest to save the lives of their families. They are in pursuit of a better life and the freedom to worship Jehovah. They hope and pray that the new world will be a place where they will no longer have to fear persecution.

I can't help but notice the magnificence of the soldiers in their multi-colored uniforms. They look like walking rainbows in gold, red, green, black, silver, and brown. They move as if they are part of a sea of color as they direct the boarding of the vessel. Their Coat of Arms are proudly displayed, representing the families of Spain. The bright-colored uniforms proudly signify Spain's commitment to extending their empire into the new world. As I near the vessel a soldier and a young companion catch my eye. It is the soldier I saw hiding the young Jewish boy to protect him from the Inquisition. "Uncle, what will happen to us when we get to the new world, how far is it?"

The ship looks strong, but the ocean looks stronger. "I have heard of boats being sunk by the ocean or by pirates boarding and stealing everything and killing everyone." "Don't ask too many questions and don't talk to anyone unless I am there. Remember our talk, you are my nephew. Your mother, my sister, passed away leaving you in my care. Padre Lopez took great risk in creating papers allowing you to travel to the new world. Remember, if asked, your military training is of the highest order. You come from a long line of soldiers starting with the great Martin, the great forefather of the Martinez's. Our name comes from the Roman God of War, Mars. From the beginning we have been soldiers and will be into the future. You are now part of the family, not through blood but through divine providence. You will act accordingly and honor the family that you represent."

The soldier, Santiago Martinez had taken a great risk in saving Jose, his new given name, from sure execution. His family had been hung in the public square after the tribunal found them guilty of heresy. Their properties were seized and became the property of the crown. There had been talk questioning the whereabouts of Jose. "We know they had a son, where is he?" Their neighbors continued. "You know that many Jews are fleeing in secret to escape justice in Spain." The crowd continued to stir the fires of hate. "The King has ordered all ships to be searched and that the cowards be taken and executed along with their benefactors." "I hope they catch him! His family! They took advantage of me when I was in danger of losing my land. I had nowhere else to go so I borrowed from them, and they charged me interest. That is against

God's law." Another voice could be heard. "I would expect nothing less from the people that crucified our lord Jesus the Christ. Kill them all I say!" The crowds grew louder as the clamor of the Inquisition grew. After all, with the Jews gone, their loans were forgiven.

I watch as the ship is being loaded. The ship has multiple levels. The loading starts from the bottom and men work their way through all the levels to the top. It is obvious that the plan is long term. All that is needed to live in the New World is being loaded. The loading of the horses is what really amazes me. They prance and they snort and their manes whip about as they are ridden onto the ship, some sliding as they walk the plank. The soldiers are adept at controlling them. I can hear the horses whinny as they try to escape.

"The heathen is afraid of the horses; they have never seen them before." A soldier yells at another as they meander through the crowd. "I heard from the family of Bartolomeo that the savages are starting to steal the horses as they see them as a gift from their God Huitzilpochtli. They believe the horses will take them to their heaven in Atzlan." The soldiers continue with their discussion. "The Aztec's religious beliefs and culture are centered around the belief that their great God will send Quetzacoatl to lead them to Atzlan." As the discussion continues the exchange becomes acrimonious. "We will convert them to the one and only truth. Jesus is the son of God, and he is the only way to God. The Pope and our King and Queen are very serious about this."

Once the ship is loaded, I watch as it is released from the dock. Some of its sails are being raised and men are rowing with oars that glimmer in the sun. The ship slowly and methodically glides out to the calm waters off the shore. The sails start going up in a symphony of sound. I hear the sea gulls, human chatter, and the splashing of the great ocean that will take them to the new world. I hear the wind as it puffs the sails into spectacular shapes that look like different phases of the moon. The majesty of the event is heightened with the emblazoned symbols of Spain's supremacy on the seas. The ship is on its way.

As I watch in amazement, I see two figures looking at me. One gleams with piercing eyes and the other with eyes of wonder. In an instant I recognize the face that haunts me in my sleep. It's the Conductor. The Conductor has his hands around the soldier's neck. The soldier is Santiago. As his hands tighten around his neck, a smirk appears on his face as if he is holding a trophy. The visions of the conductor bloodied and foreboding flash in front of me. "Run, get away from him, he's evil! Run! Get going, don't let him get you! Run! Get going, he is not what he appears to be." My words are lost in the breeze as I watch the ship sail away to New Spain.

As the ship sails away, I hear people talking about the strange things that have been encountered in the new world. I don't know if the stories are true. The people are reported to dress scantily. Their clothes barely cover them, and it is viewed as sinful. Their complexion is dark and some of them wear strange hats made from bird feathers. The more important the person, the bigger and brighter the hat. I wonder how long it will take the ship to get there and what will happen to Santiago and Jose when it does. The Conductor being on the ship confuses me. I was used to him haunting me from the Ghost Train, yet here he is sailing on the ocean. I feel a hand gently stroking my head. "Time to wake up little one, return to your place in time." "Who are you? Last time you spoke you told me I could get off the train anytime I want to. That's not true! I never asked to come on it. Why does that thing, that evil ugly thing, continue to show up? I run, and I run but he is always in my sleep. Is he going to get me? Does he get everyone or just the people that have been bad. Has Billy been bad?"

I wake up and I am looking up at our new ceiling. I hear Michael in the kitchen with my mom, the smell of tortillas, red chili and beans permeate the house. I rush out of bed and get dressed. There is no way I am going to let Michael hog the attention of my mom, the competition continues. I guess that's just the way brothers are. We are always at it, dreams or no dreams, night journeys or not, we are brothers, and this is my life.

Chapter | 15

SANTA FE

Our move to Santa Fe was now complete and we were ready to enroll in our new schools. Arthur, Michael, and I would be attending Carlos Gilbert Elementary in the heart of Santa Fe. Billy would be attending Harrington Junior High and Juan would stay and attend school in Española. I would never know why. My guess was that it was due to limited bed space in our new home. The answer we were given was that he was staying to help our grandfather. Our move had been and still was an adventure for us.

The landmark that amazed me the most was Camel Rock. Camel Rock would become a stopping place on our multiple trips to and from Santa Fe. Camel rock had been carved through the centuries by the wind, sun, and rain. We looked at mother nature's version of a camel head sitting majestically on a small hill. The head towered above the huge boulders which created the camel hump. The head sat on top of a wind carved neck. The camel look-alike was so big to us that it became our passion to conquer it, to own it somehow. We tried to climb up to the head, but it was impossible. We did manage to climb up on its humps. Camel Rock was surrounded by Piñon trees and was superimposed against the blue sky of New Mexico, the Land of Enchantment.

Even at our young age, we were enchanted, so much that we would throw rocks at the neck trying to tumble the head. Thank God we failed. "Let's see if we can knock the head off!" I wanted to see it tumble. "Are you crazy that thing is made out of rock." Arthur gave me that look that made me feel dumb. "Let's see if we can climb it, give me a boost you guys, let's see if I can get to that spot. I might be able to grab on and climb it." Billy was sure he could climb it. Time and time again he failed. The same discussion took place for a few visits then stopped. It became a spot for us to run around and play tag. Sometimes we just sat on the boulders or went exploring in the rolling hills behind it. On these occasions we watched for hawks until we were summoned back by our father.

"There's a hawk!" Michael was pointing into the sky. "That's not a hawk, that's a crow. Hawks are brown with white, and they have a red tail." Billy started walking towards it as he talked. "Look there's two, no there's three, wow, look how many of them there are!" I was watching the sky as white clouds floated lazily across it. The host of black birds stood out as they were stenciled into the white and blue. The big black birds looked menacing; they were hunting. I felt a lump in my throat. "Something is dead over there see how they are circling that spot?" My dad was explaining it to us. "Soon you'll see them go down to eat it." "Are they really going to eat it?" "Yes, they will. That's what they do, they eat dead stuff." I had never seen crows hunting like this. The closest thing I had seen were the geese that flew over the river heading south for the winter. They formed a V as they glided through the sky way up high. They made a noise as they flew as if they were talking to each other. They were different from these crows. I thought they were beautiful. I remembered the time that my dad took out his rifle and shot at them. Thank God he missed. In my young mind I did not understand why he wanted to kill them.

The plaza in Santa Fe was spectacular to us. The first time we cruised around the square it was a journey of bewilderment. My dad stopped at a few places. We walked around exploring some of the sights.

The Palace of the Governors, one of the oldest Government buildings in the United States reminded me of our home in El Guache. Of course, it was not born of poverty like ours, but of power and Spanish legacy. The architecture was the same. The portal ran from one end of the building to the other and faced into the Plaza, the square. The plaza was built as a modified fort. It was square and had an opening at each of the four corners. The original Spaniards worked the fields surrounding the plaza. They had lookouts walking the roofs looking for any approaching dangers, especially the Apache and the Comanche. If the alarm was sounded everyone would rush into the Plaza. Collectively they would roll wagons and place other barriers at the four corners to seal entry and fortify the plaza. I had grown up hearing stories about it. I wanted to go inside the Palace of the Governors and take a look. My first trip would not be the way most people visited.

I was entranced by the Indians selling jewelry, pottery, blankets, and other handmade objects. Everything they were selling had designs and colors I had never seen before. I watched the rich tourists looking down at the merchandise and at the Indians selling them. The Indians sat like stones in a row under the portal that goes from one end of the historic building to the other. They sat with their stone faces and spoke to each other in their native tongue and laughed. They sounded like the Indians of San Juan on the other side of the river from our home in El Guache. The men were not very friendly. They spoke only when spoken to about the price of an item. I noticed that most of the time it was the women that responded and interacted with the tourists. I listened as a blonde-haired woman spoke to her companion.

"Look Mildred, those are the Concha belts Tyler told us about. Excuse me, how much is that?" Pointing at the Concha Belt the lady continued. "Is that real turquoise?" The Indian just shook his head in the affirmative. "Is the silver real?" Again, the Indian shook his head. "Did you make it? It is handmade right? I don't want to go back to New

Jersey and be laughed at during our Bridge night. How much do you want for it?" The tourist laughed out loud obviously proud of herself. "You have to talk them down or they will over charge you. The Indian looked up, "50 dollars." In a high, irate voice the woman reacted. "Fifty dollars, are you crazy? Let's go Mildred, we will find an Indian that is not so greedy. No wonder they lost their lands they have no common sense." The two women walked away berating the sellers. I heard a discussion cascade down the row of the Indians sitting on beautiful handwoven blankets. Meanwhile a couple of tourists had heard the exchange and were shaking their heads in disgust. "Did I hear 50 dollars for that Concha? Can I look at it?" The Indian slowly handed it to him, keeping a close eye on him and his belt. "This is a beauty. The workmanship is exquisite. I'll take it." The exchange could be seen up and down the row of sitting Indians and standing tourists, they smiled.

As we walked around the Plaza the aroma of tacos, salsa, and sopapillas shrouded the plaza in the unique cuisine of Northern New Mexico. There was music in the plaza. Mariachis were strumming and belting out the traditional Mexican ballads. I felt like I was in a carnival. Cutting through it all was a slow-moving Chevrolet, it was a Low Rider. I was surprised. I thought only Española had Low Riders. We all dreamt of having one. This one was an old Chevy with baby moons and twice pipes in the back. The old Chevy was black. "Look at that Low Rider, I like the way they put the outside sun visor over the front window. That's a '49 Torpedo back, I've seen it in Spaña." Billy had started using the slang 'Spaña' for Española. "I recognize the guys, they're from Chimayo. I like the way those pipes sound. They took the mufflers out and are running straight pipes like uncle used to run."

Billy was talking to my dad. It was obvious that he was excited to see a car from home. "They are punks, I'll see them soon in lock up. I deal with guys like those all the time! Out here they think everyone is afraid of them because they ride together and when fights happen, they all jump in. In there I hear them when they become someone's girlfriend." Billy stopped talking about the car. It was really riding slow and low, and there were four young men sitting low, a couple of them wore bandanas. They looked mean. They slowed down and stared at us. My dad and Billy stared back. Rock and roll played in the car; it was really cool. I felt the excitement in the air everything was alive and for real.

Our next stop was around the plaza to the Lamy Cathedral. "The Cathedral stands out as its architecture does not match the other buildings in the square." My sister was full of knowledge and eager to share it with us. "We learned in our history class that the cathedral was built by the New Archbishop Lamy after Mexico lost the war with the United States in 1848. Archbishop Lamy was French, so he built this French church." Annette was one of the smartest people I knew, even smarter than a lot of the grown-ups in our circle. She loved school and every day I watched as she happily left carrying her books. "My auntie taught me the true history of it. When the new Archbishop arrived, the Spanish Clergy in New Mexico did not accept him as their new boss, their loyalty was to the Archbishop of Durango, Mexico. The clergy had been reporting to the Archdiocese of Durango for a century and resented the change. In fact, there was a priest in Taos that was excommunicated for not doing what Archbishop Lamy told him to."

I could hear the excitement in Annette's voice. "Padre Martinez refused to follow any directives issued by Archbishop Lamy and other Spanish Priests followed his example." "Are we related to Padre Martinez?" Annette had our attention. My dad interjected, "If you go back far enough all Martinez' are related." My dad always talked highly about our ancestry. Annette continued with the history lesson. "When the new French Priests arrived from the east, mainly from St. Louis, Lamy began replacing several Spanish priests with the French ones that were loyal to him. He assigned one of these priests to Taos. When this priest arrived, it added to the simmering bad feelings. Not only was the government changing hands but so was the church, all brought about by the annexation of New Mexico. It's funny, when this priest arrived in Taos and was standing outside to meet his new congregation for Sunday mass, no one showed up. Padre Martinez had started his own church in another part of Taos, and everyone was attending Sunday mass there. This infuriated the new Archbishop and a papal war erupted that would not end until Padre Martinez was dead and buried."

Annette was beaming with joy at being listened too. "The Lamy cathedral is granite in the front and adobe in the back. Lamy did not like the Adobe architecture so he started importing rock and rebuilding the church building from the front to the back so Sunday mass could continue. I guess the rock was brought from the east somewhere, and when he ran out of the church's money, he stopped replacing the adobe with rock. That's why the back of the church is not completed and is still adobe. You know that Bishops Lodge Road is named after him? He built a large house in Tesuque for himself. He spent a lot of money on himself even though the people around here were poor and could have used the help. Dad, can we go inside and see it?" "Not now." I liked it when we were all together bunched up in the car. When my dad was nice, we all enjoyed the moments. It was a good day in Santa Fe! As dad drove us home, I spoke out load in the car. "I think I'm going to like it here!" I would soon find out. Tomorrow would be our first day in school.

As Billy walked down the halls of Harrington, he noticed how nice some of the students were dressed and how many white people he was looking at. There was a mixture of cultures which included a couple of Native Americans. But for the most part they were separated by culture. Billy felt out of place. It looked as if everyone was excited to be there as they looked for their rooms. He chuckled as he heard the Spanish kids talking in a mix of Spanish and English just like in Española. Billy could hear the voices in the hallway as he walked. The Spanish people in Santa Fe, like those in the many towns in New Mexico, had held on to their culture and language in the face of the continued effort by all the gringos who did everything in their power to erase it.

Billy wandered around all day and found all his classes. He felt out of place and mad dogged any guy who looked at him too long or in a way that he saw as challenging. In Española locking eyes with someone for too long was considered a challenge and who ever looked away first was looked down upon. Billy saw some of this in Harrington as well. As he went from class to class, he started to acquaint himself with who the leaders were and couldn't help but notice how many pretty girls were around. They were giggling as they shared summer stories and talked about the handsome boys in the school. He was pleased that some smiled at him as they talked to their friends and pointed him out. It made it easier for him to be there.

All day he thought about his school days in Española. He was sad, he wanted to be there with his friends. The day dragged on. He was glad when he reached his PE class and saw the nice gym and the basketball hoops. Basketball was one of his favorite sports. As they stood and sat on the bleachers a big man walked in and introduced himself. "Good afternoon, I'm Coach Ramirez." He spoke while standing in the middle of the gym with a basketball in his hands. "Make sure all of you bring your gym clothes tomorrow. This is a list of what you will need. As you leave after class today pick one up at that desk by the door." Coach Ramirez pointed to the shiny black line stretching across the middle of the shiny wooden floor and had all the kids line up on it. "All of you, if you are wearing tennis shoes come and line up, if not take your shoes off and line up. You will never get on this floor with anything other than tennis shoes and they will be clean."

The coach was a big man. He walked with a slight limp and Billy would find out later that he had lost his leg in a bad automobile accident. He was very muscular and wore sweatpants all the time. He walked as if he knew how big, and strong, he was. His face was chiseled hard and so were his arms and legs. His muscles bulged through his sweatshirt and sweatpants. The coach was well known in Santa Fe. At the time of the car accident, Coach Ramirez was playing for the University of New Mexico Lobos.

The community of Santa Fe was very proud of him as very few locals ever made the team. It was a loss for Coach but also for the community when he couldn't play anymore. The Coach continued his studies and got his degree. He came home to coach at his Junior High School. His teams were always one of the best in the state and won several tournaments. It was well known that if you were going to play for him you were going to work hard, not only at basketball but in academics. Coach was no nonsense, and everybody knew it. Billy was not intimidated. He had grown up in a home full of intimidation. Billy smiled at this. He knew it was a piece of cake. The one he worried about was his dad. He was mean at the games. He would chastise Billy for bad performance. He would confront anyone else in the gym that he took a disliking too.

Billy noticed how the lights from the ceiling reflected off the floor. The floor reflected everything above it like a brown mirror reflecting the importance of the gym with the promise of good times. Here it did not matter who was rich or poor, only who could play. Billy could play. He was happy standing in the gym. It was the biggest of the classrooms and he felt good in it. The day had been challenging for him as he did not know anyone, and no one knew him. Here he felt excited. He was a good basketball player, and he knew it. He was good at football and baseball too. "How many of you have played basketball before?" Half of the hands went up. Billy looked at each of the teens assessing who would be the best. "You guys move over here. The ones that haven't played move over there, assistant coach Lujan will teach you the basics. Coach Ramirez looked at each of the boys and was assessing who he might recruit. His team was his life. His dreams of the NBA were dashed by getting in the wrong car at the wrong time with the wrong driver.

The coach had the boys line up and passed the ball to each of them instructing them to pass it back. He noticed how they caught it and assessed their manual control of the ball. "Half of you go get a ball and I want you to pair up with each other and pass the ball back and forth. Focus on how you catch it. Use both hands. Keep the ball in sight and watch it as it goes into your hands." Then in turn he had them step up to the free throw line and shoot. Most shots hit the rim with a few going in. Billy stepped up careful not to step over the white line.

Our dad had taught him well. One of the few luxuries we had was a basketball goal on a dirt lot. We spent a lot of time playing sports. Besides swimming in the river, we played basketball, football, baseball, boxed, and fought with each other all the time. My dad believed in the philosophy 'no blood no foul'. Our games ended up in tears for the younger ones and anger for Billy and Juan. The games with my dad were brutal. They started out as fun, but he did not like to lose, even with us. If it meant playing very physical with us, 'no blood no foul', so be it.

Billy let go of his thoughts and released a shot that floated through the air with a high arch and perfect spin. The coach was immediately impressed. "Nothing but net! Good shot Martinez, where did you learn to shot like that? Can you dribble as good as you shoot, here, let's, see?" Billy got the ball and dribbled towards the court to the left side. My dad had trained him to go left. Most young players were right-handed and by default, went to the right. A junior high school player that could go left and right was rare. Billy was good at both. I had seen my dad literally tie Billy's right hand behind his back and have him play with only his left. "Martinez, I want you to try out for the team, we need a good point guard. You have a good chance of being a starter. Next!" It continued for the rest of the hour with small scrimmages at the end.

Billy was a star! Billy felt alive the next day. The popular boys now knew him. He had new friends and the word spread. He noticed that the girls began to smile at him with that young girl gleam with sexual dreams and schemes. The next day the coach went through the same routine with football. Again, Billy impressed with his ability to catch, and run with the ball. He was very elusive. Again, the Coach Ramirez wanted him to join the team. "Billy, we're having tryouts for football, talk to your parents, I want you there."

Billy had a good year at Harrington. He was the running back in football and the point guard in basketball. I was proud when he put his football uniform on. I got to pose with him for a picture. The shoulder pads made him look strong. I wanted to be like him. He had us playing football every chance we got. The lawns at the prison were perfect as there were no fences or walls. The Penitentiary kids, or the Pen Gang, as we took to calling ourselves, took to playing, every one of our games was tough, we were very tough. We played some mean games. Our games were tackle, we didn't have any pads to protect us. Best games we had were when we played in the snow. The ball was cold, our hands were cold, our feet were cold, and when we ran, we lost our footing. Getting tackled was the most challenging. The tackler and person being tackled slid in the snow. As good or better than sledding.

During basketball season Billy started to show us how to roll the ball on the tip of our fingers. No matter how hard I tried I could not do it. Michael on the other hand was good at it. He knew it bothered me that he could, and I couldn't. It seemed as if he was rubbing it in my face. "Good job, Michael, you are really good." I stood to the side as my dad had us all go through the drill. I was the only who could not get the hang of it. I felt terrible. The look on my dad's face said it all. "Do it like Michael, how come he can do it and you can't?" Billy came to my rescue. "Look, do it like this. Bend the tip of your finger and spin the ball smoothly so that you don't knock it off your finger. Keep your finger straight and the ball balanced. If you feel the ball is out of balance, spin it with your other hand and the spin will keep it in place. Make sure when you spin it you slide your hand on the side of ball without moving it." He showed me by doing it and then handed the ball to me and I did what he said, or at least I tried to. It took me a couple of tries but I got it to spin for a bit, but I dropped it again. My dad walked away; the party was over. Michael walked away with the ball, spinning it as he did. I went outside, I wanted nothing to do with it. I knew I was a good player and I had never seen anyone spinning the ball on their finger during a game.

Billy began to make friends with the tougher boys at school. Most of his friends were the gang boys from the east side of Santa Fe. His school year was a mixture of his new city and the old. Running with the tougher boys reminded him of his life in Española. He was being raised in a tough environment as our dad brought the prison mentality home. We were being raised as miniature convicts. Billy was a good fighter, and the adrenaline rush was stronger than anything a sport could produce. He didn't realize it, but he was sliding into a life in a bigger city that was drawing him into the wrong side of town, the poor side. I noticed the change by the friends that came over to visit. Most of them weren't from the team, they were tougher. One of his friends that I was enthralled by was Pat De Vargas. He was tall and lanky and had jet black hair that he combed straight back. His hair was shiny. I recognized the smell of the Pomade he used, Tres Flores.

Tres Flores, Three Flowers in English, was a hair dressing that was popular with the Pachuco, the street gang banger. It made the hair shiny, kept it in place, and had a unique smell; that's why they called it Tress Flores. I loved his black boots. All of us wanted them, he had them. When they came over, I would smell the alcohol on them. From time to time I would smell an odor that was strange and watch as they passed a hand rolled cigarette like my grandma used to make. I watched as they laughed and kidded around. I wanted some so I went over to where they were. "Can I try that?" "This kid is crazy! We should give him a drag and see what he does." I got happy. I thought they were going to let me try. Billy let loose a kick that sent me airborne. "Get the hell out of here punk before you get it worse." I was in tears hurt by the kick in the ass, but more by the way Billy treated me in front of his friend. As I walked away filled with shame, hurt, and anger I shouted out to him. "I'm going to tell dad!" "Go ahead and I'll make sure I tell him what you did so that he can really kick your ass." That was the end of that.

My first days in elementary school were very dramatic. My brother Arthur was in the 6th grade, I was in the 4th, and Michael was in the 3rd. Carlos Gilbert Elementary was in downtown Santa Fe. The mix of students was new to me. Some of the kids came from rough neighborhoods and some of them, mostly the whites, came from the expensive side of town. It became apparent that the dominant kids that hung out together were tough and had friends or relatives in all grades. I felt like a stranger and realized that I would end up having to deal with some of them. The way they looked at me and talked to each other about me was enough to put me on alert.

My 4th grade teacher was Mr. Cordova. I found out early that his nickname was 'Porky' and that if he heard you call him that you would face the board of education, a paddle the length of a bat. Just looking at it hurt. It was worn down and smooth from years of use, or abuse, depending on how you looked at it. To me it was normal. The kids knew that he would paddle you so hard your feet would leave the ground. "Good morning students. I am your teacher Mr. Cordova. We are going to have a wonderful school year. A few things I want you to know. I am very serious about you getting a good education. Every year I get a few students that don't want to follow the rules. For them I have this." Mr. Cordova proudly displayed his Board of Education.

As typical for me, I was one of the smartest kids in class and was done with my work before the other kids. I would use this time to disrupt the other students. After a while, Porky put my desk next to his and would deal with me every time I disrupted the class. A week in I started to utilize a new trick I had learned, shooting spit wads through a straw. Porky's desk was in the back of the room facing the blackboard. He could see all the kids from the back of the room, but the kids could not see him when he was seated, except for me. I was his neighbor. Well, me being next to him, gave me a perfect view of the classroom.

"I'll be right back. I am going to the principal's office. You all sit there and do your assignments. Santiago, you work on the project I gave you." "OK, I will, I'm almost done." I liked the special assignments. The extra math problems and the extra reading kept my mind busy. Slack time was not good for me or anyone near me. As soon as he was out of the room, I started putting small pieces of paper in my mouth, spitting it into my hands, then wadding it up into miniature projectiles until they were the right size for the straw and began target practice. At first, I couldn't hit the broad side of a barn if I was standing in it. The more I fired the better I got. As the spit balls started landing on my intended targets the class started to lose its focus.

Many of the students would get very upset, especially the girls. They hated when the spit wads got stuck in their hair. "I hate him! I am going to tell my parents when I get home. My dad is good friends with the principal. My dad told me if anyone bothers me to tell him, especially the Spanish boys. I am to stay away from them." Joanna was a twin. Her brother was John. Both had blond hair and very light skin. You could tell they were related. They looked the same except for their size. John was tall and a bit plump. Joanna was thin and short. The other boys used to make fun of John, and Joanna would come to his rescue. During PE the boys started making fun of him because his penis was too small. John took to hiding from us. A few days into the classes he showed up with pride on his face and looked up at all of us and made an announcement. "My dad told me mine is bigger than all of yours, it's just in the garage." We all started laughing and John started getting teased about his being in the garage.

I did not notice the return of Porky and before I knew it, he had me by the arm. His grip was strong, and his eyes were locked in on me. He was looking at me through his black framed glasses. He had a stern look on his face. I could smell and feel his breath bouncing off my face. I could feel his strength as he pulled me out of my desk. My first inclination was to punch him but thank God I came to my senses. He grabbed the Board of Education from the top drawer of his desk and proceeded to take me to the front of the class to educate the class on the consequences of shooting spit wads.

"Listen up class. Santiago has decided that he doesn't have to do what he is instructed to do! Not only that, but he has decided that he can shoot spit balls at you and that it is okay. It's not okay!" I looked out at the class, and I could see that most of the kids were scared, almost as if they were the ones about to get paddled. I could also see that some of them were happy I was there. Joanna had a smug look on her face, she could not contain herself. As Mr. Cordova continued with his presentation, I heard Joanna giggle and quietly clap her hands. Sitting in the back were three boys from the low-income housing that had smiles on their faces, it was obvious they were enjoying my predicament. I could hear them snickering. "I knew it was only a matter of time. That guy is crazy. I guess his older brother threw blows with Clarence in the older kids play area." "Yeah, I heard he kicked Clarence's ass. They were playing basketball and I heard that Clarence got mad because Arthur was beating him at 21."

"You back there, pay attention or you're next." The three boys from the projects were hard, their environment was tough. My brothers and I had already tangled with the locals and had shown that we were a force to reckon with. I was surprised at how much better we were than most of them. There were some that were tough and we either became friends or became enemies. There was little wiggle room with the boys from the Projects, Alto Street, and the area around West San Francisco Street. These families had been in Santa Fe for centuries and the blood ran thick. It did not take us long to realize that here it was clan warfare. If you fought one you had to fight them all. We were at a disadvantage. We weren't from Santa Fe. Here it was just us and our band of misfits.

"Bend over and touch your toes. You need to understand that you are in the classroom to learn not to play and disrupt the other students. You save your playing for outside." As I bent over, I could see Mr. Cordova's pant legs and shiny shoes. I also could see that the paddle looked bigger when bent over. The room looked different. The world was upside down. The desk legs looked like sticks stuck in the mud and the kid's legs were dangling. I could see the books in the metal storage built into the seat. The girls wore dresses with bobby socks and loafers of different styles and colors. The white and black shoes stood out. I couldn't help trying to look up their dresses. My experience with girls was limited to my older sister, my mom, and my aunts, who would have beat me to an inch of my life if they had seen me trying to peek. I knew better. I thought about how scared of girls I was. I did not know how to talk to them!

Before I realized what was happening, I was airborne! It felt like my butt was on fire. Without knowing it, I was the first Hispanic in outer space, that's the way I felt. The burning spread to the rest of my body. The bulletin board on the side of the blackboard scared me as I flew passed it or at least that's the way it felt. The Crayola pictures looked like flashbacks from my dreams, but this wasn't a dream. When I landed my body hurt from top to bottom and I could feel my heartbeat in my butt. It hurt so bad I almost cried but remembered what happened when I cried at home.

"Do you want to cry? I'll give you something to cry about!" My dad had ingrained these words into all our spirits and Billy had taken up the saying. I had learned my home taught lessons well and I did not cry. I would realize later the impact it had on the class and the rest of the elementary school. Most kids cried when the Board of Education came calling. "Now go sit down and get to work. Next time it will be two." As I sat down, I felt a strong stinging vibration that was radiating through my body. I tried to lift myself from the seat but couldn't. I had learned my lesson but for how long? As it turned out there would be many more. I guess some people have a hard time learning their lessons.

Our first year in Santa Fe continued pretty much like this. Each of us in our own little worlds making a name for ourselves as good fighters and troublemakers. Arthur had established himself with the sixth graders and was friends with the rough, tough, and poor kids from the 'wrong' side of town. Each of us migrated towards that. We were more like them than the richer white kids and their Spanish counterparts. They stayed away from us. We picked on them. I guess it was our way of making up for what they had and were and what we didn't and weren't. After a while they moved out of the way as I walked through the hallways looking for trouble. I was looking for a place to drop my anger and insecurity.

It was not too difficult to find. It turns out I was surrounded by soft targets. I guess I thought they were all raised like us, survival of the fittest. As I grew up, I realized that not too many were raised like us. Time after time, I was approached on the playground by locals wanting to establish that they were tougher. They were acting like the playground was theirs. Time after time they would get beat. Then the older brothers, cousins, and friends would show up. "Try it with me," was a phrase that I often heard. Most of the time I could beat them too, but on those occasions when I couldn't, Arthur would take care of me. After a while we were the ones doing the challenging. By the end of the school year, we were in. Our training at the hands of our father had paid off. We ran the prison yard.

"Where did you get that gum?" I asked Louie. Louie was from the projects, his father, a Marine, was in prison for murder. He was blowing bubbles as we talked. He was enjoying the Bazooka Bubble game. "I stole it from the 7 to 11, it's easy. As my brother distracted the fat man, I put it in my pocket. Do you want one?" I answered excitedly. "Hell yeah, I want one!" He handed me a piece that was wrapped in a blue and white paper. I couldn't help but ask, "Where is the 7 to 11? You think we can do it?" He answered quickly. "Yeah, we could do it after school." "I can't, I have to catch the bus." Times like this is when I hated that we lived at the Prison Housing. I knew what would happen if I missed the bus and my mom had to pick me up; even worse if my dad had to pick me up. As we discussed it, I was thinking about how much things had changed in my life in a small amount of time. It was lunch time, and I was hungry.

The food we had packed was gone. Most of the kids ate in the cafeteria. We didn't have any money, so we brought sack lunches with Tortilla sandwiches. The sandwiches were made either with Vienna Sausages, Spam, hot dogs, or bologna. It depended on what we had at the time. Sometimes we came without lunch. I didn't know why but I felt embarrassed when I saw the other kids eating sack lunches with white people food. Their sandwiches were made of luncheon meats, bread, lettuce, tomato, desserts, and good stuff to drink.

"Let's go now!" I was excited. "How are we going to get out of the fenced playground without being seen?" The playground had a six-foot fence that enclosed the entire playground. The only way out was through the building, and it was impossible to make it past the hall monitor and the principal's office. Then it came to me. I remembered chasing a ball into the corner of the fence. "I saw a small hole in the corner, let's see if we can dig it deeper. All we need is something to loosen the dirt with." We were very excited to go on an adventure. As we talked, I felt good inside. I also felt a strange kind of fear, a fear that made me feel important in a way. What would Billy say? He and his friends were always doing stuff like this. We talked for a while discussing how we were going to do it. We went to where I had chased the ball. There was a small gap in the fence where it met the building. I knelt and felt the dirt. "It's pretty soft, we can use our rulers, don't forget to bring them. Someone will have to be lookout and warn us if someone is coming. Keep that nosey Joanna and her friends away, she's a rat. Let's ask Gary to help us. I can ask my brother Arthur to help us too. Let's go ask them."

Louie was hesitant. "I don't want to go through to the six graders playground. Last time I went Clarence picked a fight with me." Louie always chickened out. "Let's go, they won't do anything. I'll tell Arthur and he will beat up anyone who does." I led the way along the fence. No way was I going to walk through the middle of the playground. "Hey, what are you doing over here, go back to the little kid's side of the playground." As we walked a few of the kids taunted us but left us alone. As we walked along the fence, we made sure that the teacher on duty would not see us. We made it through and found Arthur and Gary playing basketball. We told them our plan like it was our very own prison escape, but Arthur was not interested. "Why do you want to do that? If you get caught you know what's going to happen. Dad will beat you and me for not stopping you." Arthur had the look again. I could tell he did not want me bothering him. "Every time you get into trouble, I have to clean up your messes!" The discussion went on for a while and ended with Louie and I returning to our place in the playground certain that we could do it and committed ourselves to do it. We started our own gang that day, the Thunderbirds. It was short-lived.

Chapter | 16

HOW SWEET IT IS

I t took us a few days to make the hole under the fence big enough. It took longer than we thought. One of us would dig and the other one looked out for the teachers and the principal. "Watch out, Mrs. Nyquist is coming!" Louie got on his feet. "Where is she?" We pretended we were wrestling as she came by. "Hello boys, how are you doing on this fine day? Hope you are behaving. Is everything okay?" "Everything is going good, just messing around." I was always quick with an answer. I sighed a breath of relief as the bell rang. "Run along, don't be late for class." As we walked back inside the school we were laughing, it had been close. Our pants had dirt on the knees and our hands were dirty, but we were happy. Our plan was coming along. "See you tomorrow, we'll finish it soon. I can taste the candy already."

The bus ride home was pretty much the same. Rough housing in the back of the bus was normal for us. My evening was quiet. I went to bed and slept like a rock, no journey on the night train. As I got ready for school in the morning I was in a good mood. I felt like a Pirate getting ready to board a Spanish Galleon. "Good morning, how is my wonderful son this morning? What are you doing up so early? Did you have another bad dream?" Talking to my mom early in the morning was wonderful. "No, I just got up." I walked up to her, and we hugged each other. These moments were rare, normally all of us were around and she was too busy getting us ready for school and herself ready to go clean rich white people houses. I often wondered if she cleaned houses for some of the kids in my class. Did they know she was my mom?

It was a beautiful morning and classes went on as usual. I sat in the classroom quietly, I didn't want to bring attention to myself. When the bell rang for lunch, we ran outside and met at the hole under the fence. We heard the traffic on the road behind the school. "Are you sure you want to do this?" Louie was always starting things and reluctant to finish them. "Let's go, no one will even see us! Are you afraid or what? Look there goes Sonny and Gilbert. Hey guys come here. Do you want to go with us to the 7 to 11 to get some candy? We don't have any money, so we have to go in, grab it and run. We're going to do a raid." "Really, are you guys crazy?" Sonny asked with a huge grin on his face. "Are you scared or what? No way they can catch us." I could hear the excitement in my voice. Louie shared that the guy behind the counter was old and fat and would not be able to catch us. "Hell ya, let's go! I love candy!" So now there were four of us. I was the first one under the fence and the other three quickly followed. As we walked down the street towards the 7 to 11 some of the kids saw us and started yelling at us. "Hey, where are you going? You're not supposed to be out of the yard. We are going to tell the teacher!"

"You better not, I will kick your ass!" The kids knew by now that I meant it and would enjoy doing it. We continued our quest for the forbidden candy. As we approached the store, we got strange looks from the people passing by. I was the first one in the door and the guy at the counter began grilling me immediately. "Hey young man, shouldn't you be in school?" "I am, my dad is coming in a minute. We are going on a field trip." I lied as I looked over my shoulder and saw the other three peeking in through the window. "Stand over there until your dad comes in. Where did he park? I don't see the car. Why isn't he picking you up at school?" The man started around the corner, and I grabbed a handful of candy bars and ran outside towards the school. As he chased me, my three cohorts went inside and loaded their pockets and ran down a side street and we all met at the school. We crawled through the hole in the fence and proceeded to the first and second graders playground and buried our sweet treasure in the sandbox for future enjoyment. We each ate a chocolate bar enjoying every bite and burying the wrappers on the other side of the sandbox. The bell rang and we all went to our classroom rushing in so as not to draw any attention to ourselves. I felt like a million dollars. After school I would go get my candy and take some of it home to share with my brothers.

Mr. Cordova had us working on math problems when we heard a lot of talking in the hallway. "Do you see any of them?" The principal was talking to someone. "There's one of them right there, and that one too." The principal talked to the teacher across the hall and then I saw Sonny and Gilbert being led by the principal, a police officer, and the man from the 7 to 11. They went into another room across the hallway, and I heard voices. The principal was talking to Mrs. Nyquist and then I saw that Louie was being led out of the room. My heart sank into my stomach, I knew I was next. The principal walked into the room. "Mr. Cordova it seems we have some students who rushed into the 7 to 11 and ran out with several bars of candy. This gentleman was working the counter when one kid went in before the others. He has been described as the ringleader."

"One went in and distracted him by grabbing some candy and running out. During the chase these ones here went in and loaded up with chocolate. We have Louie, Sonny and Gilbert here who have been identified as the three who went in. We're going classroom to classroom to identify the fourth." I had my head down low to the desk believing that I could escape being identified. "Sir, please look and see if you recognize anyone else that was there. I could feel the man surveying the room and literally could feel him looking at me as I looked down at my desk. "That one there, he was the first one in. When I asked him why he was there and not in class his response was that his father was parking the car because they were going on a field trip. I did not believe him and was coming out from the behind the counter when he grabbed some Hershey's chocolate bars and ran out. As I chased him the other three came in behind me and did the same thing."

Next thing I knew I was in the principal's office waiting for my parents to show up. I sat there hoping it wasn't my dad. I knew he was working graveyard and was probably at home sleeping. Sonny, Gilbert, Louie, and I were seated in the principal's office waiting for our parents to arrive. All of us were really scared. All our dads were mean as hell and we knew there was no escaping their wrath, except for Louie, his dad was in prison. In the office with us were the principal, the counterman, and a police officer. I don't know who I was fearing more, my dad or that cop. The cop was dressed in a blue uniform with a blue and black hat that looked like the one's soldiers wore. It had a shiny badge in the middle of it. The cop's ID badge had the name Saiz on it. I looked at the gun on his belt. I would hear later that this cop was known for beating people up on their way to jail. I didn't know it then, but we would get to know each other well in the future. After what seemed like an eternity our moms were all there. The principal greeted each one as they arrived and asked them to sit down. Extra chairs had been brought into the office. The principal sat down behind his desk. "We have a serious problem on our hands. Your sons have decided that they can sneak out of the school grounds and enter a 7 to 11 and steal candy. Officer Saiz please address the mothers and let them know what the legal ramifications are." "We didn't do that, it wasn't us!!" I blurted out.

Officer Saiz looked at each one of us before he spoke. He glared at me, and I shrank in my chair. He took a hard look at me. He didn't like that I had responded the way I did, he wore it on his face. I couldn't help but notice that his muscles on his arms were big. I was wondering if he could take my dad. He had taken his hat off and his hair was short and straight and brown. His face was square with shiny straight teeth and a square nose. His chin had a dimple on it like Juan's. His eyes seemed to look inside of me. I had nowhere to hide. He pointed to me and asked a question that penetrated my skin. "What is that on your face?" No matter how hard they tried, the group let out a short laugh. It turned out I had chocolate on my face. In my rush to consume some of the bounty of our piracy I had enjoyed it so much that I had smeared it on my face. Officer Saiz then pointed to Louie's shirt and asked him a question. "What's that on your shirt?" Louie had wiped his hands on his shirt when the bar he was eating melted in his hands. Again, the adults had to stifle a laugh. They probably looked at us like the dumbest pirates they had ever seen. The atmosphere went back to cold and serious. They still had to figure out what to do with us. The cop stated, matter-of-factly, "What I want to do is to charge them with stealing, arrest them, and take them to the juvenile detention center."

I had heard about the D-Home and how scary it was in there. Some of the teenagers in there had killed people. What would they do to me? "Don't you think that's a little extreme? Santiago is in the fourth grade. He gets straight A's on his report cards. I know his behavior isn't as good as it should be. Maybe if you had advanced courses, he wouldn't have time to misbehave." I was surprised at how strong my mom was talking to the cop. I guess all those years of dealing with my dad had made her tough. I loved my mom! As they went back and forth, I felt really bad. Why did I have to do stuff like this? I hated to see my mom have to go through this with me. I felt a hot tear rolling down my face. I lowered my head and wiped them off without my co-conspirators seeing me do it. The other moms nodded their agreement though they didn't say much other than the threats to their sons about what waited for them at home.

SANTA FE: A PIECE OF 'MI VIDA'

The principal and Officer Saiz stepped into the hallway and could be heard talking to each other. My mom was looking at me with those Northern New Mexico eyes. Those eyes had a historical strength and knowledge that seemed to come from the past. I knew that she was very upset for two reasons. First, here I was again, always starting trouble. Second, it was not good that she had just started a new job and had to leave to deal with her chocolate pirate with his chocolate smeared face. I did not know what was going to happen, but I had an eerie feeling.

"The principal and I have decided that this matter will be handled by the school and the parents. Boys look at me and trust me when I say that you do not want to see me again under these circumstances. Next time I will arrest you and take you to the D-home. You will not like it there! You will be surrounded by older boys that will beat you up every chance they get, and maybe worse." The principal walked Officer Saiz to the door. "Thank you, Officer Saiz, you can rest assured that this issue will be taken care of." As the cop left, the principal looked at us. "Where is the candy you stole?" The four of us kept quiet. "We can call the Police Officer back!" The principal headed towards the hallway. "We buried it in the sandbox." I knew the sooner I got passed this the better.

The four of us led the way with our tails between our legs to the sandbox and were ordered to dig the candy out of the sand. The sandbox was located at the front of the school. I knelt and dug the candy out and handed it to the principal wishing I had eaten more and hid it in multiple areas. "You know the rules. You are not to come to this part of the school." Back in the school room we were told that for the next month we would stay inside our classrooms for lunch and recess. "Get your stuff ready and go home with your parents. Come into my office first thing in the morning and I will escort you to your classrooms so that your teachers understand what happened and what your punishment will be."

The trip home was mostly quiet. The sound of the rubber against the road was deafening. It was mostly silent all the way home, except for the choice words my mom had for me. I sat in my guilt and shame. She informed me that she had no choice but to tell my father. She had that look again. When I got home my father wasn't home yet. I was glad to be home. No matter what, it was home. The living room blinds were pulled aside, and the outside light was pouring in. "Go to your room and stay there. No dinner for you tonight." I went into the room I shared with Michael, closed the door, and wept. I seldom cried in front of others except when Billy put me through one of his torture sessions. Some of those sessions were frightening. One came to mind as I lay on my small bed in tears and in fear. I felt alone.

My memories of that day were crystal clear. It had been a day much like today. I remembered the beautiful weather in Santa Fe. I made a mistake of asking Billy a question. "Can I throw them?" Billy was throwing darts at the wooden door in the garage. Our garage was small and had a storage area running the length of the garage with tall wooden sliding doors covering it. He had drawn a circle in pencil and was aiming and throwing the darts, most hit inside the circle. "You can't hit that target, get out of here." "Yes, I can, let me try." Billy looked at me with that look he gave me every time I bothered him when he wanted to be alone. "Here, go ahead and try it."

The darts I threw hit, and most of them stuck, to the large yellow wooden doors, none of them stuck to the target. "Give me those. Go stand at the door and let me throw them like they do in the circus, it will be fun." "I don't want to that, what if one hits me?" I looked at him and recognized that I was headed for a torture session. I saw that look every time. I knew better than to refuse so I walked slowly and stood at the door. "Don't move, I don't want to hit you." I stood still and could feel my heart pounding in my chest. I could hear it like the drums at the Indian ceremonies I had been to, only I wasn't dancing. I was feeling like that now, only it wasn't the darts I was afraid of. I was praying and wishing that when my dad came home, he would not be drunk.

My memories of the dart day continued. I remembered Billy throwing the darts. I shivered every time he did. I could see the darts in flight, like hummingbirds flying straight at a nectar rich flower. Bam, bam, bam, I would hear the darts slamming into the yellow wooden storage door. They were landing and sticking, they were getting closer to me. I dared not move. I begged him to let me go play, but he kept me there. I was emotionally pinned to that wooden sliding garage door. As I stood there, time slowed down, coming to a stop as I watched a dart head straight for my head. It looked like a missile fired from a ship, it came in straight, and for me, just as deadly. I felt the dart hit me in the forehead and the warm flow of blood streaming down my face. I hung my head down as if I was trying to avoid the next missile. As I did, I watched as my blood flowed down the dart falling to the concrete garage floor.

I started to cry, and Billy rushed over to where I was. "Don't be a cry baby, it didn't hit you in the eye. Go stand over there on the side of the house. Leave the dart in, let me go get a rag and I'll pull it out." He ran into the house and was back in an instant. He yanked the dart out of my forehead, put the rag to my forehead, and told me to put my head back. He kept the rag on my head until the bleeding stopped. "Don't tell mom or dad. I didn't mean to do it." This was a common occurrence only the events changed. I loved him so much I never told on him. I loved him that much that I was willing to allow him to do crazy things to me. He was my hero. Most of the time it wasn't like that. He taught me how to play basketball, football, baseball, boxing, weightlifting, and more thoroughly, fighting. He loved to put me into fights, like a trained pit bull. When we were at dinner that night, I told my mom and dad that I had run into a low hanging branch from a Monkey Peanut Tree and one of the branches had thick thorns. They didn't say anything as my dad changed the subject. My mom looked at Billy then she looked at me. She knew there was more to the story.

I was startled from my dart dream by talking in the next room. My dad was home, and I could hear him and my mom talking. At first, I couldn't make out what they were saying. I could tell it was not good, they kept getting louder. "Billy, leave him alone, he's in the fourth grade. I'm sure he learned his lesson." "Why did I have to hear about it from the neighbor?" My mom replied in an agitated pleading voice. "You weren't home!" As usual my dad spoke and moved at the same time. "Get out of the way, I'll teach him not to steal!" "No, talk to him tomorrow, he's asleep, he as school tomorrow." "Get out of the way!" "No!" "I told you to get the hell out of the way, no one keeps me from my sons!" My mom was crying, here we go again. "Come here you little shit."

Chapter | 17

BOOM

"Let me out of here!" I'm in a dream again, screaming at the top of my lungs. "Dear God, why are you doing this to me? What did I do to deserve it? Please take me out, I'll behave!" I had my eyes closed praying, crying, begging until the booming startles me into consciousness. Boom! Boom! Boom! I open my eyes and see darkness. I reach up and touch the top of a box lined with soft and smooth material. I realize that I'm lying in a soft bed surrounded by soft cloth. Am I in a coffin? The sheer terror brings wailing into my small enclosure but there is an echo that is stifling. I visualize all the dead I've seen at funerals. I had always wondered why they were being buried in boxes that were nicer than any bed I'd ever slept in. As I lay in my dark terror, thoughts of last night enter my mind. I remember that what happened last night has happened on lots of night. We were sent to our room and told not to come out. Our mom was adamant about it.

My dad was at it again, home drunk and yelling at my mom. "Serve me beans and chili and fry me some eggs!" When these episodes happened, I had a hard time sleeping. It always started the same and ended the same. It was happening more often now. One of the surreal effects on me was a feeling of throbbing in my body as if each part wanted to break away from the past and the present. In my mind the past and present were a continuum, it was all one. Often, I would feel an out of body experience. An aura would consume me and stay with me all night. I woke up smelling stuff that wasn't there. I knew I recognized the scents, but they were all jumbled together. I would search my mind trying to figure out what I was smelling. It was right there within reach, but I couldn't quite figure it out. It scared me. After these episodes I had a hard time falling asleep and when I did, I tossed and turned until morning. Now I was locked up in a coffin? How were these two connected? It was real I knew that, but how could it be if it wasn't real to anyone else. The reality of the terror brought on us by my dad was blending with my dreams.

A scratching noise wakes me up! I can hear my heart echoing inside my cushioned prison. My breathing is rapid! I hyperventilate! I hear fingers walking across the top of my coffin as they locate the handle to open my prison door. The scratching reminds me of the noises I would her in the cellar, my bedroom in El Guache when the mice were out rummaging at night. It seemed as if that life was an eternity ago and in another life. "Here I go again!" I whisper out loud. "Man, I wish this would stop!" Suddenly the door is ripped open, and the Conductor is looking down at me. His bony face is white with red blood flowing inside as if there are clear tubes running underneath his skin. I see through his bones; a river of bloody bodies is running inside them.

There are faces contorting in the blood. Many of them, I remember from my journey on the train. I see the soldiers as they lay dead on the battlefield. I see the Priest with his rosary. I see the young soldier saving the boy from the tribunals. I'm connected to all the faces from beginning to end as I'm being held connected by an invisible thread. One image is clearer than the rest. It is an image of my brother Billy as he flows nearby. His arms are reaching out for me as he pleads for my love, my salvation, my help. I am powerless to do anything. I can hear my heart wanting to burst out of my chest. Something inside of me wants to fight back but I am frozen in time.

The Conductor is standing next to hanging corpses, their blood smeared on his face. The blood is dripping like a faucet that has been left running to prevent the pipes from freezing. Now he is looking down at me with that same grin that speaks to my soul as if saying he has me. He doesn't say anything as he starts to reach down towards me. His fingers are gnarled, twisted, and bent, with his fingers pointed in all directions like the roots of the weeds we pull in our back yard. Only his fingers are alive prowling like an octopus probing the ocean for food. His head is lowering towards me. I am pulled inside his eyes through a fog. I am swirling as I tumble inside. Booming noises like canons can be heard in the walls of the abyss. I smell his breath and I recognize it. It smells like the dead decayed cow we stumbled upon when we were on one of our adventures at the river.

The cow had been there for a long time. We could see the bones under the brown wrinkled hide and the flies were everywhere. But what I remember the most was the stench, the smell of death. We had run away from death that day, the smell was back but I couldn't run away. As his hands reach my neck, I shudder at how cold they are. As the grip starts to tighten, I feel a presence in the room. A voice speaks from behind the Conductor. I recognize the voice. It is the woman who has saved me from the Conductor before. Her voice is like the soft summer rain in El Guache. I can't see her, but I feel her. I know who she is. She's old as the blue sky and bright as the stars at night. He looks back and evil flows from him, not towards me but towards her. As he turns, I am released from the viral quagmire, and I rise from the silken trap and run. The ancient words follow me as I leave. I find myself back on the train heading forward into the night.

I find myself looking out over the ocean as the train comes to a screeching halt. I am on the shore, but it is not in Spain, it feels different. The air is moist with the feel and smell of salt in the air. I am part of the quiet noise of the ocean. Sea gulls are flying overhead. As they glide above me their wings turn from white, to silver, to grey as they shift direction, and the sun reflects iridescently off their wings. They fly in unison as they dive individually into the moving aquarium beneath them for their sustenance. I am enthralled by the majestic interplay, life turning to death to provide life. They call out into an ecosystem that I am a visitor in. They are talking to each other as they turn their beaks towards the water. They can taste their catch already. I see one close to the shore and I see him with a fish in his bill. The fish is wiggling in vain trying to get away. I see the fish's eyes as the life drifts into the heavens. I can see the seagull's throat contracting in and out as it swallows the fish whole. I see behind him a host of gulls doing the same thing, like an orchestra united in the concert of life and death. Each one is in a different plane, but each is part of a bigger whole. I turn from the ocean, I am overwhelmed. I am looking at a world of green imbued with colors I have never seen before. Wild living plants are hanging from the sky, snaking up from the floor, and winding across itself in a never-ending cornucopia of sounds, images, and smells. I feel so alive I want to run and scream at the top of my lungs. The coffin is now a distant memory.

Suddenly something moves on one of the trees. It is huge! It's a snake, larger than any man I have ever seen. It is moving slowly towards a pile of living brown. Instantly the pile comes to life and brown and black monkeys are chattering so loud it scares me out of my mind. The monkeys clamor as they elevate into the trees, climbing and swinging into the canopy, into the green, blue, and white. One monkey stays behind. I notice there is a small ball at her feet, it's a baby chimp clinging to her, unable to move. The baby appears to be sick. The mother is trying to pick it up but the little one is unable to provide any assistance and it just lays there. The baby ape is looking up at its mother with a look of pure trust and love. The mother is frantic as she grabs the chimp in her arms. The mother drops the baby as it squirms out of her grasp unaware of the approaching reptile. The snake sees them and quickens from its slow slither in their direction. "Hey, get away from them, go on, get away!" I pick up a stick and head their way but stop halfway. I know I am powerless to prevent what is unfolding in front of my eyes.

I am scared, angry, and sad, I cannot take my eyes away from the scene. The mother stands on her hind legs with her teeth protruding from her mouth and her front legs stretched out in front of her, attacking the air in front of the serpent. The serpent is unfazed as it draws near with is bulging eyes focused on the baby. The serpent flickers its jet-black tongue in and out splitting into a 'Y' with every flicker. I watch its body quickly constricting forward. I have never seen a snake move this fast and look so slow. The size of the serpent hides the speed it is traveling at and how quickly it gets to its target. As the snake draws even closer the mother attacks the snake jumping on its back digging her teeth into the flesh on the back of the snake. The snake convulses and magically contorts its body and begins to wrap its mammoth length around the mother ape. The mother escapes and leaps off into the trees. The sound of a mother's pain filled moaning echoes through the forest. In an instant, the serpent wraps its huge rope like body around the stranded baby and I watch as the life is squeezed out of the baby and consumed. I see the bulge as it moves down the tunnel of death.

I am stunned and bewildered as I watch the snake swallow the baby whole. I am mesmerized as I watch the lump inside slowly moving towards the center of the beast. The snake looks at me but does not move. I realize it has no reason to, it has satiated its hunger. The snake looks at me and I recognize the grin of my nightmares. It does not transform but it sits there licking its fangs while it looks at me and through me. Now the beauty of the jungle takes on a different hue as I realize that it is alive, every drop, every sound, every smell, every view, it's all part of a whole living being. It's an ecosystem that I cannot wrap my mind around. I hear cracking and shrubs collapsing and catch sight of men riding on horseback through the jungle. Their presence feels alien, invaders from another world. The noise quiets the jungle. The silence is loud in that it is unnatural. The serpent looks at them and seems to quiet down with a look of satisfaction as it slithers away.

They are Spaniards in full armor moving slowly with a group of men, women, and children trudging in front of them. I recognize that the families on foot are not Spanish. The color of their skin and their clothing are divergent. The natives look tired, angry, and sad as they trudge their way through the green layered walls of the living jungle. They are being prodded by soldiers riding behind them. The Spaniards have their weapons at the ready and they are yelling fiercely. "Hurry it up, the gold will not dig itself. The Crown demands it from us. All the gold available from Mexico has been sent to Spain and we need more. Now we must make these savages dig it for us if we have any hope of being welcomed into the Spanish court." "Yes, my captain, we will serve the King and Queen, we will do our duty!" The replies from the Spanish Conquistadores sound like a ripple of the leaves on the trees. I can hear the chatter as the sentiment works its way down the line. The natives march on.

The native men have hatred in their eyes, the women and children fear in theirs. The men are whispering to each other as they walk. "We must honor Montezuma and attack and kill this enemy that threatens our way of life. If we sacrifice them to Quetzalcoatl, he will purge them from our ancestral lands." I crawl behind the procession and listen as they talk among themselves. I understand what they are saying even though it is a language I have never heard before. I am acutely aware of the pain and anguish emanating from the enslaved natives as they are driven forward. I see two Conquistadores that I recognize, Jose Lopez, the Jewish boy from the hidden room in the wall back in Spain, and Santiago Martinez, the soldier who saved him. They are yelling at the natives, prodding them forward with their horses gilded in their armor.

The mounted Conquistadores are brandishing the points of their swords as they drive their new slaves forward to the gold pits. The Aztecs believed that if they gave them all the gold they would go back to where they came from. I am startled by a loud boom. The Spanish are firing their harquebuses. Boom! Boom! Boom! The booms echo like a monster through the jungle. The collective panic of the jungle resonates with every burst. You can track the animals flight from the danger by the movement of their sounds. I too want to run, nothing good can come from such an invasive noise.

Growing up I had heard the story of 'La Llorana', the weeping women. It was often told late at night to scare us. "Tell it again, tell it again." The story had it that there was a beautiful young lady, Rafaela, who lived in a small town in New Mexico. She grew up poor but was known throughout Northern New Mexico to be the most beautiful and most desired Señorita for miles around. Many a suitor applied for her hand, bringing whatever dowries they could afford, they all were rejected. The father was tempted as he was poor but his love for his daughter made it impossible for him to lock her into a loveless life with a stranger she did not know.

One day a handsome stranger, Enrique rides into the small town and immediately they fall in love, they marry, and have children. The stranger often leaves his family behind to go conduct business, or so he says. Nobody knows where he goes or what business he conducts when he gets there. After one of his trips Enrique shows up and tells Rafaela that he has come for his children and will leave in the morning. She will not be going with them. Rafaela is stunned. "Why, what have I done? I have been a good wife and a good mother, please don't do this. What about our children, they need their mother?" Rafaela begged and cried for him not to abandon her and take her kids. "I have met another woman and she has captured my heart and my soul. She will be a better mother to our children than you, she comes from a wealthy family.

Take comfort in knowing that our children will grow up in a fine home with all the finery that goes with it."

That night Rafaela woke her kids up and quietly took them to the river. "Where are we going mom?" The children kept asking. Deborah, the oldest was persistent in her questioning. "I'm scared mommy, I want to go home." "I want to go home too mom!" Gilberto started crying." The children clung to Rafaela's hands as she continued to lead them down the path to the river. When they got to the shore the water was splashing against the bank. "I love you my children and I will be with you for eternity." Rafaela hugged them with all her might, kissed them on the cheek as she lowered Deborah into the water and held her down until her body stopped moving. Rafaela watched as the lifeless body of her daughter floated downstream. "Where is Deborah going?" Gilberto asked. "She is going to heaven! Do you want to go with her?" "No mom, I want to go home to daddy!" As he spoke, she took her son in her arms and cried as she lowered him into the water and held him under until he was gone. Rafaela watched as her little boy floated down stream.

She drowned them and then she started walking up and down the river crying in pain for what she had done. She would never see or hold her children again and the love of her life, Enrique was gone. Rafaela never stopped roaming the river crying. Her flesh turned to spirit, and you can still hear her crying for her daughter and her son. Immediately the people who lived up and down the river started to hear what they said sounded like a woman crying for her children. The story of La Llorona changed every time it was told. The main part of the story always stayed the same and was used to scare us into behaving. "If you do not behave La Llorona will come and take you to the river. She will think you are her kids." Every time the wind blew strong it was her song. We hoped she was not coming for us, taking us away to replace those who perished in the river. Why was I playing this story in my head right now? Two of the soldiers in the jungle were talking.

"Did you hear what happened to Cortez?" I heard the two Conquistadores talking. They sounded serious and on edge. Santiago was talking as they rode through the jungle. "I don't exactly know what happened, but I know most of the story. It all started with Cortez' arrival. That's what led to the tragic event." "Keep your eyes open, no one is to stray." Their Capitan had seen the two talking and this was his way of getting them to pay attention. They rode in silence until the Capitan was out of sight. "The Aztecs were alarmed when they spotted our King's ships anchored off their coast. Upon arrival, the Spaniard rode horses out of their ships their armor shimmering in the early morning light. They rode the first horses to ever set foot in the new world. As the natives approached, the Spaniards fired the harquebuses to warn them, and the natives fell to their knees.

Their superstition allowed three hundred Spaniards to conquer an empire of millions. After all, it would take a God to possess a fire stick that thundered, sending flames into the sky. The rudimentary firearms were used by the first Spaniards to keep the natives at bay and more so to trick them into submission. It brought to life the belief that Cortez was the long-awaited arrival of Quetzalcoatl, their God. Legend had it that he would arrive on a strange four-legged animal and transport them to Aztlan, their equivalent to our heaven. All artistic renderings showed him illuminated like an exploding star in the sky. The Spaniards ships, horses, armor, and weapons were all it took to allow Cortez and his men not only to be led but welcomed into the heart of the Aztec empire. Once inside, Tenochtitlan, the center of the great Aztec empire was conquered from within. The legend of Quetzalcoatl had become the Spanish Trojan Horse.

They immediately sent runners to spread the word. It spread like wildfire. As Cortez and his Conquistadores came on shore they were stunned as the multitude approached, fear ran through their ranks. Cortez gave the sign and the canons on the ships fired warning shots and the crowd stopped in their tracks. The talk of the natives spread like a tide through the ocean." "I have heard", responded Jose. They thought we were Gods, they had never seen or heard fire come from floating houses."

"That's correct Jose, most fell on their knees and genuflected. Cortez tried to established dialogue with the leader dressed in feathers and strange clothing. They could not understand each other. A young Indian maiden, Malinche, walked to the front. She was a linguist and could speak the hundreds of dialects of the people who were part of the huge empire. Cortez was stunned with her beauty. After a few days she could speak rudimentary Spanish and became the translator for the Spaniards. She translated for them, and they were welcomed into the heart of the Aztec Empire. Eventually, Malinche and Cortez were married and had children, two sons. When they were young boys, Cortez took them to Spain and presented them to King Ferdinand and Queen Isabella. The court was enthralled. Upon his return to 'Mechico' he told Malinche that he had been accepted into the Spanish Court and would be leaving with his sons, she was not to go."

"Why would Cortez do that?" Jose was curious and needed to hear more. "Who is to say? Early, in the morning, Malinche used the hidden catacombs to get them to the shores of the lake that surrounded the city. The catacombs were an extensive network of tunneled passageways under Mechico that were well known to the Aztecs, especially the priests. The underground passageways were used to worship their Gods. The Aztecs were driven underground by the insistence of the Spaniard that they convert to Catholicism. Is it fitting that there, in the heart of the new and old, the merger of the two empires failed? Malinche must have felt trapped." Jose spoke out in a sad voice. "Is this what my parents felt when they left me behind?" Santiago continued the story as he made sure the natives did not stray. "When Malinche got to the lake, what must have been her thoughts? After all, she is the one who made it possible for Cortez and his three hundred to pass through the heart of the Aztec Empire. She was being betrayed by the man she loved and served. I can only imagine the shame and the guilt." Santiago continued. "I am sure that she was standing on the shores of the lake and had nowhere to go. In front of her was a wide expanse of impassable water. Behind her certain loss and possible death. Once Cortez left, she would be shunned by the Spaniards and her own People. I guess to her there was no other option. She wept and she hugged and loved her sons. "I love you with my entire being and cannot bear the thought of you leaving to a strange world and being treated as less than human. You come from a powerful people! I cannot allow the evil invaders to make a spectacle of you or the empire you come from! One at a time she gingerly drowned her sons in the lake. Immediately after their death she began to wail so pitifully that the heavens seemed to hear her. She roamed the shores of that lake crying for her sons and the life she had been promised. Her wailing flowed over the still waters off the lake and could be heard for miles around in all direction. The water transmitted her pain so that all could hear. Her wailing was heard by all the people around the lake."

The two split up as they see two men trying to slip away. As I follow through the growth, we are at the perimeter of an empty field and the smell of rotting flesh fills me with disgust and to my surprise, Jose is looking at Santiago as they ride past. They are part of the contingency of hell on Earth. I remember the image I had of them as I was on shore in Spain. The image of seeing them sail away from the Spanish port was strong. I listen as Jose talks to Santiago. "These natives attacked us two weeks ago, we had no choice but to retaliate. It is God's will that they dig for gold so that Spain can reclaim her power. I do not like this but understand it must be done. I am glad that you and I have been chosen to join Coronado's expedition to find the legendary seven cities of gold." Santiago thought for a moment. "I too am ready to leave.

I see natives getting sick and dying by the hundreds. If we don't kill them or work them to death, disease does. It sickens me to see what we inflict on them, they asked for none of it!" "I know, but we are bound by honor to serve the Crown and we must do so."

As I listen to them, a familiar feeling flows through. Standing in the middle of the multitude of dead natives is a creature I recognize, the familiar phantom, the Conductor. He is covered in blood from head to toe as if he is dressed in it. I shudder, he looks at me and recognizes me. The blood is dripping from his skin, his body is sponge-like, the blood soaked into his bones. Will I ever escape this nightmare? How long is he going to be there and how is this related to my life? I have come to realize that my nightmares are tracking my daily life. It's as if I'm living two lives at the same time. I shudder at these thoughts. I fear how I, at such a young age, could have these ideas and see such evil. Yet I know that there are good people and beautiful places.

How can the two exist together? The gentle voice is back. "One builds, the other tears down. One loves, the other hates. One laughs, the other cries. One saves, the other destroys. How can a person do such good and yet be the vessel for evil? The love of God overshadowed by the greed of men. You are doing well, stay strong." I accept that she is gone, she never stays for long. I wondered out loud where this duality was taking me. I worried about why these thoughts were within me. Where do they come from? How can someone as young as me have them? I see Priests and nuns working, their silhouettes contrasting with the wild fauna, digging graves, blessing the corpses of the dead, and burying them in the jungle from which they came.

As the Conquistadores continue, I can hear the voices from inside the jungles green canopy get louder and louder as they move through. Instantly we are in the midst of activity at a level I had never seen before. I feel a presence in this camp that I am becoming familiar with. I look around and see a figure circling around the perimeter. No one else notices him peering in. I see him rubbing his hands as if waiting for a steak at a top end restaurant in Santa Fe. As is the pattern, his gaze finds me and begins to move in my direction. I start moving away and find myself in the entrance of a deep cavern. I stand in awe as I see the haggard natives passing buckets of dirt. The assembled line is continuous, and the people break my heart. Life is gone from their souls. They move without feelings. A few of them reflect a simmering hatred for the Spanish oppressors who are controlling their world, all in search for the golden rock. They know that the Spanish have conquered Montezuma from the center of the Aztec Kingdom. They have merely changed from one oppressor to the next. One ruler sacrificed them to the Gods, the other to the golden rocks. I can hear wailing from the inside of the earth as I turn and run.

As I run through the jungle the quiet beauty of the lush green gives me hope. How could something evil catch me in here? I had not done anything that gave life a reason to turn me over to the Conductor but neither had the natives dying by the thousands. I run faster, faster, and faster than I have ever run before. I remembered my flight and escape into the river so very long ago. Once again, I feel the warmth of the familiar spirit that had saved me in the past. "Turn left at the next fork and you'll see a tunnel. Take the tunnel and you will be back on the train. It is very important that you get on it, you cannot stay behind. You will see a group of nuns towards the back of the train. Sit in their midst. The Conductor will follow and know you are there. The nuns have fallen prey to the humanity from which they came, but there is still enough goodness among them to protect you as you travel north." I do as she instructs, and her kindness warms my being.

She feels familiar to me as if she has been with me from the beginning of time. She is older than the jungle and has a purpose in protecting me. I find the haven in the train among the nuns and feel strangely at home, like I do in my bedroom, familiar and comforting. At the same time there is a foreboding, waiting for hell to break loose. The train starts its familiar journey through the mixture of faces and the places flowing through time and space. The panoramic view enthralls me, but I hope to wake up any minute. I see the Conductor approach and growl as he stands in front of us with anger in his eyes. He cannot get to me. The nuns hold hands with me as I sit in their midst. Their circle is more than the conductor can penetrate. "Do not let go. We are not strong enough if we separate. We must watch and rotate our sleep if we are to carry the promise of God to those who await us." The Priest who I had seen earlier on the train is seated in front of us, his rosary in his hand. The Conductor smiles as he passes. It becomes obvious that the Ghost Train carries the lust for all things coveted by humanity. I feel my life slipping away like the old tire sleds in the snow in the hills by our home. As I slide, I see Billy entangled in a web, the conductor is licking his chops!

Chapter 18

OLD CHEVROLET

"Get dressed we're going for a ride!" Billy demanded of us as he and his friends laughed. They always came in like a whirlwind, a dust devil. We were back in El Guache for the summer. The school year had been challenging for all of us. We had all made new friends and experienced life in a different way. Now we were back to the beginning. I felt as if we were back in time. The image of Billy in a web echoed in my heart. He was in his world here. This is where he was the happiest. They were talking excitedly. "Man, I had a good time! Do you think we'll get caught?" Little Billy was laughing but had a look on his face, he was anxious and scared. "I don't think so. How will they know it was us?" "Billy, that was a good idea, you're crazy bro! They know your dad, so they fell for it. How did you talk them into paying us to clean up after the dance?"

They were all talking at the same time, one thought flowing into the next. "My dad is one of their best customers." Billy and his friends were at it again. "Man, those girls from Medanales were awesome. We're supposed to meet them next Saturday at the High School." "What time bro?" Little Billy was starting to question himself about hanging out with these guys. He did not want to go to jail. "I pick the one with the green eyes!" Miguel was smiling. "Yah, but does she want you." Suddenly, some guys I didn't know came into the house. "Put them in the kitchen." Billy was walking towards them. They were carrying cases of cokes. I had never seen so many cokes. "It's about time you guys get here. What took you so long?" Billy was walking towards them with a smirk and his hand was quickly filled with a coke. "The truck broke down on the dirt road. We're lucky we got it started." I recognized Ricky, he played on the same baseball team as Billy. Ricky was excited. "What are we going to do with them?" "Right now, we are going to drink some. Let's go you guys. Let's unload some of these, then we will figure out what to do with the rest." Billy looked at us. "Do you want some or not? Let's go!"

Ricky handed us each a couple. "Here you go boys, drink as many as you want, we have a bunch of them." It was a blast! "This is one of the best nights in my life!" A guy I had never seen put a case down, grabbed a coke and began to drink it. He finished it quickly and opened another. I could hear a lot of talk coming from outside. "We have to find a place to hide these." "I know, each of us can take a few of them home and hide the rest in the shed we have at our house." Jimmy had been around as long as I could remember. "Let's put ours in the cellar for now, you guys can come for them tomorrow." In an instant the cases were put in our cellar.

They had attended a dance at the National Guard armory. The guy who was in charge, Tito, owned a bar and I guess he was the one who had sponsored the dance. Part of the benefit to him was that he was the one who sold the alcohol and cokes for the dance. After the dance Tito wanted to do a lot of clean up right away because he was leaving town the next day. He asked Billy and his friends if they wanted to clean up. "Billy, how's your dad? I saw him last week at the bar. Haven't seen him since. Listen, do you guys want to make some money?" Tito was hoping Billy and some of his friends would do it. Billy responded for the group. "What do you want us to do?" "Mr. Trujillo is going to stay here until this place is cleaned up. I know its late, but it must be done tonight."

"How much are you going to pay us?" Billy wasn't really listening, he wanted to earn some money. "How does five dollars each sound?" Nothing else had to be said. The job was finished by four in the morning. Billy saw that the cokes were still there when they were done cleaning. Before Mr. Trujillo locked it all up, Billy and his friend had gone to the back and unlocked one of the windows. They went for a ride came back and made sure everyone was gone. Billy climbed through the window and unlocked the back door. In an instant the truck was loaded. We drank coke for a few days and then they were gone. While we were drinking the cokes, we thought we had died and gone to coke heaven.

Billy's year had gone really well. He had starred in football and basketball. We went to all his games and my dad was his biggest fan. "That's my son!" He shared this with anyone in hearing range. "I taught him to play like that." I wondered why he had to take credit for that. I often saw Billy with girls now. He looked really happy. One time when we were in church my mom was looking for him. Billy had a habit of disappearing. "Where's your brother?" My mom was strict about church. I had asked why our dad didn't go to church with us. I never got a straight answer. "You guys go find your brother. Not you Michael you stay here with me. Tell him he better get over here right now." My mom was mad. She had seen Billy earlier in the back of the church talking with some girls. "Look at your brother, he is becoming very popular with the girls. Look at how they flirt with him. He'd better be careful, or he'll be a daddy soon." My mom was smiling when she said it, she wasn't smiling now. She was proud of her oldest son, but she worried about him. He acted more and more like his dad every day and it scared her. Between sports, girls, and street friends, Billy was on top of the world.

Now it was summertime, and Billy was playing baseball. As the short stop he was the key to the success of the team from Hernandez. They were winning most of the games. "We're going to take state this year!" Their coach would predict after every game. It was exciting to go the games. There were parties in the stands and in the parking lots during all the games. Often there was more swinging taking place in the parking lot than in the game. The fans were mostly family members from the two opposing teams. They drank and partied during the games, and it usually ended up in swinging, hitting, and yes, strike outs. During the fights the players would normally stop playing. They were not happy about it. You could see a look of disappointment coming from the players. All they wanted to do was play baseball. Sometimes the brawls would erupt around the players themselves and move out into the stands. These were dangerous as bats and balls became weapons and it escalated to full blown warfare. When it got to this point you could see as it moved like a tidal wave into the stands and behind the back stop. I saw men and boys lying on the ground severely injured from these and everyone would pack up and leave as fast as they could. My dad was usually in the middle of the brawl.

Billy was the star and my dad the number one fan. After the games, my dad would go celebrate with his friends and Billy with his. The team from Hernandez would eventually win state representing Northern New Mexico, beating the highly favored champs from Southern New Mexico. Billy as the short stop was magnificent. His speed to the ball and accuracy with the throw was the talk on both sides of the stands. The one thing that really stuck in my mind was how different the two teams were. The team from the North was mostly Spanish and the team from the south was mostly white. The game meant more than a trophy. The results were used to justify prejudices and fuel the already strained racial tensions in the state. "We kicked their ass! Those gringos didn't know what hit them. Billy, that was a bad ass catch you made in the sixth inning, the bases loaded. No one else could have made that catch." The coach was beaming, ear to ear. "Smiley, you pitched a hell of a game, almost a no-hitter. All of you were great. Next year we will do it again."

I tossed and turned that night. It was hard for me to fall asleep. I was afraid to dream. I knew if I slept, I would be on the Ghost Train, and I didn't want to take a journey to that place. Slam, boom! "What the hell is wrong with you, leave them alone they are all asleep." I recognized grandpa's voice. He was angry. My dad yelled back. I recognized that voice too. "Are you going to lend me some money or not?" My dad and my grandpa were arguing outside. "I already lent you some, 'cortale', stop, it's late!" I heard more commotion as the arguing got closer to us.

I pulled the blankets over my head to hide. "Adelida, get in here and make me something to eat." The lights came on in the kitchen. "Billy it's late, the kids are asleep." "I don't care this is my house." I could hear my mom cooking and I could smell the sweet aroma fill the house. It was different though. The air was pungent, it was a mixture of the essence of our food, our fear, our anger, our hate, and yes, our love. The night ended.

My school year had gone pretty much the same way after the candy raid. The memories of that day would follow me for the rest of the year. Billy had been extremely strong on me. "How can you be so stupid. Don't you think that if they saw kids, they would know you came from Carlos Gilbert?" I had paid dearly when my dad got home. I got one of the beltings my father was quick to give. When we saw the belt come off, we knew the punishment we were about to receive would be swift and painful. We prayed that he did not escalate the physical punishments with punches, pulled hair, and sometimes kicks on the ground. It was as if all of us were being punished. All of us shared in the pain, the one receiving it and the ones that had to watch. We were living a life of contrasts, the outside and the inside. The outside called us out and the inside held us in its death grip. The battle raged in its daily extremes and daily dreams.

It was nice to see Juan at my grandfather's house when we arrived in El Guache. During the school year we saw him on our trips to El Guache. Every time we saw him, he looked different, wild. He didn't talk to us that much except to help us and try to protect us from ourselves. "How have you been doing in school?" Juan asked the three of us. I didn't have to explain my chocolate exploits to him. He already knew what had happened, but he let me explain it anyway. He didn't seem to be impressed as I bragged and told my story. He knew my grades were always good, and my behavior was mostly bad. I continued with my tale. "My mom always asks me, what is wrong with you? You're lucky I don't tell your father about your behavior at school. I spend as much time in school as you do! My mom gives me the same speech every time." Juan walked away shaking his head.

I knew that my teachers were the ones that were saving me from I didn't know what, I just knew it was bad. My teachers were quick to point out how impressed they were with how smart I was and at the same time how dismayed they were with my dysfunctional behavior. "He keeps disrupting the class. We've taken to giving him extra work to keep him busy but that doesn't always work. Are there any serious issues at home we need to know about? We've noticed that his father never attends these meetings." My mom's reply was always the same. "My husband works at the State Penitentiary at night and sleeps during the day. I keep him informed. He too is concerned."

I was brought back to reality. "Come on, hurry up you guys!" We all rushed to get dressed, the excitement filled the air. At first, I thought we were in Santa Fe but realized where I was as soon as I opened my eyes. I was back in the old mud brick house with my brothers. I could smell the old dirt bricks, the stains on the ceiling woke that part of my soul. I was happy, my parents were both in Santa Fe and I knew that when Billy and his friends woke us up, we were going to have an adventure. I had been practicing the guitar and had learned some new songs. My favorite was 'Gloria'. I couldn't wait to play it for Billy and his friends.

As soon as we stepped outside the fresh air hit us and the beauty of the of stars and their brilliance was magical. I could hear the water in the acequias flowing, singing to us like an old friend who would always be there for us. I remembered the ocean from my dreams. Was this river the oceans child on its way home? Was its movement connecting me to that journey on the Ghost Train, taking me to and from the past? Questions like this one were becoming normal to me. I never forgot the evil smile that was present on this journey or the soothing voice that watched over me. The two were like the canopy of stars. The promise of the blinking star light was always surrounded by darkness.

My brother and his friends ran ahead of us in the starlight, laughter filling the air. Parked under the huge pear tree was a black shadow with starlight reflecting from its side. It was a car. I did not recognize it but knew it was an old Chevrolet, a Torpedo back with baby moon rims. We were taught early all the makes and models of the cars around us. "Hurry up and get in!" I loved being with my brother and his friends when they were having this much fun. The stories they shared about the things they were doing made me wish I was with them. In a way I was. I was part of it, always at the end of it. Their stories were always about things that were exciting, some of them illegal. But still, I wondered where this adventure would end up.

As I got in, I noticed that the interior was torn in spots and the stuffing was popping out of holes in the seat. It smelled like my dad's car when he was drinking. As I got in the car, I kicked an empty can of beer. I worried a little bit. In my life, anytime alcohol was involved bad things happened. I heard the starter grind, and the old Chevy came to life. Before I knew it, we were cruising on the dirt road, Prince Drive. The windows were open, and laughter filled the interior of that old Chevy. I couldn't help but wonder where the car had come from. We

SANTA FE: A PIECE OF 'MI VIDA'

were the only car out on the road. It felt wrong in a way, but it also felt good to be where I knew we weren't supposed to be. The car stopped a few miles from our farm and the three of them got out of the car, laughing, and bragging about their exploits. I could hear them talking. They were excited, they were going to meet some girls the next day.

When they were done my brother came to my side of the car. "Get out and come over here." Everyone got quiet. The night was still, the stars were bright, and the moon was nowhere to be found. I got out and followed him to the other side of the car. "Get in and start the car." I could hear Miguel and Antonio laughing. They were used to my brother picking on me. I guess I was their entertainment. Like the time they came home from one of their escapades and Billy decided to polish up on his shooting skills with his BB gun. At first, I did not know what he wanted to do. "Take off your shirt and start running. I'm going to start shooting on the count of three." I thought he was kidding but the look on his face said otherwise. "You're crazy, I'm not going to do that. I'll tell my mom and dad on you! I don't want to! Do it to one of them!" I had no problem volunteering one of my brothers for this. "Go ahead and tell. I'll say that you snuck into the Sinclair's and stole their ice cream out of the freezer and gave it to the prisoners that were cutting the lawns. What do you think will happen then?" It never failed, he always won, and I ended up doing what he said. It's amazing how much you can remember when you're getting ready to become a running target. My memories of the ice cream heist flew by in an instant.

The Sinclair's lived across the street from us in Santa Fe. Mr. Sinclair was the prison plumber. His wife was a tiny thing, but she was very nice. Mrs. Sinclair wore glasses and always wore her hair in a ponytail. We used to make fun of her. She had a squeaky voice that came out of her perfectly round face. They did not have any kids so she would invite the neighborhood kids to go have ice cream with her.

We had never seen so much ice cream. They had two freezers in the garage storage area. One of them was almost all ice cream, every flavor imaginable! "Now come on kids, grab a cone and pick a flavor." These words were music to our ears. The summers were hot, and the ice cream was cold and sweet. I always got the chocolate. "No wonder Mr. Sinclair is so fat." We would joke among ourselves. He was the fattest man I had ever known. He walked like a horned toad we were catching except he walked on two feet. They used to keep the storage doors locked and the ice cream safe. We never went over when he was there. He was gruff and we didn't want anything to do with him.

We had become friends with the convict trustees that worked on the prison grounds and the area around our houses. We used to hang out near them and watch them work. They cut the grass, trimmed trees, and repaired anything that needed it. They never went inside the homes though, after all, they were convicts. "I can hardly wait to get out of this joint bro! My old lady is waiting for me. You know how they are. They'll last as long as they can, but if it's too long they'll have a Sancho in no time." The convicts always laughed and joked with each other. Every now and then you could feel the tension in the air. "How much time do have left?" "Did you hear what happened in cell block four last night? Pepe got shanked! He had to be transferred to Saint Vincent's hospital, he's in critical condition. I guess Hyena did it. "Hyena is crazy bro. I stay away from him!" "Hyena threatened to kill Pepe."

"Hey, you two, shut up and get back to work." The Guard in charge of the detail normally let them talk, but his time he didn't. We listened to this stuff every time we were around them. I found it strange because they looked and talked like our family members and our friends. They were like us in so many ways yet all of them had done some really bad stuff and were in prison. I always felt sorry for them. They talked and laughed among themselves, but you could always feel the tension under the surface, especially when the guard was telling them what to do.

"Hey, you guys, do you know how lucky you are? That ice cream looks good. I can't remember how it tastes." This convict was younger than the rest and always had a smile on his face. "Here, you can have some of mine." Without thinking I walked in their direction to share Sinclair's ice cream on a cone. "Hey, stay away from them? You can't give the convicts anything. If I catch you trying to again, I'll have to tell your dad, you don't want that." "Come on Esquibel, what's it going to hurt, it's ice cream!"

The convict was young, and we really liked him. He always talked to us. "Make sure you stay out of trouble. It sucks in here." I think that was the day we decided to get them some ice cream. The summer days were long and hot. "I think it's time for us to get them some ice cream." Arthur made up his mind and there was no hesitation on my part. "How are we going to do that?" Michael and I looked at each other as if we understood. We were going to go on another adventure. Arthur pointed across the street at the Sinclair's house. We spent the rest of the day planning it. My main concern was getting caught, how could we do it and get away with it.

The next day we snuck into the Sinclair's garage, the storage room was locked. We looked at the top of the doors, there was an opening at the top. Juan joined us and came up with the idea to boost me up so I could crawl in and drop down to the freezers. It took a few tries, but I was finally lifted high enough to crawl in over the top. I dropped down to the tall freezer then to the smaller one, then to the floor. Arthur was right behind me. His movement was fluid like the brown and white Roadrunner roaming our neighborhood with a wiggly striped lizard dangling from its mouth. "Hurry up! We don't want her to catch us." Juan had come to Santa Fe for the summer. My parents would soon find a way to get him to live with us. I opened the small freezer and grabbed a box of ice cream and tried to throw it through a gap at the top. It smacked into the door and fell back towards me making a loud noise as it hit the wall and fell to the ground. "Be quiet, dumb ass! Put them on top of the big freezer then throw them through the top!" Arthur was on me in a minute. He took the half gallon of wonder and delight climbed on the small freezer and tossed it over.

It took me a while, I had to take them out of the small freezer, put them on the floor, close the door and put them on top of the little one, climb on the little one, put them on the big one and toss through the small opening at the top. "Quick get out of there, I hear her in the kitchen." I threw down the fourth box of ice cream and pulled myself through the gap and was helped down. We each ran off with a half-gallon of ice cream. The only ones happier than us on that day were the prisoners we shared the ice cream with. We knew that the guard got into the vehicle every day to eat his lunch and the prisoners sat in the shade and ate theirs. We got a spoon and Juan snuck it to the young convict and dropped it near him. The convicts ate their delight as quickly as they could. We had hidden ours in the back of our freezer. Later that day we invited the pen gang over to our house. We ate the remaining ice cream and found the empty box and spoon left behind by the prisoners and disposed of the evidence.

Mr. Sinclair came over that afternoon to talk to my dad. My dad wasn't home, he told my mom that we had stolen ice cream from them. My mom called us in and asked us in front of him. "Did you boys steal ice cream from the Sinclairs?" Our reply was always the same. "No. it wasn't us and we don't know who did." Since no one had seen us except the prisoners, we got away with it, we were never invited over for ice cream again. Not too long after that the Sinclair's moved away. Before they moved, Mrs. Sinclair avoided us like the plaque. It made me sad every time I saw her outside with her little hat. She had been nice to us, and we had messed it up. I was not surprised that we did. I guess it was our way of entertaining ourselves.

SANTA FE: A PIECE OF 'MI VIDA'

My flashback returned to Billy and the BB gun. I was more afraid of my dad than running from a BB gun with real BB's. I took off my shirt and laid it on the ground. "Are you ready? Make sure you move side to side so it will make it harder for me to hit you." This advice would serve me well sooner that I thought. "Wait, wait, why do you have to shoot at me? I can put up some cans for you!" "One," I started running as fast as I could, zigzagging as I ran, waiting for the third count. "Two," and then I heard the puff of the BB gun. He had not waited for number three. The shots started coming quicker, I heard the lever of the BB gun every time he reloaded. He had not hit me yet when I noticed that the sound of the BB gun was getting closer.

Billy was chasing me as he shot at me. His friends and my brothers were hysterical, "Look at that guy go." "Hey Billy, what's the matter, is he too fast for you?" I finally felt a sharp sting on my back. It felt like a bee sting, then another one. I fell to the ground and started crying. "Come on Santiago, I was just playing with you." He tried to calm me down. "Later on, I'll take you to Reggie's and buy you a coke." I knew it would not happen. I stopped crying and went back to put on my shirt. I felt the sting from those BBs for a long time. It was amazing how these memories that took hours and days to accumulate could pass through me in seconds. They came at me like a swarm of bees.

My thoughts were back on the fact that I was sitting in the driver's seat in the old Chevrolet, and I could barely see out the window. My feet could not reach the peddles. "Why do you make Santiago do crazy shit all the time?" Antonio asked and Billy's respond did not surprise me. In a way I was proud and eager to please him. "Don't worry about it, he's a tough little dude." As they talked, I remembered the times he would put me to fight boys a little older than me. It never failed that he would put us to fight. Maybe if I had lost some of those fights, he would have stopped doing it. I would never know. As I sat in the driver's seat, the car turned off. My brother did not notice at first, he was busy with his friends. They were alive and pure in everything they did. Most of it felt right, magical, especially at night. The beauty and the silence were a perfect pool to reflect that pure innocence that belongs to the young, even when it's wrong in the eyes of society who does everything in its power to condition it away. Too bad that the youthful exuberance often put them on the wrong side of the law.

"Did you turn it off? Push that button and turn it on." Billy pointed at the button on the dashboard reaching over me to show me where the button was. As he did, I saw that he had moved the shifter down. I could smell the liquor on his breath and the excitement flowing from him. Life just poured out of him. He was my brother and I loved him more than anyone I knew. I sat there in that car underneath the canopy of stars and there was no other place I wanted to be, except maybe in the back seat. I reached over and pushed the starter button and the car lurched forward. "Move over." I was glad he was getting in with his friends. You could hear my sigh of relief in the darkness. He put the car back in neutral and turned it over. The small straight six-cylinder engine came back to life. Billy put the car into the granny gear and let it roll forward. I could feel the Chevrolet as it crawled down the dark, bumpy, lonely dirt road.

Suddenly, he opened the door, held on to it as he jumped out and started running alongside the car as it crawled forward in the granny gear. "Get behind the wheel, hurry up! You better not let it crash." All I heard in the car was laughter mixed with exclamatory apprehensions. "Get behind the wheel, you better not wreck. Just do what you see dad and I do! Just steer it in a straight line, keep it on the road." "Este vato esta loco, this guy is crazy." His friends were jostling with each other and with my brothers as the old Chevrolet chugalugged down Prince Drive. I was frozen to the wheel and then I started feeling good as I was getting the hang of it. I could hear and see Billy running alongside laughing, encouraging me, threatening me, and coaching me. Just as I was ready to take a bow, Billy reached in and turned off the lights.

SANTA FE: A PIECE OF 'MI VIDA'

"If you wreck it, I will kick your ass for the next month." Now the party in the car came to a sudden halt. "Come on bro, if we wreck this car we are screwed!" Billy ignored them as the cacophony of remarks, sighs, warnings, and dismays grew at the same time as I froze behind the wheel. It took a moment, but I saw the side of the dirt road where it was piled up with dirt, rocks, and debris. I got too close, Billy let go of the wheel as he tripped and fell. I continued into the embankment and the car came to a screeching halt, sputtering as it died. I could hear Billy laughing in the darkness behind us and felt the deathly silence in the old Chevrolet. I was wondering if I was going to get my ass kicked. I never did find out where they had gotten the old Chevrolet.

The next day our dad showed up bright and early. He was in a good mood and very happy to see us. He and my mom looked happy, and they had bags full of food. I liked it when they were like this, it was like a ray of sunshine breaking through the dark billowing storm clouds always about to unleash a thunderstorm. It was a beautiful summer day, and I knew we would be working, but it did not matter. A day like this was priceless. The events of the night before were still fresh in my mind. In a way I was proud of myself and loved my brothers for the things we did together. We always seemed to find ourselves in situations that were exciting and dangerous, but we almost always got each other out of it, sometimes against tremendous obstacles. I wondered how long it would be before we got ourselves into a situation where we wouldn't be able too. I worried about Billy, he was gone more often, and I knew that him and his bros were drinking, fighting, and looking for trouble all the time. Why didn't he stay with us more often? I missed him when he was gone and found myself doing daring things trying to be like him. We spent the day tending to our crops and our orchard with the highlight of the day being a lunch with all of us there together, laughing and talking and just being in the moment. Why couldn't it be like this all the time?

Our summer was a journey back and forth between Santa Fe and Espanola. I was liking Santa Fe more the longer I was there. For one thing, we didn't have to work as much. The schools were bigger, and the diversity was awesome to me. I had more interaction with Gringos in Santa Fe than in my prior life combined. I was amazed that some of the rich white girls liked me even though I did not know how to interact with them. I came from a male dominant world. Five brothers and a Correctional Officer who worked in one of the most dangerous prisons in the country. We were Spanish machos. We had inherited the Conquistadores' culture that drove us towards conflict. What we had missed was the fact that the world had changed, and our culture had been slow to change with it. Our isolation in Northern New Mexico had created the perfect place to retain our ways even though many of them were self-destructive. My sister was in a quandary. The older she got the more the old values came into play. My dad started to comment on her interaction with boys. My sister was becoming a woman in this male dominated world.

Chapter | 19

KNIVES FROM THE SKY

C orrectional Officer Billy Martinez was a force to reckon with. His need to dominate all those who were around him created some very troublesome events. In one way or another they consumed all those around him. "Adelida, have you seen my keys?" "Let me get them. Billy used them to get something out of the trunk." The Lieutenant was putting on his uniform. His uniform was very important to him. He looked professional dressed in light blue trousers, matching long sleeve shirt and tie. What he was most proud of was his military style hat that was formed out of blue cloth and topped off with a shiny silver badge and a shiny black visor. His mustache was always perfectly trimmed adding to the look. He had always wanted to be a State Trooper, but he fell in love, had kids, dropped out of school, and went to work for the Prison. "If you can't beat them join them." He often said this when talking to others about his career choice. He regretted getting married so young.

Many Northern New Mexico residents worked at the Labs in Los Alamos. Billy Sr. had been one of them. He had become disillusioned when he saw that the Spanish employees did all the low-end jobs, and the rich Anglos had the cushy high paying jobs. "Pinche Gringos! I'm tired of them telling me what to do. They talk down to us. They forget we were here hundreds of years before they showed up, now they think they own it!" Billy had discussed his disgust with anyone who would listen until one day he told them where they could put their job and if they needed any help putting it there, he would be more than happy to help, and he walked out. Now he was his own boss as long as he was walking the tiers inside the prison. The higher ups seldom went in there, it was his world, and he was large and in charge. "I'll see you later." He said good-bye to Adelida, stepped out into the yard of his prison home dressed in his prison uniform. He made an impression as he walked, he had hit the big time.

It had been a long week for Lieutenant Martinez. Staffing was poor, more often than not, several correctional officers were calling in sick or just not showing up. The long days due to overtime and working their days off was getting to them. Adding to the stress was the fact that the facility was overcrowded leading to poor morale among the employees. They were dealing with increasing violence in all sectors due to the inability to properly enforce prison rules. The Prison was one of the largest employers in Northern New Mexico and hired mostly the poor Hispanics from Northern New Mexico with minimal education and training. "Here comes another one." Officer Martinez was caught in a revolving door of training new incoming guards and processing the outgoing guards who were looking for something better and safer. "Why am I the one that has to train them? What are those cowards in the Wardens office doing?" He resented this but had no choice. He trained all the new guards selecting the toughest to be on his crew. His goon squad, as they were known, were highly feared inside the walls. Many a convict dreamed of and vowed to kill Officer Martinez if given the chance.

"Lieutenant Martinez, inmate Campbell is at it again." Captain Ortiz was in the conference room with several correctional officers. "We have a tight schedule today. After staffing the gates and the towers we are at half-staff on most of the sections. Martinez, you will take the lead at the maximum-security wing. You will have to release the inmates in rotation. Do not let them out to meals, the yard, or to their work assignments at the same time. Make a visit to inmate Campbell's cell the first thing you do, let his rotation be the first."

"Yes, Sir Captain! I'll see to Mr. Campbell again. Some people just don't learn." "Martinez, a slip, trip, or a fall is not really the way to address these issues." Captain Ortiz relied on Lieutenant Martinez but knew about his tendency towards violence with the inmates. He understood the difficulty in dealing with so many convicts with so few guards. It was like herding cats except these were lions and bobcats, there was no room for the weak, they got eaten in this place. He coached him and admonished him, but he overlooked it. He knew it was a necessary evil. Most correctional officers under his command were afraid to implement the hard rules and hold the inmates accountable but not Lieutenant Martinez. He was good at it and seemed to enjoy challenging the worst the state had to offer. "It's not my fault some of these pieces of shit can't walk!" Captain Ortiz let it go. "Okay, get to it. Be safe out there. You know how sneaky the inmates can be. Don't get caught up in a situation that will prevent you from going home. Better them than us."

The Penitentiary of New Mexico's architecture was like a telephone pole with several wings extending out in a perpendicular fashion. Facilities like this were built to house minimum and medium security level inmates only. The structure due to the numerous 90-degree angles created by the outward extensions, created unsafe conditions with too many blind corners. Due to funding, it had become necessary to put all inmates in this facility, including murderers, sexual predators, child molesters, protective custody inmates, and a psychiatric ward. The limited staffing and overcrowding created a very dangerous environment for anyone stepping foot in the facility. The Correctional

SANTA FE: A PIECE OF 'MI VIDA'

Staff was inadequately trained and underpaid further aggravating conditions that were cruel and unusual in the way the prisoners were treated. Unfortunately, it became the norm for both inmates and correctional officers.

The fact that most of the correctional officers were from the poor Spanish communities in northern NM created an additional issue. Most of the convicts were related to or were known by the guards. The Constitutional prohibition against 'Cruel and Unusual Punishment' was nonexistent in this facility. The law was ignored due to conditions inherent at the facility. The conditions were largely unknown to the state and local decision makers as most of them didn't care. If news of the abuses remained in house nothing was done to change it. The use of solitary confinement was extensive with inmates suffering multiple physical abuses on their way down the dark stairwells leading to basement of the facility. They remained there until they healed, or the next victim needed the space. The criteria used was driven mostly by the prejudice of the correctional officers. Best not to get on the wrong side of them.

"Lieutenant Martinez, what's the plan for Campbell?" Officer Williams asked as they walked. "That black Son-of-a-bitch continues to disrespect us and is involved in all kinds of illegal activity. I guess he thinks because he's as big as a tree we won't do anything and most of the time he's right. A lot of you are afraid to go in there, not to worry I got his ass. I still don't understand why they won't let us carry batons. The idiot is sentenced to 30 years without parole. That's a life sentence. The boy has nothing to lose." Officer Williams was the only black guard and had established a relationship with Terrance Campbell. Officer Williams knew that Lieutenant Martinez was not going to allow it to continue any longer. "How many times have I asked you get him under control? The last time I put him in the hole you came to me and promised you would straighten him out. Well, here we go again! Only this time, don't even think about coming to his rescue."

Officer Williams did not like where this was headed. "Don't worry boss, I'll take care of it." Lieutenant Martinez had not stayed for the rest of the meeting with Captain Ortiz. His mind was not there. His thoughts were on his life outside. He regretted the events with his family. Too many times he didn't remember what he had done. The damage in the house, the bruises on his wife and kids, and the deathly silence in the house were the clues as to what he had done. Now here he was dealing with this. He could feel the anger rising in him. He had tried to understand how simple things with his family put him in a trance like state that often times resulted in domestic violence over simple tasks not done. The same thing happened in the facility, except in here, there was no remorse.

Lieutenant Martinez was the correctional officer that was feared more than the craziest of inmates. Sometimes it appeared that the only difference between the guards and the convicts was the uniform. Lieutenant Martinez was 5'11 and weighed in at 200 pounds and was as mean as a rattle snake. As they walked through the top tier the familiar noises from the prison echoed through the facility. The noises never changed only the faces making them did. As some of the prisoners were released, they were replaced by fresh meat or by those returning from the outside world unable to function in society. The majority would go back into small communities that afforded very little opportunity. Jobs were scarce.

Most of the time the prison noises were ignored and accepted as part of the prison hierarchy. The young handsome ones that didn't have family in good standing in the joint usually became surrogate girlfriends. The painful crying and screaming would in time become silenced by their acceptance until they could form alliances and become what they had hated, part of a prison gang.

The clanging of the security doors as they moved from one section to the next echoed through the facility, reminding prisoners and correctional officers of the futility of escape. The only difference between guards and convicts was that the guards got home release to self-medicate with large amounts of alcohol and whatever stress relief they adopted. The interior of the facility was a drab grey and the low lighting gave it a sinister ambiance. Lieutenant Martinez was part of a series of images that included different people, places, and times, all sharing a cell in a Cosmic Prison. The cells were uniform, and the iron bars were like windows into the worst of humanity with rays of sunshine barely visible. Most of the inmates managed to hold on to some compassion even in the face of each other's societal and personal wrongdoings. Not all of them were evil but all of them had done enough wrong that here they were like a stew of bad ingredients simmering in their tainted broth.

As the Correctional caravan moved towards inmate Campbell's cell, their number got smaller as most of them peeled off to their assignments glad to avoid what was surely going to be a dangerous confrontation. As they arrived at the cell there were several inmates looking down to the ground level standing in front of their cells. The facility was in a buzz, this confrontation had been in the works for a long time. Lieutenant Martinez could feel it in the air. "Keep a close eye on these punks, make sure none of his people get close."

Inmate Terrance Campbell had moved from Missouri to play football at the University of New Mexico in Albuquerque, the Duke City. After a lackluster career he had decided to stay in Albuquerque. There were very few black families in New Mexico, and he liked the fact that he was bigger than most of the locals and he liked mixing it up with the Spanish women in the city. It did not take him long to get involved with several other blacks living in the War Zone, a part of Albuquerque known for gang activity, including drugs, prostitution, and other assorted crimes. The black gangs earned some notoriety in this part of town though they were outnumbered by the Spanish gangs and played it close to the vest to avoid extermination. "Keep your eye on the prize my brothers, the young chickee's, the good drugs, and the power that comes from those who control them, that is going to be us!" This was Campbell's motto on the street and in the joint. "This cell block is our neighborhood! No one comes in here to take anything from us and that includes the pig guards!" These words portrayed Terrance's lifestyle and it was a continuation of his life on the streets.

Terrance had become one of the main gang bangers in Albuquerque and created lots of enemies as his black crew started using teenage black males to recruit the young Hispanic females in the high schools. He had them sell marijuana and other drugs and had them bring the proceeds to him. They would lure the young girls out using proven flirtation practices and introducing the naive youngsters to drugs. Then the young girls were methodically turned over to the older gang members who proceeded to hook them on Heroin, sexually abuse them, and then put them on the street. Terrance enjoyed his time training the young girls.

His world fell apart when he did this to the daughter of a major player in the notorious 14th street gang. 14th Street was the wrong one to mess with in Albuquerque, 'Burque' in street talk. The 14th Streeters started tracking black gang members as they left their homes robbing them, taking the drugs and cash, and inflicting some serious physical harm. They left one to roll around in a wheelchair as a sign to the others. He had been shot five times with a .45 caliber revolver, how he survived nobody knew. They continued to hunt Terrance until they found him in a vulnerable place, shooting him multiple times and killing a member of his crew. Terrance was laid up for months and returned with a vengeance doing a drive-by and killing the younger brother of the leader of 14th street. He was arrested, tried, and sentenced to 30 years in the New Mexico State Pen. A contract was put out on him, and he knew it. Luckily it was common practice to house the inmates by race, known affiliations etc. This practice reduced the violence and allowed a level of self-management reducing the stress and risk to the guards. Many shady deals were ignored in return for a twisted loyalty to the guards. Sometimes murders were ignored as they were part of the process of removing those convicts that were enemies to both.

Lieutenant Martinez was standing in front of Terrance's prison cell. "What seems to be your problem? Did you forget what happened to you the last time you wanted to play this game. When will you understand, in here, you do what I tell you to do, or you pay the price? I guess you like the hole. If it wouldn't have been for Officer Williams vouching for you, that's where your sorry ass would be now." Lieutenant Martinez knew that he had to establish dominance in this world to survive. Campbell replied with a snicker. "I remember, just like I remember all of your little Spanish girls I brought over to the dark side. Was one of them your daughter?" The inmate grinned and stood tall as if he was reaching for the sky. His muscular black arms and large rock like head screamed violence. Lieutenant Martinez stepped forward into the cell.

"Let's go, you're supposed to be at your post in laundry." In an instant, the door clanged shut behind him. "Not this time fool, I'm not going to the laundry. I know where you're really taking me, I'm not going to the hole, I'll kill you first!" Lieutenant Martinez realized that the officers had been distracted by a disturbance a few cells down and no one was there to open the door for him. In perfect unison with the clanging door, inmate Campbell jumped up and hit the light cover above his head. The light shattered and two knives fell to the floor. Campbell, like a black leopard, sprang into action. He picked them up from the floor and in an instant rushed forward stabbing Lieutenant Martinez with the knives. "You don't know how long I've waited to kill you. We call you Chilly Billy because you're always trying to stick it to someone."

Campbell's movement was controlled as if he was on the prowl. He spoke and attacked at the same time. His years as a gang banger and as a convict had made him tough as nails and methodical in his violence. "You'd better kill me, black son-of-a-bitch!" Lieutenant Martinez stepped aside just as quickly, but not quick enough as he felt the two knives cut into his upper torso. "How do you like it now Chilly Billy? I'm going to kill you and toss your body over the rails." It was amazing how Campbell could talk and attack at the same time. Billy stepped aside while grabbing the mattress and using it to fend off the knife attack.

He was lucky, the first two stabbings were superficial. He could feel the warmth of the blood as it flowed down his skin, like syrup rolling off a pile of pancakes. He felt as the knife reached its mark several times. His fear turned to strength. He had to choose one or the other, he chose strength fueled by fear. He saw his family flash before him. He vowed that if he got out of this alive, he would stop the assault on the ones that he loved. Terrance Campbell was seeing his life flash before him as well. Martinez was tougher than he had anticipated. "Kill him!" "Stab him in the heart!" The comments were flying from all directions. The prisoners were blocking the walkway, they all wanted him dead. "Move back, move back all of you!" The guards were moving in. They had gotten word to the control center and were in the process of shutting the facility down. "All of you, back to your cells now!"

The strength of inmate Campbell allowed him to drive hard with the knives which resulted in the knives penetrating through the thin cheap mattress. The mattress did not stop the knife, it merely reduced how deep the knife went into the flesh. Campbell was pressed up against the mattress which pushed it up against the Lieutenant's body. The knives were able to inflict multiple stab wounds, painful but not fatal. Lieutenant Martinez could see the hatred in Campbell's jet-black eyes and ebony skin. The strength of the man showed through his prison clothing, muscles bulging as he stabbed away. Campbell was like a tempest in the shape of a man. He could see the intent to kill as clear as the full moon in El Guache. Campbell threw one of the knives back over his shoulder using his left hand to grab the mattress pulling it away. As he did, the pressure of the mattress against his body subsided just enough for Lieutenant Martinez to slide from behind it causing Campbell to be pulled forward into the bars by his own weight and force. Both men responded immediately to the pressure change, each responding in an instant.

Lieutenant Martinez, had seen the TV on a small stand next to the toilet when he walked in. Most cells were laid out like this. He had often wondered why they allowed TVs in the cells. In a fluid motion, he picked up the TV slamming Campbell with it in the head right as the convict turned around posturing to continue the attack. The inmate fell to the ground and began to crawl towards Lieutenant Martinez in attempt to finish the job. Campbell was still clutching the blood-soaked knife in his hand. In an instant, the Lieutenant was standing over him. "Nice try you piece of shit!" He struck him with the TV again sending glass and plastic in all directions. "So, you're going to kill me?" He asked as he struck him again.

Lieutenant Martinez' shirt was covered with blood; he could feel himself weakening. The TV was in shambles so he did the next best thing and started kicking him as hard as he could making sure that a couple were well placed to the groin area. "You won't be molesting little girls anymore. In fact, I'll see to it that you become the little girl. You're really going to like your new tier in cell block three." He knew that 14th street ran that cell block. It wouldn't matter how big this inmate was, he had a price to pay for killing one of their members and molesting one of their daughters and for being stupid enough to ignore the prison hierarchy in which Lieutenant Martinez was the top dog.

"Lieutenant, are you Okay?" Correctional Officer Williams rushed in. "The facility is locked down and all inmates are in their cells and accounted for. Sit down and take it easy, our medical staff and an ambulance are on the way." The attempted murder was over. Inmate Campbell was put on a gurney and carried out to the ambulance with a severe concussion and multiple injuries. A small group of Correctional Officers were gathered at the cell entrance where the Lieutenant was at. "What took you so long?" He was staring at Officer Williams. "It was almost like you wanted Campbell to kill me." Officer Williams responded. "Sir, I would never do that." The medical staff were applying bandages to the wounds and then he was escorted and placed in an ambulance and taken to Saint Vincent's Hospital in downtown Santa Fe. Lieutenant Martinez had been stabbed 11 times and had taken on an aura of notoriety as everyone read about it in the local paper, the Santa Fe New Mexican. Life for all of us would change as his notoriety grew. He had become a legend in his own mind, and in some cases, a legend in the minds of others. His vow to stop the abuse of his family disappeared as he celebrated his newly found fame.

The New Mexican printed a story about the event giving a step-by-step account of the incident. It was great for us. The kids in the neighborhood and at school treated us with a bit more respect. Maybe they understood why our passion always involved fighting and compet-ing in one fashion or another. Our dad's strength rubbed off on us and we walked a little taller and became more aggressive. Our life patterns continued with our aggressive behavior escalating in conjunction with our dad's drinking. We had a lot of freedom as our parents were gone most of the time. Would that happen to us? Would we become our dad or could we escape from Alcatraz? Only time would tell!

Inmate Terrance Campbell spent a couple of weeks under guard in the hospital. He had gotten use of the phone to contact friends and family about his condition. He was overheard asking several of them to come and visit him in the hospital. "You know I don't have any money to send you, I'm in prison. Can't you borrow some, I really need to see you." Terrance had come up short, he was on his own. His gang banger buddies had abandoned him as well. He had grown up that way. He never saw his father, and his mother was a heroin addict. Funny how that had worked out. He had become what he hated.

As Campbell lay in bed he thought about his life. He had done to young girls what had been done to his mom. He knew that when he was taken back to the joint his life expectancy was short. Would Lieutenant Martinez follow through with his threat to assign him to the cell block run by 14th street? He had no reason to believe that he wouldn't. Officer Williams walked in with a look of disgust on his face. Campbell recognized the look of resignation. "I guess I'll stay here as long as possible. Can you get me out of here? I have some money stashed away, close to Ten Grand. I'll let you have it." "Are you Crazy?"

Officer Williams had been assigned to monitor Campbells Recovery. "Why in the world would you pull a stunt like that, I had you covered?" Officer Williams was irate. He had done his best to save Terrance from himself. He knew what the consequences would be. Nobody messed with the Lieutenant without suffering. The fact that he carried eleven stab wounds did not bode well for Terrance. "I'll talk to you later brother. Don't be in a hurry to heal, stay in here if you can. I'll see if I can get the Lieutenant to limit his wrath to placing you in the hole on bread and water for a while."

Terrance stayed in the hospital for a couple of weeks despite all his efforts to stay longer. He feigned headaches and memory loss, but the doctors were under pressure to release him to the Department of Corrections. After all, they had medical staff that could take over. Terrance was released and he was paraded around the facility in full shackles and placed back in his cell. "Looks like bother Williams hooked me up. Now I just have to keep a low profile and stay away from the

Lieutenant." Campbell had just muttered these words to himself when he heard what he dreaded the most. "Get up scum bag, time for you to finish what you started." The Lieutenant was looking down at him and four other officers were with him. He felt the sting as a Billy Club came down on his head, his world went dark. The official report stated that Terrance had attacked the correctional officers while they were taking him downstairs to the hole, and he had fallen down the stairs breaking several bones on the way down. Due to staffing, it took a few days to get him medical treatment during which time someone had forgotten to deliver his meals and most of his water. A few days later he was taken to the infirmary and treated for several serious medical conditions.

Terrance was kept in the infirmary isolated from the rest of the convicts. It took him a couple of months and then true to his word Lieutenant Martinez assigned him to cell Block three. Due to his weakened condition, he was unable to fend off his new cell mates. The Lieutenant smiled as he heard Terrance screaming as he was repeatedly sodomized for killing one of 14th Street's family member. A few days passed and Terrance Campbell's dead body was carried out of the facility to the morgue. The reason for death was listed as blunt force trauma and multiple stab wounds. Eleven stab wounds had been inflicted on Terrance. No one was ever prosecuted for the murder, no one claimed the body.

Chapter | 20

TURN

M y head is turning. I know that my body is lying in bed and
yet I feel myself in a whirlpool of color. The red is the base
color with yellows, greens, oranges, purples, whites, blacks,
and their magical blend swirling in my mind. My thoughts are the
colors twirling and mixing as they swirl downward like the water after
the toilet has been flushed. I hear voices breaking into the contorting
rainbow. I recognize them as they fill the space around me. I try to
ignore them. I hear metal on metal and realize that the Ghost Train is
moving through the swirl, the colors are the time, people, and places
mixing into the reality of the train's journey. Is it reality or surrealism?
I don't understand, and yet I understand that I don't. The colors light
up and glow and I know that I am headed towards understanding. Part
of me doesn't want to go. The depth of my thoughts trouble me and
in a strange way, excite me. I am but a boy and yet I am starting to
understand the enormity of my journey towards understanding.

As we swirl, I am brought to a high level of awareness as I recognize
the face of evil. He is in the colors that are swirling. His face melts
and merges with the colors. "Here we go again!" The swirling turns
into sounds, they have the same resonance. Now they turn into smells.
Now my body is swirling in the colors. The swirling has become me,
and I have become it. Everything is turning in and out of a world of
mixture. It is beautiful except for the face of the Conductor.

The swirling rainbow continues as the train comes to a halt. I hear a bell ringing breaking the silence of the night. The passengers get quiet as the doors open. New passengers get on, a few get off. I get scared looking at the death in the eyes of the new riders. The new riders are part of the swirling, the colors of the young and old and all ages in between. Some of them are laughing as they board the train some are crying, and others rest as others look for a place to hide. I see images of dreams and nightmares greeting them at the door and taking them to the back of the train where music and laughter permeate. I dread what their dreams are and how they are being fulfilled. Others that get on are harder to figure out. Some are somber as if in deep thought.

A man boards the train with a book in his hands, he is searching for something. He looks in my direction and smiles, he walks towards me and then through me. We meet in the middle of each other, I feel it. He walks toward the caboose he wants to know what makes it tick. The train starts clanking into the whirlpool of color, turning over unto itself. The colors are life, but they are blending with death. The train makes another stop. Once again passengers get off and others get on. The process happens again, and again, and again, as if the train is going back and forth between the old and the new.

As the train approaches the next stop, I know it is different. As new passenger's board, I overhear their discussions. "The new Viceroy of New Spain, Mendoza, has decided to send Coronado north to explore and expand the Spanish Empire. They are gathering 400 Spaniards and some native allies to make the journey." "I wish I was going!" A young Spanish Conquistador is speaking to an officer. "And I young man, wish that I wasn't going but how can we refuse to make this journey? We have made it this far. This is our opportunity to make a new home. Who would have thought that our journey over the vast ocean would bring us to this? I am torn between the two. Do I stay in the safety of our new home or go off and find the New Spain? Anyway, I have no choice, my King and Queen will decide." The older soldier looks familiar to me. I recognize the two sojourners as they board the train. It is Santiago Martinez and Jose Lopez. It feels like an eon ago that I was in the dark room and in the jungle with them, they have aged.

Jose is a full, grown man, tall and handsome with a full Beard. "What are you doing on the train? Why are you on the train?" I am talking to them but remember that they can't hear me. I hear a voice, but it is not coming from inside the train, it is inside of me and outside of the train. I recognize the woman's voice. It's the voice of hope and strength. "Remember where you are little one. I know you are scared but you are performing well. If the Conductor doesn't consume you, your purpose can be fulfilled. Few are given this view, and even fewer make it through. I see you are growing in wisdom." I ask the same questions in a different way hoping to get answers. "But who is he and why does he eat people and how does the train move the way it does? Can I get off the train and stay off?" "Be patient. Our future is tied to our past. It is a continuum. If you want to change the path of your life in the continuum, you must understand it. You are not there yet."

I can feel myself tossing and turning. I am trying to wake up but the tossing and turning becomes the motion of the train and puts me back into a deep state of sleep. They continue to discuss their new adventure. The two want to travel north in the quest and yet here they are in front of me on the train. How could they be alive and on the train at the same time. The more I look at Santiago the more I think of Billy. It's as if his spirit is in this man. I look at him in full uniform and see a warrior who's volunteering to go into battle and leave his family behind. They are surrounded by noblemen and are married to their daughters; all with visions of riches and vast holdings. You can hear the excitement as several knights plan their explorations north, to the New Spain. They all serve the same kingdom but explore their own glory and riches. The competition between them is fierce. These proud and noble men would be the first to set foot in what is now California, Arizona, Colorado, New Mexico, Oklahoma, Kansas, Florida, and several other states in their longing for the prizes that they envisioned. They seek gold, and they seek glory.

"I am glad that I married Victoria and have my beautiful kids. I, Santiago, will serve Viceroy Mendoza well. As the first Viceroy, Mendoza will honor those that serve the King and Queen and bring favor to his family and those loyal to him. To protect our family, we must never forget that we are descendants of Mars, the God of War. We have a proud heritage of being warriors. Many of us have died valiantly on the battlefield while those of us who have survived have taught our offspring what it is to be honorable and for our enemies to fear us. And now the Martinez's are on their way north in search of the treasures that are rumored to be up there."

Santiago was talking to quell the anxiety he was feeling over making the journey to the unknown. Jose replied to Santiago's comments. "The jungle fever took many good men. I have heard that several of them saw an apparition, they describe it as the bones of the dead filled with the blood of the living. The priests performed many exorcisms for these men, saving their souls before their descent into death. Praise be to God and his son Jesus Christ." I blinked and they were gone. The two were on their way north to Cibola in the continued search for the legendary seven cities of gold. My spirit is in turmoil, the colors swirl in turmoil, turning into images that come and go. I have trouble keeping up with them.

Santiago Martinez had come to be part of the Viceroy's family as he had married the younger daughter. He came to understand his great love for his home in Spain but did not regret his request to come to the new world with the young Jewish boy he had saved from the Inquisition. The Moorish occupation of Spain had lasted for eight hundred years. During this time, the blood of the Jews, Moslems, and Spanish had become one. He had three legacies running though his veins.

In Mexico City, the Capitol of New Spain, the streets were filled with laughter and excitement. The first children were being born in the new world and Santiago was proud that he was part of this New Spain, this new world. Their occupation was changing into settlements that were unique in their origin and he witnessed how easy the Spaniards were becoming one with the earth. It truly was a sight to behold, but at the same time, his heart ached due to the death he saw in the process, both Spanish and Native. The Natives were paying the bigger price as their legacy was being destroyed, supplanted by that of an invader.

As these visions pass before me, the train comes to a screeching halt. As I step out, I behold the most beautiful vistas I have ever seen. As far as the eye can see in all directions the blood red, blue, and white sky goes on for eternity. I look up and see birds flying in a phalanx, dancing in the atmosphere. The daylight moon above shimmers like a pearl, white and translucent. They are in perfect unison as they do their collective ballet in the sky. The sky is multicolored, the whirlpool of colors is magnificent, it takes my breath away. There is a red penumbra where the sky meets the earth. It's in a magical world filled with the mysteries of life. I watch as other birds began to join the silvery reflections swimming in the sky.

They fly in circles as they move in unison across the sky. They glide over the earth, scanning as they migrate from north to south, then east to west. I hear them over head and want to cry. It is so beautiful and sad at the same time. As they fly directly over me the collective flapping of their gray and silver wings reflects the sun back to the earth. The song of their wings sound like the magical sound that emanates from a flowing stream. I think about the parallel, both are part of something bigger than themselves. In an instant, they are gone. I can see their shadow as they migrate away. I want to grow wings and become part of that magical troupe, but I know it will never be. I want to fly home.

I am aboard the train again headed north with Don Juan de Oñate y Salazar. Coronado's journey had served as a reconnaissance of the northern lands and many Spanish expeditions and settlements would follow. The train shoots forward with a violent screech. It reverberates like the voice of a witch crying in the night. Like La Llorana crying for her dead children. "How do I know all this I ask myself, and why can't I remember it when I'm awake?" The train passes through several pueblos and meets up with many nomadic tribes that do not welcome the strange men. They are confused, afraid, and angry at the invader riding strange four-legged animals dressed in shiny coats of the sun.

Oñate was known as a harsh man, and it reflected in his treatment of the inhabitants of the north and of his men. It was well known that he was not happy. He had not wanted to come to New Spain, but as a Knight of the Spanish Crown he had been ordered to do so. He did everything possible to avoid conflict even though he welcomed the skirmishes that resulted in death. His number one priority was to establish a colony in the lands of the north. He did not know it, but he would go down in history as one of the first Europeans to establish a settlement in the new world. Oñate knew that if he found riches, his place in the Spanish court and all that went with it would be his. He would not let anything, or anyone get in his way.

As they traveled north, a small band of natives waited in a narrow canyon. When the Conquistadores passed through, they were attacked from the upper ledges with an onslaught of arrows, boulders, and other debris. The Spaniards were amazed at the quickness with which they were attacked and how accurate their bows delivered their arrows with deadly force. A few of the Spaniards were killed and several were wounded. "Fall back we cannot defend ourselves where we are! They have the higher ground! We must hurry!" The attack continued as they withdrew. They found an area outside the canyon that was safe, set up camp, and assigned sentry duty. The natives would have to take the only path going down to attack them. A few tried but were quickly repelled by the Spanish horsemen. Their retreat was successful, and they camped for the night.

"It goes against everything I believe in to attack the native people of this region, but we cannot allow these savages to attack the King and Queens contingent. As you saw today, they occupy the high ground overlooking the canyon. I need 25 volunteers to circle behind and secure our passage and honor those that died in their brazen attack." Oñate spoke to his men, their faces illuminated by their campfires. "Captain Martinez, you will command the contingent. Be ready to head out in the morning. Volunteers, report to Captain Martinez in the morning." This would be one of many confrontations with the natives on their way to the Rio Arriba, The river up above.

As they leave the meeting Jose speaks with his benefactor. "I am your first volunteer. We have been together from the beginning, and we must accomplish this together." Captain Martinez answers him by saying. "Jose, you must not come with me. We do not know the forces that await us. You must think of your family that awaits your return. I cannot allow it; all will have been for naught." There is a finality to Captain Martinez's words that saddened and angered Jose. How could he do this to him? He owed this man everything and could not envision a way that he would stay behind. "I must find a way to go with my surrogate father. I cannot abandon him, he never abandoned me." Jose was muttering to himself as he prayed next to the fire and laid himself down to sleep. He knows in his heart that it is his duty to fight for God, country, and his family.

The Spaniards wake to a spectacular sunrise! There is a bright orange and yellow silhouette against a sky of baby blue that gives the day a peaceful beginning that contrasts with the impending battle. They must move forward to ensure that Spain's Conquistadores are free to head north and claim its territories in the name of the King.

Captain Martinez is mustering with his 25 volunteers and goes over and gives Jose a hug. "I will see you soon my son. We are on a mission of God for our King, we cannot fail. I understand your anger at not being allowed to join us. As you grow in wisdom you will understand." Jose stands in silence as he watches the troop mount up and ride back in the opposite direction of the ambush. The plan is to take the high country and circle back on the natives. As soon as they are out of sight, Jose readies himself and his horse and heads out tracking the movement of the troop ensuring that he will not be spotted. He knows he is disobeying the orders of his superior officer and adoptive father but his love and devotion to Santiago and to his family is stronger than the fear of the consequences.

As I dream, I am on the horse with Jose. I feel what he feels, see what he sees and do what he does. We are moving uphill and we are on his heels. I can't help but notice all the possible hiding places as our steed maneuvers through the pine forest with its rock formations and natural rise and fall of the mountain. We can hear the hoofs of the horses in front of us. The tumbling of stones down the hill rumbles like thunder as they hit the ground down below. The horses are antsy as they maneuver up the narrow trail. As Jose watches the soldiers go around a corner a chill runs through our body. He hears strange bird calls permeating the mountain. They are coming from all directions.

The birds are primal using their calls to communicate their presence. In an instant, his comrades are under attack from all sides. They have ridden into an ambush. Jose watches as Captain Martinez leads the charge. The Conquistadores attack with their swords and lances and begin to kill and wound the native forces. Using the horses and battle armaments they encircle and begin driving the natives to a drop off at the cliff's edge. The Warriors are from the Pueblo of Acoma, the Sky City. They are fierce warriors and are giving as much as they are taking. Santiago can hear the natives discussing in their own strange language and he spots their leader who is adorned in buckskin and strings of blue turquoise beads. It is obvious that the Chief is a great warrior. He is firing arrows at an astounding pace. Santiago witnesses several of his comrades take hits to the armor with a few arrows finding their way through the crevices where the armor joints are present. He can see blood stains where the arrows have found their mark. Some of the arrows are jutting out and are imbedded in the Conquistadores' bodies with blood trickling off the feathered end.

I can feel sweat dripping down my face unto the pillow. I toss and turn as I wipe it off, but I continue to ride with Jose. "Turn them to the right!" Captain Martinez orders. To the soldiers on the left he orders them to "turn them to the left." He knows that if he can move them all to a center position it will give him a tactical advantage. In a well-coordinated assault, they manage to drive at least a dozen over the edge. Their screams echo through the canyon as they tumble to their death. The natives keep coming with a vengeance. The continued onslaught begins to take its toll as the skirmish rages on. Several of the horsemen begin to withdraw as the wounded begin to fade in the saddle. Some are falling off only to be hoisted up by their comrades and are moved out of harm's way. Jose moves up the hill and surprises several native warriors slashing and cutting them down from atop of his horse.

He spots his benefactor and mentor as he is being attacked from all sides. The horse is bloodied. Jose watches it fall to the ground nearly crushing his surrogate father. Jose rushes to his side, dismounts and begins the tedious process of fighting off the natives with every fiber of his being. The backdrop of the battle slows time down. The dark green trees rising form the deep brown earth reaching towards the heavens strengthen him. He is maneuvering from position to position to turn his defense into offense. He begins to drag his surrogate father down an embankment having to continually stop and fend off the attackers. The embankment is covered with sand and gravel and Jose uses it to slide the captain down quickly. The natives must come down carefully to avoid sliding down and being impaled to death by the sword in Jose's hand. Jose finds a semicircle created by large boulders and puts Santiago up against the rocks and begins trying to dress his wounds. There is a lull in the attack, but they both know it is not over.

Santiago looks up and sees the Chief standing at the top of the embankment pointing to him as he begins to sing in a strange blend of foreign words and cries that seem to flow from the earth. Santiago can't help but notice his surroundings again. He sees the spotted earth, the marriage of the browns, tans, whites, with the dark red Spanish and Native blood. The chief continues with his prayers as he looks up to the heavens with his bow in one hand and his arrow in the other. The totality of this time in space is overwhelming. The world has stopped as lives are becoming one with it. A silence has fallen over the earth. Jose makes his way in front of Santiago vowing to protect him with his life if necessary. Santiago can hear his breath in unison with Jose's and he can feel his heart as it tries to beat its way out of his body. The silence is loud and deafening as the Chief stops and the world stops with him.

Suddenly a group of warriors start their slow slide down the embankment. The battle rages on behind them. Santiago moves forward as the arrows start to fly. He has regained some of his strength. He knows that the makeshift bandages applied by Jose have stopped the bleeding. His son has given him time to get his mind clear. The fall from his horse knocked him out. His body is in pain, he sees where the arrow entered his body and where Jose has broken if off leaving the arrowhead inside of him. His location in the semicircle provides cover from the aerial onslaught and the natives have no choice but to enter directly in front of Santiago. The first warrior appears dressed in a loin cloth with a medicine bag strapped to his waist. His dress is all derived from buckskin. His skin is as brown as the clothing he wears. The spear that he carries is the same color as the hand that holds it. His hand and his spear are one.

The native does not move but just stands there. He is looking at Santiago and Jose as if he has seen an apparition. "Save yourself Jose, I will finish this. Tell my family I love them and that I died with honor. You have a family to get back to as well. You are young and will see many more battles. Fight your way out and get back to Oñate." Just as he utters these words, he hears Jose as he tumbles to the ground. An arrow has found his heart. Tears flow down his face and as quick as lightning, the Acoma warriors are upon him. Santiago attacks the first warrior that enters the rock enclosure and cuts him down with his sword. The others begin to attack Santiago and he slays several before he feels a poignant warmth in his body. He hears Jose groaning as death hovers above him. Jose looks up and sees Santiago in a fight for his live. He hears the thunder, feels the cool rain on his face, and sees that the Chief has moved to a knoll giving him direct sight towards Santiago. Santiago has kept an eye on him and moves quickly towards him knowing that if he kills the Chief the battle will end. The Chief let's go an arrow and Santiago and Jose watch the arrow fly in slow motion. Jose can see the V shaped arrowhead spinning as the feathers on the shaft kept it straight and true. The chief's arrow pierced Santiago in the center of his neck.

Santiago falls to the ground with his face towards the sky next to Jose and cries out. "You must not die! I love you, my son!" His wounds have drained him of energy, he is powerless do anything but wail. Santiago lays there as the rain and his tears fall to the earth mixing with the blood of Jose who lies dead beneath him. The essence of their lives is soaking into the soil becoming one with the new world. The rain is refreshing on his skin, and he can see the individual droplets as they fall. They shine like diamonds on the neck of a beautiful woman as they glisten and glitter in the sunlight.

His life flashes before him. He remembers his childhood in Spain and the people and places he loved. It is strange that the only things he remembers are those that he loved and the wonderful places he saw. The last image he sees is his family. Smiling, he can feel the warmth of their love as his body grows cold. His vision clears and he sees the chief looking down at him singing to his God thanking him for victory in this battle. The chief is holding Santiago's sword, it does not belong to him anymore. The blending continues. The Chief pierces through the armor taking Santiago's life.

As I lay there living this nocturnal life, I see a swarm of birds coming towards me only these are not white flowing as ones that I dreamt of earlier. These are dark black birds. They are moving like a black storm headed towards me. The images of battle are gone but I know it is not my last nocturnal battle. The angry black birds approach me, and I see them gather and explode in front of me. I watch them becoming a face that I have grown to hate more than fear. It's the Conductor. The black swarm seems to look down at me, and like the tip of the native's spear, they dive from the sky with the apparition narrowing as it approaches me. When the Conductor's eyes are ready to enter mine, I scream in a panic and fear. It puts me in a downward spiral. I find myself falling deeper into the abyss. The darkness is so thick that I cannot tell where it begins and where I end. I wake up screaming and then I feel a hand on me, shaking me.

Chapter | 21

WHISKEY MASON JAR

"Wake up Santiago, wake up!" My eyes open and Billy is standing in front of me with a look on his face that speaks volumes. It's as if he knows where I've been and what I've seen. He looks strangely familiar. For a moment I'm looking at Captain Santiago and he is looking at me, but...but... how can that be? It wasn't Captain Santiago! I had just seen him die in my dream. We were back in Santa Fe. All of us were going to school again. The students from our neighborhood had been reassigned to a new school, Agua Fria Elementary. Agua Fria is a small community south of Santa Fe founded in the 1700's. I liked this school better than Carlos Gilbert. It was smaller and the students were not as aggressive, at least until we got there. It didn't matter what school we went to; our aggression went with us. I instigated a lot of the conflict. I was accused of being a bully sometimes, but I justified it. My response was, "I'm not a bully, they're just a bunch of chicken shits." I didn't realize that what was normal for me was frightening for most of the other kids in my school; even the ones that hung out with me.

Billy was now attending Santa Fe high school and was no longer involved in sports. He started bringing friends home that were more like the ones in Española. I liked them, especially Frankie. Together they made quite the team. They both had swagger and laughed a lot. Based on their discussions, they were fighting and drinking and chasing girls and they seemed to be on top of the world. I continued wanting to be like Billy. As a kid in the fifth grade, I was doing everything I could to be like him. I started hearing my parents talk about my brother more often. Billy had taken to ditching school and taking his Santa Fe friends to Española to party and raise hell. On several occasions my mom, and sometimes my dad, would go get him and bring him home.

Often, he would wake me up as he was crawling out the bedroom window. The windows were small and very close to the ceiling. They were placed this way as a security measure. Our proximity to the prison made us vulnerable to escapees. It would be difficult for them to crawl through and get into our home. Billy would move the bed under the window and crawl out. I often wondered where he went. I wanted to go with him. I remember the first time I woke up and saw him doing it? "Where are you going?" "Shut up and keep quiet. If they hear you and come in here, you are going to get a good one."

I was assigned to Mr. Chavez' class. Mr. Chavez was a big man with a beard and a beer belly. He had an oval face and the beard made it look long. He appeared to be calm. He acted like he had a secret, and it was a good one. He was very strict and from the beginning he kept a close eye on me. I could tell he liked me. Several times he would call me to the back of the classroom. "Are you done with your math problems?" "Yah!" My response was always short. I soon learned he was going to put me to work. Mr. Chavez had several cows, and when he butchered one, he would let the skull sit in the sun until the skin and meat dried. He would then boil it to soften and remove most of the flesh. Then he would bring the skull to the class and have me clean it down to the bone.

It was a very tedious job, and frankly, I was the only one that would do it. The hardest part was breaking a small bone at the base of the scull where it joined the neck. "Take your time Santiago, keep it quiet. Don't disturb the class. See this area right here?" He pointed to a spot on the back part of the skull towards the bottom. "Use this screwdriver and hammer, tap on it until it breaks. Go ahead, tap it." I placed the skull sideways, put the screwdriver in the semi-circle and hit it lightly with the hammer. "Good, not too hard. Tap it until you feel it break and tap it until you break all of it off. Why do you think we are doing this?" "I don't know. Do I really have to do this?" I looked at the rest of the kids in the class and I just wanted to sit at my desk. "You're the one that keeps getting in trouble. You can do this or go see the principal, your choice."

I watched as Mr. Chavez left the room and came back with a bull skull that was decorated, it was beautiful. I couldn't believe that it had once looked like the one I was working on. He went on to explain to me that he had a small ranch and that he raised cows. Once again, he explained the process to me. I almost responded that I understood but I let him go over it again. He had noticed that I was squeamish when I broke the thin membrane on the skull we were working on. "Now, don't get scared, the reason you have to break the little bone at the bottom of the skull is because that is where the brains are. If we leave the brains in there they will rot and smell."

"Hey, you kids sit down over there! Now, when the bone is broken use this small metal and dig in there and take out as much as you can. You won't get it all but use your finger around the edges and wash the rest out. Hey, I told you kids to sit down over there. Brian, get over here and help Santiago." Mr. Chavez went back to the front of the classroom and left me to clean the skull. Brian watched me. "That looks like Potted Meat." Brian watched as I struggled through the process. I found out later that Mr. Chavez would take the skull and turn it into a work of art and sell it to the tourists and that he made some money out of it. I never looked at Potted Meat the same.

Mr. Chavez was like my dad in a way. I usually did what he said but I continued to slip into my aggressive habits. My entire life was being molded by them. I was surrounded by them. I struggling to figure out who I was. My happiness depended on it. Funny how it seldom brought happiness. I often reverted to the essence of who I was. Being paddled at school for misbehaving was common. It was something I was familiar with. I kept calling the paddle the Board of Education and Mr. Chavez took to calling it the same thing. Once I mentioned it the first time, I was paddled with it. This one was humongous with holes drilled into it. Anytime someone got paddled their name was written on the paddle. After the first time a tick mark was placed near your name.

Two names began to emerge, Brian and Santiago. Brian and I became close friends. He was a blond with blue eyes, thin, with a sarcastic smile and laugh. Him and I were always getting in trouble, like the time we went swimming at the Municipal Swimming Pool. One of the prettiest girls in our class Vicky, also a blond, had a tremendous crush on me. Brian knew about it and for some strange reason he enjoyed it. I could see the gleam in his eye. He was up to something. He had a plan, and I knew it. He liked to set me up and enjoy the show. His younger brother was Michael's friend, so we were tight. "Vicky likes you." Brian kept teasing me like this. "What? How do you know?" I pretended I didn't care, but I did. "I heard her talking to Elizabeth yesterday." I walked away with a knot in my stomach. I was afraid of girls. I was usually mean to them to keep them away.

Swimming day was exciting for us. I liked that there was a train parked in front of the pool. I wondered why it was there and how they had gotten it there. There were no tracks. The train looked like the Ghost Train. I was glad I had learned how to swim in the river, I was excited. We got to the pool and were given instructions to stay in the shallow end. There were lifeguards in and out of the water, some of them were teachers. While we were at the pool, Brian convinced both

Vicky and I to get out of the pool and go outside and sit down. Several students had not been given permission to swim by their parents, so they sat outside. Before long Vicky and I were under our towels. Brian was enjoying the show, urging us on. He wanted us to touch each other. I guess we wanted too as well.

Vicky put her hand into my trunks. I felt her cold hands touching me. It excited me in a strange way. I put my hand under her bathing suit and felt between her legs. I could feel her shiver as I found the opening and slipped my finger inside. She grabbed my hand and pulled it away from her. She held my hand. On that day we started the awkward transition to sexual beings without knowing what we were doing. We were in the fifth grade. As we were exploring each other, the swimming coach came along and in an instant our fling was over. We were taken to the bus while the class finished their swimming lessons. They put Vicky in the front seat and me in the back seat. We were both ashamed that we had been caught and made to feel foolish and dirty. We were both teased a lot, her more than me. I beat up a few boys that were teasing her. This pretty much put a stop to it.

The school year went on this way with Brian and I continuing to add tick marks on that paddle. Mr. Chavez told us that whoever got the most would earn the paddle at the end of the year. That was all Brian and I had to hear. The challenge was on. I quickly learned to gauge when to disrupt the class. I made sure I determined what kind of mood Mr. Chavez was in. He didn't swing as hard when he was in a good mood. Brian was oblivious to this, and he received a lot of paddling that would make him turn red as a turnip. Mr. Chavez tried to use reverse psychology on us by making it a contest. My guess is that he didn't think any kid would be dumb enough to get paddled on purpose.

Towards the end of the year we were tied, and we had to determine who was going to win. Brian and I decided that we would compete for a week and whoever got paddled the most would win. Part of the game included asking Mr. Chavez to paddle us, he was enjoying it. The sting got stronger and stronger closer to the end of the school year. I went first. In response to spit balling, Mr. Chavez paddled me so hard I was airborne. I could feel where the holes in the paddle were. It felt like bee stings, hundreds of them at the same time. Brian went next, he got one as painful as mine. He turned so red I thought he was going to explode. We both took one more and that was enough for me. Brian won the paddle, and it was as if he was taking home an Olympic Medal. I always regretted not winning it. I hated to lose, especially to my friend Brian. I often wondered what happened to him, he did not return to school the following year. They had moved, and I would never see him again.

As the school year continued my reputation in the school yard continued to grow. I was always being taken to the principal's office. I started to get a following and was committed to proving how strong I was. One day while we were at recess, Bruce approached me. "We should run away from home!" He was very excited as he proceeded to give me the reasons why. His father was a Korean War Veteran who had lost his leg. Now he owned a junk yard and worked on cars for a living. As was common practice in those days, he subscribed to the belief 'spare the rod, spoil the child'. He believed it so much that he was very generous with the rod. I guess Bruce was convinced that we could make it. After I agreed to run away from home with him, it became a group project. Several of our elementary peers were on the planning committee. "Are you really going to run away? You're not afraid? You know you are going to be in deep trouble. My dad would kill me!" Sharon was going on and on, she was more excited than we were. "Let's get you what you need. Where are you going to stay?" I looked at Bruce and wondered, "Do you know a place?"

The planning went on as more of the kids started to learn about the plan. We were at the far end of the playground looking over the fence at the empty lot every day for morning recess talking and laughing.

We were getting excited, and the plan was starting to unfold. There we were at the end of the playground where only the most daring of the kids went. The tough kids owned that part of the playground. In our case, the same was true for the last six seats on the bus. Bruce and I decided that we would leave on Friday, that way we wouldn't get in trouble for not being in school. We had no idea where we were going to go or what we were going to do when we got there. It was early Spring and there was still a chill in the air. Friday came quickly, and we met at the fence again to go over the details. Sharon had put together a plan to bring us supplies.

They brought us some food that consisted of Spam, tortillas, and potted meat. "Here, I stole some from my dad, you guys will need it to stay warm." Sharon spoke with pride. She was tempted to go with us. She spoke while she handed me a small Mason Jar with whiskey in it. I took it not knowing what to do with it. I hid it and the other supplies under a pile of dry leaves, remnants from the fall season. David told us about a place not too far from the school in the foothills nearby. It was a semi-circle of boulders where we could sleep. We went to class; the afternoon went by slowly. As the bell rang, we walked outside and the kids that did not have to catch a bus followed us to the stash. It was cold out and I noticed that Bruce had a much nicer coat than I did. I did not care. It was time to run away. To me it was an adventure. I didn't think about what the consequences would be. I was ready to go.

"Let's go to the boulders first, we can put all this stuff away." Bruce looked worried, so I took charge and led the march into the foothills. We walked on the side of the main road for a couple of miles and got off on a bumpy dirt road. We crossed an arroyo that was sandy and desolate. Not a sign of life was to be seen except for a couple of pitch-black ravens flying overhead. I could hear their gruff caws like grinches in the sky. It was as if they were warning each other that we were headed in their direction.

There was a part of me that wished I could go with them. Their presence in the silence was mystical. I wanted to be free. I felt like I was in a prison. I had very little control over what happened to me. When I took control, it landed me somewhere the world didn't want me to be. The consequences restricted me even more, the vicious cycle continued. Here I was again, headed for the boulders looking for adventure and for freedom. Bruce was following close behind me. I didn't really know him that well. Him and his older brother rode our bus. They were very different from each other; they argued a lot. Bruce was very quiet. I could see that he was tough under the quiet and we were slowly becoming friends.

We found the smaller dirt path and started our gradual ascent up into the hills. The ground was rocky and there were multiple areas where the sand had washed unto the trail. I slipped and fell. I landed with my palms down and felt the sting and the warmth of the blood flowing from my hand. I was face down and looked to the right and saw the road leading to my school. I wanted to go back but it was too late. I couldn't bear the thought of having to face our planning committee and explain why I had chickened out. I had landed on ground that was made of mixed sand and small rocks. The rocks were beautiful. They each had their own personality and looked like jewels. I picked up a few of the prettier ones and put them in my pocket. I got up and started moving up the trail.

The committee was waiting on me and I needed their approval and was willing to sleep in the boulders to get it. Before I got fully up from the ground, a stink bug lifted its rear end and let me have it. The stink bug was jet black and had a huge body and a small head. As it raised its rear end into the sky it looked funny. Its legs seemed to grow in the back and shrink in the front. I wanted to catch it but thought better of it. The smell was more than I could handle. "How can something so small stink so big?" I asked Bruce who was standing behind waiting for me to get up. I didn't wait for an answer.

As we climbed, I noticed that the pine trees were getting bigger and closer together. There were large rocks scattered throughout. The quiet was deafening and the wind had a biting chill to it. I was under dressed but I knew that we had matches to start a fire. "There they are, we made it!" Bruce got animated as we walked into the enclosure. "Let's put all our stuff in the corner over there." He pointed and walked to an area where two large rocks made a corner. "Let's go find some wood and start a fire. It's going to be cold, and we have to stay warm." I had been camping with my dad a few times and began to emulate what I had seen him do. "See those small rocks over there? Let's make a circle and we can put the fire inside it." The rocks were tall and provided shelter from the wind. We could hear it howl and I got worried. I could see the same feeling flash across Bruce's face.

The rocks we gathered for the fire were heavy for their size, but we managed to get them into a circle. "Let's go find us some wood. We will get this fire going quickly. We have to find enough to last the night." Then I realized a cold fact. "We are going to have to sleep on the ground." I had seen my dad make a bed out of Piñon branches. "Let's collect the wood and then we can cut off the branches. "I have this." Bruce produced a pocketknife. I wished I had a knife. After an hour or so we had our fire blazing, it was awesome. Every time we got up; our shadows would be cast unto the boulders; we were in our own little world. I started to move around to make my shadow dance on the rocks. The light reflecting on the boulders changed colors, from dark brown to a tan almost white. My shadow was pitch black. I was performing a play and the boulder circle was the stage. Bruce was laughing but for some reason he just sat near the fire and watched.

"Let's go to the 7-to-11 on Osage, we can buy some candy." Bruce had reached into his pocket and pulled out some dollar bills. "Where did you get that?" "My dad pays my brother and I sometimes to take off parts from the junked cars to sell." "We already have candy over there." I pointed to the stash in the corner. "I don't like those candies. I want a chocolate Hershey's Bar." "Hell yeah, let's go." I could taste the chocolate in my mouth. I wanted a Hershey bar like my dad got. We left our things in the corner, including the whiskey in the Mason Jar. I had smelled it and tasted it. I did not like it, but I did notice the warm tingling as it went down my throat into my stomach. I figured I would drink some more later if I really needed it to stay warm.

As we stood up and got ready to go, I looked up at the sky and the stars almost made me cry. We couldn't see the stars at the Penitentiary, the lights were too bright. Here I was gazing up. It took me back to El Guache, a simpler life. Santa Fe was great, but I was having a hard time fitting in. I felt like a stranger everywhere I went. I was homesick, for a home that would never be again. As we started to walk, I saw my family working our small farm, brown from the sun, laughing as we picked on each other. The sound of the wind was the sound of the river. I missed our river. The memories of our explorations hunting for the perfect willows to make bows and arrows, slingshots, spears, and tools to dig around on the bank looking for whatever flowed as we walked. I almost fell as I remembered swimming and the trials and tribulations I went through to learn how. Billy's face lit up in my mind. I missed him! We were seeing less and less of him. We were not told what he was doing. What we knew came from overheard discussions and from him and his friends when they were around.

We went down the trail, slipping and sliding as we did. The sun was gone, and the air was getting colder. The darkness had become a thick cloud. The stars reminded me how small I was. "Maybe we should go home, my dad is going to be really mad." Bruce was quieter than normal. I could hear that he was scared and worried. I had seen that look many times in my family. My response was one of false bravado. "Let's check it out, we can go home tomorrow. I can hardly wait until we tell our class that we made it at least for one night." All I was thinking about was that Hershey bar. I seldom got candy. My mouth watered as we walked. As we walked, I remembered our 7-to-11 chocolate raid last year. This time we wouldn't get caught.

"Check it out, that car is cool!" We both stopped and watched as a white and shiny car rolled by us. The car was different, it had a small window on the side of the roof and there were two people in it, there were no back seats. "That's a 56 Thunderbird, we have one in our junkyard. My dad says that only rich people can buy those. I hope I can when I'm older." Bruce was back for a moment but in the back of my head thoughts about tomorrow slowly crept in. It was getting colder and darker. It felt as if we were getting in too deep. It started to dawn on us that we had been stupid to have ever done this. Our childish fantasies had taken over and here we were in the middle of nowhere. The walk to the 7-to-11 was further than I thought. I was learning that driving in a car made the distance feel shorter. Cars with teenagers started passing by and one of them stared at us as they passed by. I wondered why they didn't like us.

We kept walking on Osage up towards Saint John's Catholic church. I had made my First Holy communion there shortly after our move. The 7-to-11 was next door to the church, and I was familiar with it. "Look, we're almost there." I was reassuring Bruce. I could see the fear in his eyes. Bruce's response was more of a decision than a response. "Maybe they'll have a phone, and I can call my dad. Do you want to call yours?" I wanted to go home too I just didn't want to admit it. I had been through a lot, and I knew I would make it through the night. "It won't do me any good, we have a party line and Monica and Suzie down the street are always on it. I get on sometimes and if I'm quiet I can listen to them talk. Girls are funny, they talk about the boys they like but when they see us, they pretend and act as if they don't." We continued walking in silence. The night was growing as we walked. I was thinking about how good it felt to have the kids around us at school help us. They were walking with us in a way.

My thoughts were shattered like glass falling on concrete. I heard a loud angry voice and saw Bruce fly in the air at the same time. "What the hell do you think you're doing?" I felt my heart start to race as I imagined the evil that was attacking us. I looked back and saw a white man with a straggly beard rushing towards Bruce yelling at him. "Get up you little son-of-a-bitch, let's go! Did you really think you would hide from me?" "I'm sorry dad, I was walking to call you." "Shut up and get in the car! You, what is your name and where do you live?" He grabbed Bruce yanking him to his feet and in a single stroke turned him and shoved him towards a car that was down the street. I could see the exhaust fuming in the night, like my breath was. I did not know what to do and got ready to run. "You get in the car too. I won't kick your little ass, I'll let your father take care of that. Don't make me ask you again. What is your name and where do you live?" I could see it in his eyes, there was a hunger in them. I got in the car, told him my name and where I lived, and then kept my mouth shut.

The ride to the Penitentiary housing was one of the longest I ever experienced. Bruce was crying and his father was quiet, but you could hear him loud and clear. His silence spoke volumes. We drove in silence. I was wondering what would happen to me when I got home. I thought my dad was the toughest man I had ever known, but Mr. Lassiter was a close second. His demeanor was serious and no nonsense. His limp was pronounced but it was part of him, and he carried it. I found out that he had lost his leg in the war. I wondered how he had lost it. His overalls were stained and frayed. I could see that he worked extremely hard, his junk yard took on a whole new meaning for me. It was dark outside, and I could see the stars through the window in the back seat. There were very few cars on the road. When we arrived at my home, Mr. Lassiter walked me to the door with Bruce in tow. He knocked on the door. "Come in." I recognized my dad's voice and was glad it wasn't the agitated one.

"Good evening, Mr. Martinez." Mr. Lassiter was stoic and firm in his stance and spoke in a strong voice. "Good evening, who are you and why is my son with you?" My father responded while getting up. "When my son Bruce did not show up this afternoon on the bus, I knew something was going on. I have spent the last few hours searching for him and found these two walking on Osage." My dad looked at me with a look of disappointment, not of anger. "Obviously these two are not good for each other and I must insist they not buddy around anymore. I am asking for your cooperation on this matter. I will share it with the principal tomorrow."

I was surprised by dad's response. "Okay, have a good night." Mr. Lassiter firmly grabbed Bruce by the hand, they disappeared into the night. I heard the car drive away and my dad told me to close the door. "If you don't want to live here go ahead and pack some things and leave. Until then, go to your room and don't come out." As I walked to my bedroom with my tail between my legs, I had a feeling of sadness. I could see that my family was having a great time playing checkers. I had picked a terrible day to run away.

The following day things were back to normal, at least for me they were. I was used to getting in trouble, paying the price, and moving on to the next one. It was Saturday, we did our chores and played basketball for most of the day. "Did you really run away yesterday?" Where did you go?" "Was it cold?" "Did you guys drink the whiskey?" The questions came faster than I could answer them. The kids from the neighborhood were excited. The Pen gang was back at it, playing, fighting, planning, and just hanging around with each other. The questions continued all weekend. Arthur was quiet about the whole thing. He was thinking about how much he disliked his brother Santiago. "That punk is always getting into trouble and then we have to get him out of it." Michael watched with amusement, but he was not happy. "Here we go again! Santiago thinks he's the best at everything." Arthur continued talking about his younger brother. "I have to talk to him! He gets dad mad, and we end up paying for it too." He thought about how he was going to put it as he watched Santiago prancing around.

On Monday we were surrounded by our planning committee wanting to hear every detail. I never heard another word about my journey into the foothills from our parents, but we did from the principal, and worse for me, from Mr. Chavez. The entire school must have heard the crack of the paddle meeting my dumb ass. Maybe they heard it all the way in El Guache. My grandpa probably thought it was going to rain on a sunny day. We are all shocked when we saw Mr. Lassiter walking into the building with Bruce in front of him. We barely recognized Bruce. His head was bald, and it was two tones! His face and neck were brown, and the top of his head was white. It would have been funny if not for the look on Bruce's face. He looked miserable and he did not lift his head to look at us. I was sad for him and wondered why my dad had sent me to my room for the evening and let it go. It was one of those times when my dad showed me compassion and love, it brought tears to my eyes. Fifth grade at Agua Fria Elementary continued for the rest of the year. My grades were the highest in the class while the ticks on the Board of Education continued to grow. I kept running wild in the playground, and I kept pulling brains out of cow skulls.

Chapter | 22

BLOOD RED AND BLACK GALAXY 500

I still remember when my dad bought his shiny new 1967 Galaxy Five Hundred. School had just ended for the day. As I walked to the bus stop Billy intercepted me and walked me to the car. I was happy to see Billy. I walked like I owned the place. "Billy, what are you doing here?" I thought something was wrong. As we walked, he was looking around. "Where's Michael?" "He's probably on the bus. His teacher lets them out early to get them on the bus." Billy didn't answer my question. "Where's the bus, we have to get him, dad is waiting for us, hurry up." We found Michael in the bus sitting in our reserved seating in the back. "Let's go, dad is waiting for us." He heard the excitement in my voice, and he hurried up and got off the bus.

As we left the bus I was confused. I didn't see my dad. "Where is he? I don't see the truck." "Just follow me, you'll see. Hurry up he is going to take us to the Lotaburger." We picked up the pace now that we knew it wasn't bad. Billy walked towards a car we didn't recognize. Dad got out and had a smile that we didn't see very often. "Hey boys, how do you like my new car?" Juan and Arthur were already in the back seat. "Michael, get in front with us. Santiago, you get in the back with your brothers." "I could feel the jealousy surround me like a dark cloud. Times like this is when I wanted to pound my younger brother.

My dad always put him before me, and I hated it. I wanted to be up there sitting by Billy.

As we approached the car, the sounds of the after-school rush exploded. I wanted all of them to see our car. I recognized some of the kids and yelled to them. I was beaming with pride and happiness. I couldn't help but notice how pretty it was. It was the prettiest car I had ever seen. The car was shiny red on the bottom with a shiny black roof. The back end sloped down. It looked like the slide in the playground. The back lights were rectangular and sat above a beautiful chrome bumper. I couldn't believe it when Billy opened the passenger seat and pushed the front seat forward and ushered us in. Before I got in, I ran and looked at the front end. I thought it was beautiful. It had a full grill, double headlights, and had a bumper that curled around each end of the fenders. I got in and it was roomy inside. "Let's go!" You could see the pride in my dad's eyes. It was easy to see this car was a dream come true. He had totaled his Mustang on one of his drinking escapades with friends and this was the replacement.

I enjoyed riding in the car every chance I got. I watched every time we went out how my dad drove it. The shifter was on the steering column and when he wanted to go fast, he shifted it with ease. He let Billy drive the new car. "Billy, give a little more gas, you're driving too slow." It went like this for weeks. It was a peaceful time in our house. We were getting ready for the weekend, and I heard my dad ask my mom. "Where's Billy at?" His tone was not a happy one. "I don't know, he was gone this morning when I woke up, he's probably in Española again. Why does he want to be there so much? We have to go and get him. I'm afraid of what's going to happen to him. Your brother Gilberto called me and told me that Billy was at your dads and that he did not like the things that he was hearing. I don't know if he is still there."

Española was a small town and eventually everybody thought they knew everybody else's business. "Why don't you go get him, he's your son." "If you didn't protect him and baby him all the time maybe he'd be in school right now!" My dad was oblivious to the fact that his example was the catalyst for their son's behavior. My mom's voice was shorter and faltering. "How dare you accuse me of that. If you would stop taking him out drinking with you and your worthless friends, he wouldn't be doing this. You're the one that has taught him how to be a drunk!" In an instant, I heard a loud series of noises coming from inside the house. I heard the series of sounds I knew too well. First was the 'slapping of my mom's face, then the crying. The totality of the echoing and blending of these noises was terrifying.

I could hear her crying. Where had she gone wrong? My mom's feelings towards my grandma and my grandpa, harbored disappointment, and resentment. If she had been allowed to stay in school like she wanted to, she never would have met Billy and none of this would be happening. She felt guilty thinking these thoughts. If her life had been different none of her children would exist. She often drove away the regrets and focused on the blessing of her kids. Right now, it felt as if she was living in a hell all her own. We were all in our own hell. Because we were in our own hell, we were oblivious to hers. "Don't ever talk to me like that again Adelida!" He glared at us as he stormed out of the house. We all rushed to mom's side and helped her get up. At times like this I hated my father and wished I was older so I would be able to stop him one way or another.

Meanwhile in Española Billy was hanging out in the world that he loved. "Hey Billy, you in there?" It was Antonio and Miguel pounding on the old wooden door to our ancient house in El Guache. "Come in." Billy answered as he got out of bed, still hung over from the night before. They had been out on the town last night drinking with anyone who would provide them with alcohol. Most of their days were spent at one home or another where they ate, rested, made plans, and gathered in the evening. They would then head out looking for their friends and spontaneous adventures they had come to love. They loved each other and stuck together no matter what.

For the first time Billy had used my dad's name to get booze on my dad's credit. A common practice for liquor establishments was the sale of alcohol through a drive-up window. It was the norm for us to be in a car with any of our relations as they pulled up to the drive-up-window and bought their drink of choice. One of the most prominent pass times was cruising. It was common to cruise around drinking, meeting people, and hooking up. When the liquor ran out you would pull up to the drive-up-window and purchase more alcohol. This created situations that resulted in a lot of accidents. Too many times the driver was so drunk they couldn't walk and yet, they would drive up and buy more alcohol further impairing their ability to drive. Billy had grown up cruising with my dad, his cousins, and his friends. As the oldest, he was the apple of my dad's eye so why not share the same credit at the bars?

"What do you guys want to do tonight?" Billy was interrupted by my grandfather. "Billy, como estas mi jito?" My grandfather was a good man and had seen his son do some terrible things to us. "You need to go home. You know how your dad is. You do not want to provoke him. It is better if you go, school is very important." Grandpa looked at Antonio and Miguel as he spoke. "This place is not good for you. I have seen many young men destroy their lives due to the drinking and the violence that comes from it. The sheriff came to visit me yesterday. You know he is my first cousin. He is getting pressure from the State Police. They are questioning why they keep arresting you and nothing happens. They are threatening to go to the State Attorney General and file their complaints." "I don't want to go back and live with my dad. I hate him and can't stand to be around him. And my mom! Well, she just lets him abuse her. Why doesn't she go to the cops?"

Billy was thinking about all the abuse my dad had inflicted on his family. He had seen my dad leave the bars with other women who were just as drunk as him, after all, dad had bought them drinks all night. His thoughts continued as he spoke. "Why does he treat them better than my mom?" Billy often wondered about this when he waited in the car or in a strange living room. Too often he sat there hearing the sex sounds coming from the bedroom or even worse from the backseat. He had been there one time when dad had opened the trunk of his car and had sex with a woman in there. I guess that was an advantage of having a big trunk. "And do what, where will she go with all of you?" "Okay Grandpa, I get it. We will be careful! I promise that I won't get into any more trouble. Let's go." Billy and his friends took off walking. They would hitch hike into town. The rides were usually immediate, most of the people on the road knew them.

During this time my dad was planning a trip to Española to pick up Billy. He wanted to go right away but couldn't. The penitentiary correctional staff rotated working schedules. First, they worked days for a few months, then evenings for a few, and graveyard shift for a few. We all had to adjust our schedules as well. My dad was on days now. It was Friday and we were looking forward to the weekend. We were still shaken up. Our mom was in obvious pain and our dad acted as if nothing had happened. As soon as we got off the bus and walked home my dad was at the door waiting for us. "Let's go, we're going to Española to get your brother." My mom got into the front seat. She had taken a day off from her new job as a custodian for the State of New Mexico. "Can we stop at Lotaburger?" "Not today! Adelida, go inside and get some tortillas and Vienna Sausages, we can eat them on the way there." The trip to Española was quick. The Galaxy 500 was smooth and fast. My dad got pulled over often but most of the time was given a warning. He would get out and talk to the cop and show them his badge and it worked for him. The State Police Officers had come to know him. They would tell him to slow down and let him go. Dad drove fast when he was upset. We all knew to be quiet.

When we got into Española, my dad and mom were talking about where Billy would be. I recognized the look on my mom's face. I knew she was praying that Billy would come quietly but she had noticed of late that Billy Jr. was rebelling against his father's authority, and it scared her. She was having us light candles at church and making us pray for our brother. Now here we were watching as they decided the order in which they would visit the homes and hang out places of Billy and his friends. First, we went to our property in El Guache. "Have you seen Billy?" My dad was talking to my grandpa. "Has he been here?" My dad asked without allowing time for the answer to the first question.

"He's been sleeping here. I make sure he has food to eat and that he is okay. He doesn't want to go back to Santa Fe, he likes it here." My grandpa was aware of why we were there. "It doesn't matter what he wants. I'm taking him back one way or the other." "Let him be for a bit, he's okay for now. He's not doing anything that you don't do!" I got scared for my grandpa. I wasn't used to anyone talking to my dad that way and getting away with it. My dad hadn't started drinking yet, so his response was controlled. "I do a lot of things that maybe I shouldn't do. But just because I do them doesn't mean I want my son to do them." My grandpa turned and walked into his adobe home shaking his head as he walked. He was saying something in Spanish, but I couldn't hear what he said. When my dad got back into the car, I could see that he had not liked the words he had just heard.

We went house to house looking for him. The intensity of the search increased every time Billy wasn't there. All the parents knew my dad and did not want any trouble with him, so their responses were short and to the point. "We haven't seen them in a couple of days. If we see him, how do you want us to get in touch with you?" "Just tell him to call me and I'll come and get him." We went to Antonio's house and his dad was home. "We haven't seen him or Antonio since yesterday. Have you tried Patricia and Mary's home? They have the hots for those girls." I could hear the laughter; Antonio's mom was the best person ever when she was sober, but she got crazy when she drank. She had a way of making us laugh. "Chi" as she was known was a unique person. Her home was always open to all of us.

We could see that there was a beautiful woman underneath the blood-stained eyes, wind-blown hair, and ragged skin. We hung around there a lot as Billy was Antonio's best friend and Moises was Juan's. I had seen her really drunk many times and she was scary. Her face would turn blood red, her eyes popped out of their sockets and looked like red and black marbles. When she walked, she talked to herself and swung her arms and wiggled them in the air as she paced their old adobe home looking for booze. Thank God she was sober today. I felt sorry for her. She always went out of her way to welcome us and feed us. I did not like her husband very much. He was a little man with arthritis and walked hunched over and was shriveling up. Without her, he would have been in bad shape. He bossed her around and was abusive towards her, but she never left his side.

My dad seemed to have cooled off a bit but was still highly agitated. As we drove, I was hoping that we didn't find Billy. I feared what would happen if we did. I could see my dad's mood darken as we got closer to town. I recognized the pattern, when he got frustrated, he dealt with it by imposing violence on the source. It was getting dark, and we had to stop and get gas. I heard my dad mumbling to my mom about that dumb ass costing them money that they did not have. As he got out my mom mumbled to herself. "Less money for you to spend on your friends and whores." Good thing she said it without him hearing her. As my dad got into the car, he unleashed a narrative on how worthless my brother was. He turned his wrath on us warning us what would happen to us if we didn't stop getting into trouble. "I brought you into this world I can take you out." His tirade continued. I could see my mom's lips moving and I knew she was praying for her son, for us, for herself, and for my dad.

Pat and Mary lived in a small house right next to the Española High School. As we pulled up, there were several boys and girls outside listening to the radio blaring from inside the house. Most of them had beers in their hands and I could tell that a lot of them were drunk. The laughter was in direct contrast with the mood in our car. If given the choice I would have chosen being with them. "Let's go to the game tonight it's going to be a blast." A teen dressed in a tight-fitting T-Shirt was talking to a small group standing near him. "Did you go to the sock-up last week? I didn't see you." The young teens were talking to each other about all sorts of things. They looked happy but I knew what happened when alcohol was involved. The good turned bad the later into the party it got.

I had been around it my whole life. I had already started drinking and I was in elementary school. I would watch as beers were left on the table. I would sneak drinks when I could get away with it. After all, 'real men drink, and the more they drink the stronger the man they are' was the motto around me. I wanted to be a hell of a man. I recognized some of the kids in the crowd and saw a couple of older men mixing in with them. As we pulled into the front yard several of the people in the crowd pointed to us. I could see a hush cascading through the party as they seemed to move to the sides simultaneously. The wave of movement was like the parting of the red sea, only my dad wasn't Moses.

I was happy that Billy was nowhere to be seen. Out of the corner of my eye I saw Antonio hurry past the gaggle of youth and rush inside. "Miguel, is Billy here?" My dad had gotten out of the car and walked to where Miguel was talking to Mary. "Hello Mr. Martinez, how are you doing this evening?" Miguel looked as if he was talking to a ghost. He looked over at us and got a worried look on his face that he tried to hide underneath his million-dollar smile. My dad wasn't buying it. "Is Billy here? I've been looking for him all day. Has he been with you? He needs to get back to Santa Fe and to school! What's going on with you guys? Every time I turn around, I'm getting you guys out of trouble. Do I have to kick you guys in the ass to make you understand?" I could see the color on my dad's face changing from a dark brown to a tinged red while Miguel stepped back in apprehension as he responded. "You know how he is. He does what he wants. I don't have anything to do with it. He's my best friend and if he shows up, I hang out with him."

These words had barely left his mouth when we heard Billy's voice coming from the door of the house. "Hey dad, how is everything going, hi mom!" He showed no sign of fear or any other emotion. He appeared to be happy to see us. My dad on the other hand was not happy to see him. "Are you already drunk? Get in the car, let's go." Billy's response was not the one any of us wanted to hear. "I'm not getting into the car. I'm not going anywhere. I'm not doing anything wrong!" Billy was talking very firm. Everything was in slow motion. We all cringed as dad's voice revealed his anger. "I said let's go! You have to get back to school, you haven't been home in days. You're 15 years old and it seems like you're doing something wrong all the time. You have to stop drinking. You're too young to drink so much. Now get into the car and let's go!" My dad was now moving towards my brother. I could feel the tears rolling down my face. I knew that something bad was going to happen.

"Please get in!" I heard my mom pleading with her son. "Let's go home, tomorrow we can figure out what we are going to do." I could hear the love and the fear in her voice. The rest of us joined in, pleading with my brother to get in and go with us. It became apparent to me that he was drunk. He was looking at his friends as my dad moved forward. "Go with your family Billy, we'll see you soon." I recognized his girlfriend Pat and could see the fear and love in her eyes. "Don't worry, everything is okay, let me talk to my dad." Billy looked at my dad then at us. "I don't want to go dad, I like it here, these are my friends. I'm not from Santa Fe, I'm from here." As he spoke, the voices of his friends started piercing the dark like a fluid blanket surrounding my dad and my brother. All of them were urging him to go. "We'll see you when you come back bro!" The same sentiment was spoken by several of his friends who were stepping back from the fray. As they stepped away my dad and Billy were standing in the vacuum. "Get in the car or I'll get you in!" I knew that the talking was coming to an end. My brother was stubborn and now he was drunk. My heart sank as I listened to what my brother was saying. "Then you're going to have to get me in."

In an instant my dad grabbed Billy by the arms and yanked him towards the car. The car was a two door and my dad had set it up to get Billy in the back seat so that he wouldn't get out and run first chance he got. I could see their bodies gyrating as my dad struggled to get Billy into the car. My brother was not hitting my dad, but he was not giving an inch. I could tell how strong Billy was by how hard my dad was having to work to get him into the car. My dad managed to get Billy to the door of the car. "Get in the car I told you! You are going to get in the car one way or the other!" The world came to a stop as my dad continued to move Billy towards the back seat of car. He finally had him up against the car. The door was open, but Billy would not lower his head and get in, my dad's voice was loud now.

All of us in the car were begging them to stop. I started crying begging Billy to get in. My sobs fell on deaf ears. In an instant, my dad started punching by brother and I heard as Billy's head hit the roof of the car, the edge where the door met the cab. The blow weakened Billy and my dad got him into the car. Blood was flowing down my brother's face. The silence was so thick I could feel it on my skin. I couldn't help but notice that the blood was the same color as the Galaxy 500. My heart ached for my family. Why did it have to be this way? My tears flowed all the way to Santa Fe. "I'm not going to stay with you. As soon as we get to Santa Fe I'm coming back." My dad responded in Spanish. "You better not, next time I won't be so nice." I sat next to my brother all the way home. The blood ran down his face and the tears ran down mine. The scar in my heart would last longer than the one on his face. The Shiny Red and Black Galaxy 500 lost its magic. The Galaxy 500 had become the Ghost Train. A cold shiver ran down my back as I looked around. The Conductor had to be near!

Chapter | 23

THE PRINCE AND THE DWARF

"What are you doing here 'carñal', my brother? Your dad is not going to like it. Man, he kicked your ass. I thought we were next!" Miguel and Antonio were happy to see their best friend, but they had been given a scare by Billy Sr. last week. The families had become very close, but they were always leery of Billy's dad. When drunk, he was dangerous. Miguel had gone home after the incident. In his heart he knew Billy would be back, but it worried him. Billy was getting more daring and his escapades more dangerous. Lately he had been staying away from Billy making excuses about why. He was worried about his friend.

Antonio on the other hand was loving it. He didn't like being home. His mom was always drunk, and his dad continued with his gambling. Billy was from El Guache, The Prince, and Antonio was from El Duende, The Dwarf. Miguel was from Herñandez. "I wonder why the Spaniards gave these communities these names?" I had heard adults discuss this as they laughed speculating why, especially El Duende. Miguel and Antonio watched as Billy walked up to them. There was a guy with him that they had never seen before. "Who's this vato," Miguel asked. Billy got a big smile on his face. "This is my bro from Santa Fe. He's a good dude, bro, he's crazy. So, what's up? You guys want to go do something?" Billy was back.

The new guy, Frankie, was quick to join in. "Billy's been telling me about the swimming hole in the river, what's the name again?" He was tough like them and enjoyed the thrill of living on the edge. He was a couple of years older than Billy and he was impressed by Billy's willingness to cross all the lines. They had met one day at school when Frankie was walking outside headed towards the Plaza at lunch time. The school had an open campus and most of the students walked to eat and mingle in the city square. As he was walking, he saw Billy in a fight with one of the local 'Cholos', a street thug, a gang banger. Most of them liked being called that. It meant they were revered and often feared. They seldom were alone and messing with one meant messing with them all. He was impressed at how quickly Billy was getting the better of Harvey, but noticed that the others were ready to jump in. Frankie was well known in the Santa Fe gang scene.

He rushed into the circle yelling. "Let them fight it out!" "Be careful ese,' you don't want to mess with us!" A tall muscular Cholo spoke up. He was dressed in old khaki pants and was wearing an unbuttoned long sleeve shirt exposing a white T-Shirt. You could see a large scar running across his chest. The scar got wider as it ran towards the middle and shrank as it got to the other side. "No, I don't, but you don't want to mess with me either! Let them fight it out, unless you think your boy can't handle it?" Frankie did not move forward, but he didn't back away either. "Harvey, take this guy out." The Cholos backed off and in no time at all the fight was over. Billy and Frankie were inseparable from that time forward.

"Sounds good to me. Let's go pick up Little Billy, he's at my house. We got really drunk yesterday and he was still asleep when I left." Antonio looked at Miguel. "You ready to go?" "Let me go inside and let my mom know." Miguel spoke to himself as he went inside. "I probably need to tell them that I can't go!" He had been dating Pat's older sister and he knew that they had fallen in love. On several occasions Billy and himself had double dated with the sisters and he really enjoyed those times. They were filled with happiness and a different kind of excitement, the kind that only comes from young love. "What the hell, we'll probably end up at their house anyway." Miguel walked into the kitchen and the smell of freshly made tortillas filled the air. It was strange how that scent united the Spanish Community in Northern New Mexico. You could smell them at family gatherings and community events. The uniting scent of fresh tortillas was ever present.

Miguel walked up and hugged his mom. "I'll be back, I'm going with Billy to Antonio's, they're waiting for me outside. I'll be back later." Without waiting for an answer, he grabbed some tortillas and headed for the door. "Be careful and stay out of trouble. Be careful around Billy. Your dad talked to his friend Joe, the State Trooper. According to Joe, Billy is getting in deep." Like most mothers of young Spanish males, she worried about her son. Parents were aware of the dangers they faced. The different communities were initially settled by families. Conflicts grew over the years. Family feuds took hold. It was the Spanish version of the Hatfields and McCoys. Some of the familial disputes lasted for generations. This created a violence stronger that gangs in the big cities. "I will mom. Don't worry mom". Miguel was out the door.

"Let's go guys!" Miguel handed each a tortilla. "Where's the butter bro?" "I give you a tortilla and you want me to butter it for you?" Billy was always challenging the group. "If you don't want it, shit, give it to me." Antonio knew it wouldn't happen. Too many times they went hungry as they traveled from place to place, being young and enjoying it. The four of them walked to the highway and put their thumbs up and out. They are well known in this little town and were picked up and given a ride immediately. They were headed north to El Duende, then they would head out to El Guique.

Frankie was enjoying the camaraderie. "What does El Guiche mean? You already told me about El Guache and El Duende." No one seemed to know what El Guiche meant. To us it meant a natural swimming pool. They were dropped off at the 'T' and walked the short distance to Antonio's house. The door was open, they walked into the kitchen where Little Billy was seated eating breakfast. The smell of fresh tortillas filled the air complemented by the sweet aroma of red chili, eggs, and fresh pinto beans. The four of them welcomed each other and the excitement filled the small kitchen. Frankie was introduced to Little Billie. Frankie became one of them that day. "Billy, you and your friends sit down and eat breakfast." Chi immediately went to the wood stove and started cooking the fresh eggs. She was sober this morning and was cheerful as she took care of her boys. She was a surrogate mother and they all loved her. Their love for her was tremendous, even when she was drunk and swinging her arms to the heavens, red faced and swollen. There were times when each of them had wanted to protect her from her husband.

The house was like most of the homes in Northern New Mexico, made of adobes. Most of the homes had been built one room at a time as the family grew. Sociologists labeled these family units as an extended family since three to four generations lived in the same dwelling. You could see where rooms had been added on as the family grew. The building materials were the same, but the age of the mud showed where they were different. The mud bricks were plastered with mud made from calciche and straw. As time and the four seasons wore down the mud, sheets of the mud plaster would peel off. The community would join in and repair the walls by adding new mud and straw plaster. I often saw them doing this to the old Spanish missions as well. The buildings were almost as old as the dirt they were made from. They looked as if they sprang from the earth. I would learn later that the initial Spanish settlers integrated some of the architecture used by the Moors.

The entry to the house had a small step made of inlaid rocks. The kitchen was small and homely. Like our home in El Guache, the bathroom and the well were outside. The two huge cottonwoods in front of the house provided the perfect amount of shade during the hot summer months. This house was unique in that the kitchen was the largest part of the house and the bedrooms flowed out of the kitchen. The bedrooms did not have doors but were in a straight line and were connected by a long, dark hallway. There was no privacy as you walked down the hallway passing the beds and drawers that were sequential. The rooms were scary to me. The rooms were small, and the beds took up most of the space. There were holes and cracks in the walls. The roof was tall with the vigas holding up the ceiling and the roof.

Entering this house was like going back in time, a blast from the past. The home reflected how poor the people were. They made do with what they had and with what they didn't have. My brother and his friends loved it. Here they were free to be what they wanted. They were not judged. It was always exciting as it became the meeting place for all their friends. Sometimes it became a place to hide from the police, parents, and enemies. In darker times it was a place to heal from the damage inflicted by the life they led and driven by a freedom they chased. It was a doubled edged sword! Their quest for freedom became a prison, they were caught in a web of self-destruction, they just didn't know it or wouldn't acknowledge it.

Chi could barely contain herself, taking care of her boys was one of the few things that gave her true joy. In a world of suffering, their youthful exuberance took her back to a better day when she was young, beautiful, and full of hope. Now here she was, married to a cripple in a wheelchair that treated her like dirt. "Sit down, sit down, let me make you some breakfast! How are you doing my son?" Antonio's mom loved all the young men and boys that always filled her home. She always made it a point to make them something to eat. There were very few rules. She loved them all, they provided an escape from a life that had chosen her. The boys joined in and enjoyed their breakfast and planned their day. "You guys think Tony is home? Let's get going, he's probably home right now." "You guys finish your breakfast first. What are you doing out all the time? Be careful out there." Antonio got that look of disdain. He was ashamed of his parents and sometimes he couldn't hide it. Antonio's dad hobbled into the kitchen to join them. Whenever he heard them in the house he enjoyed sitting down and talking to them. He had grown up hard and poor and he was still living that life. He had really bad arthritis and could barely move.

He talked as if he was a philosopher. As he spoke his shriveled fingers gestured in the air creating the sense of a sad comedy. He told stories to share lessons. He enjoyed playing the part to anyone that would listen. It was difficult for young teens to take him seriously. They all knew about his abuse of Chi and his love of drink and gambling. "Como están esta mañana? How are you guys doing this morning?" Without waiting for an answer, he sat at the old table and motioned for his breakfast. As he sat down, he put his cane against the table and pulled out a bottle of Tokay Wine. Esto me cura, this heals me!" As he took a swig, they all noticed the crunched shriveled fingers. They looked like they were made of small rocks glued together. Everyone knew it was time to go. They pushed away from the table despite Chi's pleas for them to stay longer. "We have to get going, we have to meet Tony." Billy was out of his chair and out the door, the others were right behind him.

Tony was their age but had been driving a long time which made him a very desirable friend. Tony's dad had been killed by a gas explosion that destroyed the family home killing his father. The gas company had acted quickly and paid them more money than the poor in Northern New Mexico ever possessed. Tony's mother took the money and bought a home with running water, indoor bathroom, and lights in every room. They sold the few acres they owned for a fraction of its worth like many others in the valley. They were land rich and money poor. The inherited property for many of them was a liability rather than an asset. The taxes were a drain on their meager earnings.

Every small town had a small store run by outsiders that often gave credit to the poor landowners encouraging them to spend freely. When they were unable to pay, they seized their property. Tony's parents were in the process of having theirs taken away when the tragic explosion took place. His mom was glad she could be rid of it. The little she got added to the proceeds from the settlement with the gas company. She did not understand that she was selling it for a fraction of its worth and that another piece of the Spaniards legacy was being lost. The Spanish had fallen asleep at the wheel. Their isolation had kept them reliant on and attached to a way of life ill-suited to succeed in the capitalism invading their world. Billy, his family, and friends, like most of the young in Spanish Northern New Mexico were caught between the two worlds.

Billy and his friends enjoyed cruising with Tony in his new car, they felt like celebrities. Everyone checked them out when they cruised. All the girls wanted to ride with them which led to multiple hook ups for the young macho men. The new Ford Mustang had a hopped up V8 engine. It had a four-speed transmission with a pistol grip shifter. It was the coolest car these boys had ever been in. Their first stop was a drive-up-window to buy beer. It always surprised me that Tito's bar sold them alcohol knowing they were underage. Tito knew all his patrons and felt safe selling to their kids. His dance hall was a party place for the area and Billy's dad often took his kids there and sat them in the corner while he drank and frolicked. My brothers and I had been playing guitars for as long as we could remember. Often dad would talk Tito into letting us play during intermission. The crowd loved us. We were young but we were very good musicians. More times than not our dad would pick fights with one or two other drunks at the bar, and they would often end up outside. We all remembered one incident when the bar closed, and the party moved outside. We are all told to stand to the side and stay out of the way.

My dad's retelling of the event always went the same way. "Do you guys remember that guy from Medanales that called me out for talking to his wife? I told him it wasn't my fault that she was looking for a real man. Give me another beer." "We remember bro, you took that fool out!" My dad's first cousin Joey was always with him as long as my dad was buying the liquor. "He was dumb when he invited you outside." Joey was doing what he always did, fueling my dad's ego. "He didn't know who he was messing with. When he told you 'Let's go outside and see if you can back what comes out of your mouth' I knew what was going to happen. I couldn't believe the idiot had called you out. Well, he asked for it and you gave it to him."

My dad knew that my mom hated Joey as she blamed him for my dad always being at bars. My mom often paid the price for sharing her feelings. She would not have been surprised to see that we were there late at night watching our dad fight. The other man was bigger than my dad. He was dressed in faded jeans and a long sleeve khaki shirt. He was big with a square jaw and thick eyelashes with a flat nose. It was obvious that he had met up with some fists in the past. His nose was flat and crooked. Anyone looking at him could see that it had been broken at least once. My dad always remembered the details every time he told the story. It did grow a bit with every telling like a flower when it was watered. The State Penitentiary had taught him to remember small details. His life and those of the correctional officers that worked for him depended on it. During his ego driven narratives, he gave as much detail as possible to hold his audience's attention.

As he told his stories, we had our own memories of fear mixed with pride. I remembered this night clearly. We stood silently close to my dad's friends as they yelled out encouraging words. We watched as my dad and the other man circled each other. They reminded me of two Lobos circling each other. The night was dark and cold, the two men looked menacing as they prepared to do battle. My dad and his adversary stalked each other. The moon was shining and appeared to be dancing with the clouds. The night was magical. The clouds lit up as they covered the moon. In and out of the clouds the moon danced. It was a light show like I had never seen before. During one of the dark cloud driven blackouts my dad rushed the other man in a swift motion and the two went at it.

I saw my dad's blow hit the other man in the jaw and instantly there was no sky only two men that looked like animals. A strange feeling came over me. I felt fear sweep through my body. The man threw a kick that caught my dad on the leg. "You chicken shit, we said we were going to throw 'chingasos', blows, with the hands, not kicks. Okay, let's go!" The man rushed in, my dad side-stepped him and made a move so fast I didn't see it. The man was on his back and a kick to the face followed. We all watched a flow of dark blood reflected by the light of the moon.

My dad hadn't noticed that one of the man's friends had circled to the side of him. "Billy, watch out! A punk is coming at you from the left." Joey was animated as he pointed to a shiny object in the man's right hand. Everyone in the circle looked and saw the knife shimmering in the moonlight. My dad saw it and took his shirt off in a hurry wrapping it around his arm. The two started circling each other. The other man began waving the knife to cut my dad. "I'm going to cut you into little pieces. You guys from El Guache think you're better than everybody else!" With these words the man stepped closer. I could see a look on his face. He glanced at me, and I saw a familiar grin. "We're a lot better than you punks from Medanales. I see your cousins every day in the 'Pinta', the Penitentiary. They turn them into little girls." The man screamed and stabbed with the knife. It struck my dad in the arm, but the shirt trapped the blade and my dad punched him in the face.

Instantly another man went at him catching him with a blow on the chin. As my dad stepped back from the blow, I saw Joey grabbing something from the trunk. "Billy!" Joey was holding a crowbar above his head making a motion like he was going to throw it. My dad looked at him and shook his head yes as he circled away from the two attackers. Joey tossed the bar towards my dad. We all watched as the bar floated through the air. It was a perfect throw. Dad caught it and in a single motion swung and caught the knife wielder on the side of the head.

It was as if the electricity had been cut off. The man melted into the black, landing with a thud. "Now, what were you saying?" The other man stepped back. He had seen enough. "No more, that's enough." "Okay, just don't ever mess with us again." I felt relieved. I saw Joey and another man patting my dad on the back. I wondered why none of them had backed my dad up when they were ganging up on him. Joey did throw him the bar but had not stepped into the circle. Maybe my mom was right. My dad bought the beer, and all the others did was drink and enjoy the ride. I never liked Joey after that. I saw through his fake smile as he held up a beer my dad had paid for.

Now here they were, Billy and his friends pooling their money at the same place. How much do we have?" Tony made them buy the beer, after all they were in his car. They bought a case of Schlitz Malt liquor and before they knew it, they were in El Guiche by the river hanging out. El Guiche was so small that if you blinked you missed it. The magic was the river that flowed right next to highway, the water flowed slow and deep. There was a secret swimming spot known to the locals. Eons before a huge boulder had rolled down the hill and fallen into the river. Over the years the river had carved away at the dirt under the rock creating a huge hole around the rock, perfect for swimming. There were a few spots like this up and down the Rio Grande. This one was much bigger than the one near our farm. The rock was normally under water. To find it one had to park on the side of the narrow road, cross a fence and find the barely visible ripple on the surface.

"Throw me one over here!" Billy motioned to Frankie. "Here it goes, don't miss, the river will take it, we only have a case." The five were in the river in their underwear, whooping and hollering, splashing around, and using the underwater rock as a diving board. They glistened in the sun. Their young, muscled bodies embodied the beauty of life. They were unaware that these days were fleeting. I had heard my grandfather talk about his youth. The stories he told made it obvious that he had lived in a different world.

The now antique horse drawn wagon under our tree had been a standing testament of that time long gone. On one of our summer-day adventures we had taken to destroying the wagon just for fun. His anger and his pain had taught us a painful lesson, a little late for the wagon. We didn't realize that the past flowed into the future, the two were one. That wagon had been a reminder of grandpa's past, and we had taken it from him. We were always doing things like that. "You're only young for a short time and old for a long time." My grandfather often shared his wisdom with us. I wish we had paid attention.

As the young boys enjoyed their reverie in the slow-moving river, a car approached slowly. The car was a blue lowrider with four very brown low riders inside. The 1960 Chevy Impala was low to the ground, and it looked magical to the river swimmers. It was a baby blue with metal flakes that reflected the sun and made the baby blue shimmer. The wheels were smaller than stock. They were the highly coveted Cragar Rims. "Check it out, the boys from Cordova, what are they doing here? Remember, we got into it with a bunch of them! Pay attention and see if they stop and get out." Billy's words were not necessary, the group had turned silent and still. "Let's go see what they want." Frankie was unaware of the feuds that existed among the small villages that surrounded Española. Española was in the center of all the small towns and villages. It was the hub, and they were the spokes. "Pass me another beer Little Billy." "Here you go bro, what do you think?"

Little Billy was tossing and looking at the same time. "I think we better stay out here and see if they come back!" Earlier that day Antonio had reached into his pocket and pulled out a small pistol. "I'll stay out here bro in case those pussies come over here." Antonio walked on the river's bank, they sat next to his shirt and pants. The Lowrider came to a stop and the four low riders inside looked out over the river assessing who was swimming in the water. Billy listened as one of them spoke. "Are those the punks that beat up Carlos?" "It looks like them, let's go see if they want to try it with us. We owe them a good ass kicking." "Not now." The front seat passenger spoke. "We'll catch them down the road." The baby blue Lowrider slowly drove off, sparkling in the sun. It looked ominous to Billy and his friends. All of them understood it was not over.

The boys swam in the river all afternoon, their joy was overwhelming. As they got out of the river, they were discussing how they were going to get some more beer. They were just getting started and their plans included partying well into the night. "Let's go to Tito's!" Billy knew there was a wedding dance going on. "I know what to do, we can trick Tito and take the beer. When we get there ask around about who got married. We can then go in as if we know them. Antonio you and Miguel start a fight. Tito will have no choice but to leave the bar and the drive-up-window to stop the fight. When he does, the three of us will take some beer and a couple of bottles if we can!" Billy smiled, he remembered Santiago and his friends pulling a chocolate raid at the 7-to-11 in Santa Fe. The group of five were alive with anticipation. Each of them praising Billy for his craziness and planning. The plan worked perfectly. They laughed all the way back to Antonio's. "Let's change our clothes and get going." "Sounds good to me, but let's eat first. After they had changed their cloths and eaten dinner, they were off cruising in Española. As the night wore on, the traffic on the streets was reduced to the cruisers.

My grandfather used to admonish us that only the devil was out passed midnight. Billy and the boys were extremely drunk and out of money and out of gas. They decided that it was time to go home. "Drop me off at the Horsemen's Haven. The waitress gets off at two. She wants me to take her and do the nasties." Antonio laughed, obviously anticipating the action that lay ahead. "Okay bro, we'll see you in the morning. Say hello to the waitress. Let us know what she serves you for breakfast." They all laughed as they said their goodbyes. Billy and his friends went home only to wake up and have Antonio's family knocking at the door. "The Staters came by looking for Antonio. I guess he got into it with some guys from Cordova and he killed one of them." The dad was intense holding on to his cane. The mom had red splotches on her face.

"We talked to Sandra, the girl he was with. Sandra told us that when they were walking out to her car, a baby blue Lowrider pulled up to them and started threatening him. He told them that they better get away from him or pay the price. According to Sandra, they parked, got out, and walked towards him and threatened him." "Let's see how tough you are without Billy here to protect you?" Antonio boldly replied. "I don't need Billy to take care of a punk like you. I'm not stupid. I know it's not going to be a fair fight, there's four of you. I'm warning you, if you take another step towards me, I'll kill you!" "According to Sandra, Antonio pulled a small pistol pointing it at the guy in the front. Did you know he had a pistol?" Billy looked at the parents and shook his head. "I told him not to stay alone, but you know how he is. He told me he had one. I thought he was kidding, he never showed it to me." Billy lied, he did not want them to know that he had seen the gun and had not done anything.

Antonio was a couple of years older than the others and had a mind of his own. During the next few days, he was nowhere to be found. After a few days the word got out that he had turned himself in at the Tierra Amarilla Courthouse. The man he had killed had a brother that worked at the Española jail so he couldn't turn himself in there. After Antonio shot the man, the others ran back to the car in a frenzy, they were yelling. "We'll be back, we are going to kill you!" Antonio rushed off and word had it that he swam across the Rio Grande to get to the other side and followed the riverbank back to El Duende where he hid. It took him a full day to get home. The riverbank was thick with growth, and he had to get into the water several times to make it through. He slept on the ground in a panic. He knew he was in deep trouble. There was a hole inside, he knew it was not going to go away. "What am I going to do?" He wept as he slept.

He got up from his slumber. "I've got to run, it's time to say goodbye." He spoke to the river. The vision of the man he had killed flashed as he ran. The eyes had pierced through the night, his anguish and disbelief permeated the night air, time stood still. He looked into eternity and saw this man's life flowing backwards as if returning to his ancient past. The dark deep flow of the blood oozing out of his chest through the shirt into the dirt was stuck in his soul. The young man was dead. The red morning sky at dawn reminded him of the life blood that had flowed as the young man's life had ended. He had seen a lot in his short life, and he knew his life would never be the same. He prayed like he had never prayed before believing that there was a God. He began a conversion to Jehovah Witnesses that would transform his life forever. When he awoke from his journey all he heard was the clanging of metal doors as he sat in his cell. He sat on the dirty metal cot and wept. Then he wiped away the tears and got ready to survive what waited for him. He was on his way.

"He was sentenced to serve 2-to-10 years for involuntary manslaughter. Billy and his friends were shocked by the news. "Did you know he had a gun?" Miguel asked them all. Little Billy responded. "I kind of suspected it, he kept talking about what would happen if those low riders from Cordova messed with us." "I knew he had it, he showed it me." Billy had seen it and wished he had one. Guns were hard to come by. Antonio had traded a transmission for it no questions asked. "It's too bad that it went down this way. I hear the dead dude's family is talking revenge all over town. We took one of theirs, they are going to take one of ours." Miguel knew people from Cordova. He had a cousin of his that had married into one of the main families up there. They were on fire!

Someone was going to pay! Billy spoke to calm them down. "My dad and the other correctional officers will make his time as easy as possible. My dad had a talk with Antonio warning him not to talk to him or even say that he knows him. If he does, they will label him a rat and he will have to be put into segregation with the rats, queers, and anyone thought to be involved with law enforcement. I heard my dad talking to one of the guards he met at the gas station. They are going to make up something about Antonio that is bad and put him in the hole so that the convicts will see him as one of them. It will make his time easier." The talk went on for a few weeks until it became a side note.

My brother's problems began to escalate. I was scared for him because I knew he had no fear. I wondered why God didn't answer my prayers and bring Billy back home. I saw him sporadically between our visits to El Guache and his to Santa Fe. He would come around with his friends, sometimes the old crew, sometimes with new friends, sometimes with both. I guess my parents had given up on keeping him home in Santa Fe and in school. My Grandfather became his surrogate father but had no chance of controlling him.

It was a bright sunny day when Billy and his friends rolled up in a couple of vehicles. It was mid-afternoon. "Juan greeted them as they got out of the cars. "We're out of food Billy. You were supposed to get us some. Dad and mom gave you money to buy us some." Billy quickly came up with a solution. He had us wade in the irrigation ditch till we got to a few properties up. Instead of stealing cherries from the tree, he sawed off a couple of branches and we floated them down the irrigation ditch to our home. Next, we snuck into the neighbor's yard and took some rabbits. We cooked them outside. It was gourmet to us. My parents had taken us food and money for food, but Billy and his crew had a heck of an appetite.

Chapter | 24

THE BEAT GOES ON

It's pitch-black in my room. I'm extremely tired and even though I fight if off, I slowly drift to sleep. I've been having premonitions and I don't want to sleep. "I don't want to get on that train!!! I don't want to see the conductor, or the passengers!!!" In my dreams I travel through the universe of time, not understanding. "I just want to stay home!!!" The voices in my head grow louder and stronger as I fight to stay awake. I ooze back into the Ghost Train like lava flowing out of a volcano slowly flowing downhill. I want to stop but I can't. I'm keeping up with a figure ahead of me. No matter how fast I run I can't keep up. It's Billy again. I see him getting deeper and deeper into the fog. It is pitch black yet there is a glow around him. I follow him as he boards, the train starts to move. I run and grab unto the handle near the door. I am being pulled forward; the handle is ice cold. I can't hold on much longer. I feel my fingers start to release and I feel the warmth on my hand as I am pulled into the compartment.

The fog is lifting. I look out the window as the train rolls north, passing large piles of burning debris. The smoke and ash rise to the sky then settle on the ground. Images flash as we pass through. I see the face of the Conductor looking at me wearing that grin of longing on his face. He has something in his hands, it's the medal of Saint Martin. I can swear it's the one I gave to Billy. It's very shiny as if the Conductor is holding a star in his hand. The train slows and I notice a young man sitting on a horse looking on as Native Americans are herded into a line. At the front of the line is an iron clad soldier with a sword and a fire canon. The natives have come to fear the fire stick. They have seen it splatter a person like smashing a pumpkin on the ground, moist pieces flowing in all directions. As each man is brought forward his foot is placed on a brownish red rock. The native families watch and cry out in their native language, some wailing and some cursing. A few of the males rush forward to protect their family members and are cut down by the Spaniards. Their foot is cut off and sealed with the fire. Their screams and wailing echo through the empty space surrounding the Acoma Pueblo, the Sky City.

Acoma Pueblo is comprised of several mud structures built on top of a mesa. There is one way in and one way out. The Spanish Conquistadores have fought their way in and taken it. The screams are having an impact on the entire pueblo. You can see the hatred in their eyes, those who stand, sit, and prostate themselves echo their screams to their god, waiting for a great chief to arrive and drive the Spanish from their land, they never come. The spirits of anguish flow through the cabin of the train from the outside, they become a part of it as they are living bricks on a wall. Hot tears roll down my face. I see the Conductor jump off the windows he has been clinging to outside the train. His movements are like a Walking Stick on a tree branch as he moves to the front of the train. He has been perched on the outside with his head turning 360 degrees viewing it all. The Conductor hops over to the pile of legs and grabs one in each hand with a smile of vengeance. The pain, anger, and sadness have become part of the Ghost Train.

I hear a voice floating in the air. "It looks as if you are questioning why the train continues on its journey north. Out of fear the natives attacked and killed some of Oñate's family members. I hear your thoughts, why do families kill each other? Instead of forgiveness and understanding they choose to kill." I feel the warm hand on my shoulder, it comforts me as I sit apart. I recognize the voice. "You must hold on and not lose faith." The voice disappears as quickly as it arrived. The wheels grind forward. Once again, I see an apparition that looks like Billy. He is surrounded by voyagers laughing as they pass a bottle around. The train is traveling through red liquid, pain and suffering permeate the walls that imprison us. I think about the young soldier that is watching as the feet are being cut. I recognize him, I don't know how, he is the son of Santiago Martinez following in the military path of generations past. In the back of my mind, I wonder why the train keeps moving. I see a white light breaking in front of us, fighting to cut through the swirl of red.

I notice that passengers have changed. I see a hint of hope on their faces. I see babies in mothers' arms, the shade of their skin is darkening as the train moves forward. I see that the priest's demeanor has also changed. I hear two talking to each other. "Saint Francis of Assisi showed us the way, all life is sacred. Our struggle continues, the trials and tribulations of man keep this train moving." "Yes, and we must keep moving with it, we are the only thing that stands in front of annihilation of all that is good." As the train moves, I realize that the good is always there. Why do we focus only on the evil? Have we always had to focus on that? My young mind reflects on my life and the lives of my loved ones. We focus on the bad because it is the force that wants to destroy us. The good nourishes us but the bad threatens to destroy us. I am learning amidst the Conductor's continued pursuit that there is no escaping the duality of who we are, who we have been, and what we will be.

Once again, I rush out of the train only to find myself in chaos. I see families packing, running, all of them are scared and urgent. "Hurry up, let's go. Leave it, the Indians are slaughtering families. "The savages have turned on us, after all we have done for them! After taking them from their paganism into the warm hands of our lord Jesus Christ. We offered salvation through the love of our King, our Catholic Pope, and the Franciscan Friars and now they slaughter us likes dogs." Their cry echoes through La Villa Real de la Santa Fe de San Francisco de Assisi. I know from my aunt and uncle that in English it means, The Royal city of the Holy Faith (Santa Fe) of Saint Francis of Assisi.

I look up towards the heavens and see a bird I have never seen. I hear my dad's voice. "Look on that tree, that's a Red-Tailed Hawk. Look, the colors are different from the Eagle I showed you guys last week." My dad was always showing us the wonders of the earth like the horse head image in the Sangre de Christo mountains and the cliff dwellings in Bandelier. But this bird he had never pointed out to us, and it was above me now. As it hovers, it looks like a kite my neighbors fly. The wings are spread out from the body. The body is on fire and the wings look like the flames are burning to spread out its power. I can see that the bird is old. There is chanting floating through the wind. I listen as the chanting comes from the four directions. I see the Zia symbol on our state flag and understand what it means now.

The firebird is releasing its flames like the lines extending out from the Zia Symbol and feeding into each other creating a circle. The chanting sounds sad as if it is crying out asking for the return of something lost. The Firebird shoots fire down to the earth and the few buildings built from wood begin to burn, adding destruction to the carnage. I look up and I follow the migratory trail of the fleeing Spaniards and some of their native converts. The smoke from the burning is highlighted by the brown and green background of the surrounding mountains. The fire has spread to some of the trees, adding charcoal to the mix as trees are consumed. The fire is alive as it dances from tree to tree. As I look up, I think I recognize the mountain from its steep incline.

I do, it's where the Cross of the Martyrs is. We went there a few days back. The views were awesome as we looked down at the panoramic view of Santa Fe. We checked out the metal cross. The metal cross that sits atop the mountain is a testimonial to the events the train has brought me too. On our visit, I noticed that there were names of priests forged on a plaque that is part of the monument. I recognize now that those are the priests that are being massacred as they flee the city. The inscriptions on the cross are being formed in front of me. When we saw the cross, we noticed that names are followed by the names of the surrounding pueblos where the priests were assigned to convert the natives and where they worked and loved them as well. They were overtaken by a simultaneous attack on the Spanish occupiers.

The Firebird has lowered in its hover and is breathing fire over the chaotic scene. He gets bigger as more Spaniards die in the flames. I can see the Indians dancing around chanting to the Firebird. The dead number in the hundreds. Some of the bodies are being trampled by the desperate evacuation. A trail of blood marks the death marching out of the city. The firebird continues to grow as it hovers directly over me. I start to cry and scream out for it to go away. The shadow drifts down over the high city as I watch. I look up at the mountain and see a soldier that has turned and is looking at the carnage, it's Billy. I open my mouth to call out to him but before the words come out, he turns and rides away. The chanting is slow and loud, and it feels as if it is echoing through me. I have heard the chanting before at some of the pueblos during Christmas. The one in Taos stands out. As the blood smoke rises, I am taken to a Christmas past celebration in Taos.

It is near midnight in Taos, and we are seated inside the small catholic church that is across from the ancient pueblo structure in the Taos Indian Pueblo. Once again, I am awake in my dreams. I feel my body, but my spirit seems to have escaped. Even though I am young I sit in awe of the contrast between the ancient and the recent. Two worlds sitting next to each other, separate and apart, sharing the same time in space. My thoughts are confusing as I sit through the ritual of Midnight Mass. The Priest is of Spanish descent but most of the congregation is Native American.

"Let's go, hurry up." My mom is leading us out of the church, we become part of the human tunnel that is forming a path from the church to the cold midnight air. There are several 'luminarias' outside rising out of the snow. It is quiet, the crowd is waiting for something. "Here they come, what are they going to do?" Arthur reflects the wonderment we are feeling. "Be quiet and pay attention." My mom was very forceful when she had to be, that was every time she took us out into the social world. 'Boom, boom, boom, boom, boom! The echoing of the drums unites us all, Anglos, Spanish, Indian, and a mix of tourist and visitors.

The procession is moving slow to the beat of the drums, and we are all part of it. The drums are speaking to us, drawing us in to an ancient place. "Why are they dressed like that?" Michael's curiosity got the better of him. His voice is too loud as those around us turn and look at us, some of the looks are not friendly. My mom reaches over and pinches Michael, he knows what it means. The pinch is a reminder of what will happen if he continues. "Where is your brother?" As she asks the question, she looks over at Juan who has been enjoying the procession. He hasn't heard her or is pretending not to hear her. She nods at Arthur gesturing for him to get Juan's attention. "Did you see where your brother went?" "I saw him talking to some girls, they were walking that way." Juan points with his chin towards the back of the church. "Go get him, tell him to get over here or he will hear from his father. We will not wait for him when it's over, it's a long walk back?" The last statement worried me, there was a foot of snow on the ground.

I wake as I hear our home come to life. I rush out of bed. It is calming to my spirit. I am home. Something doesn't feel right, it looks like if I am at home, but I know something is wrong. As I step into the small hallway, I smell it. It is dark and damp. I hear heavy breathing coming from the living room. I inch forward and see Billy on top of a girl, or a woman, he is naked and moving on top of her. He is unaware that I am there, but the woman looks at me and smiles as if she has caught a prize. It reminds of what it felt like when we caught fireflies and kept them in a jar. Billy notices that she is looking at me and his face contorts into the white blood-filled skeleton I have come to fear. I turn and I run. I am back in Taos. Boom, Boom, Boom, Boom! The drums continue beating in unison with the flow of life. As the drums boom, I am reliving some of my life and remembering how important the celebrations of Christmas have always been to us. Everyone goes to church and often visit the surrounding pueblos. Each has a unique celebration as they blend our catholic celebration with their traditional beliefs and spiritual manifestations. "Stop complaining and pay attention."

My mom is glaring at Juan and glaring at us. I stand there in a white night, cold. I wish I was home. Juan has come back from looking for Billy. "I couldn't find him. He is nowhere to be seen." What he doesn't tell her is that he found him kissing with a girl and told Juan to go back and tell mom he didn't see him. When Juan reminded him of what mom had said Billy's response was not a nice one. "Go tell mom what I told you and make her wait for me or else you know what I'll do to you!"

Some of the natives stay in the church and the rest of us wait outside. We all stand in a wonderland covered with the moon illuminated snow and the moon illuminated sky. The people look like statues in the bright light that is being reflected off the snow. I am confused! I just saw this! I feel like I have seen this before only now it's from the past. In an instant I hear the chanting and the chief of the pueblo is leading a procession out of the church. I see that most of the natives have a trance like look on their face as they walk by. I see that they are walking with an air that thickens as they move further from the church. Instantly, huge piles of logs and sticks are set on fire turning night into day, melting the snow around them. The area in front of the church is now brown and wet, like a dirt island in the middle of a white sea. I had noticed the stack of wood earlier; they were at least ten feet tall.

"Those are 'luminarias', see how big they are? It means luminaries because they light up the sky. The ones we put up in the paper bags with the candles inside are called 'farolitos', small lanterns. It really makes me mad when the gringos call the luminarias 'farolitos', they're dumb and they continue to do it even when we explain it to them." My mom's explanations come to me all the time. The procession is moving away from the luminarias. I start to follow when one of the Indians tells me I can't. I would find out later that they were on the way to their Kiva where they would spend the night praying to their ancient Gods. Outsiders were not allowed. They still harbor resentment towards the Spaniard for defiling the Kiva. Upon their arrival, the Spanish Conquistadores had used the kiva as a makeshift corral. I feel the blood coursing through my body. I feel the drums as the procession moves forward in time. They are a part me but so is the harsh Spanish presence. I am two rivers of blood becoming one.

Boom, Boom, Boom, Boom! I am back to the smoke rising from the city of the Holy Faith, Santa Fe. The cries of the Spanish continue as they run for their lives. They see their new life go up in smoke. As they flee, they watch their new homes burn. The wailing of mothers for their children being murdered join in the cacophony of the drums, the Conductor hovers. He watches as 400 men, women, and children are murdered. Native unrest had been growing for decades as the Spanish Settlement grew in its oppression and conversions of their people.

Po'pay had grown up seeing, hearing, and living with the cries of his people. He was from 'Ohkay Owingeh', San Juan Pueblo as named by the Spanish. San Juan was on the other side of the river from us in

El Guache. We had engaged in many a shouting match with them. In a subtle way the battle taking place on this night journey was still being fought. Billy had encountered them a couple of times when he swam across the river. I had worried about him. We could see the fire in their eyes all the way across the Rio Grande separating our two worlds. I heard a priest on his way out of the burning city. "The wrath of our heavenly father will fall on the heathen attacking his people. Po'pay has led this rebellion and the mighty sword of God will find him and strike him dead and cast him into the pit of the burning inferno."

Po'pay led the revolt. Through a series of secret meetings, he had devised a very unique method of synchronizing the united revolt of all the Pueblos. In accordance with the agreement, he sent runners to each Pueblo with a piece of rope. Each rope had several knots tied into them. Each rope had the same number of knots. "We will strike together as one. Our people have suffered enough, we must drive the oppressor out of our land forever. The battle must be swift! They must not be allowed to leave to ensure that they do not go south and bring more soldiers and settlers to our lands." The strongest young men were sent out to deliver the ropes. Each of them got to their assigned Pueblos on the assigned day to ensure that they all attacked on the same day. Each pueblo was to untie one knot every day. When they got to the last knot they were to rise and drive the Spanish out of their land.

The revolt almost failed. The Spanish caught the runner from the Tesuque Pueblo and tortured him until he revealed what the knots meant. In response, Po'pay sent out runners to update the plan and the attacks occurred one day early. The natives stole the horses from the Spanish in Santa Fe so that they could not flee. In the end, all the Spanish Settlements were destroyed with 400 dead, including 21 out of the 33 Franciscan Friars. On the way out the Spanish Priests took the Statue of 'La Conquistadora', the Virgin Mary with them. La Conquistadora would lead the way back in the reconquest 12 years later led by Don

Diego De Vargas. The 'Entrada', the reentry into Santa Fe became a yearly event as a celebration, the Fiestas. The Fiestas symbolized the peaceful re-entry into Santa Fe and as a reminder to all of the resiliency of the Spanish Empire.

The Franciscans had done a lot of good in the Pueblos and most of them treated the natives with love and compassion. Sadly, some of those in leadership got overzealous in their attempts to wipe out the native religions. By forbidding their worship and destroying artifacts and art related to their traditional religious practices they maligned the Pueblo leadership. Spain was on the brink of withdrawing from the north due to the disappointment over not finding the riches they anticipated. The gold promised from the legendary Seven Cities of Gold had turned out to be a myth. The cities had turned out to be pueblo buildings made of mud with mica embedded in them. The mica reflected in the sun and the Spanish scouts sent to recon the area had seen them from a distance. They feared getting any closer. The reflection of the sun integrating with the brown earth gave the impression that they were made of gold. When they returned to what is now, modern day Mexico, they spread the news. There were entire cities made of gold! The Spanish migration north was underway, led by the Conquistadores, the Franciscans, and later, the settlers. The Franciscans convinced the Crown not to abandon this part of the world. The Franciscans convinced the Crown that the church was doing God's work.

The Spanish Crown was convinced that wealth was not to be found and sent word that they were to abandon the settlements and head south, the cost was too high. The Franciscans increased the number of conversions and petitioned the crown to maintain the settlements as a gift and testament to the Lord and Savior Jesus Christ. The Crown was convinced and agreed, so the conversions continued. In the process, the Spanish Alcaldes, the Mayors, of the settlements began to tax the Natives for their labor, agricultural products, and other items of value. There were many Spaniards that worked to put a stop to the abusive treatment but were silenced when some of them were taken back to Spain and brought in front of the Inquisition and charged with heresy. The natives in their resentment began to attack the settlers. The nomadic tribes were the most ferocious as they were always on the move. The Spanish soldiers had a hard time retaliating, they couldn't find them. The revolt put an end to it as the native's began destroying all evidence of the Spanish.

As they flee Santa Fe, I can see several bodies of massacred priests, men, women, and children in a pile. I am standing in silence as blood falls from the sky. I am mortified as I watch a dark cloud approach the dead. The dark cloud is hovering over them and is morphing into the Conductor. He eats their flesh as he mocks me, smiling as his body turns redder with each bite. I see swine, birds, and insects join in the feast. I turn and run as the train begins to move.

I remember the words of the spirit lady. "Don't get left behind, you will have to stay here forever!" There was no way I was going to stay here. I run for my life, faster than I have ever run before. I grab unto a handle on the back of the train and am lifted into the air. I feel a warm hand grab and pull me into the train. As I land aboard the ghost train, I see the grandson of Santiago Martinez, Guillermo Martinez (Billy), smiling at me through the bloody red window of the fleeing train. He gets smaller and smaller until he is a living dust particle sitting on his gilded horse. He is a part of the Conquistador procession fleeing Santa Fe. The statue of La Conquistadora is leading the way out, the way she had led the way in.

Chapter | 25

HERE I GO AGAIN

"Wake up Santiago, you'll miss the bus!" My eyes opened with a joy that was hard to contain. My mom was looking down at me, her love warming me and saving me from the terror and uncertainty of my night on the Ghost Train. I jumped out of bed. School was a safe place for me, most of the time. I felt important there. I felt free there even when I was acting like a bull in a china shop. Unfortunately, I often did a lot of damage, leaving others to clean up my mess. I did pay for the damage, one way or the other. I got out of bed and my younger brother Michael was already eating breakfast.

Michael challenged me on everything until I was driven to kick his butt. The only problem was that I was always treated as the one at fault. Through all this, we were always there for each other. He started as many fights as I did. Him and his little pack of friends were always around. Many times, I came to their rescue, more times than that, I was around to keep the fight fair. Michael was a tough little kid. Many times, his friends were the younger brothers of my friends. I was in the sixth grade, and he was in the fifth.

"Hurry up, we are going to miss the bus!" Michael yelled as he ran out the door. I ran after him, and we got on the bus. The bus driver admonished and warned us to behave. The current bus driver was the owner of the buses. We had driven so many bus drivers away he had to drive this bus himself. Some of things we did were truly amazing and disturbing like the time we created a special holiday for ourselves. "My brother will be right here. He forgot his books." Michael implored the bus driver, Buddy. Meanwhile a couple of us were putting a board with nails under the rear tires. The nails were driven through the 2 x 4, so that the sharp end stuck out enough to puncture the tires.

"Glad you decided to join us. You know what time you have to be here, next time I'll have to leave you. It's not fair to the rest of us to be late because you can't make it on time." Buddy pulled the lever and closed the door. We smiled all the way to the back of the bus. Some of the kids from Cerrillos had seen us doing our dirty deed but were afraid to say anything. "You guys are going to get into trouble one of these days and will not be able to get out of it." Buddy was a nice guy. He had long wavy hair that he parted in the middle. He tried to give us good advice. We just laughed and noticed that Buddy was looking at us through the rear-view mirror waiting for us to sit down. The bus lurched forward, and we were on our way. We heard as the board hit the side of the bus, the tires had picked up the board with the nails. A quiet excitement filled the back of the bus, we were pulling over to the side of the road.

"All of you, stay on the bus." We had traveled almost to the two miles, the 'Y" where Highway 14 merged unto US 285. We watched as Buddy walked to the rear of the bus shaking his head. "Listen up, we have a flat tire." As planned, we had stopped the bus requiring Buddy to figure out a way to get us to school. We waited for another bus to pick us up. As we sat in the back laughing, patting each other on the back, Buddy confronted us. "Did you do this? Is this what you were doing while I was waiting for you?" Buddy was angry but he was also sad. He had been nice to us. I liked him.

Juan stood up and took a single step forward. "We didn't do anything. Why do people blame us every time something happens?"

As he spoke Arthur, Michael, and me stood up. "Sit down right now or I will throw you off the bus and your parents will have to figure out how to get you to school every morning." I saw a new side of Buddy that morning. I could see he meant it and that he could do it. We sat down. "Remember, we didn't do it." We turned it into an adventure. While we waited for another bus to pick us up, we acted up and played around with each other. Buddy had to get a ride into town leaving us on the bus with a warning to stay inside. All the kids complied except for the pen gang. As soon as we saw Buddy climb into the car we piled out off the bus and started clowning around.

We crossed the barbed wire fence and began looking for lizards, horned toads, and snakes. We found them all, including a rattlesnake. We were very familiar with their hiding places. Arthur had picked up a stick and began to poke into the high desert bushes and we heard the rattle that always reminded me of death. In a short time, the snake was dead. Juan had the rattles, another one to be put into dad's guitar. Buddy got transferred to another bus after that. We heard later that he had given the owner an ultimatum. If the owner didn't move him, he was going to quit. The Pen Gang had struck again! The owner was driving the bus.

Our mischief continued. The bus driver was furious. His disbelief and disgust were written on his face. This was one of many scenes that were played out on our trips to and from school. We had taken over the bus and picked on the other kids all the time. We threw spit wads, wadded up paper, and just bullied everyone on the bus. I felt sad. I had a very good friend that lived south of us in the small village of Cerrillos. On one of our escapades, he became the victim. He looked at me and I could see the hurt on his face. I lost a good friend that day. The other 20 or so students on the bus detested us but were afraid to confront us. The pen gang was more than they could handle.

We laughed and caused trouble every day. On several occasions we were confronted and threatened with expulsion from the bus. The problem was that they couldn't tell who did what and we didn't tell on each other. Eventually our antics quieted down a bit once our parents had to meet with the school. They were at the point that we knew it was time to stop it for our own good. There was no pranking our parents. My dad wasn't into spanking. His corporal punishment was Penitentiary style to be avoided at all costs. The following year Eddie attended St. Michaels, a Catholic School. His parents had made the decision to separate him from us.

"Santiago, come up to the board and do the first math problem for us." Mrs. Taylor spoke with a gentle authority. She was my favorite teacher ever. I could tell she cared for me. She spent time with me and shared advice. She sat me in the front of the class and called on me every day. "Very good Santiago, I see you have been doing your homework." I never knew where she was from. She wasn't from the tumultuous world I came from. She was kind and very smart.

Our room was decorated with the work we produced and all of us kids were represented. She would make us all line up and take us outside on nice days. We would sit around the playground, and she would hold class outside. One day as we sat out there, she asked us questions about what we wanted to be when we grew up. A lot of the kids answered enthusiastically. "I want to be a doctor!" "I am going to be a lawyer!" "Not me, I want to be a basketball player!" The dreaming continued with some of the kids wanting to be a nurse, a policeman, a soldier. My classmates all answered in a jumble, speaking all at once with their dreams and aspirations. "How about you Santiago, what do you want to be when you grow up?"

It felt strange to me that I had never thought about that. I was too busy surviving the present, the future was short term, day to day. My future was what was I going to find when I got home. I kept quiet for a long time; the only sound was the movement of my class waiting for an answer that never came. It wasn't very often that I didn't have anything to say. "Okay class, time to go inside and get ready for lunch." Mrs. Taylor rose and led us back to the classroom. I had an uneasy feeling. I felt lost. What was I going to grow up to be? I guess I just wanted to grow up and have a family that was not in pain all the time. It was as if we took turns creating our own misery. I thought about how every time life started to brighten for us a tragedy would shatter it like a rock busting through glass. Time to clean up the mess again with our blood, sweat, and tears. I guess I just wanted it to end and hoped that something better would begin. Only time would tell.

"Who were you laughing at today in class, punk?" When I didn't respond to the questions of my career plans, Carlos from La Cienega had made a comment to the kids around him. I could hear them laughing. I felt the anger and shame as I turned my head to look at him. He ignored me but I knew what was going to happen. Carlos was very dark complexioned, darker than me and built like a tree trunk. Him and I had almost bumped heads a couple of times but always managed to walk away. "I wasn't talking about you, but I'm not afraid of you." He sneered as he walked towards me. "Let's see bro." I walked towards him at the same time. As soon as we were face to face. He swung so fast I didn't see it coming. I could feel the warm blood in my mouth as I staggered back. He smiled as he rushed me and kicked me just missing the family jewels. I felt the pain move up my body. I muttered through the pain, unbelieving what had just happened. "Is he going to beat me up?" Carlos rushed me again. I swung hitting him on the side of the head.

I felt a sharp pain shoot through my hand all the way up to my head. In an instant Carlos was on the ground. I had knocked him down. "Get up, let's finish this!" "Santiago, what do you think you're doing, come here this instant." The other sixth grade teacher was walking towards me. Mr. Jimenez was a nice teacher. He was tall and wore black framed glasses. He did not look very nice as he closed the gap between us. "Let's go, you're going to the principal's office. We are going to call your parents and have a serious discussion about your behavior. Why do you feel the need to settle your differences through violence?" All I could think to say was that Carlos had started it. I was hurting inside, and my hand was throbbing. I wanted to cry but I had been trained not to. In my world if you cried it only got worse. "I don't believe it! You seem to be the one that starts most of the fights out here, let's go to the office." I stood still, after being told repeatedly to go with him to the office. I would not move. "Do I have to carry you?" A crowd of students were standing around. I noticed that Carlos was up on his feet, looking down at his feet. My hand was still throbbing, man he had a hard head.

Mr. Jimenez grabbed me by the arms and picked me up and started walking towards the office with a trail of kids behind us. "Let me go, put me down!" I kept yelling. I reached out and tried to wiggle loose. When I did, I hit him in the face knocking his glasses off. He stopped and put me down holding on to me as he reached down and picked up his glasses. He put them on and started walking, dragging me to the office. His face was red and angry. "I can tell you right now if you continue behaving this way, you will be dead or in prison before you are 18 years old." I was already in prison, no one could understand. Mrs. Taylor, was standing inside the outer office of the principal's office as we walked in.

"Sit down right there and wait!" "What happened Mr. Jimenez?" "We'll discuss it later." He rushed into the principal's office without answering her question. I could hear Mr. Jimenez through the walls, then he stormed out. The principal took me into his office with Mrs. Taylor following behind us. "Tell me what happened." I sat there with my head straight and tears rolling down my face. Here I was again. I did not respond. "Tell us what happened Santiago." Mrs. Taylor joined in. I sat there quietly; I knew they would not believe me. "Go sit out there, we are calling your mom to come and get you. I could see the sadness in Mrs. Taylor's eyes. Her look hurt me the most.

It took my mom a while to get there, they called her work and since she didn't drive, she needed to get a ride to the school. "What did you do now Santiago? Do you want me to get fired? I can't keep leaving my work because you keep doing these things. Your father is not going to be very happy; you know I have to tell him!" The principal heard my mom and asked her into his office. The bell rang and Mrs. Taylor left smiling at me as she did. My mom was in the office for what seemed like an eternity. "Let's go, they're sending you home for today and tomorrow, you can come back Monday." She did not wait for a response she just nudged me through the door. "Over there!" We turned as she pointed to our neighbor's car. Once again, I felt like I was on the road to hell. I didn't care anymore.

I resolved myself to the punishment that would befall me. It had happened so many times I knew it would be physical pain, embarrassment, harassment from my brothers, and pain and compassion from my mom. I wanted to cry and scream at the same time. I felt so alone I could hardly stand it. I wished Billy was around, he always found a way to make it better even if sometimes it was with strong words and every now and then a good shove, a slap on the back of my head, a kick in the ass, and if it was really bad, all the above. I knew he was on my side, and I really wanted him around me today. He had been gone for a few days. He was with my grandfather more than he was with us. My parents had relented and let him live and go to school in Española. The discussion in our house about him to others was that he was living with grandpa and attending Española High School. The story sounded good although most of us knew he had stopped going to school. I realized I was on my own. I knew my mom loved me, but I also knew she was powerless to save me from the punishment that would be inflicted when my dad got home.

SANTA FE: A PIECE OF 'MI VIDA'

The weekend had gone okay. My dad asked me about the fight and wanted to know if I had won. I explained to him and showed him my hand. He took the time to discuss what I had done and that it was not the right way to handle things at school. "Your mom is going to lose her job if she has to keep going to school because you can't seem to behave. Go get my belt, it's on the bed." I walked slowly to his room. I could feel my entire body shake. I felt like a man walking to the gallows, dead man walking. "Hurry up, I don't have all day." Flashes of past beltings filled by mind. I could feel it in my belly. I could hear the change in my dad's voice. His voice got meaner and meaner as time passed, this was a pattern as his frustration of having to deal with us grew. I knew his frustration was growing and changing into anger.

Having to deal with this only served to wind him up, it wasn't good for me. I grabbed the belt and walked back into the living room. I was aware of my surroundings. The Montgomery Ward furniture, our new TV, and my dad standing there fuming. As soon as I handed it to him, he grabbed me by the hair and began whipping me with it. My cries echoed in the house. When he was done, he sent me to my room. I could hear the expletives as I walked by. I was used to the names I was hearing. I saw my mom standing in the hallway, a look of sadness on her face. My brothers had all gone outside, they wanted no part of it.

School continued pretty much the same way with one small change. I stopped challenging the boys on the playground. "Can I go to the bathroom?" I asked Mrs. Taylor. "Go ahead Santiago, make sure you come right back." The hallway was empty. I could see all the kids in their classrooms. Each class was unique and learning in their own little rooms with their own little books and their own little pictures and papers hanging on their own little wall. As I was done using the bathroom I opened the door to go back to my class. I saw Scott walking down the hall and without thinking closed the door and stood against the wall so that when the door opened Scott would not see me. It was quiet in the bathroom. I was excited to play a trick on Scott. I was friends with his older brother, and I thought Scott would be cool with it. The door started to open, it felt as if time had slowed down. As the door opened, I could feel my heart race. As a result of the incident with Mr. Jimenez I had been in the dumps. I felt like my old self again.

As Scott cleared the door, I grabbed him from the back and put a small folding knife I used to carry close to his neck but far enough away to where he could see it. As I did, I was enthralled by how shiny it was. I felt powerful and liked the feeling. I guess it was the opposite of what I felt at home or anytime I was with my dad. Scott's response was nothing like what I expected. He started to scream and shake in a way I had not anticipated. Now I was as scared as he was. I released him and pushed him away. "Scott, it's me! I was just messing around, don't tell on me! I'll make it up to you! I don't want to be in trouble again!" Scott looked at me with a face in shock and fear that made me feel smaller than I had ever felt.

I saw my life flash before me, and panic and sadness came over me. Scott opened the door in tears and ran down the hall to his classroom. I walked outside of the building and started walking towards the spot in the hills that Bruce and I had used as our short-lived runaway refuge. I didn't make it very far. I walked slowly, I guess I wanted to be caught, accepted, loved, and forgiven. The exact opposite was about to occur. The rest of what happened that day is a blur. My mom showed up again. I heard strong discussions in the other room, and I was back in our neighbor's car on my way back to the Penitentiary.

The scene at home was the most severe I had experienced in my short life. The belt was not enough to satiate my fathers need for revenge or whatever drove him to inflict that level of violence on us. I heard him and my mother having several discussions about me. The school had told my mom that I was not to go back until they figured out what they were going to do with me. They wanted to expel me for the rest of the year, but the rules and their experience did not address events like this. Michael showed up on the first day of my exile with my books and a list from Mrs. Taylor on the work she wanted me to do. The list was quite extensive, but I was glad that she still cared. It felt like she was the only one that did. I was left alone every day as everyone else was at work or in school. The days seemed to last forever. I was given a list of chores to do, and my mom checked my homework when she got home. Every day when I was done a silence came over the house. I was alone with the images of the sky over the Ghost Train as it moved forward through time. I knew there was good in the world but in my life the need for warfare seemed to obscure and overcome it.

"What are you doing here?" Billy asked as he walked in the door and saw me in the kitchen doing my schoolwork. "Are you sick or are you in trouble again?" I got up and ran to him and hugged him like I had never hugged anyone before. He nudged me away. "What's wrong with you, what have you done?" I hadn't noticed that Miguel and Frankie King had walked in with him. They both laughed and I did not know why. "Wait here, I'll be right back." Billy went into his room and then into my parents' room. I got scared just watching him go in there, we were not allowed to go in there, none of us had ever had the courage to go in there when my parents weren't there, much less when they were. If they didn't summon us into their room, we were to stay out. We knew my dad kept firearms and knifes in there. I was in awe when he took out his rifles and took use into the mountains so we could watch him shoot them. My dad let Billy shoot them and was amazed at how accurate he was.

Billy walked in there like it was his room. "Stop doing this dumb shit, you have to go to school and do good." I followed them outside and the three lit up their cigarettes and started talking about their plans. "Let me try that." I had followed them outside. Billy grabbed me by the shoulder. "Get inside and stay in there!" As I walked inside, I felt a stiff kick to my ass. I turned around crying more from the pain in my heart than from the pain in my ass. "I'm going to tell dad, why did you kick me?" "Go ahead and tell him and I'll tell him you were asking me to let you smoke." I knew he had me, I sadly went inside and laid down on my bed. "What's wrong with me?" I was alone again. I was a sixth grader, and I was alone!

After a week or so my mom came into my room after dinner. "Tomorrow morning get dressed. We're going to a meeting with the School Board." I didn't know who the School Board was. The ride in was quiet with my mom talking to me. She loved me and wanted me to get an education. "You're so smart, why do you continue to act this way? I know your dad is mean to you guys, but he really does love you." I sat quiet. I was thinking about how a man could love you and treat you like that, you, and everybody you loved. We arrived at a large building that was not at the school. "My name is Adelida Martinez, and we have a meeting." "Yes Mrs. Martinez, go down that hallway and it's first room to the left, they're expecting you."

As we walked in, I saw that people were dressed in suits and nice dresses. They were seated around a large table. I could tell it was serious. I was not used to being surrounded by men in suits. They looked mean to me. I got closer to my mom. I heard someone come into the room. I turned and was surprised and happy to see Mrs. Taylor. She walked up and greeted my mom. She bent down and talked to me. "Good morning, Santiago. Don't worry everything will be alright. We've missed you at school." I almost cried. I loved Mrs. Taylor and I felt that she loved me. I did not believe that everything was going to be okay. I was trapped, there was no way out and I felt myself disappear.

"Please sit down." The man in the middle motioned for us to sit down in chairs on the opposite side of the table. "We have read the principal's letter describing last week's event. We have also spoken to Scott's mother and her concern for the safety of her son. Quite frankly, we are at a loss to understand why this type of behavior has continued. Our inclination is to expel Santiago for the remainder of the year and require that he attend a different school next year. Before we make our decision, we want to hear from you, Mrs. Martinez. We want to understand why your son behaves this way. The level of violence he exhibits is very troubling." I looked up at my mom and felt sorry for putting her through this, she looked small. My mom was five feet tall and slender. She was small to begin with and I had put her in a situation where she looked even smaller. I was very angry with myself. I felt like a failure and at that moment I was wishing I had never been born.

"First, I want to apologize for Santiago's behavior. I know it doesn't make it right, but he was playing a practical joke on that other boy. He never intended to hurt him. Sometimes Santiago doesn't understand that what is funny to him is not funny to everybody else. His father works at the State Penitentiary and our home is in Prison Housing. My husband and I both work and unfortunately, he spends a lot of time isolated with only a few families to associate with. I think that Santiago wants and needs attention that apparently, he is not getting it at home. His older brothers like to horseplay a lot and Santiago is often on the receiving end of it. The level of the horseplay has taught him to be a little aggressive to protect and assert himself. His brothers don't do it to hurt him. He's their brother and gets caught up in the rough housing. Santiago's future is in your hands. Santiago understands that what he did was stupid and has promised us that he will never do it again." I was proud of my mom. She wasn't small anymore. I felt better, knowing she was on my side. As she spoke, I saw her differently. She could be tough and yet in front of my dad she shrunk. Here in front of these men she was strong and articulate.

"May I say something?" Without waiting for an answer my teacher continued. I am Mrs. Taylor, and I am Santiago's sixth grade teacher. I have been working closely with Santiago this year and I have seen potential that is rare in a child of his age with his unique challenges. I want to show you something." Mrs. Taylor handed each board member a copy of my report card. "Please notice that his grades are straight A's. Santiago is a gifted student and I have been working with him to modify some of his inappropriate behavior. Now please look at the right-hand side of the report card rating him on his behavior. You can see that he has gotten unsatisfactory ratings on his ability to work well with others, follow instructions, cooperate, etc. But if you notice, at the beginning of the year his ratings were straight Unsatisfactory, but he has shown improvement. It would be a mistake to take him out of school right now. I will commit to this board that I will monitor Santiago very closely for the rest of the year. I have spoken to Scott's mother, and she is willing to allow it if Santiago stays away from her son. I will guarantee this as well. For the rest of the year, if we agree, Santiago will stay in for recess and lunch and work on extra assignments in my classroom. The school year is two months from completion. I strongly suggest that Santiago be allowed to return to school. Again, look at those grades!"

"We will adjourn this meeting and discuss this very seriously. We will notify you by the end of the week and let you know what our decision is." We left the building with Mrs. Taylor holding my hand. "Mrs. Martinez, is it okay if I talk with Santiago for a minute? I want to give him his assignments for next week." My mom nodded stating that it was okay. "Do you understand how serious this is and how bad what you did to Scott is?" "Yes." "It's okay, I am sure we will work this out. Did you hear what I told the board, you can't go out to the playground for lunch or recess. Do you think you can do that?" "Yes." "Okay, it's a deal." And with a smile that warmed me, we shook hands on it.

"Here's your work for next week. When you come back to school, I want you to bring the completed work to me, do you understand?" "Yes." I took the assignments and walked to our neighbor's car. Minnie was one of the nicest people I had ever met. She was always there for my mom. She knew what my dad did. She lectured me all the way home. I was back in school the following week and did what I promised Mrs. Taylor. I was sad at the end of the year when I said goodbye to her. My fond memories of her would follow me for the rest of my life. I had grown to love her. She had treated me as if I mattered!

Chapter | 26

SHARING THE HEARTACHE

"Oh my gosh... did Miguel tell you that they locked Billy up again?" Pat was having a serious discussion with her older sister Mary. Pat was struggling with mixed emotions. She felt as if she was being pulled apart. She was young and was in the midst of her first love and everything that comes with it. "Yes, I heard what happened? What do you think about it all?" Pat's eyes looked sad to her sister. She knew her well and had seen the red puffy eyes before, she was worried and scared. "I really thought he was going to change but down deep inside I saw this coming. I tried warning him. But of course, he did what he wanted to do. I love the fire in his eyes, the excitement in his heart, the fact that he's so spontaneous. I didn't realize that it would get to this point. Now all I can think about is where it all went wrong. I think his drinking, partying, and going out looking for trouble with his friends is his way of coping with all his dad puts him through. I hate his dad! He takes him out with him, it always ends up with Billy getting hurt. I wish I could help him. I can't stop blaming myself."

"It's okay, you cannot blame yourself! You have tried your best. He chose not to listen. Now he's realizing that his actions have consequences." "It's just different though. We've been through so much together and I truly thought he was different. The change that I have watched him endure is so unlike him. I hope that this is a wake-up call for him. I'm so scared for him... no one deserves this. He's strong and I know he can take care of himself but that bad attitude gets him into more trouble than he likes to admit. I think he likes it." Pat's feelings were poignant and to the point. Mary knew she had to choose her words wisely. "Don't worry about it so much, you're strong enough to handle it. I know you'll be able to get through it."

"I know, but mom is getting started. I know she's worried about me, but she has no room to talk. She keeps telling me about all the things people are saying about Billy and the rumors that he goes out with his friends and is with other girls." Mary was aware of the rumors, and she worried too, Miguel was always with Billy. If Billy was doing it so, was he. Mary had asked Miguel several times. "Are you cheating on me? Rose told me she had seen you and Billy with some girls swimming in El Guiche, is that true?" The answer was always the same. "Get her over here and let her say it to my face. We went swimming at the rock and they were already there. Don't worry about that, I love you." Mary believed him or wanted to. Sometimes it was easier to believe.

"Well you know how they are? I got a huge 'I told you so' from my mom but that was expected. Sometimes I wonder if I should have listened to them in the beginning." "Don't say that! You love him, don't you?" Mary and Pat shared glances. "Of course, I do, I'll do anything for that man. But it just puts me in a hard place. I don't know what to do anymore." Pat buried her face in her hands. "I'm so torn between him, my family, my morals... even myself! He's starting to lose sight of what's truly important to him and I don't know if there's any coming back from that. Things have been worse with our parents too. My mom has been mad at me because she knows that things with me and Billy have gotten more serious. When she found out about all of this, she could barely look me in my eyes. You know how tough my dad is! He doesn't face his own problems! I'm so lucky to have you, you get it, you know. But morally, I feel like what I'm doing is wrong."

Pat was clearly in distress and Mary let her continue. "Knowing the right time to follow your mind, and your heart is so hard, especially when it comes to my beliefs. They shove this whole 'honor your mother and father' and all these rules down our throats but it's so hard when your parents aren't honorable people. But one thing I can tell you is that I really love Billy! This whole thing has been so hard for me. It frustrates me even more because I know his friends are quick to make him do stuff at the spur of the moment. These 'bros' seem to get him into more and more trouble, and he doesn't see it!" Pat knew that all of this sounded like a lot to her, but this was her life now. All this madness was hard to see on the surface but to Pat, it was a lot worse in her head and in her heart. So much was constantly going on in there, but she chose to tell so little of it. Her sister was all she had, the only one she could talk to that listened, comforted, and didn't pass judgement. Billy and Miguel were best friends and the sisters loved them. I guess you could say that they were all in it together.

"It's okay! I completely understand. It's a lot when you have so much going on and such little support. The thing with our parents is hard, but you always have me, your sister if you need me!" Pat was so glad to hear Mary say that, she felt so lucky to have her. Mary continued to share with her sister. "Just do what feels right to you. Don't worry about our parents, don't worry about the rules, do what YOU want and what feels right for YOU! You have to remember that at the end of the day, you're the one living your life. Live it the way you want to whether it's with Billy or not. Just remember why you fell in love with him." They both sat in silence for a few seconds and then she continued. "And his friends? I know it doesn't help that he has all those idiots that talk him into doing stupid things. I have the same problem with Miguel."

"You're right. Thank you so much. I just need to focus on what's important!" By this point, she felt numb. "Oh don't get me started on all of them, you know how guys are with their 'bros'. You know what's worst of all? It's not fair to me! Who has always been there for him? Me! But them 'bros' mean everything to him. Were his 'bros' there for him when he went to jail? They all ran off and hid cause they knew they'd be next! I was there for him through it all. But he forgets that." Mary got a few words in edge wise. "Well maybe you should remind him!" Pat knew Mary was right, she did need to remind him. She was a bit nervous to say it, but she said it. "I'll Make him remember why we are together in the first place. I have always been so good to him and loved him the way he needed. Maybe if I remind him of that, it will change things and we won't be in situations like this again. I've tried, I've really, really tried! It doesn't work anymore. I've cried to him, I've yelled at him, I've tried keeping my cool and just talking to him! But look where we are!"

Mary loved her younger sister and really wanted to help her through all of this. "Well you can't forget that our parents raised us this way for a reason even if they don't do it most of the time. Now you can't lose sight of who you are! I know that you love him. I know you've done so much for him. I'm not going to say he's changed you, but you aren't who you used to be." Mary was concerned for her baby sister. She had never seen her like this. She was extremely grateful that they were having this discussion. It was good for her to hear it. She was having the same issues with Miguel although not to the same level. Billy was the alpha. He was the one leading the boys into the truly dangerous situations, and they kept following him.

Pat talked to herself as she walked away. "I can't believe she said that to me! What does she know? I know she's going through the same thing with Miguel. How is that not hard on her too. She has changed, it's normal to change, right? How can she keep herself together so well? This just isn't fair anymore." Pat spoke these words in her head, she was exhausted and just wouldn't fight with Mary. Pat walked away; she had heard enough. "All people do is lecture me about how he has changed me and my life. But I like who I am when I'm with him so why does it matter? They keep saying the same thing. "We only tell you these things because we love you. The things we say aren't coming out of anger, they come from our hearts. Listen to us, it's for your own good!"

The two sisters went about their own business for the rest of the day. Both carried the love and anxiety for their young loves. Pat went to a quiet place at the end of her street and broke down. Her sobs were painful, the heavens listened as she wept. She had dreamt of their life together and wanted it more than anything else in the world. This would be the first of many heartaches, the universe was sharing the heartache.

Chapter | 27

TREES IN TESUQUE

I t was a beautiful day in El Guache. The sun was up in the eastern sky looking out over the Española Valley. If the sun were an eye of God, it would have beheld one of the loveliest sceneries on the planet. The Rio Grande shone like a glass ribbon winding its way through a green wave of life. The old homes were interspersed with the newer homes being build due to the continued migration of Anglos into the valley. Most of them were from the northeastern part of the United States, Texas, and other surrounding states. I heard a lot of negative talk about them. "All they do is steal our land." "They come over here with money and think they are better than us." "Why can't they stay where they came from and stop bringing their ignorant beliefs of superiority to our beautiful valley?" The divide between 'us and them' seemed to grow every day and it was reflected in our school. The cultural clash hung heavy in the air.

The newcomers were often at the receiving end of physical intimidation, and we were on the receiving end of psychological intimidation as they laughed at our dress, our language, and even what we ate. We often hid our burritos out of shame. The 'gringos' brought lunch in nice lunch boxes, or they ate in the cafeteria the whole time snickering at our tortillas. "Often times I would hear them talk about us. "The Mexicans should go back to Mexico." I used to wonder why they said this. I was Spanish not Mexican. Several times I had to teach them a lesson, both in the classroom and the playground, sometimes in the halls of the school. After a while they learned to stay away from me, though sometimes I yearned to be part of them. They looked so much happier than I was. My aunt used to say that the people that were moving here had money and that they treated people poorly anywhere they went. "They are jerks everywhere they go. Their money makes them act that way."

Like everything else in life, the ugly was ever present in the beautiful. I got along with a lot of the white students. Often, I was called out for being a traitor to my own race. I wondered if the eye of God saw it that way and why he allowed it to exist. Faith was never a complete explanation to me. If we were created in the image of God, well, did God have the ugly running through him? I got in trouble when I asked questions like this, so I stopped asking them out loud. How could a loving, caring God allow my family to suffer and destroy itself. I saw people I knew go into church and kneel, stand, sit, sing, and chant and then I would see them living a life of the opposite of what they were being preached to in church. It would take me years to understand that life on our planet was bigger than any religion could capture or understand. Meanwhile the outside world started to squeeze in us, we were being invaded.

I grew up in two worlds, the old and the new. The new included the Ed Sullivan show, Andy of Mayberry, Gilligan's Island, Dragnet, and many more. We never saw anyone that looked like us on TV, and if we did, they were the bad guys. When I was in El Guache a lot of it went away as I was back into the ancient, the Spaniard Legacy of my family. My life seemed normal there. The orchard imbedded in the alfalfa, the running water through the acequia, our adventures to the river, the sing song of our Spanish language, interspersed with English words. The 'new language' in parts of Northern New Mexico came to be called 'Spanglish'. It was almost spiritual, yet there was a part of me that missed the livelier interaction in Santa Fe. I found out that I was born in Santa Fe, it felt special to me. As I maneuvered my life through these two worlds, I felt like I was being torn apart.

We had been in El Guache for a few days and seen Billy for short times during those days. On this Saturday I woke to see that Billy had spent the night and that he did not look good, he had obviously had a hard night. I was happy to see him. I noticed that he looked older. He was stirring, twisting, and churning while he slept. I could feel that his spirit was troubled. It reminded me of the eddies in the river, churning but not going anywhere. Billy sat up and looked around. He saw me looking at him and nodded his head. "Hey little brother, how are things at home?" "Okay I guess, same old stuff." I always tried to be bigger and tougher with him. "You're not doing dumb shit like you know how, right?" I kept quiet, I wondered why he told me not to do stuff that he did. We stopped talking as he laid back down in bed. By this time all of us had gotten up and we were moving about. It was nice to be together with my brothers again. We never seemed to notice that my sister wasn't around that much and when she was, she was seldom with us. Her and Billy had bad feelings towards each other. Billy got preferential treatment from my dad and mom, and he used it to get away with picking on his older sister and ignoring her when she was assigned to take care of us. Lately it had become easier for her. Billy was seldom with us in Santa Fe. Billy was pretty much with grandpa on a full-time basis, or should I say, he was supposed to be. His friends and Pat had become his family.

Billy lay on the old, stained mattress trying to sort out what his life had become, wondering where it would lead him. Things were changing around him at an alarming rate. His heart was troubled, he felt alone. No matter how hard he tried he had something inside that drove him to seek danger as if a spirit drove him to look for adventure, a quest, a soldier's desire to fight. "I hate that son-of-a-bitch," was becoming more and more prevalent when he thought and spoke of our father. He often ran into dad in town. "Hey, what's going on with you guys?" When he ran in to Billy and his friends, dad acted like he was one of them. Billy resented it. He knew what was behind the jovial persona.

Much like everything else, it fed his ego, especially when he was drinking and with his friends. The young bucks fed his ego because they feared him. They praised him and told him what he wanted to hear. "Do you guys want a beer?" Billy and his friends always said yes. "Let's go to the Saints and Sinners." The Saints and Sinners was a small bar on the main drag. My dad often went there to drink and often took Billy and his friends with him. Billy would spend his time shooting pool winning beer. Often it led to fights as the older men resented getting beat by a 'young punk'. Often, they would get their actual asses beat by the same 'young punk' or by his dad. Last night had been one of those nights for Billy. He and his friends had left early. "Where are you going, we can go to the Delta Bar if you like." "Nah, thanks dad we have some people we have to meet."

Billy lied, he had to leave. Dad was sitting at the bar with a woman who was giggling, dad was buying her drinks and touching her under the bar. "Oh Billy, you're too much, I bet those prisoners know better than to mess with you." "Ricky, bring us another drink!" Billy knew where it would lead. He had seen it before. He had heard dad laughing with his friends as he shared his conquests. "If the car is rocking don't come a knocking!" Billy hated him for it. He knew that mom was at home and would receive the opposite when dad got home. Billy often had these thoughts and this morning they were extremely strong.

Billy and his friends had gone out and partied the night away. They drank until they started dropping like flies. Billy was the last to go. Today as he opened his eyes, he looked up at the old ceiling, it was stained with years of water leaks and dust from inside the old adobe home. Most of the square panels sagged from the weight. The square panels were a grungy blue with small strips of wood holding them together. The ceiling had always been there, the old life-beaten panels. He saw images imprinted by the weather stains; a horse head, a snake, an apple, a cloud, they were part of him. His head was throbbing, and his throat was parched.

Guilt, shame, and sadness wreaked from his body; he was trying to remember what he had done last night. The last thing he remembered was leaving from the Saints and Sinners. He couldn't remember but he knew it wasn't good. He knew he would find out later when the pieces fell in his lap like they always did. He inched out of bed and walked outside. He covered his eyes as the bright sunlight broke through the fog. He could hear the protective music coming from the birds using their song to warn other birds away from their trees. Even the birds had a duality to them. How could such a beautiful song be a warning to other birds? He drove those thoughts away. He wasn't in the mood for philosophical meanderings. His soul was craving relief, he didn't know from what or how he would satisfy the craving.

Billy was feeling like he was at the point where everything that had been important to him was gone. He knew he loved his family, but he was always separated from them even when he was with them. His friends and girl friend had become his primary group and he was starting to see them going off in a different direction. He had seen a lot on his young journey and unfortunately his dad was driving the train he was on. All he wanted to do was get off. He had seen a father that spent more money and time with his friends, drinking, and chasing women then he did with his family. Often when the party was over, he watched and experienced our father going home and resenting his family to the point that it turned physical. Were we a chain around his neck? Billy thought about this a lot. "Are we being punished for being a weight around his neck?"

SANTA FE: A PIECE OF 'MI VIDA'

He had decided that anything that was important to his dad, as his elder son, he would not do it anymore. The joy was gone. "It's always about dad and his friends. When I do good, he brags and when I do bad, he goes off on me!" Billy often spoke these words to anyone who would listen. He loved his dad, but sometimes he hated him. Little did he know that he was becoming a different version of what he hated.

Billy had given up sports, school, and almost his family. The love he had for his younger brothers showed that he still cared about them but felt powerless to help them. His life had become a prison to him, he did not see a way out. He was on a downward spiral, and he thought and felt like there was no way out. Billy had chosen to go with the flow, he was on a one-way journey to a place he could not identify. The momentum downward grew stronger the further he fell. His spirit felt like it had boarded a train and couldn't get off and stay off.

He continued his journeys on the Ghost Train, he felt wanted there. He worried! He could swear he had seen me board behind him. He wondered why I followed him. Billy worried about that. He knew how easy it was to become addicted to the wine, women, and song. He knew there would be a price to pay. He just didn't know what that price would be, but he knew it would be spiritually expensive. Billy was an old spirit. He knew that the ancients lived inside of him. It made him fearless while at the same time the love of his heritage fought for him and his life.

"Good morning!" Grandpa's voice startled Billy. "Good morning!" Billy mumbled as he walked back into the dirt home and came out with a water bucket. It was a new day. Billy walked to the ancient well and pulled out a bucket of the dark cool water, a gift from the earth. He poured it into the transport bucket, lifted the bucket to his mouth and sucked it into the void in his being, man that water was good. "How are you doing today son, is everything okay? You look like hell. Have you had anything to eat? Your dad came by looking for you last night, did he find you?"

"Yeah, he found us last night. We went cruising with him and Jody until he started getting crazy. We snuck out of the bar, found some friends, and did our own thing. Actually, I am hungry, do you have anything to eat grandpa?" "Yes, come on in, I'll fry some eggs. Do you think you can help me do some work today? I could really use some help. Ever since you guys moved to Santa Fe, most of the work around here has fallen to me. Your dad comes by to say hello and to sleep when he's too drunk to drive but he doesn't lift a hand to help. Thank God, he brings you guys over for the summer to help." "Yeah, I'll help, let me know after breakfast what you want me to do."

My grandpas' home was smaller than my parent's bedroom in our small home in Santa Fe. He had everything he needed in his humble abode. His old wood stove was already going. You could hear the crackling of wood as it heated the small room making it unbearably hot. The smell of the Piñon wood was intoxicating. He fried some eggs for Billy and gave him some coffee. The coffee was good this morning. My grandfather would usually use the coffee grinds several times until the coffee came out almost clear, coffee was expensive.

Billy was lucky this morning, it was the beginning of the cycle. The coffee came out of the old tin coffee pot, hot and black. It was amazing that in the year 1968 there were people still living off the fruit of the land with a little assistance from family. They were stuck in time. The flow of their lives followed that of the earth. They lived their lives like it was the 1800's, still Colonial Spain for them. After breakfast, Billy took the basin that grandpa used to wash and shave, and the bed pan from the side of grandpa's room and walked to the outhouse to dump it. We were inside eating powdered milk and cereal. Why didn't we get eggs?

As Billy walked, he thought about his girlfriend Pat. He was having inner turmoil over his feelings for her. He didn't know what love for a woman was, but he knew his feelings were strong for her. "Don't go with your friends tonight, let's go to a movie." She was putting pressure on him to stay with her. "Please don't go out so much and if you do, be careful. My parents got really upset when the Sheriff came looking for you guys last week." "Let them, they haven't caught me yet." Billy smiled as he remembered running from them last week and losing them as he ran through an orchard and got lost in the bosque. His uneasiness towards last night returned as he entered the outhouse. He remembered the fight with Pat. They had been at it more lately, she was changing. The fun Pat was gone and the nagging one had taken her place.

The outhouse was a small wooden structure with two holes cut on top of a bench that served as toilets. We all laughed the first time my grandpa referred to it as the throne. The seats were assigned. The one on the right was for the adults and the one on the left was for us. When we used the bathroom, we carried a roll of toilet paper with us. We never left it outside where the weather, dust, or bugs would get to it. I used to think that my grandfather was a well-read man. There was always a pile of newspapers and magazines on the right-hand corner of the twin seats. One day I inadvertently walked in on him and saw that he had pages of newsprint in his hands. I saw that he was rubbing them back and forth in his hands until they were pliable, they became his toilet paper. I wondered if some of the words were left on his butt as he wiped. He had to be frugal, he was land rich and money poor like so many in the Española Valley. "Get out of here 'negrito'! Knock before you walk in stupid! Don't do it again!" I got out of there in a hurry. I had never seen an adult on the seat before.

We were supposed to lock the door when we were in there using the hook that went into the half circle holder. The whole time we were in El Guache, using the outhouse was always scary to me. During the summer I used to look down the hole and see spider webs. I was fast at doing my business. I was afraid of having a Black Widow bite me. "Don't forget to use a stick and get rid of the spider webs before you sit down. The Black Widow is poisonous." This was a common admonition. I didn't have to be reminded. During the winter the wood was cold. We were told not to sit down but to squat and to keep our butt slightly above the wood but not to let it touch. I didn't have to be reminded of that either. A freezing butt was a cold reminder if we ever forgot.

"Okay grandpa, what do you want me to do?" By this time, we were done eating and joined them outside. Billy spent the morning and early afternoon helping grandpa move and chop wood, release and guide the water in the acequia. We did what we always did. We did what we were told to do as we did our part. It was hot and the orchard was calling for water. Billy thought about all that had happened in that small little farm. Ditches had to be cleaned, trees pruned and all the other tasks it took to run a small farm. He laughed when he remembered riding El Gordo in the rain. Man, those were good days!

Early in the afternoon a Sheriff pulled into the driveway and the sheriff got out. "Buenos dias Abelino, is Billy here?" Billy had spotted the sheriff and slid behind the wall telling grandpa what to say. "I'm not here and you don't know where I am!" Billy slipped into the old adobe house, cringing when the screen door let out its rusty wail as he closed the door. He watched from the small window in the door. He watched as the sheriff and grandpa talked to each other. We stood off to the side and listened in, it was exciting in a way, we had never seen the Sheriff drive unto our property. "Emilio, como estas? How have you been, haven't seen you around for a while, how is business?" Grandpa's greeting revealed nothing. "How are your parents?" Everyone knew everybody in the valley or someone in the family.

The sheriff answered our grandpa. "You know how it is around here, trying to save people from themselves. The old timers are doing well, thanks for asking. You should go visit them. They would love to see you. You guys go way back. Let me tell you why I'm here. Someone broke into Tito's bar last night." Our grandpa responded with astonishment. "You don't say! I can't say I'm surprised! You know he sells liquor on Sundays even though it's against the law and most of that is to minors. Very greedy that one." "I know cousin, but burglary is still a crime, and when there are witnesses, I can't ignore it!" Our grandpa got a perplexed look on his face. He had a feeling in the pit of his stomach that Billy was involved. "What do you mean? What does that have to do with Billy?" It was obvious to the sheriff that the tone had changed. He had to be careful how he approached it. The sheriff knew Billy Sr. well. They had bumped heads a couple of times. They had decided that they would keep their distance from each other. "Two Rattlesnakes won't bite each other," they joked. "There are too many rabbits around."

"Someone saw Billy and his friends running from the building early this morning. The witness lives near the bar and they were getting ready to take a trip to Texas. He heard loud noises coming from the bar. He watched through the window and said he saw three males running out of the bar, each was carrying a box." "How does this neighbor know it was Billy? Does he have night vision, is he an owl?" Grandpa was getting upset and Emilio could see it. "Billy and his friends have been getting into a lot of trouble lately, they are drinking and are getting out of hand all over town. I've had to stop them several times for fighting, being drunk and disorderly, trespassing and all the other dumb things they're doing. I'm getting a lot of push back from Judge Salazar. The judge is taking a lot of heat from the State Police. They are asking why they keep arresting him and nothing happens. I guess the State Police have arrested him a few times and the paperwork disappears. They are not very happy and are pushing it up the chain. You know that as long as it's one of my sheriffs dealing with them there isn't a problem, but I can't control the State Police."

"You guys need to get Billy under control. My wiggle room has lost its wiggle. He needs to turn himself in so we can clear this up. Tito is very upset, and we know he will not let it go. If you get a chance have your son talk to Tito. If they can work something out, we can let this go. Maybe if he pays him for the booze that was taken it will be enough, but I doubt it. Word got to him that it was Billy and his friends that stole the cokes from the National Guard Armory too. Billy better be careful, or he'll end up in prison. With his dad working there it will be a living hell. They'll probably have to move him to another state." "Billy left earlier this morning. It couldn't have been him! He was here all night."

Grandpa knew in his heart that it was Billy, a dark cloud of sadness and fear came over him like the clouds rolling in right before a thunderstorm. He hadn't noticed the actual clouds rolling in and it started to rain. They could hear the thunder in the Sangre's, it started to pour. "OK, let him know I came by and that I need to talk to him about last night and a few other incidents that have to be cleared up." "Okay cousin I'll let him know. Hopefully I won't see you later primo, have a nice day." "You as well cousin, my regards to your familia." The two men laughed as the Sheriff got into his black and white police cruiser and slowly backed out, looking at the house as he left. Grandpa shuffled into the house where he found Billy sitting on the steel framed bed. Billy had a look that was failing to mask the understanding that was creeping in about what he had done last night. He wore an underlying look of defeat on his face but also a look of defiance. He was at war with himself and the life that surrounded him. So far, he was losing.

Grandpa stopped and listened for a while to make sure the County Sheriff was gone. He knew Emilio, sneaky one, that one. Emilio's influence was growing in the county. His political machine was very powerful. Anyone wanting to win an election for any state office had to work with him. Without his support there was no way they could win Northern New Mexico. Emilio was known as the Patron, the Boss. It was rumored that anyone that crossed him paid for it, either the defiant one or a member of their family. I heard my dad, and his friends talk about some brothers from Tierra Amarilla that were running a campaign against him citing several examples of Emilio's abuse of power towards those not aligned with his party. The story told was that the two brothers were stopped for a traffic violation as they drove through Española. "Get out of the car and put your hands on the hood." "Why, we haven't done anything?" As the Deputy kept them leaning on the car the Sheriff began to search the vehicle. "Well, well, well, what have we here?" Rumor had it that the sheriff planted drugs in the vehicle, arrested the brothers, had them convicted, sentenced, and sent them to prison. If you were on his side, you got favors like my dad. If not, you got what the two brothers got. There was no middle ground.

Billy could feel the silence permeate his being. He was worried, his thoughts were going a hundred miles a minute. He was starting to remember the events of the evening. "Is it true?" Billy sat quiet. Billy loved his grandpa. He showed him more love than his own father. "What happened my son, is the sheriff telling the truth?" Billy said nothing as the events of the previous day and night began to force their way into his memory. His grandpa's voice disappeared as the voices from the night called to him. He remembered the discussion that had started their day, they were reminiscing about our cousin Norman. "They found him outside the bowling alley in his car, he was shot in the head, his rifle was in the car. They are saying that he killed himself." "No way!" Billy was in shock. He had grown up with Norman who was a few years older than him. Norman had just gotten back from Vietnam and the word was that his head wasn't right. I had recently been paying attention to all the news on TV detailing the war and the protests against it. We had several family members and friends serving or who had served in the war. The way they were being treated by the protestors were making everybody angry in our community.

"Rich man's war, poor man's fight!" I heard my uncle say several times. He was a principal at a local high school, having graduated from

Stanford University. My dad used to make fun of him and my aunt. She was a teacher and had graduated from Stanford as well. My dad used to call my uncle our aunt and our aunt our uncle. My mom hated it as we all laughed. The discussion around Norman's death continued throughout the night. Billy and his friends started drinking early that day. They all respected Norman and looked up to him. It was hard for me understand why TV protestors would do that to people coming back from a war. Between Martin Luther King, the Brown Berets, and the war protestors, I was challenged as I tried to make sense of it all. I was enthralled when I heard what they were saying and why they were doing it. None of it was real to me except for Vietnam. Vietnam was everywhere as more and more local teenagers were being drafted.

Billy and his friends spent the afternoon and evening drinking and reminiscing about Norman. "He's the best organ player I've ever seen man. He played with the Defiants, the Morphomen, and a bunch of other bands!" "Remember that '66 Nova Super Sport he had, man that car was fast. I wonder what Lola is going to do with it?" "What bro, you can't buy it anyway. The best you can do is go buy some more beer." "With what, my good looks?" "You can't pay with those! They'll charge you extra!" It went on like that for a while. "Man, I can't believe he's dead. Vietnam is crazy! All of us will probably get drafted." "Billy, where is Frankie?"

Miguel had become friends with Frankie. "He's in boot camp bro. He left last week. He's crazy, he volunteered." "That's dumb bro, from what I hear it's the chicanos and blacks that are being sent over there doing the fighting. The rich white boys are running to Canada. They're a bunch of punks. I'll tell you what bro, I don't want to go. I want to stay here and take care of all the women left behind." They all laughed. "If they draft us, we won't have a choice. Let's go to town and check it out." Billy was growing restless, and he needed to stop thinking. The best way to stop thinking was to get the party going.

They had a friend, Pedro, who lived at Apple Valley, a low-income housing unit. They decided to go and visit him. They decided to go and visit him. Usually when they went to see him, he wasn't there or was in the middle of something. On this day they felt like they had hit the jack pot. Pedro was home partying with some friends who Billy had never met. They all introduced themselves and Billy, Miguel, Little Billy, and Gilbert started drinking with them. They passed the hat and took a collection. By pooling their money, they came up with enough to buy a case of beer. A couple of Pedro's friends drove off to buy the booze. "What have you been up to bro?" Billy was talking to Pedro. Billy and Pedro had hung out when they were with their dads, but they really didn't know each other that well. "You know, same old stuff. I have some good weed! Do you guys want to smoke a joint?" Pedro didn't wait for an answer, he lit it and passed it.

"Hell yeah!" An enthusiastic response came from everyone in the room. Marijuana was very expensive and hard to come by. Before long all of them had a good buzz and then the alcohol got there, and the party really took off. Miguel and one of Pedro's friends started talking trash to each other and before they knew it, they were fighting. The fight was heavy. They both had grown up tough. In an instant it had turned into a full-blown brawl. A loud shrill was heard and Pedro fell to the ground bleeding from his stomach. Billy and his friends ran out of the house before the others in the house could recover. Billy held a bloody knife in his hands as they ran away. He couldn't remember if he had stabbed the guy or just picked up the knife to take it. The level of inebriation was such that the memories disappeared into thin air.

"Do you think he's dead!" Little Billy was pacing. His brother was in prison, that was the last place he wanted to be. They ran to Pat and Mary's home as it was close to Apple Valley. The sisters were always there for them and had hidden them more than once. They loved Billy and Miguel and they showed it; they were part of whatever the two friends did regardless of how serious. The cops had been there more than once looking for them and the sisters had covered for them. "We gotta get out of here, can you give us ride to El Duende, we can go to Antonio's house." "He's in prison, don't you remember?" Billy responded, "I remember, we still hang out there sometimes, his mom still takes care of us. We'll hang there for a bit." Billy was scared but at the same time he was exhilarated, the rush of the fight was still surging. The sisters were already moving. "While we're there, you guys can do us a favor and check at the hospital to see if Pedro made it. Man, I wish that hadn't happened, my dad is going to be really mad." Billy was walking towards the car.

Billy knew his dad and he knew how loyal he and his friends were to each other, after all, he put them first ahead of his own family. In a way he was glad it had happened. Was he attacking his father through everything he loved? "Let me go ask my mom if I can borrow the car to give you a ride." As the oldest of the two, Mary was the one that got the car every now and then, being careful that nothing happened to it or to them. She knew if it did, never again would she be able to borrow the car, so far so good. "Let's go, I have to be right back." The ride to El Duende was short and sweet. The sisters waved as they drove off. The worry and love were written all over their face.

As they walked into the kitchen they were greeting by several people. Billy was surprised to see Juan sitting at the table with Johnny, Antonio's younger brother. Juan stood up and did the 'bro' handshake with them all. He was close to their age and often hung out with them. "My boys, come on in, come on in, it is so nice to see you." Antonio's mom was always happy to see them. "Hey bro, has my dad found you?" "No, why?" "I don't know, I saw him talking to grandpa and he got into the car talking about how you were going to end up in jail if you didn't cut your shit out." "The hell with my dad, he's got no room to talk. I've seen what he does!" Billy walked outside as he spoke the words.

Billy and his friends hung outside for a bit and then decided to call one of their friends to come and pick them up. Peter rolled up in a '56 Belair with Baby Moon hub caps. His cars were always sharp. Peter had quit school to work with his dad at the garage. "Hey Peter, how's it going?" "Same old shit brother, working and working, my dad keeps fixing cars." "What happened to you guys?" "What do you mean?" Look in the mirror bro, you guys have some healthy bruises, who did you throw down with?"

Billy glanced into the mirror and rubbed his cheeks. He had some serious bruising and a fat lip. His ribs hurt every time he laughed. It reminded him how tough Pedro and his friends were. He dreaded having to go at it with them again. He knew Pedro and he knew it wasn't over. "We threw with some crazies from Apple valley. Do you know Pedro?" "Yeah, I know that vato, he is known all over the valley. Be careful, I hear those guys are crazy. Anyway, where are we going?" "Let's go get some beer, do you have any money? We'll pay you back." "No sweat, I got paid for a job today."

They spent the rest of the night drinking, going from drive up window to drive-up window. When all the drive-up windows were closed, they were all drunk out of their minds. "Let's go break into Tito's. That punk takes us every time he sells to us because we are underage." Miguel was slurring his words. It didn't take much to convince the inebriated bunch. Peter parked down the street and waited with the engine running. In an instant the group was back whooping and hollering unaware that the neighbor had seen them. They made a couple of trips bringing bottles of whiskey and Tequila. "That's enough, let's go." They drove off and drank until early morning. They dropped Billy off and drove off with all the bottles they had stolen. They would meet in a couple of days and drink some and sell the others. This was not the first time they had done stuff like this. They were starting to get a reputation. Their bragging about their adventures was spreading the word and in a small town, it spread very quickly. My dad found Billy a week or so later and convinced him to go to Santa Fe for a few days while he talked to his connections in Rio Arriba County. No matter what, when Billy was in deep, he was there for his son. This time it was too little too late.

"I'm sorry Billy, your son has brought all of this on himself. How many times have we gone through this?" Billy Sr. sat in Judge Salazar's office. The judge was related to us. "Primo, you know how many votes I got you to put you in that chair! We go way back, we're familia! We have always taken care of each other! This is my son we are talking about. I'll make sure he stops." "I understand primo but it's too late. If I sit in front of the State Judicial Committee, it won't matter how many votes you got me or how close we are as familia. I will be removed from the bench. Too many other people depend on me for justice and compassion for their families. I can't let one person that has gotten chance, after chance, after chance ruin it for all of us. The best we can do is get him to turn himself in and we can work on the sentencing. He can enter a plea and we will honor it. We will reduce the sentence, preventing any serious jail time. He probably will have to do some time, but we can make sure it is in the county jail. If he continues, he will probably end up in prison. I'm sorry primo, it saddens me to see your son like this. He's the best athlete I've ever seen."

It was nice to have Billy back. After a few days you could see him pacing with anxiety. I tried to get close to him, but he told me to leave him alone. "I want you take your mom to work today, take the Galaxy 500." My dad was trying to entice him to hang around Santa Fe for a bit. Drop your mom off and come straight home, you can pick her up when she gets off." "Okay," was Billie's only response. When my dad got home from work that afternoon he was in a good mood until he saw my mom roll up in her friend's car. "Where's Billy?" "I don't know, he didn't show up to pick me up." "That son of a bitch, he is going to regret this." As he changed out of his uniform, he got a call from the State Police that his car was found in Tesuque and that it was in bad shape. Our mom started to sob. "What's going to happen to my son?" Billy was breaking her heart. She remembered the beautiful baby she held in her arms a lifetime ago. "My son won the Gerber's Baby Food Beautiful Baby Award!" It was true. She was so proud of that. All her children were beautiful, and each was talented in their own way, but she knew she had a special place in her heart for her eldest son. Her face lit up as she bragged to anyone who would listen.

"You should have seen that car." The owner of the small gas station in Tesuque was explaining to my dad. "I have never seen a car traveling that fast. This hill is very steep as you know. That car was moving. All I saw was a red streak! I couldn't tell what kind of car it was, just that it was bright red with a black roof. In an instant I heard a loud bang, then another, then another. I ran to the scene, and I saw some young boys running from the car. The car hit several trees. Thank God it was not a direct hit. Looking at the wreckage it's hard to believe that anyone walked away. Was that your son running from the car? Is he okay?"

My dad thanked him without answering his questions. "What am I going to do with Billy? He is going to kill himself and those dumb asses that are always with him." As he drove to El Guache to find his son, he couldn't get the amount of damage done to the trees and his car out of his mind. Billy was leaving his mark, just not the way anyone wanted him to. Now here we were in our neighbor's car. My mom sat in the car unable to control her tears. She hated her husband for what he had done to her family. She knew in her mind that her kids were all gifted and wondered why her husband could not and would not see it. He had the making of a small empire right in front of him, yet he gave his best to drunks and whores and his worst to his family.

The crash became the talk of the town. Word got out and a lot of people made a special trip to gawk at the wreckage, it was truly a sight to behold. On the passenger side of the Galaxy 500 it looked good as new, but the damage to the other side shattered the illusion of perfection. It was a visual manifestation of my life, the beauty within shattered by the inertia of my families troubled life. "Did anybody die?" "Look at that car!" "That's the worst I have ever seen." The gawkers were amazed at what they saw. The junk yard holding the car had placed it like a trophy right in front of the building. I was worried about my brother. I would find out later that they had hitched back to Española and not missed a beat. They were on the run and did not realize that a net of their making was unfolding

Chapter | 28

SINKING

I am dreaming again. I scream into the black. Dark red bubbles flowing in a sea of black. The dark amoebas morph into a contorting sea, deep dark menacing. They stand out as they mutate in and out of different shapes, twisting, turning, slowly sinking, and scary singing. I try to fight and swim out of the sea of red only to find myself on the train again. One minute I am on the train, the next, I'm floating inside one of the bubbles surrounded by a throng of bubbles, each one changing. I notice a sea of faces starting to materialize, each bubble becoming a face. I am aware that the faces come close to me and flow away with another right behind it. Then several of them approach my fluidity and permeate my being as they are a part of me, but they are transitory.

"You made it through some terrible times, your spirit is strong." I see the face of my guardian, the beautiful woman that pulled me out of the water many train rides ago. Her face is clear as the water we drink. It sparkles as its waves reflect love. "Where am I?" My voice is trapped in my fluidity! "I can hear your thoughts, no need to talk. You are not ready to fully understand the meaning of your journey but know that I am here with you. The spirit that has taken you on this journey is life itself. The phantom that surrounds you in your sleep is present for us all. For whatever reason he has exposed himself to you.

He will contact you soon. Fear is his essence. He will come near, do not despair. I will be there to protect you. Your love is strong, stay inside it and you will see!" "What will I see? Why me?"

As her voice goes quiet, I feel a loss inside. I look up and see that the bubbles have lined up and are flowing towards me in single file. The first bubble approaches and a face swirls in the bubble. I recognize the face of the young man that died in the arms of Martin of Tours. One by one the faces from my journey approach as a red haze, each in their own bubble, each a metamorphic phenomenon. They meld from a red liquid to a face that has defined my dream journey. Once again, I know that I'm dreaming but this time I don't want to wake up. One by one the red fluid bubbles go by. The faces flow, disappearing into the night. The one escaping the Spanish Inquisition, the one crossing the ocean to the new world. The images continue. I see the movement through the jungle on the Spaniards way to the conquest of the Aztecs. I see the one moving north in search of the legendary Seven Cities of Gold. One bubble stands out, the face of the fleeing soldier watching Santa Fe burn. I know I will see that face again. The faces continue their mutation, permeating the very essence of my existence as they move northward to Española, to El Guache. The train of red comes to a halt. I now am very aware of the silence that surrounds me.

The bubbles line up, and I notice that together they have become the Ghost Train and I feel the train slow its movement. The steel wheels wail as they grind slowly forward. As the train creeps in its crawl, there within its slow motion I see faces of people that have moved on from the Santa Fe Rebellion. I see as they march back into Santa Fe, they are being led by Don Diego De Vargas. Once again, the Spaniards wear the armor of glory. I see faces, these include people from the previous stops, they seem to know each other. How can that be, aren't they all from a different space and time? As I look out the window, I see the soldiers and citizens changing.

The soldiers look on as the Armor falls to the ground. They are lighter now and I notice that the weapons they carry into the future have become pistols and rifles. Some of them are wearing ammunition belts crisscrossing their torso and wide brimmed hats to block the high desert sun. Now the weapons are flying in the sky, death pours from the heavens. I see images from beneath, as they float up, they are encircled by a clear membrane. I watch as it wraps around young faces in soldier's uniforms. The membrane becomes a circle as red flows in like water into a glass. The weapons are changing, chariots of fire, birds of prey shooting fire, hand-held rifles with bursts unending like water from a hose.

In an instant, the train passes through a time warp. The Conductor is smiling at me. His gory red countenance stirring fear and hatred in my soul. "Haven't you done enough?" His face contorts and he has an evil grin on his face as he starts to laugh. The laughter is like nothing I have ever heard. His macabre laughter and song shock the heavens. I hear as his thoughts become mine. "I have to take you back to visit a young man that was loved by and feared by many." This is the first time he has spoken directly to me. I drive the thoughts out and regain my awareness. The train slows down, and I feel the movement as it stops and hovers in place. Am I outside or inside the train? I look through a glass where all things are happening at the same time. One thought is starting to form, it's all connected. The past and the present are all connected somehow. I am older than my life.

The Conductor's laughter shatters me as the train comes to a halt. Something has changed. I feel him, a connection has been made, what does he want from me? I see a huge dark red and black molecule speeding towards me. A darkness takes over the ether, now I am the only orb in the dark. As the blackness approaches, I have a familiar feeling, here we go again. Right before it gets to me a bright light illuminates the black orb and I see that it is traveling towards me. The bubble has once again become the train. The train is smashing into the red bubbles. I watch the red blood explode every time the train demolishes one of them. The entire world seems to be bathed in blood. I am being brutally tossed around in a cyclone of blood. The cyclone's walls are preventing me from escaping! I am trapped, and again I find myself being pulled into the abyss.

I become a bundle of fear tied together by the thread of impending death. As I scream through the night flight the bright light reappears and I know that there is a good force involved in saving me. I have been flowing through the dark for what feels like forever. My soul yearns to flow in the light not the dark, the good not the bad, the love not the hate. I have tasted the light but lived in the dark. The piercing of the light is a kernel of hope inside of me. I hope it's enough. As the Conductor appears before me, I feel his ice hands on my heart, it is cold, hard, and evil. I feel life oozing out of me, I start to cry, begging for life.

I hear the loving voice! It frees me from the grip of fear. I am thrown to the back of the train. "Stay here till you get to your next stop. It will not be your last stop, but you will remain there for a considerable time. You must know that the definition of your life will be determined there. You will have to choose between several paths even when you are not aware that you are choosing. You are very young and will not understand why life is as it is. You must endure the hardships, though it might not feel that way. If you persist, good will come into your life in small pieces. Accumulate those, they will be the light that leads you out of darkness." The melodic voice comforts me in the Ghost Train as it heads towards where I don't know. "I will be at your side to save you from folly, but I cannot dictate how or which path you pick for your life, only you can do that. Seek wise council, you will excel at whatever you do. If you want to know success, ask someone who has attained it. Do you understand? You cannot change your past but understanding it can change your path to your future. Your past will bring strong forces to prevent you from reaching your full potential or to help you reach them. You must run from it and embrace it at the same time"

I wake up shooting up into a sitting position trying to figure out where I have been. It is raining and I look up at the sky and see every drop. The rain is a wonderful retreat. I can smell the newness in the air, it is refreshing to my senses and my spirit. We are spending less and less time in El Guache. My father has lost all interest in farming. He goes to Española on his days off but it's not to work the land. My mom has taken on three jobs. We see her during the day for a bit and seldom on the weekends. When she's home, she does laundry, cleans our house, ensuring we have everything we need. There is always food in the refrigerator. "Go play outside!" Many times, she would lock the door. She needed her quiet time. The soap operas on TV allowed her to escape her dysfunctional life. She often told us the story about how she met our dad, her mood was always sad yet hopeful. "I met your dad while I was at work cleaning the home of your uncle Manuel. It was one of the many jobs your grandma had me do." Her story continued. "I often think of what my life would be like if I had not met him. When I first met him, he was very nice to me. He worked in Los Alamos and took the bus up there every day. He didn't have a car, but he rode a horse around El Guache. I used to ride piggy-back with him, he was a true cowboy. The problems started when he bought his first car. He stopped riding his horse and eventually sold it. Before too long his behavior began to shift towards cruising and everything that came with it."

School began with me going to Harvey Junior High, a school for Seventh and eighth graders. It was exciting! There were kids from several elementary schools attending and I was lucky that I had attended two elementary schools. I knew quite a few people. The hallways were the social gathering place, and a lot of interaction took place there. On my first day I met Antonio Ortiz. I would find out later that he had been held back and considered himself the toughest kid in school and behaved that way. Antonio was muscular for his age. He was as tall as me and I had the same class as him for first period. As soon as I walked into the classroom, he walked up to me and challenged me. Antonio had brownish hair and wore glasses. I could see that he had a lot of facial hair for his age. He looked a lot older than me. I was a bit scared of him. "Do you think you're better than us. You walk like you think you're pretty tough!"

His confrontation was immediate, but I knew what it was, he was showboating in front of the other students. I responded the way I had been raised to. "Get out of my face before I kick your ass." The classroom grew quiet. The teacher hadn't walked in yet. In an instant, Antonio pushed me and rushed me. The fight was on. He was very strong and quick. We wrestled, punched, and kicked, knocking desks over. The fight was pretty much even. We were stopped by the teacher before we could finish it for good. Antonio and I became good friends after that.

We ended up in the principal's office. The principal greeted Antonio with a sarcastic smile. "Not again Antonio, are you starting off where you left off last year? Do you like it here so much you want to stay another year? See that chair, go sit there, we'll discuss this in a while." Then the principal looked at me. "What is your name young man?" From here it was all the same things. He explained the consequences if I was going to behave this way. It was my first day and I was already in the principal's office, it would not be the last time. "Go back to class and remember, I don't want to see in my office again."

In my life, love and happiness existed in the cracks of aggression. The school year went on and once again I was always in turmoil. I saw kids that I thought were normal who did not act physically aggressive and at times I wish I could be like them. I felt good in school. I was at peace most of the time as I enjoyed learning, I was good at it. I enjoyed the freedom and the excitement, but too many times I reverted to the values of my upbringing. I enjoyed the power and brotherhood it afforded me. I was always the first in and the last out. I often fought their fights and some of them started taking advantage of me. I was good at it and got positive reinforcement for it. Learning and fighting, what a skill set that was.

Harvey was an open campus and we walked out to the plaza every day. Lunch time was a very exciting time. Every day we got to mingle with kids in the heart of the old capital. Near the school was a small bakery where a lot of the kids hung out eating pastries and forming social circles. I never had money to buy anything so after a while I had a group of girls from Casa Solana buying me Long Johns. Long Jones were pastries the size and shape of hot dogs. The pastry was covered with chocolate on the top and had a sweet white filling. I loved them. The girls would laugh and dare to me to stuff a long john into my mouth and eat it. I became quite good at it. The girls fed me long johns for a long time after that. I guess they enjoyed the entertainment. I was an act in the circus of life, the cream filled Long John Eater. I really enjoyed the attention plus I got pastries I couldn't afford.

Sears Roebuck was next to the Bakery and the parking lot became the place where most of the fights took place. "Meet me at the Sears parking lot" became the battle cry. "Hey what's up bro? Can you back us up? The clowns are meeting us at the Sears parking lot. They messed with us last night, today we'll see!" This type of interaction became common place, it had become a spectator sport. If you wanted to be known, a few wins here was one way to do it. The Sears parking lot became like an arena. The older kids from the high school were often involved so it was only natural for us to involve ourselves. We immersed ourselves in the pond, like fish in water, we reveled in it, we were in the water.

Our journeys into the plaza exposed us to a lot of activity. The plaza was a gathering place for the residents of Santa Fe. The TV aired story after story about Martin Luther King, The Black Panthers, Equal Rights, the Hippies, the Chicano Power Movement, and the War in Vietnam. There was electricity in the air. Being young during these turbulent and exciting times was invigorating and permeated everything we did. It drove us to increase our aggression, our exploits often took us to the edge. We had more luck than brains, we survived to fight another day.

We used to sit on the benches and watch the cruisers go by. The Lowriders became our favorites, they looked and behaved like us. They would cruise by riding low and slow. Every now and then I recognized a car from Española. I would give them an enthusiastic greeting. Our energy was mostly diverted towards fighting, there was a lot of "gang warfare' among the Spanish families and neighborhoods. The use of weapons became normal. I excelled in this world. I became known for my ability to fight and willingness to cross the line where few dared to tread. Many a time I would bite off more than I could chew and had to be saved by my brothers and our friends.

"Santiago! Santiago! Come here!" It was Billy cruising by. "Get in, let's go for a ride." He didn't have to tell me twice. "I'll see you guys in a little while." I didn't wait for a response from my friends. I got in the back-seat of the 1956 Belair. Billy and his friends were happy to see me. I was happy to see them. Instantly I grew two inches. I was in the middle of strength. As we cruised, I looked around, I wanted everyone to see me, to see how strong I was. "Are you still playing the guitar?" Miguel was smiling as he asked me. "I remember when we woke you up and Billy made you play and sing for us. He made us put money in the hat for you that he kept." Miguel was at it again. The laughter filled the air of the '56 Belair. They were talking about all they had done. I saw Billy shake his head when the discussion turned to all the people that were looking for them which included enemies and police.

"How is everything going Santiago? How are you doing in school? I better not hear that you're not going, do you understand?" "Yeah, I understand, how come you don't go to school?" I regretted it as soon as it came out of mouth. "Maybe you think you are really tough now little brother. I don't answer to you or to anyone else anymore." Billy was talking to me, but I was old enough to know that he was talking to everyone in the car. "I'm going to go into the Marines. Frankie went, and I want to go to. I just have to get mom and dad to sign for me. I told them that Frankie enlisted in the Marine Corps. Those guys are the baddest! If they see me in Española again, they will arrest me and lock me up." "You're crazy bro! Have you seen what's going on over there on the news?"

His friends were all commenting on how brutal the war looked on TV and how the soldiers were being treated when they got back and how many young men were being killed or wounded. "Don't go!" I was pleading without realizing it. "Just come back to Santa Fe, they won't find you here." Billy responded as they pulled up to my school. "I'll see you later punk, stay in school, you're a smart guy, don't make me come looking for you." My heart sank as he drove away. I had felt his sadness. I knew he was feeling like he had nowhere to go. I wanted to go with him so bad it hurt. I had a horrible day and night and it showed at the Sears Parking lot from that day forward.

Chapter | 29

LUNCH TIME

"They caught Gilbert stealing at the Safeway!" Michael and his entourage were running towards me. "He's in the manager's office, they are going to call the cops." I ran to the Safeway and without thinking, walked inside asking where the office was. As I got close to the office, I saw Gilbert sitting there with a worried, scared look. His dad was as crazy as mine. "What the hell do you think you're doing?" I walked into the office and started yelling at Gilbert as I slapped him on the side of the head. "How many times has dad told you?" "Who are you? You need to stop yelling. I'm getting ready to call the cops! They can take you to jail with him!" "I'm sorry sir! My brother has been doing this kind of stuff for a while. My dad is going to belt him until he can't walk! Last time he didn't walk right for a month. Let me take him sir, I promise you, he will pay for it!" The manager's response was terse. "I don't know, shoplifting is a very serious thing, it's a crime." "Well, it's up to you. If he goes to jail, I don't want to be around when my dad has to get him out. My dad works at the State Pen, and he is always telling us that if we do dumb stuff, we will end up in there. Let me take him, my dad will take care of it." The manager was quiet for what seemed like an eternity. I could see that Gilbert was alert, he knew me. He was getting ready to run out.

SANTA FE: A PIECE OF 'MI VIDA'

"Okay young man, take him with you but he is never to step foot in this store again." I felt the sigh of relief coming from Gilbert. As we got up the manager spoke to Gilbert. "You are very lucky to have a brother that cares about you. Listen to your parents. I'm sure your dad cares about you. Stealing will only make your life miserable. Your dad is right, there are a lot of men in prison because once they got started stealing, they didn't stop. Don't you become one of those." "Thank you, sir, I won't!" "Let's go". We walked out the door and starting walking fast in case the manager changed his mind. "Don't let him see us laughing, just keep walking." As soon as we rounded the corner our little gang of ruffians was there waiting for us. They could not believe that I had gotten Gilbert out of there. We laughed and we laughed. I walked around like I had won a thousand dollars. Word spread like wildfire. My reputation was growing, but not in a good way. "Why did you have to slap me so hard?" Gilbert was thankful that I had saved him from the wrath of his father, but he was also a hurt that I had slapped his head so hard. "The manager had to believe it. Why did you get caught? The slap had to be hard to make it believable." We were old beyond our years, and we enjoyed it.

A few days later it was my turn to go into the Safeway and get our lunch. The bell had just rung ending the day. We still considered it lunch as most of us had not eaten. We had started a requirement for those in our group that had started off as a dare. As I opened the doors and walked in the store, I did a recon and saw where the workers were. I walked to the pastries and got a package of cinnamon rolls, a large bag of potato chips, and a large bottle of Dr. Pepper. As I started to walk out the door, I heard a voice behind me.

"Hey, what do you think you're doing?" I recognized the manager's voice. Without turning to look I took off running making sure I did not lose our gourmet meal. The school buses were a block away at the mid high and I had to get there. From the time we were let out of school and our bus left, we had a half an hour. I knew they were getting ready to leave. I could hear the manager yelling at me. "Stop, I'm going to call the police!" I did not stop. I knew if he caught me, I was going to jail. My mom would go get me, and my dad would take care of me. I realized that the manager was not going to quit until he caught me. Mid high was a block away from the Safeway. I was fast. Images of Billy shooting at me with a BB gun played in my mind, his training was working.

As I rounded the corner of Grant Street to West Marcy Street, I could see the activity where all the buses were lined up. The buses had assigned parking spots and I knew exactly how to get to mine. The buses looked like a row of yellow corn in straight lines like our orchard. I zig and I zagged as I worked my way through the buses trying to confuse the manager of the store. I could see the recognition on the faces of several kids as I flew by. Some were perplexed as they saw the booty, some were laughing and pointing, others were pretending not to see. They wanted nothing to do with it. I ran into my bus and headed to the seats in the back of the bus. I got on the floor at the back of the bus. "Sit down and hide me!" "Why, what did you do now?" My brother Arthur had that sound in his voice, he was clearly agitated. Before I could answer I heard the manager as he got on the bus. "Did a kid just run in here carrying a coke?" I was grateful that the bus driver was not in the bus yet or he would have given me up. The drivers congregated outside before doing a head count and he had not seen me board. No one answered until Arthur spoke from the back of the bus. "No, we haven't. If you find him tell him to share."

All the kids on the bus started laughing as the bus driver showed up at the door, it was time to go. "Can I help you with something?" The manager turned to see a not too happy bus driver waiting to leave. "I'm looking for a little truant that shoplifted at my store, the Safeway down the street. I thought I saw him run this way." "Did you see him get on my bus?" "No, but I saw him as he ran around those buses and then he disappeared." "Well, I wish I could help you, but I have a schedule I have to keep. Good luck, I hope you catch him." The manager reluctantly got off the bus and kept looking over his shoulder as he did. The bus driver pulled the handle, closed the door, and drove off. I stayed under the seat until we were a good distance from the school. We ate the treats on the way home, laughing all the way, it was like a party. "Don't laugh so loud, the bus driver keeps looking back here!" Arthur was still agitated but after a cinnamon roll, some potato chips. and some Dr. Pepper he calmed down and enjoyed the ride home. I felt like a pirate! This was one of the best meals I had ever eaten. The excitement mixed with the sweetness of the Dr. Pepper was euphoric. I remembered the chocolate fiasco from Carlos Gilbert. I did not realize that the seriousness of my behavior was escalating.

My friends and I continued to walk to the plaza every day for lunch. It became our thing as we walked, laughed, fought, flirted, stole, and rough housed. When we were lucky, we would be picked up to go cruising with our older brothers, friends, or anyone who would take us. We had started to play hooky in the afternoon. We started drinking and smoking weed. We thought we were cool! We were in the seventh grade! The old Spanish Fortress had become our playground. It had protected our ancestors and had served as the seat of the Spanish government. Now here we were everyday walking in what had become the social center of the locals and the retail center for tourists. I should have known that it would not last.

"Santiago, where have you been, do you have an excuse for being absent the last three days? Mr. Ortiz had been a teacher for ten plus years and had seen it all. "I've been sick, here's the letter from my mom." "Why have you only been sick from your afternoon classes? I talked to all your teachers. Let's go, we're going to the principal's office. Let's call your parents and straighten all of this out. The rest of you, go to chapter ten and start reading for tomorrows test." "What are you doing out there on the streets in the afternoon. Nothing good is going to come from that. When you're here you are a very good student." We arrived in the principal's office, and I had not said a word. As I walked out of the classroom, I noticed all the students looking at me. "Is Mr. Lopez in?" Rhoda the secretary was busy at her desk. "He'll be back, he had to step out for a bit." She looked at me with the look people that cared about me had. She knew me and shook her head from left to right. "Santiago, sit down over there." Mr. Ortiz left with Rhoda's assurance that she would go get him as soon as Mr. Lopez came back.

As I was sitting there waiting, it felt as if I was in jail. I hadn't been in jail, but I had been inside the prison to get haircuts and had heard the metal security doors CLANK behind me. I felt the apprehension as I sat. "What did you do now Santiago? You're such a good boy, why do you do this yourself?" Rhoda was a very nice lady. She had gray hair that she wore in a bun and had a loving face. Rhoda was nice to all the kids. I sat there and didn't answer, I was tired of explaining myself. How could I answer? I really didn't have an answer. I liked the life on the street. "I need to use the bathroom." "Go ahead but come right back." Instead of the bathroom I went straight out the front door and headed for the plaza. "Fuck that shit!" I sat in the Plaza. "I knew that by now they had called my mom and told her I had walked out. It was my dad's day off. He would be waiting for the bus, for me, this time it would be bad. As I sat there a brown Buick passed by. There was a gringo driving it and he smiled and waved at me. I ignored him but he came back around the plaza and slowed down and stopped in front of me. There were people on the square but no one thought anything of it, it was a common practice.

"Hello young man, it's a beautiful day to be outside. Listen, I'm from out of town and I'm looking for someone to show me around." "Why are you telling me?" I wasn't in the mood to deal with another adult, especially a white one. "I'll pay you, all I need to know is where the Cross of the Martyrs is." Thoughts started running through my head. I hardly every had any money and I knew that the white people did. I didn't want to just sit there and wait for the bus. "I can do that, but I have to catch my bus at three. "Alright, let's go!" I stepped off the curb and went and circled the car through the back and noticed that the license plate was not from New Mexico. As I got into the car the driver was moving stuff off the front seat.

"Thank you for agreeing to show me around. I'm from out of town and have heard some wonderful things about Santa Fe. I am thinking about moving here. Are you hungry? My name is Joe what is yours?" "I'm Santiago and yah, I could eat." "Do you know a good place?" "Let's go to Bert's Burger Bowl, its down the street. Go around the plaza and go up the next street." As he drove, I noticed that he wasn't very big. He had on a checkered sweater that stood out, it was red and gray. I would have gotten my ass kicked if I ever wore a sweater like that. His hair was brown and long and looked messy. "Turn here and go down a bit you'll see it on your side." I had heard that the food was really good, I had never eaten here. On the few times we went out for a burger it was always at Lotaburger with my dad.

Bert's parking lot was almost empty, there were only a few cars there." We went in and I ordered a hamburger, fries, and a Dr. Pepper. The line inside was short so our order was placed quickly and before we knew it, our order was ready. "Let's go eat somewhere else where we can enjoy our meal. I heard that the Cross of the Martyrs has a great view of Santa Fe, do you know where it is?" I answered as I licked my lips. "Yah I know where it is. Do you know where the Post Office is?" I could smell the food on my lap. I couldn't wait to sink my teeth into that Bert's Hamburger. I reached into the sack and took a couple of French Fries and slowly put them into my mouth. The hot salty potato strips were one of the tastiest things I had ever tasted. I took a drink

ERIC SANTIAGO MARTINEZ

of my ice-cold Dr. Pepper as Joe nodded and drove towards the Post
Office. I gave him instructions and we headed north on Bishops Lodge
Road. "Turn here." We took a right turn on Kearney Road and drove up
the steep hill. The houses on both sides of Kearney were small, most
were old Spanish architecture. At the end of the steep climb, we turned
right and then right again. Joe drove on the dirt road and parked. The
Cross was below us and we had a great view of the city. As we ate,
I started to get some weird feelings as I caught Joe looking at me in
a strange way, like a cat getting ready to pounce on a rat.

"It is really nice to meet you. It gets lonely when you're by yourself
in new place. Do you get lonely? I could really use a friend. I will treat
you nice if you want to be my friend. We can eat anywhere you want,
and I can give you some money so you can buy yourself some things
that you like." I didn't answer I was too busy eating. I was hungry.
I hadn't eaten since breakfast and the Bert's hamburger and fries were
really good. Joe got quiet and started eating his and then I noticed him
start to move over towards me, slowly. He put his hands on my leg.
"I really like you, let me touch you and when we're done, I'll pay you
and take you back to the plaza." As he said this, he put his hand on my
crutch and started working the zipper on my pants. His face got weird,
it's as if he was another person. He had a hungry look on his face, and
it wasn't for the hamburger and fries. He was licking his lips. I could
see the top of his head as his face got closer to where his hands were,
he was moving faster now. I noticed that he was bald on the top of his
head.

I felt my heart start to pound even faster and harder and my face
got hot. Instantly, I slammed my knee into his face. As his head shot
upward, I reached over and opened the door. I started punching him
as he tried to grab me. All the fighting I had done during my young life
came into play as I punched him in the nose and saw the blood spray
out of his face. "You little shit, why did you come with me, you knew

what we were going to do!" He was yelling as he got out of the car and headed for me. I was surprised at how fast he was. I ran towards the embankment that led down to the cross. We had been here several times drinking and smoking weed. I looked over my shoulder and saw that he was chasing me. There was a steep path that led down off the hill, and I was on it in an instant and instead of running down the curvy path I went straight down sliding most of the way. As loose rocks and dirt followed me down, I looked up the hill and saw him looking down at me. "I'll find you and we will finish what we started!" I saw him turn and he was gone.

My slide down from the Cross ended on Paseo De Peralta. I sprinted the short distance to the Federal Building next to the Post Office and jumped over the brown wall. I used the metal railing running on top to lift myself over and ran towards the building. I was running as fast as I could. I knew he was on his way down. What I didn't know was whether he would come looking for me. As I ran, I thought of my dreams. I was always running from something evil, down deep I was glad that I hadn't been caught...yet. There was an alcove on the east side of the building created by three walls. This alcove was a place we often went to lay in the grass and smoke weed. We knew where all the good hiding places were. We were oblivious to the fact that this is where the Federal Courthouse was and that some of the windows looking down were judge's offices. I crouched in the furthest corner and waited.

I saw Joe or whatever his real name was passing by looking around in slow motion. I could see his head rotating as he scanned the area, he was looking for me. I kept watching as he rounded the corner. I stepped out of the alcove and walked along the edge and saw him go past the Post Office. He crossed the intersection and kept going straight away from me. I sprinted to the bus stop and thanked my lucky stars that the buses were already there waiting. I shared my story on the way home. My brothers and friends were fuming. Juan was adamant. From that day forward I was seldom alone. I knew that if we saw him again, we would kill him or make him wish he was dead. I learned an important lesson that day. Trust the people around you that are like you. I made it home that day and paid for my truancy. The beatings always hurt but I knew that it lasted for a short period of time and then it was business as usual.

Chapter | 30

VISIT TO THE MUSEUM

I stopped ditching school, for the most part. On our daily sojourns into the plaza, we were happy-go-lucky. We were young and felt like we were on top of the world. The music from the cruisers, the strange people walking around looking for deals, and the students on lunch break were invigorating. A group of tourists caught my eye as we walked. I listened as they interacted with each other. I understood the English they were speaking but had to pay close attention to decipher what it meant. The words were the same, but it was a different language, from a different world. "Look Mildred! The Indians are selling jewelry and stuff. I promised Gwen, I would take her some pottery!" We heard this time and time again as they looked right through us. Sometimes I couldn't help myself and did something to make them see me.

On this day as we walked in front of the Plaza Bar. We would often hear laughter and heated discussions echoing from inside. We stopped and listened and laughed at how crazy they were in there. Most of the customers we saw going in and out were locals and we got a kick out of how crazy some of them were. Many times, we saw men stagger out blinded by the bright sunlight. One of my favorites was a man known by the name 'Cantiflas'. Cantiflas was a character well known from

SANTA FE: A PIECE OF 'MI VIDA'

a Mexican TV station. The character Cantiflas was a short heavy-set man who wore his clothes loose and had a comical look about him and his role was very silly. The Santa Fe Cantiflas was dark and brooding and didn't like his nickname and let you know it if he heard you use it.

"What the fuck are you looking at?" He had just walked out of the bar and was talking to himself as much as to anyone in his vicinity. We started to laugh as we saw a group of blonde-haired, blue-eyed tourists almost choke on their burritos and cross the street to the grassy square. They were bewildered as they looked at each other with a concerned look on their faces. As they hurried across, a Lowrider almost hit them. "Hey, gringo, watch where you're going!" "Hey 'carñal', do you guys have a beer? How about some 'mota'? I know you have some I can smell it." Cantiflas was trying to score. "I could use a good joint right about now bro." Cantiflas had zig and zagged his way to the lowrider and was talking to them as if he knew them. The Baby Blue Impala was stopped in the middle of the road. The two young Spanish men in the car were in no hurry. They had nowhere to go and all day to get there.

"Get this dude a beer bro." I saw the passenger reach down and pulled out a Coors. "Here you go bro, be careful with the cops, they don't like it when we drink in public." I kept looking at the scene, to me, it was beautiful. The soft murmur of the high performance 327 motor, the laughter of our little crew, the exchange between the bros on the street, and the look of shock on the faces of most of the white people on the plaza made me proud to be Spanish. We owned the plaza even if the rich owned the buildings, it was ours and it always would be. "Bueno bro, got to roll." The sleek blue machine rolled off like a magic carpet on wheels shining in the beautiful New Mexico sun, low and slow, ready to go. We had been here for centuries, and we acted that way, we weren't visitors looking for a deal, we were for real.

The Plaza Bar was situated in such a way that part of it was a lounge and part of it was a carry out liquor store. Both were run by the same person. The Bartender spent his time in the lounge until someone came into the packaged liquor. There was a door giving him access to the liquor store. When someone went into the liquor store a bell on top of the door would sound and the bartender would go into the liquor store and deal with the customers. As we stood in front of the bar watching the day unfold, Little Andy and Mike McDonald stopped. They looked at each other and nodded. "Let's do it!" I looked over at them and saw them laughing. "What are you guys thinking of doing?"

Mike's red hair sparkled in the sun as he moved back and forth, he was always ready to join in the fun, many times initiating it. It was strange how we had a lot of animosity towards the gringos, but Mike was like us, except red. Mike had become part of our little crew. He had flaming red hair and I had seen him around but had not interacted with him until the day he ran past us being chased by a group of kids from the projects and Alto Street.

I saw that he was strong. He had a look of determination on his face not one of fear. His long red hair was moving side to side as he ran. For whatever reason I stepped in front of Eugene and his friends and asked in a loud voice as they stopped chasing him. "Why does it take so many of you to handle one guy?" I recognized most of them and knew I could take them, and if not, one of my brothers could. There were a couple of older ones, Eugene was the toughest of them. I knew right away what was going to happen as my friends got closer to me. The other kids had seen the commotion and a crowd had gathered around. I could hear the whispers in the quiet anticipation. For that moment in time, all of us, friend and foe were frozen in time. That moment was worth any result that would follow. My dad often admonished us by explaining that rolling stones eventually ran into each other. Here we were, we had run into each other.

The leader of their pack was Eugene. I had seen him around and knew him well as he was Little Andy's older brother. Eugene quickly approached me with an attitude. He was two years older than me, and I recognized the look on his face, he was going to beat me down in front of the whole school, or at least he thought so. He didn't say anything as he took a swing at me. I had seen it coming and I knew it was on. I dodged his blow and returned with a series of punches that took him by surprise. I saw the look on his face as he realized he had bitten off more than he could chew. Often, I was underestimated by those that were older than me. They didn't realize that age was a number, and the skill and temperament were not always an accurate measurement through that medium.

My upbringing was serving me well on the streets. He came back at me with a kick, and I grabbed it and used his momentum to pull him forward. He landed on the ground with his hands and knees saving him from full frontal contact with the ground. I could hear the reaction from the bystanders as he hit the floor with a loud thump. "In jiu jitsu you use the other persons momentum against them." My dad's words echoed in my head as he had trained us. "They train us on this so that we can handle the convicts. It works but you still need to use your boxing skills. One more thing, if you get them down, don't let them get back up." I maneuvered to the side of Eugene and kicked him on the side of the face as he was trying to get up. As he went back down, I broke my dad's rule. "Get up punk!" I knew I was center stage and it felt good. Eugene made a fatal error and got back up. Before he was fully erect, I caught him with an uppercut, and he went back down.

"Don't get back up bro!" Before I could finish my sentence, I felt a hand on my back. "Let's go, here comes the principal." Mike had turned back and was thanking me by saving me from a trip to the principal's office. As we walked away, I saw the principal and a couple of teachers nearing the crowd. Eugene got up and walked away. I couldn't help but notice that Mike was wearing Beatle boots. The Beatles were at the top of the charts and the mania around them was something I had never seen before. I was wishing I could have some of those boots, but it was not to be. Mike became one of my best friends that day. He was a tough kid when he wasn't running for his life.

Mike's father worked in Los Alamos. The labs had been key in the development of the Atomic Bomb. They lived in a nice house in Tesuque, and it was obvious they had money. "Thanks for saving my ass today. Those guys have been after me for a few days." I knew that the issue with Eugene was not over. Eugene lived in a dangerous part of town, and he had several brothers, stacked by age, they resembled us. They were a dangerous bunch. They were from Santa Fe, and we would have several confrontations with them down the road. We were at a disadvantage. We were the outsiders. They were a large family with a lot of historical relationships.

Now here I was watching as Eugene's younger brother, Little Andy, got down on the cement sidewalk directly in front of the Plaza Bar and Liquor Store. It was happening so fast we didn't have time to plan anything. We kept a look out as they executed their plan. We got lucky, there was no one around to notice. "Hurry up before someone see's us and calls the cops!" I was getting nervous, the last thing I needed was to be arrested. My confrontations with my dad had gotten more violent. I didn't want to imagine what would happen to me if I ended up in jail. Andy looked back and up at me; he was having the time of his life. Little Andy pushed on the door quietly, as he slowly opened the door a couple of inches making sure the bell didn't ring. Mike reached up and held the bell at the top of the door opening the door so that Little Andy could crawl in.

Mike was tall for his age and had no problem reaching to the top of the door and holding the bell. We all watched as Little Andy crawled and grabbed a couple of bottles of whiskey and crawled out. "Let's go you guys! Let's get out of here." I feared being caught. "Hide the bottles!" Mike was directing traffic. He had come up with the plan and done it, so we went along with him. Two of us tucked the bottles against our side and the others walked in front of us so that no one would see our bounty. The chocolate pirates had become whiskey pirates. "Have you ever had whiskey before?" Andy was laughing as we walked. "I have, it's pretty strong. Do you guys want to drink it or sell it?" I remembered the Mason Whiskey Jar.

There was a Sock Hop Dance scheduled for the afternoon in the gym and all of us were excited about it. "Let's find a place to drink some!" I pretended like I knew all about it. I had seen my dad and his friends pass a bottle around. It was funny watching the faces they made as they took a swig and passed the bottle. I had seen how they got, talking louder, challenging each other, and often fighting with each other. I felt a twinge as I remembered when I saw my dad beat up my uncle. "Where can we drink some and hide the rest for later?" Mike was ready to go. As we talked, we looked through the metal gate of the Museum. I had been curious about the old stagecoaches inside the yard. "Let's go in there, we can sit down inside, no one will see us." Without hesitation Mike and I helped Little Andy and Gilbert up and over, then we climbed over the gate.

We all clamored into one of the stagecoaches and opened the first bottle of strong-smelling liquor. I was the first to tip the bottle back and take a good look at it. I had never been this close to one, much less own one. The bottle was dark and kind of scary to me. As I unscrewed the lid, a powerful smell wafted up into my eyes and nose. The smell made me gag. I held the bottle up away from me. "This stuff stinks! Why would anyone drink this stuff?" "Because it gets you drunk bro!" Gilbert reached out and took the bottle. "I'll go first." Gilbert put the bottle up to his mouth and took a small drink. His neck and head bopped downward then upward. "Damn, it burns! Who wants to go next?" Little Andy grabbed the bottle and took a big swig. I could smell the Jack Daniels in the air. "Whoa, that stuff is good! I can feel it in my stomach!" Mike went next and had pretty much the same response. "Here you go Santiago, take a drink, it isn't that bad once you swallow it." I grabbed the bottle and took a small drink and held the bottle for a while then took another. We passed the bottle around sitting in one of the stagecoaches in the outdoor exhibition. It was surreal sitting there with our whiskey. The seats were hard, and we sat facing each other. "Be quiet, don't talk so loud, they'll hear us!" Mike was looking around and you could see a worried look on his face. "Don't want anymore, my head is spinning, I feel like throwing up." Gilbert had started to slur his words. "Me too, I can't go home drunk, my mom will kill me."

"I don't want anymore, I'm feeling dizzy." The exchange continued for a bit as we sat there feeling the whisky take over. "Give me that bottle over here, I'm feeling good!" I grabbed the bottle from Mike and took a long slow drink. "You're crazy, we have to go back to school! You better hope they don't find out that you're drunk." We tried to jump back over the wall into the street, but we were too drunk. We wobbled inside the museum and found the exit without being challenged. We went on our way to the school and the Sock Hop, then it went black.

"Hey bro, do you remember what happened yesterday?" I stood there with the Pen gang. I was suffering from my first hangover, and it was a painful one. My mouth was dry, my head hurt, and shame oozed out of my pores. I had dodged a bullet. My dad was in Española and my mom had left early to go to one of her part time jobs. I could remember some of what had happened. I remembered dancing on my knees. I was so drunk I couldn't stand up. "I remember some of it, what happened?" "You were really drunk, wanting to fight with everyone." "You were really drunk bro! You drank most of the whiskey!" Gilbert was enjoying himself. "You danced with Charlotte until she left you. You should have seen the look on her face! You are lucky she didn't kick your ass bro!"

"When you were on your knees dancing everyone stood in a circle with you in the middle, some were laughing, most of them were

SANTA FE: A PIECE OF 'MI VIDA'

making fun of you. She walked away from you with a look of disgust and humiliation. Do you remember Mr. Saiz grabbing and picking you up off the floor? You started punching him. He went and got Salazar. He lifted you off your feet and carried you out of the gym like a sack of potatoes. It was funny bro, you kept trying to wiggle free. You looked like a fish on a line being pulled out of the water. It was funny. The sock up was cancelled, and we had to go back to our rooms. What happened in the office?" I heard Gilbert ask the questions, I really didn't want to know the answers.

"I don't remember very much. I know the police came and got me and took me to the Detention Center. My mom went and got me, brought me home and I guess I passed out. Thank God my dad isn't home. He is going to be mad! My mom was! I guess they told her I was expelled and that I was never to step foot in Harvey again." The discussion continued. "So, what are you going to do? That's crazy bro!" Gilbert piped in. "The other bottle is still in the wagon. We should go get it." "No way, my dad is going to kill me." "Charlotte hates your guts. You know that Mr. Saiz is her uncle?" "I didn't know that. All I know is that she will never talk to me ever again. Did I really start punching him?" "Yeah, you did, you got him good a couple of times. You could see the bruises on his face. They stopped the dance. A lot of the students were not very happy with you. As soon as we saw you dancing on the floor, we tried to stop you, but you wouldn't listen."

Gilbert continued smiling as he continued. "We moved to the back of the crowd. We didn't want to be taken with you. You drank too much. We are all glad we stopped when we did." Gilbert was shaking his head in disbelief. I stood there with nothing left to say. I felt a knot in my stomach. I was ashamed and scared. I felt alone again and knew it was my fault. I also knew that when my dad got home, I was in for it. My brothers were relentless talking to me about how stupid I was and what was going to happen to me when dad got home. My mom said very little to me when she got home. I could see the disappointment, layered between the love and anger on her face. I thought about how my life seemed to be strange. I was looking through a glass wall wanting to be on the other side of it, where the normal kids were. Every time I thought I was going to make it passed the wall, I ran up against it. The wall kept me in, feeling frustration, shame, pain that turned into anger. The result was living in a world devoid of hope. Would it ever end? Would I ever get to the other side of the glass wall? I felt trapped.

I never knew what had been said at whatever meetings my mom went to. All I knew is that the expulsion was permanent, and they had come up with a plan to keep me in school. The bus we rode to school stopped at the high school first then went to Mid High where we got off and walked to Harvey. De Vargas Junior high was right next to the High School, and it was decided I would be transferred to that school. "This is the last straw for your son in the Santa Fe schools. If he has another incident you will have to enroll him in a different city. We do have St. Michaels here in Santa Fe but it is a Christian Brothers school. This would be a very good alternative as he would get the individual attention he needs. However, it is problematic in that they charge tuition, and you would have to set up transportation." So, it was decided, De Vargas Junior High was my new school. Every day the bus would drop kids off at the High School, then stop in front of De Vargas. The bus door would open, and one student would get off, me. Once again life had found a way to keep me in school.

De Vargas was totally different from Harvey. It was new, and the environment was almost the opposite of Harvey. Many of the students were from Dale Bellamah, a middle-class neighborhood though a few students were from the low-income projects nearby. I was tired of the trauma and decided to focus on going to school. My year at De Vargas was probably the best year of my young life. My new friends were friendly and got along with each other. There was very little fighting, boozing, and acting stupid. I joined the basketball team and did really well. I was living my life on another planet where the sun shone, and the birds sang. My dreams of the Ghost train went away during this time. The whole time I was there I was involved with my new friends. It was difficult for me to truly engage because we lived so far away. Little by little I was being pulled back into my world of tragedy, sadness, and pain. I saw Billy a few times. I heard whispers from my mom and anyone that visited that Billy was running out of room to run. The judges in Rio Arriba were pushing for him to get out of town. They knew if he didn't, he would end up in jail. Not a good place for someone whose father worked at the State Penitentiary.

Chapter | 31

WAKE UP CALL

"Time to get up if you want to eat!" Clang, clang, clang, the metallic sound of two pieces of metal coming together echoed throughout the Española jail. "Hey Billy, wake up bro, time for breakfast." Pedro had been in jail multiple times and knew his way around. The opening of the doors to the cell block got Billy's attention, the guard greeted Pedro. "I don't believe it! Pedro, last time you were here you told me you were done with the nonsense, 'que tienes', what's up with you? What are you in here for this time?" The jail guard was shaking his head back and forth as he spoke. He was laughing. Pedro didn't know if the laugh was out of caring or out of mockery. "They say I stole a car. I didn't steal it! This guy I met at the Saints and Sinners Night Club asked me to drive him home in his car, he couldn't even stand up."

Pedro was partially right. His challenge was going to be explaining why a day later he still had the car. "Oh really, you expect the judge to believe that story? How many times have you been in front of the judge this year? You know Judge Salazar is tired. He's been taking a lot of heat from the State Police. He can't let you guys just come and go because he knows your family. And you Billy, what are you doing hanging around with this crazy fool?" Billy was awake laying in the bottom rack. "Your dad works at the prison. You know what will happen to you if you get

time, right? They'll probably move you to another state and those fools
will find out from these fools who you are. Don't be stupid, 'pendejo'!"
Billy didn't say anything, everyone was telling him what the dangers
were if he ended up in prison, he was tired of hearing it.

"So, what's the word, has my dad been told that I'm in here?"
Billy was defiant. He knew that through all the anger and impatience,
dad always showed up. "I don't know, you guys were arrested after
midnight. What's the phone number, I'll give him a call. You know
your dad and I go back a long time, we're 'primos', first cousins. Our
families both come from the Salazar's, your dad through his grandma
and me through my dad. You know he's not going to be happy. Your
father is one mean, mean man. Story is that his brothers didn't treat
him very well. Every time I saw him, he was alone. Your grandma, his
mom, was crazy, so was her family."

The guard was bored. "You know she was Fresquez. Your familia
through your grandma's side are from Santa Cruz. They are all crazy as
hell. They drink and they fight with anyone in the vicinity, normally
with each other as most people stay away. Anyway, I'll call your dad."
As he walked away Billy asked, "Can you bring us a little extra food,
I haven't eaten since breakfast yesterday." Billy could feel the hunger
pangs that combined with the hangover and after-effects of a night
obviously gone bad. The guard came back in a few minutes. "I talked to
your mom, she'll let your dad know. You are breaking her heart. Here
take this, don't say anything, I'm not supposed to bring anything in."
Billy grabbed the burrito and inhaled it, he was starving, and he was in
a mess. This was serious and he knew it.

A few days passed and Billy was still locked up. Pedro was out
of there the following morning and Billy continued to wake up in jail.
Billy had expected to get out as well, he always did. This time he was
surprised he was still locked up. People had been warning him to no
avail. He was in his personal river running through space and time and

was being swept along as if a force had him and wouldn't let him go. As the days slowly passed the jail guard often brought snacks and reading material. Billy knew the other prisoners were not being treated that way and he began to hear about it.

"Who are you bro? I've been in prison. We don't like it when someone gets too close to the guards. Most of the time they turn out to be rats. Are you a rat? I'll make you my girlfriend." The prisoner laughed an evil laugh. The way he talked to the other prisoners it became obvious that he had done time. Billy noticed him right away. The tattoo tear drops under his eye told him that this prisoner had done some serious time. Some said that each teardrop represented a life taken and some said every teardrop represented a year locked up in prison. "Who's your dad 'ese', maybe I know him. Is he a punk like you? Maybe I'll see you in the shower, I can hardly wait!" The verbal assault continued. Billy ignored him. He hoped that no one who knew him showed up. He knew that if he was identified as the son of a correctional officer at the prison, his life would become a living hell. He would be grouped with rats, child molesters, queers, and any type of incarcerated law enforcement. Every bone in his body wanted to confront this guy. Hopefully, he would see this loudmouth outside. One could only hope.

The Española jail was a small square building with a small central control office where administration was located. The cells were in the back of the building and were accessed through a steel door that could only be opened by the guards. The loud clanking of the ancient steel doors was enough to scare you out of your pants. The individual cells held two to four inmates. Billy and Pedro had been assigned to a double cell. The smell was horrible. The facility was grungy, it stunk of dirty humans and their waste. The facility held both adults and teenagers as there wasn't a juvenile detention center in town. Some of the young ones could be heard crying, especially at night.

After Pedro was released, Billy was in the cell alone. He had moved the mattress off the top metal bunk to the bottom. He had discovered a yellow liquid oozing out of the mattress. It gave Billy the creeps. Pedro had slept on that mattress. "There's shit coming out of this mattress!" Billy announced to the guard. "Don't worry about it, we'll get to it. Until then, use the other one, or sleep on the rack without a mattress." "When does Salazar come in?" "He'll be here in a little while. I'll let him know you want to see him." Just as the words had been spoken, Salazar walked in.

"I talked to your dad yesterday, he's having a hard time getting you out of here. They charged both of you with auto theft. I guess in your adventure you totaled a stolen car. They are also charging you with hit and run. When the cops tried to arrest you, you idiots fled and wrecked the car. My young cousin, what will become of you. When your dad can't get my uncle to ignore the charges, you know it's serious. Your dad is working on it, I'll keep you posted." Billy hung his head and returned to reading one of the books he had been given, 'The Cross and the Switch Blade'. Billy read that it's possible to take the wrong path and still turn his life around. "I wonder if I can do it?"

Billy was down and out; he knew he was digging a very deep hole for himself. He saw it in the sadness that had come over his mom and dad. He had been gone a long time from his family. He wanted to go back but felt as if he could never go back. The reality began to set in. What was he going to do? Where was he going to go? What was going to happen to him? These and other questions began to run through his mind. Images of the war in Vietnam were becoming common. He saw the young soldiers on TV, and they reminded him of himself. The smiles they had during the battle somehow made him smile. How could they smile when they were facing an enemy trying to kill them and they were trying to kill the enemy. He felt a yearning in his heart as if he was being called. He knew several young men who had gone off, some had come back in a box.

"Martinez, let's go your dad is here." Billy heard the jingle of keys as the guard took them off his belt and jiggled one in the door lock to his cell. The key rattled and the door squeaked as it opened. "Take care young man, you better understand that you are at the end of your rope, don't hang yourself with it. The system can't bend for you anymore. Do what your dad says, he knows." The guard talked to him as he opened the steel rod door and walked him to the front where his dad was waiting.

"Why do you want to join the Marines son, you are too young?" Billy was talking to our parents. "You aren't old enough to enlist, you're not old enough and I won't sign for you." My dad was adamant about this. "You are scheduled to meet with Judge Salazar next month, he put it off as long as he can. You will have to spend some time in jail! You just dug the hole too deep. Don't worry we'll make it out of this, just don't get into any more trouble." Billy had gotten a letter from Frankie King. Billy respected Frankie and he saw the Marines as his way out. "Frankie is in the Marines, he's doing alright. He's saving his money and is going to buy a new car when he comes home. I could do the same thing, plus it would get me out of this mess." "I still don't want you to go."

"How about you mom, what do you think?" She took some time to think and then answered. "I think that when it's our turn to die it doesn't matter where we are. God knows what his plan is for us. The way I see it, you could die on the streets over here, especially the way you are living. It's up to your dad whether we sign for you or not. I do know from the news that a lot of young men are getting killed over there. Some are coming back missing limbs. When they get back, they are being called baby killers by the hippies who are cowards and are running away to Canada. Why are you so set on going if no one appreciates it anyway?"

"Mom, it's not about them, it's about me. I want my life to mean something! I'll probably get drafted anyway. I am going to go one way or the other. It's dumb for me to go to jail before I go." Often the military was a way out for troubled young men. Judges often used the military to prevent jail time for them. The judges gave the same rationale Judge Salazar was giving him. "If you join the Marines, I won't have to sentence you to jail."

Over the next few weeks Billy continued to pursue his desire to enlist. He was getting antsy hanging around the Prison Housing, but he had no choice. If they caught him again, he would not get out of jail. He had too many charges pending and his parents couldn't afford bail. He missed his friends and life in Española but deep down inside he knew he had to get out of there while he still could. He knew that they had done all kinds of crazy shit. He wondered what would happen if they found out about the rest of the crimes he had committed. Would they add more charges and send him to prison? Billy had noticed that his friends were all going off in different directions, he had been noticing it for a while. "Mom, you have to sign for me, don't you understand. I really want to go. I turn 18 in a few months! I'll probably get drafted anyway!" His mom loved him so much her heart ached.

Her anger towards Billy Sr. was growing. He's the one that took him out and showed him how to drink and do whatever he wanted to do. "Children want to be what they see." Her sister told her every chance she got. "Are you surprised that your sons are all headed down the same path as that worthless husband of yours?" "Don't talk about Billy like that, he is still my husband." She would always defend him even when she knew in her heart that they were right. "I'll talk to your dad again and see if he'll change his mind. Until then, stay out of trouble." She knew her son and she knew that he was not going to let it go. As he walked away, she felt a pang. What if he went and she lost him to that stupid war? She was angry that a country that did so little for her family found it so easy to send them over there to die. What was she going to do?

Billy was on a mission! Something from deep inside was calling him, he knew he was a soldier now, he had just been fighting the wrong war. "Why can't I make them understand, I don't want to be here anymore?" Pat was listening as the love of her young life poured his heart out to her. Billy had hitch-hiked to Española, he had to talk to Pat. "Just think, when I come back, we can get married and start a life for ourselves away from this place. I don't want my kids growing up here. Most of the people that stay here are living in the past." He had lost his family, at least that is how he felt. He watched as others built a family for themselves. They were getting married, going off to school, leaving to find work, or working their family properties to support themselves and their families. Billy wondered, "What am I doing?"

"What have I done Pat? Where do I go? I feel out of place, my life has become hollow! I have a hole in my heart! You are all I have now, I have nothing to offer you. Do you understand why I have to go?" Pat reached over and wiped the tears off his face and ran her hands over the scar that ran over his right eye. She remembered when his dad had come over and forced him into the car slamming him against the roof. She had cried that night. She felt his pain and she was powerless to help him. She was feeling that way now. "I don't want you to go Billy. We could get married! I can go to work!" Billy interrupted her. "And me what do I do? I don't want to work in the mines or the potato fields like the Mexicans that cross the border!" Pat knew it was done, he was going to go and that was all there was to it.

Chapter | 32

AGAIN

B illy was determined to make something more of himself and make up for all the harm he had done. As he walked the five miles to El Guache he thought about how much Pat loved him. Memories began to surface. He remembered what had happened to land him back in jail. He had been sitting around with grandpa. It had been nice, just the two of them at peace with each other. These moments were rare, and Billy was enjoying every moment. "Grandpa, what do you think about me going into the Marines?" "I've heard about you wanting to do that. Most of the young men that go don't come back. For what? The Gringo doesn't care about us. Our family has been fighting wars for as long as we've been alive, way back."

"Our name comes from Mars the Roman God of War. We've believed that it is our duty to do so. God tells us 'Thou shalt not kill' but we don't listen. It's up to you. It's obvious to me that you are going to do whatever you want. Let's not talk about it right now, let's have some breakfast. I have some fresh eggs, tortillas, beans and red chili and we can fry some papitas to go along with it. What the hell, I'll brew us a pot of fresh coffee." The two sat down and Billy ate the best breakfast he had eaten in a very long time. "I love you grandpa, thanks for always being there for me." "I love you too 'mi jito'. I love you too my grandson. Don't forget that wherever you go and whatever you do, you take a piece of 'Mi Vida', my life, with you."

Billy continued remembering the events of that night. Pedro had picked him up in El Guache. "Hey bro, you want to go for a beer?" "Of course, what do you think?" Billy as usual agreed without hesitation. This had become who he was. He was always ready to go. He was known as the guy who always went and never backed down no matter what. "Nice car bro, where did you get it?" "You'll never believe it. I was standing outside the Saints and Sinners the day before yesterday and this 'vato' comes stumbling out of the bar. A couple of guys follow him out. I heard them talking about rolling him. 'Quick take his wallet, he's been flashing cash around all night. Look at him, he can barely stand up'! I didn't like what I was hearing."

Pedro continued, "The little one rushed up to him and pushed him down. The old man had grey hair and obviously was unable to defend himself. Both of them started going through his pockets. I couldn't believe what those two were doing. I yelled at them, hey, what do you think you're doing? They turned as I yelled. I wasn't going to let them take advantage of this guy. The big one turned and walked away from the old dude. 'Get the hell out of here before you end up like him'! I locked eyes with him. Right now, you don't know who you're messing with. What did that dude do to you? You should have seen the look on their faces. The two walked up to me. They looked funny but dangerous. One was big and the other one was small, like a midget bro."

Pedro laughed as he continued with his story. "Before they got too close, I rushed the little one and pushed him into the big one. The little one fell to the ground, but nothing happened to the big one. This dude was big bro. I got ready to get my ass kicked. I heard a voice behind me. 'Hey Maclovio, leave him alone!' It was your dad. Man was I happy to see him!" Billy responded in a voice filled with disappointment. "I know how he is. How bad did he hurt that pendejo?" "They didn't fight, your dad walked up to him and shook his hand and set him straight. 'This is one of us. You mess with him you'll deal with me'. Your dad saved my ass!"

"Anyway, the two pendejos went inside after talking trash with each other. I flashed them this before they split." Pedro laughed as he pointed his middle finger towards the sky. "I lifted the old guy off the floor, he could barely walk bro. I'm glad I was there to help him out. "I know who they are now, they're always with Felix and Rudy." Now Pedro really had Billy's attention. "Those two brothers are always out looking to screw someone." Billy was remembering the exchange at the swimming hole. "One of these days I'll take care of those pieces of shit; they've messed with me one too many times." Pedro was worried, he had seen that look on Billy's face before, it often led to trouble. "Anyway, the old dude passed me a twenty and told me where he lived and asked me to drive him home. For a twenty I'll drive you wherever, let's go. I took him home in Velarde and was going to hitch it back when he told me to take his car and bring it back the following day. Well, here I am, still in his car. I'll take it back tomorrow bro let's go party!"

As they drove around town, Billy was remembering Felix and Rudy. Ever since the day he and his brothers were swimming at the rock the relationship had become hostile. Every time they saw each other an exchange took place. "The only reason we don't kill you is your dad." The brothers always confronted him every time they saw him. Billy's response was always the same. "Come on, don't worry about my dad, you'll need a doctor when I'm done with you!" And so, it went. One night Billy was caught between them at a dance at the National Guard Armory, he was pretty loaded. He had gotten lucky that night. Pedro just happened to be driving by and pulled over, recognizing Billy. "Remember the night you pulled over just in time? If it wouldn't have been for you, they would have hurt me bad. One of these days I'll take care of them."

"There they go!" "Who are you talking about?" Pedro responded not knowing what Billy was talking about. "Rudy and Felix, see them up ahead. I can tell by the way they walk, swinging their arms up to heaven, talking to themselves more than to each other. Turn in that side road and turn off your lights." The Mares brothers, Felix, and Rudy were often seen walking down the road. They were scary looking; they were tall and lanky and walked like the wind. They resembled witches but looked much more sinister. "Open the trunk, Pedro!" Billy was out of the car and at the trunk in an instant. Pedro got out and opened the trunk. Billy fished around until he found what he was looking for, a tire iron. It was on now! Billy took off running after the brothers in the dark. It was pitch black outside, so he had to let his eyes adjust. Pedro was close on his heels, they had to be careful. The two brothers were known to fight dirty having stabbed more than a few. It was rumored that they had killed a couple of guys by stabbing them and then pounding them to death.

When the brothers disappeared around a turn, Billy made his move with Pedro on his heels. "Hey, you fuckin' little whore, let's see how bad you are now!" Billy rushed forward with the tire iron at the ready. In an instant Felix turned around and slipped to the left catching Billy with a right as he moved. "I've been waiting a long time, where's your dad at punk?" The two were circling each other now. Pedro and Rudy were going at it, full blast. Billy's world slowed down. It was so dark; all he saw was the dull ribbon of the dirt road and the gleam in the eyes of Felix. Billy wondered if he had just made a big mistake. It was too late now. They were in a bubble floating through space. Inside the bubble it was clear as day. The dark existed on the outside. He could see the chrome knife shining like lightning in the sky. Felix was the toughest of the two, he was stalking Billy with the knife.

Through the side of his eyes Billy could see that Pedro was winning the fight with Rudy. They were on the ground and Pedro was on top pounding Rudy into the dirt. The bubble slowed the motion inside. It was slow, the motion permeated the inner circle. Felix lunged at Billy with the knife. He was quicker than Billy and the cut was true, he cut Billy on the arm. As the blood started to flow Billy could see that the face dancing around him belonged to a force that was old as the night. His night had started out great, promising heaven and now delivering hell. Felix had that grin as he moved in. "I told you I'd get you, now I'm going to kill you." As Felix moved in Billy swung the tire iron catching Felix in the arm. As Felix moved back, Billy attacked striking with the tire iron, landing blow after blow as Felix stepped back trying to avoid the blows. Billy could see the flashing pain from Felix filling the bubble. The last blow was to the head and Felix went down, the bubble burst.

They left the two brothers in the middle of that darkened dirt road. Billy remembered the feeling, the bubble had burst, and he had been thrust from it to find himself clubbing Felix with the iron, blood oozing into the dirt. "Stop It bro! Let's go! Don't kill him!" Pedro had grabbed Billy and led him towards the car. They drove the half mile to grandpa's house, jumped into the ditch to wash off the battle grime. They tossed the tire iron into the irrigation ditch. "You might have killed him, Billy! You were possessed, you just kept hitting him!" "I hope I did; he's been messing with us for a long time. Let's go get a beer." The two-drove listening to the music playing on the radio. It had already been a long night. As they cruised into Española, they heard a siren and saw the flashing lights on the police cruiser behind them. "I hope they didn't find Rudy and Felix! I hope you didn't kill Felix! I wonder why they are pulling us over!" Pedro was speaking loud and fast, clearly worried about what was going to happen to them.

"Don't let them catch us, punch it, head back towards El Guache, we can hide in the bosque!" It didn't take but an instant for Pedro to gun the SS. The car bolted forward; the high horsepower engine roared to life. With tires squealing, adrenaline pumping, the race was on. Pedro made a fish-tailing U-turn with Española PD in hot pursuit. The police officer could not keep up with the Nova SS and the duo was getting further and further ahead. As they approached Dead Man's Curve, a worried look came over Billy. Billy yelled, "Watch out!" In an instant the car was airborne! The car went over the embankment! The car landed and lurched forward repeatedly slamming into the hard cold earth coming to rest on its roof on the dirt road below. All four wheels continued to turn as if it wanted to keep on rolling.

Both Billy and Pedro were in shock and bleeding. A State Trooper had seen them fly by and joined the chase. He got there as Billy and Pedro were crawling out of the mangled steel. "Get on your stomach, both of you!" Without hesitation they took off running. Billy knew the Trooper would not shoot. Billy couldn't run very fast; he had hurt his knee and had bruising all over his body. It didn't take much effort for the Trooper to run him down. He pushed Billy down to the ground and handcuffed him.

Chapter | 33

LET IT RAIN

B illy came home from boot camp after 12 weeks and he looked so different. He looked happy. He was in his Marine Corps Dress Blues and he looked like something out of a movie. I knew what I wanted to do. He shared stories with us about his experience. One of the things he shared was the constant statement of the Drill Instructors. The statements about how long Marines on the front lines survived had troubled him. According to Billy, the Drill Instructors kept telling them that most of them died within a few months. I could see a strange look behind the smile. It was as if Billy knew he wouldn't make it back. As a high school dropout, he was a grunt, Infantry. He would be face to face with the enemy on the front lines. "Nothing is going to happen to him he's too tough!" My dad said it often like he was trying to convince himself. I was so impressed the day Billy asked dad to borrow the rifle. Billy did the rifle drill they had taught him. The precision was amazing. His body was solid, the only thing moving were his arms and the rifle, his gaze never moved. We all stood around watching, the silence was golden. That was our Billy. The collective pride and amazement filled the air. After a couple of days Billy went off to Española. "I have to see Pat."

I hadn't dreamt in a while, but I could feel the fear every time I went to bed. The few times I did dream I couldn't remember the details. All I could remember was running from the Conductor, and Billy on the train enjoying the things that I feared. I was afraid that if I boarded the train, it would put him in the hands of the grinning, blood dripping monster of my dreams. I woke up fearing what would happen to me. I was starting to see that my life was driven by the fear of my haunting dreams, the love of my brother, my dad's continued abuse of my family, and lack of physical and emotional love from my mother. We knew she loved us, we just wanted her to show it, to live it.

My night journeys seemed to mirror my life. The years of my dreams mirrored the days of my life, only my dreams were much more intense and were getting stronger and more violent. I worried about what was next. What would happen to my brother? I sought solace in the love of my mom, but she was mostly gone working all the time. Where would my life's journey take me? What would happen to us? My young mind was stretching, trying to wrap around the complicated relationship between the past, the present, and the future.

Before he left to Española, Billy pulled me aside and talked to me about how I was doing. I stayed quiet as he spoke. There was an urgency in his words. "So, what's going on with you? Are you still having those crazy dreams? Remember, they are only dreams. Have you told anyone about them?" I replied, "No, you told me not to say anything, but my mom is asking me about them. I wake up screaming sometimes. I worry about you. I see a creature taking you on a journey of pleasure and sadness, and I'm along for the ride and he sees me watching you, following you, trying to protect you, do you see him?"

His answer was clipped with a foreboding undertone, like he was hiding something from me. "I don't see anyone, let it go." He was a Marine and his power flowed from him, I felt it! Juan, Arthur, and Michael joined us as we played basketball in the back yard. Billy was aware of the reality he had created for himself. He was going away for a long time. News on the TV showed where he was going. We saw it every day. We saw the helicopters dropping the young soldiers and Marines into the jungle, the battles, and the dead, Vietnam. We watched as they were treated with hate when they got back. I hated the hippies with their dirty long hair and big mouths. Every time I saw them on the TV, I thought of how they had killed my uncle in El Rito. Hippies were cowards to me.

My life went on as usual, always on the edge, always pushing the limits, and always answering and paying the price. For such a young person, I understood and did things that few my age did. Even the Pen Gang started to drift away. My life was like the burning of Zozobra, the paper mâché monster that was burnt every year for the Santa Fe Fiestas representing the purging of all our sins the year before. And like Zozobra, right after the purge the sins began to pile up again to be burned the following year. In my case, the burning took place several times a year. It never went away. It was a process, the process of life and death, pain, and pleasure and all the things imbedded in these.

The fiestas were always an exciting time for us. No matter what we did during the day, late at night is when the real action took place. For the most part, by 10:00 PM anyone with any common sense left the Plaza. Late at night after a day of partying, the gangs, clans, and the crazies would walk around the plaza looking for trouble. We were involved in several clashes that invariably left some badly injured. The excitement of it made me want to do it over and over again. Many who I ran with resented and regretted being with me, to quote some of them, "All you want to do is fight!" I never questioned why I liked it so much. I just did it! Maybe it was because I was good at it! Most people want to do things they do well. I was born and raised in a violent world. I loved to fight and hang out with the misfits. It was amazing how many of us there were.

I thought of Billy a lot. I didn't see him until the day he left. I walked with him to Highway 14 where a military convoy picked him up and took him back to the Marines. I thought about how important he was that all those green military vehicles would park on the side of the road and wait for him. I was so proud to walk with him through the rattlesnake infested field. He was in his uniform carrying his duffle bag. I walked with my chest out, I pretended to be a Marine. "Go back now, I'll see you next time I come home." I didn't say too much; I knew he meant it. I stopped and watched him walk the rest of the way throwing his duffel bag into one of the trucks, climb aboard, and leave me. I started to cry. I was unable to control my sadness and my fear. It felt as if my life had just walked away. I was heartbroken. I carried the pain and sadness into everything I did and everywhere I went. My anger and aggression grew. I lived where few dared to tread. I was on the other side of the line that most people were afraid to cross. It was only me and the other few who found themselves on the wrong side of life.

It had been a long day for me. It had rained for most of the day. My brothers, our friends, and I had been out in the rain all day. I fell asleep that night and could feel that my spirit was uneasy. I was walking through the family orchard and farm in El Guache. I was back to the first time I had followed Billy through the brightness of the full moon and through the fog rising from the footsteps of the old train tracks. It felt strange, different, it felt as if I had gone full circle, but I knew my journey wasn't over. I was with Billy walking through the fog. This time he was walking taller rising above the fog. I was expecting him to tell me to go away like the good old days, but he didn't. I felt strange, I was used to a tense Billy, my brother who was always on the edge. I liked this one better, but it gave me a strange feeling.

As we got on the train, I saw that the passengers were different. I recognized a lot of them. Norman was sitting in the first seat, no sign of the self-inflicted gunshot wound to the head upon his return from Vietnam. I noticed in the corner that my two uncles were sitting there smiling at each other. My Uncle Donald who had been shot point blank in the chest and my Uncle Roy who I watched die of alcoholism at the Veterans Hospital in Albuquerque. On and on the faces morphed before me. I was trying to understand. As the train got ready to go, I heard a whistle blow as if I was very far away.

Everyone on the train looked and stared at me. There were no expressions, just the faces from the past. I knew they were long gone by the looks on their faces and the clothes that they wore. I couldn't stop myself from wanting to be wherever the train and Billy went. For the first time, Billy talked to me as the train clanked away to a place I knew nothing about. "Let's go home Billy I don't like this place. The Conductor scares me." Billy responded. "You have to fight him, soon he will offer things that look good, don't fall for it. Don't do what I have done, look where it has me. It's too late for me but not for you." My dreams made me sadder than I had ever been.

"I have to go now little brother. I can't go home with you now. I will always be there for you. If you need me, see me like you do right now. You are the only one that came to me now that I'm ready to leave my body behind." I responded with curiosity and apprehension. "I don't know what that means! Mom and dad, Annette, Juan, Arthur, and Michael can see you too if you come home. We all miss you and want you to come back. Please come back Billy!" I felt the tears flow as I begged my brother not to leave me. Everywhere I went I felt safe because in my heart I thought I could call him, and he would save me. "Remember I love you and always have. Don't forget about school, you have to go. You're smart, stop getting into so much trouble. I'm sorry for all the things I did to you that weren't very nice." "Where are you going?" I was on the edge of a full-blown panic attack. I was clinging to him trying to stop him from going. Don't go! Don't go! I want to go with you!!! I was crying and screaming at the top of my lungs, I was in agony. I felt Billy's hand let go of mine and I cried, and I cried, and

I cried. I wanted to die with him. I knew he was leaving us. I felt alone in a great chasm of darkness.

The last image I remember from that dream was the Conductor looking at me and at my brother, chilling. He was looking at us at the same time as if he had two sets of eyes. I watched Billy's blood dripping from his heart into the Conductor's hand. I felt a shiver. For the first time I stared back at him, and we locked eyes. I knew I couldn't escape the Conductor, but I also knew that I wanted to fight him, not run away from him. I didn't know how but I knew I would. I ran as fast as I could in the rain. I felt a gentle hand on me as if it had my entire being wrapped in fingers of white. "Do what your brother is asking you to do. All of humanity pays for what it does through the generations. It's a continuum. In that continuum all of it is one. You are but one in a series of many. Your journey back will make sense as you grow older. Where you are is bigger than the people around you. They are but a small link in the chain of time. I know you can't understand this yet, but if you pay attention, you will."

I could hear voices calling me through the dark fog. "Santiago, wake up!" I could hear the voice trying to break through. The voices sounded worried. "Go get your grandpa, hurry up!" I could feel hands shaking me, talking to me. I recognized a voice, strong yet gentle, my mom was there with me. "What's going on over here?" I started to come back to my life. I was shivering and crying and yelling, "Billy, Billy, Billy, don't go!" My grandpa was sitting on my bed. "Billy is okay. I got a letter from him yesterday."

My grandpa was talking to me in Spanish telling me that sometimes people visit us from the spirit world and that maybe that is what was happening to me. "It doesn't matter what we do, there are some things we can't control." I felt myself sit up and I had uncontrollable spasms coming from deep inside of me. "Here, have some water and let's go outside." As my mom was walking me out, I saw my dad standing in the doorway to his room with a look of disappointment. I had seen that look before. "Nothing has happened to Billy, he's too tough. Those slant eyes aren't good enough to hurt him." I saw him turn and walk away. I felt weak but deep down inside I knew that what I had gone through with my brother was true, he was gone. I would never be the same. A new chapter in my life had begun. Many would pay the price for my pain and my anger. As I walked, it started to rain.

Chapter | 34

BROKEN HEART

The fog rolled into Plieku Province in South Vietnam. It was time for Billy's platoon to recon the area north of their base camp. The fog was thicker than usual. It reminded him of a long time ago when Santiago had followed him to the spot where the train used to run through their property in El Guache. His journey had been a challenge, his life emphasized how easily a life could turn based on the accumulation of small choices. His choices had all been in a fog, as if he was aboard a force that had swept him away. Away from his home and all the people he loved and who loved him. He thought of a poster he had seen once. The devil was standing with a pitchfork made of steel with knives pointing to the sky. The devil was menacing and had a smile on his pointy chinned face and blazing eyes. The devil's ears were short like the knife prongs on the pitchfork, his tail flowed like a lasso. The poster had a caption that read, "PAY ME NOW...OR PAY ME LATER." "I guess I'm paying now, or is this later?"

He had finally worn down his parents, they relented and signed the papers so he could enlist at age 17. What had he been thinking? His hard headedness and poor understanding had brought him to the jungle of death. He didn't understand why they were there. All he understood was that since he had arrived here the Vietcong kept trying to kill him and he kept trying to kill them. He had stopped counting how many had fallen because of his ability to hit what he shot at.

At first, he felt bad, but as he spent more time, he just became numb. He knew it was kill or be killed. He remembered the words a Drill Instructor had used to train the recruits. "You've heard it said that there is no greater honor than to die for your country. I say make the other son-of-a-bitch die for his." His thoughts kept going back to this, realizing every day that maybe he had killed before. Images of Felix laying in the dirt road of El Guache came back. Rumors had it that he was brain dead and that his mom was nursing him. In a way he had killed Felix. He didn't think about why anymore. Now it was all about how he would survive and make it home.

It was a bone chilling and muggy morning. He felt it in his bones and in his soul. The rain reminded him of El Gordo. The killing, butchering, and eating of El Gordo had sparked something in him. In love there is pain and sometimes the people that are supposed to love you and protect you are the source of the pain. As a member of the Third Marines, Billy often led the platoon into battle. He had shown an uncanny ability to smell out the enemy. "Hey Martinez, what's for breakfast? You better feed us if you're going to lead us!" Corporal Harris loved the 'Biscochitos', the sweet cinnamon cookies that Billy received in the mail from his family in New Mexico, they arrived like clockwork. Even when they arrived broken, they were in high demand. Mom continued to send them and got other family members to do the same.

"I want some of them cookies Señor Martinez! We will need our energy today. Rice Paddy Daddies are out in force. I hate those gooks and don't know why I was sent here to kill them. They never did anything to me. Hell, I had never heard of Vietnam! Look around, the majority of us are black and Hispanic. I love America, but she doesn't love me. I wish I could have run to Canada like the rich white boys, but no money bro. This is a rich man's war and poor minority man's fight. I Love it!" Corporal Harris was always cracking jokes but there was an honesty embedded in those jokes. He made you laugh, think, love, hate, and regret all at the same time.

Corporal Harris was from St. Louis, Missouri, Misery as he called it. He had grown up in one of the most violent ghettos in the city. Corporal Harris was a strong black man, ripped and ready to fight. He had a reputation for his ability to survive the bungle in the jungle. He had taken Billy under his wing. "How old are you? You look like a boy, what happened mama kick you out?" They had been tight ever since Billy arrived in country and he kept calling Billy out teasing him and teaching him. Corporal Harris had survived more engagements than anyone else in the unit. He had seen young men come and go. "They came by helicopter and leave by helicopter in a body bag."

This had become Corporal Harris' remark every time they flew the dead out. Corporal Harris had been a hard-core gang banger and was surprised at how the Marines had taught him that he wasn't all that. "I'm serious, do you have any of those biscochitos? Man I love those things!" Billy walked over and handed him a few laughing at how he always mispronounced the name. "You better learn how to say it right bro or you won't get anymore." Billy had come to love and respect him. They had come from two different worlds and now lived and shared the same one.

"Hey, how about me Devil Dog? I'm a Martinez too!" This Private Martinez was from East Los Angeles and like most of the young men and boys serving in the Marines, came from a tough environment. Billy laughed at him every time he told someone where he was from, it wasn't East Los Angeles, it was 'EastLos'. "I only have a few more." "Why do you share with the black brother and not with your brown brother?" Billy relented and gave him a couple. Some of the other Marines that were close enough to hear the exchange called out wanting some. Billy had to ignore them, the bischochitos connected him to home and he wouldn't give them all away. The cookies were a staple of the

Spanish settlers in New Mexico, especially during the holidays. As he ate them the memories of the mouthwatering aroma of home came to life. Memories of his mom in the kitchen mixing them, fixing them, and cooking them. As he remembered, it filled his heart with joy and sadness. It made him question, again, why he had forced the issue to enlist and follow his friend Frankie that was nowhere to be seen.

"You're new in country little brother!" Corporal Harris had spoken to him when their relationship had started. "Me, I'm halfway home. All we have to do is survive the bad enemy, who like us, are fighting a war for others because they are poor and seen as expendable. I heard that a politician, I don't remember his name, when confronted with the statement 'why did this country have the poor Hispanics and Blacks fighting a rich white man's war and what was he going to do to solve the problem responded that sending us over here to die was not the problem, it was the solution. Getting us off the street reduced crime. Now as to our survival, don't ever forget that The Vietcong can smell us in the bush. The humidity brings out the scent of our diet through our sweat. Eat as much fish as you can, that's their diet. When you go into the jungle go with the flow. You have to become one with it to survive it. If not, it will take you and make you part of it forever."

The survival lessons continued into the night. "The jungle has its own language, walk slow and pay attention to anything that is out of place. Listen for the silence, it means that something has quieted the wildlife. Flow like water, don't you be the force that silences it. The enemy will wait and pounce like a tiger. Watch out for the growth that looks different. Look for disturbances in the dirt and growth around you, if it looks different, that is where the land mines are. Look for depressions in the ground, it might be an entrance to the underground tunnels they use to move undetected. Look at the leaves, if they have droplets and its quiet, it's probably agent orange. Stay away from that shit bro. They say it's safe, maybe for them, they aren't out in the shit."

The lessons had gone on and on. Billy wrote home in his letters about how Corporal Harris was teaching him how to survive. His letters made his mom happy, dad not as much. I could see it on their faces as they read the letters to us. My dad was skeptical, especially when he found that Billy was trusting a black man with his life. The only blacks he had come in contact with were incarcerated and he viewed them all the same. There weren't that many in New Mexico. Billy had come to love Corporal Harris. Billy finally had a big brother.

Billy was thinking about what to write in his letters to his brothers, especially to Santiago. Billy came to realize that he had been a bit rough with him. Thoughts of his visit home from boot camp filled his mind. He had spent most of it somewhere else, Española. He had received a Meritorious Promotion out of boot camp due to firing Expert at the range, maxing his physical fitness program, and serving as the guide for the platoon. The Guide was the recruit up front leading the Platoon through its drills and carried the platoon's identification flag. The guide held the flag straight and high creating unit pride and loyalty as it became a symbol of the unit and reminded the recruits of what they were becoming, Marines. It was a leadership position and highly sought after.

"Martinez, where did you learn to fire a weapon?" Drill Instructor Waters had asked? He was tough and prided himself on the fact that his mother was Mexican. Was that why he was tougher on Billy? "Get on your face!" These words were feared by the recruits, it meant you were about to do push-ups and bends-and-thrusts until you dropped. If you dropped, you did more for dropping. "How are you going to handle the enemy if you can't handle me?" The Drill Instructors constantly drilled this into their heads, body, and soul. That seemed like such a long time ago. He often thought he had fallen asleep and woken up in hell.

Once in country he looked back and realized boot camp was nothing compared to what was going on in country. Vietnam was primal. Life was precious and death was its enemy and was always staring it in the face. Billy missed home, he wondered what Pat was doing. "Don't worry about your girlfriends or your wife, Jody is going to take good care of her!" The DI's repeated this often as well. Often times it was true as the long deployments resulted in broken marriages and broken hearts. This was a wake-up call to the future Marines, focus on your training if you want to survive, home will take care of itself.

Corporal Harris liked Private Martinez. He reminded him of his younger brother who had been killed by a rival gang in the Central West End neighborhood. "Hey Martinez, what did you do that they took your rank, that's fucked up man. What little they give they find a way to take it back. A fellow Marine mentioned that you were promoted out of boot camp but here you are, back to Private." Billy didn't like to talk about it. He remembered, before sharing it with his brother in arms. When he was on leave after boot camp it was different. The Drill Instructors had made it clear that the grunts, foot soldiers, were the first to go. "I know I'm not coming back mom. Marines like me, poor and high school dropouts go to the front lines. Our Drill Instructors told us that most of us won't survive." Billy knew in his heart that it was true.

Billy spoke it out loud to his mom, but he really was trying to come to terms with it. What if this was the last time he would see his loved ones? "I know my son, that's why I didn't want you to enlist. I relented after your continued persistence and trouble with the law. We picked the lesser of two evils. I hope we chose right. The thing is, with the way you were living you could have died on the streets here. I believe our death is already determined by God, the best we can do is to serve him before we go. We are all proud of you my son, and we pray every day that you come back."

Billy saw his home differently now, he felt like an outsider. Even though he spent his time with his friends and a little with his family, he was different. He remembered the look on their faces when he did rifle drill. He did the trick moves, kicking the rifle on the butt and spinning the weapon around, handling it like a cheer leader handled a baton. He had seen the look in their eyes, he knew in his heart that this could be the last time he saw them. He took solace in the fact that they respected the Marine he had become.

Billy looked at Corporal Harris and began to tell his story. "When I was on leave from boot camp getting ready to go to jungle training, it dawned on me that I would not see my home, family and friends ever again. I remember the last day there. I had contacted the local National Guard and they just happened to have a convoy passing in front of my parents' home on highway 14. They agreed to pick me up. My little brother, the pest, walked with me across the field to the highway. I could feel his sadness. I saw tears rolling down his face. His sadness was making me sad. "Go back little brother, I'll see you next time I'm home. I remember his words like if it was yesterday. "I don't want you to go, I want to go with you." "Where I'm going you can't go. Remember what I've been telling you about school. You're smart, don't make me come home and kick your ass. As I walked away, I didn't look back. I didn't want Santiago to see me cry. Those steps are the longest and heaviest I have ever taken. I asked for this even though everyone tried to talk me out of it. 'You're only seventeen' they all kept saying, yet here I am."

Corporal Harris responded, "You're lucky my brother, you have a family to go back to. When I left St. Louis, there was no one there to see me off. When I went home, I couldn't wait to get out of there. My homies had been my family for a long time, through the violence, the drugs, the chicks, and the cops. They were the only family I had. My mom partied and was never around and when she was, she was high on drugs and booze. I couldn't stand to be around her, especially when she brought the fools home." Corporal Harris spoke with a voice that showed no emotion. He had come to terms with it. "I won't go back to that! I saw through the bullshit when I was there. No way I can go back to that."

Corporal Harris told anyone that would listen, "If I can survive Central West End, I can survive this. Those bloods in the hood don't play. The Drive-byes remind me of the ambushes over here. The Vietcong do have some badass weapons and tactics, all that means is that I have to up my game." Corporal Harris talked out loud into the jungle but in the deep recesses of his soul he knew that very few Grunt Marines made it home. Thirteen months was a long time to be in the jungle with people trying to kill you. He came to relish the few times they were given a few days to recuperate.

Those times were the best they would see while in Vietnam. They went into the Ville and enjoyed the local cuisine! The young Vietnamese prostitutes were in high demand. The race was on to get there early and pick the best, although in the end it didn't matter. They all craved human contact that was free of violence and provided a small reprieve from the reality of war. There was danger lurking as some of the young women were used as bait to attract, rob, and sometimes kill the young Marines. Corporal Harris had taught the ropes to Martinez. They stood guard as each took their turn, Corporal Harris usually went first.

Billy continued reliving those painful days. "I reported to Camp Lejeune early and hung out on base, eating good chow, going into town, relaxing before advanced infantry training. The whole time I was there I was scared and lonely. I knew it wouldn't be long before I was in the suck, Vietnam." They continued their discussion. "Anyway, I didn't want to be there, so I went AWOL. I didn't care. I was being a dumb ass. I thought I could get away, who cared about me? I hitched all the way back to New Mexico. When I got there, everyone was surprised to see me." As they talked Billy could feel the damp fog creeping into his bones. No matter what he wore the cold and heavy wet Vietnam air seeped in, he could feel rain droplets floating in the air. A Marine from Portland, Oregon called it liquid Sunshine.

"It was crazy bro. As soon as I got there everybody started asking me questions. "What are you doing, the MPs are going to come for you!" We partied everyday bro. I was acting like it was my last day on earth. I didn't want to come over here bro! I regret every day now even though I would do it again if I could. I wish I was there now. All it did was worry everyone that knew me. My time with my girl made it worth it. As soon as she saw me, she lit up like a luminaria." "What the hell is a lumiario?" Billy forgot he was talking to a brother from St. Louis and laughed at the mispronunciation. "It's a huge bonfire that is lit on Christmas Eve in New Mexico. It's a Spanish tradition that's part of the way we celebrate Christmas." "Sounds cool little brother maybe I can visit someday." "Anyway, my girl and I spent a lot of time together, the best in my life. I miss her! I have to get out of here and make it home, we are going to get married."

Billy got quiet for a moment. He could see Pat's smile and feel her warm body against his. They had made love a few times whenever they could find a private place during his stolen time. It had been wonderful for both of them. He remembered Pat's compassion and yearning, "I love you Billy, please come back to me." "Don't worry I will, I love you too. Here I bought this when I finished boot camp, it's real gold." Pat took the ring and started to cry. "I can't take this, it's yours." The ring was a Marine Corps class ring with an emerald in the center. The emerald was Billy's Birthstone. US Marine Corps surrounded the stone. There was an eagle globe and anchor on the sides. Pat said it was the most beautiful thing she had ever seen or been given. She did not know that it had cost him almost a month's pay. The young lovers laid in each other's arms for hours, sometimes without saying a word. They were joined for life now and they both knew and felt it.

Billy remembered a discussion the young lovers had shared. "You have to go back Billy even though I want you to stay. I heard my dad talking to my uncle. He was telling him that they are going to throw you into prison and label you a deserter. I heard them talking and I got in trouble when I yelled at them. 'He's not a deserter he just wanted to be with me one more time before he went to war'! My dad turned on me in front of my uncle, it made me even madder. 'Get out of here and never talk to me like this again'! My dad was really mad at me, but I don't care. I love you and I don't care what anyone says. I'll be waiting for you when you get back." "The time with her was magical and tragic at the same time bro!" Billy was laughing with Corporal Harris. "I'm like Jethro from the Beverly Hill Billy's, I'm an eighth-grade graduate."

"As soon as the MP's showed up looking for me my dad took me up into the mountains and hid me. Every other day he would deliver food and let me know what was going on. "Your gonna have to go with them. You wanted the Marines so now you have it. The State Police, the Sheriff, and City Police are all on the look-out. They will find you. The longer you stay out here the worse it's going to be when they do." "I know dad, I'm sorry for all of this, I just know I'm not coming back. I wanted to spend a little more time with all of you. Tell my brothers and Annette that I love them and that I'll see them in a year."

This was the closest Billy had felt with his dad in a long time. "Don't worry you'll make it back, just do like I showed you. You're the best at everything you do, just be careful and keep your head down." "My dad never told my brothers what was happening. I was worried about them especially Santiago, the sensitive one. Eventually my dad convinced me to give myself up. I knew the gig was up. The trip back was the longest of my life. They let me ride without chains. I guess they saw I wasn't going to be a problem. They court-martialed me and took my rank and restricted me to base. Now here I am brother, tracking gooks and ducking!" They both started to laugh, they were glad to have each other.

The moment of peace was shattered! Boom, Boom, Boom, rat-a-tat-tat, "incoming, incoming!!!" The base camp came to life as fire was returned into the jungle. It was a common practice to receive mortar and rifle fire from the enemy. The attacks would come at all hours of the day and night. The Vietcong were masters at hit and run. Sergeant Baca was walking the perimeter barking orders. "Get your gear ready, we are going out to find those pieces of oriental shit and kill every one of them." Rat-a-tat-a-tat, rat-a-tat-a-tat, the sound of the return fire was a constant to the Marines. In an instant they were all in their predefined positions peppering the jungle with a barrage of heavy machine gun, M-16, and mortar fire.

Their Captain was on the phone requesting air support which more often than not did not show up or showed up late. The exchange was short and was over as quickly as it started. They were familiar with the extreme boredom followed by the intense death raining through the air. The extremes caused a lot of Marines psychological issues. You could hear it in the aftermath. The hatred of the enemy and the desire for revenge for their comrades who lost their lives for a war became normal for them.

Sergeant Baca was still walking around keeping the Marines focused. By stressing the Marine Corps' attention to detail and adherence to the strict personal hygiene requirements, he kept their minds busy. This kept the Marines focused to avoid the setting in of extreme feelings caused by the constant threat of death. Sergeant Baca was from San Antonio, Texas and had grown up in the cultural shadow of the Alamo. He was a good Marine and amazed those he led with his ability to face heavy fire on his feet yelling out to his Marines. "Let's go Marines, time to get to work. Martinez, you've got point!" "Hey Martinez, what's for breakfast?" The cat calls started. It was a ritual that lightened the mood in the fog that enveloped them more often than not.

The fog came to represent the ever-present presence of the enemy. They were hard to see as they blended in with their home, the jungle. "If you're going to lead us you have to feed us!" The verbal therapy continued. Billy gave it as good as he got. "Yeah, open up a C-Ration and eat some beans. I've seen you shoot. You're better off farting in their direction, the way you stink it up they'll run for cover!" As usual the Marines getting ready to go out and kill and possibly get killed laughed in unison and piled on whoever was the object of their humor. You could feel the tension as they got ready to go out and recon, find, engage, and kill the enemy.

As the platoon moved slowly through the thick growth Billy could hear the life noises. As he moved, he was aware of the snub-nosed monkeys swinging through the canopy, babbling their warnings. He knew that if they became overactive there was something in the jungle they did not trust. The direction of their movement was an indicator to him, a sign pointing in the direction of the disturbance. Right now, it was them.

Billy had come to know the species of animals that lived in the jungle, the apes, tigers, birds, elephants, bears, water buffalos, pythons, and myriad of other life creatures that surrounded him. Billy loved to watch the Great Hornbill as it flew in search of food, safety, and a mate. Billy often wished he could be one and fly away. It's strange curvature bills and mane created the illusion of three yellow curved scythes like the one Billy had grown up using to cut the alfalfa glistening between the trees in the orchard. It's multicolored wings, white wing tips and tail feathers made it easy to spot. Its call was like no other bird he had experienced. It was magical to him. He wanted to fly like the Hornbill anywhere out of this jungle of death. How different it was from his home. He had to remind himself to stay alert and integrated with his surroundings. His life and those of his Marine brothers depended on it. As they crept forward Billy heard the silence and ruffling up ahead. He held up his hand and his platoon stopped and lowered themselves and got ready to engage. Every sound, every movement, escalated their collective awareness.

"What do you think? I felt it too, maybe you need to go forward and check it out. We'll wait here." Sergeant Baca respected this young Marine. Martinez, of all the Marines under his command, was the best. He had a way of finding and engaging the enemy that was abnormally brave and bordered on the reckless. Before he got a response, Billy was on his way, prowling through the jungle fauna. Billy was low, looking through gaps in the growth and when necessary, he would raise his head just enough to see what lay in front of him. He could hear his heart beating. He enjoyed living on the edge. His violent upbringing had prepared him for the challenge.

He felt responsible for saving those following him. Through his tour of duty, he couldn't shake flash backs of crying, pleading, crashing, hitting, slamming, and all the other sounds of a home being destroyed by the patriarch who was supposed to be protecting his home. This was a higher level of that violence. He loved his father but hated him even more, there were times he had wanted to kill him. He chose the streets instead. In an instant he spotted movement and a pair of eyes peering through the growth. He felt a presence all around him. Everything in his body was alive. He got ready to engage. His finger tightened the trigger of his M-16. He remembered the Platoon that was waiting on him a football field behind him, he started a slow backward crawl.

"There's gooks right in front of us, 100 yards or so. They are waiting for us. I couldn't get close enough to see how many." Billy was breathing hard. "Let's pull back and come up with a game plan." Sergeant Baca called his platoon together and discussed their situation. "Set up the mortars on the edge of that clearing. Radio base and let them know we are ready to engage an enemy of unknown size and that we are requesting air support." In an instant all hell broke loose. The sound of Russian AK-47's and Chinese Mortars erupted. The transformation of the jungle was instantaneous with dirt, leaves, and dead bodies strewn throughout. The Marines took cover and started returning fire.

The Mortar crew and machine gun crew were at it. It felt as if the battle raged on for an eternity. Billy was crawling forward when he came face to face with a young Vietcong. There was a moment of hesitation as the two looked at each other as if they were looking into a mirror. Both were 18 and if they would have met outside of hell, they could have been friends. The young Vietnamese had a similar background, poor, abused, and helpless. Billy's heart sank as he saw the young boy's head explode from the concussion of Billy's fired round. Kill or be killed!

Billy heard the helicopter gunships approach the scene and was grateful as the jungle in front of him was set ablaze. The Vietcong and North Vietnamese Regulars started to withdrew. As he swung around, Sergeant Baca looked at him as a mortar exploded nearby. All Billy saw was the flash as Sergeant Baca was blown to bits. Billy felt the pulse as the atmosphere covered him in dirt and the dead Marines blood. He was tempted to run to him, but the battle raged on, and he knew it was too late. He always got the feeling that every time his fellow Marines died someone was watching the carnage and, in some way, causing it. Why did it happen? He didn't understand the forces behind it. The more time he spent in combat the stronger his feelings of helplessness and anger for both sides grew.

The Gunships had done their job. The enemy had retreated leaving the dead and wounded behind. The battlefield was a buzz with medics responding to the calls for medical attention and fellow Marines comforting their comrades. He could see the darkness of death fall over them. Death had come and taken some away. "I must be going crazy! I keep seeing that face leering at me, mocking me. Where have I seen him before and why is he around every time I kill or watch someone die?" Billy was called back to reality by the call to move forward into the death zone of the enemy. He detested what would happen next.

"Curu toi, Curu toi!" A young Vietnamese boy was begging for mercy. "Save me, save me." Tears rolled down Billy's face as he looked down on the blood-spattered body of the young boy. Billy had seen enough death to know that the young Viet Cong Soldier would die. He felt the death of Sergeant Baca. As the vision of Sergeant Baca being blown to bits came to him, he felt both pity and rage. His anger became the force that thrust the bayonet through the young Vietnamese boy's heart. The boy looked up at him and smiled. Billy looked on as life drifted up from the corpse. He felt the freedom of it wondering if he would meet the same fate.

As he continued through the silent death zone, those that were in a similar condition received the same release. Those that had frozen under the blanket of death and surrendered were rounded up and transported to base camp where they were transferred to the POW camps. The toll to the Marines was heavy. The brotherhood, the Devil Dogs, Leathernecks, Jar Heads survived for each other and their fallen comrades. Reinforcements arrived and a camp was set up and preparations were made to pursue the forces that had ambushed them. The perimeter was set, the password was shared, and the dead and wounded were evacuated. It was a long silent night. They knew tomorrow was going to be a long day.

Chapter | 35

THE SILVER STAR FLIGHT HOME

"How are you holding up Billy?" Corporal Harris had set up next to Billy. "You did good today little brother you saved a lot of lives. Too bad about Sergeant Baca, he was a good Marine. That dude was crazy! I told him to duck every now and then. Very few heroes survive. Not me, I want to go back stateside, time for some loving for this Marine. That was scary, there were too many of them! I've seen it before; the Vietcong were not alone this time. Did you notice all the North Vietnamese Regulars? Like the Captain shared with us the other day, there has been a lot of activity on the Ho Chi Minh Trail, they're coming by the thousands. Let them come, I got something for their ass."

Corporal Harris grabbed his nut sack and laughed into the night. Billy laughed with him but didn't have anything to say. The laughter sounded hollow masking the fear they all felt. "Well good night Devil Dog. Remember what I've always told you. Keep your dick hard and your powder dry." And just like that Billy was asleep. His sleep was restless. His dreams took him back to all the things he had done knowing they were wrong as he did them. The promise of good things through the alcohol, the drugs, the women, and the violence had delivered misery. He had been tricked by a force larger than life. A power ancient and dark had made promises it never meant to keep. Billy wept in his sleep, the Conductor's face grinning as he reached down and touched Billy's heart. He owned it and would soon claim it like all the others that been promised heaven only to receive hell. Billy's ancestors had been soldiers like himself. His legacy had been written eons ago.

Billy was awoken by the sound of M-16 fire and loud voices in the dark. "He didn't give the password! He didn't give the password!" The base camp was in turmoil as all the Marines scrambled to their assigned battle formations. Billy slept in his gear, so he was up in an instant. He grabbed his weapon and fell into his foxhole and took up his position. He waited for Corporal Harris to join him and when he didn't, he was puzzled. That wasn't like him. In an instant Billy realized that the fire he had heard came from within their encampment. "Please don't let it be Corporal Harris!" Billy cried out into the night as he crawled out of his foxhole and moved towards the chaos in the night. "Medic get over here, we have a Marine Down! Get over here, now!!!" The orders rang in the night. The Marines realized it was another incident of friendly fire. It was well known that several combat deaths were caused by friendly fire, some by accident and some to save lives by removing idiots that kept leading Marines to their death by their bad decisions. The high level of tension, especially in the bush, tended to make everyone trigger happy.

As Billy moved closer to the downed Marine, he saw that it was his loyal friend and brother Corporal Harris. Billy walked away like a zombie. He didn't want to get too close. He didn't want to deal with the death that was taking a piece of his life with it. "No, no, no!!!" Billy fell to the ground and wept as he punched the ground beneath him. Months of enduring the nightmares of combat came out in a flood of emotions. "Why did I ever come here? Everyone tried to talk me out of it, but I insisted! The story of my life, 'mi vida', one fuck up after another!" Billy was chastising himself for being part of the death all around him.

Corporal Harris had become like a brother to him. Billy swore to the heavens that the enemy would pay, there was no other way. "Get up Marine and get back to your post." The Platoon commander knew the pain of a Marine surrounded by dead brothers. He was known for being tough, he knew he had to be. He watched as the Marines under his command went out day in and day out and faced the enemy as their comrades died in their arms and the enemy died in their sights. Billy was up and back to his post. His heart had hardened, and the value of his life had diminished with the death of Corporal Harris. Billy got on his feet and wiped the tears off his face, ashamed to be seen that way. "Don't ever forget Martinez, Marines die but the Marine Corps will live forever. You will get your shit together and tomorrow we get some payback." The Platoon Commander walked away into the cold dark Vietnamese night.

In the morning, the Marines prepared to go into the jungle. The orders had come down that they were to proceed up a nearby canyon and determine the presence of the Vietcong and the size of the force. Once again Billy was point man and slowly and methodically wove his way through the thick jungle. He felt very uneasy, he could feel an aura around him, it was surreal. He could see himself in his mind's eye as if he was looking through liquid glass. As he moved, images flashed before him, his family, his friends, and happier times at home. Corporal Harris' death was weighing heavy on his heart, his life had been a flash in a pan. He remembered El Gordo, his pet pig, the love he had for him and the deep sadness when El Gordo had become meat in the center of a cultural celebration that went back in time for generations.

Images of his first love, his first beer, his first joint, and all the firsts he had experienced in a short period of time wove simultaneously through every fiber of his being. Somehow, he knew his life would be cut short, another first. He had done a lot of living in a short time. At eighteen he was fighting for his life, his family, and his fellow Marines.

He felt bad, remembering the way he had treated Santiago, his loyal little brother. "I'm glad I told my parents that if anything happened to me, they were to use the military provided insurance and send him to St. Michaels High School and take him out of the street mix." Billy's lips weren't moving, it was as if he was talking to himself, a Billy on the other side of the liquid glass was listening.

Corporal Harris had gone off to use the restroom in the dark. The protocol was to alert the Marine Sentry that you were going to the field latrine and were required to use a password when you came back. According to the Sentry, Corporal Harris walked back without speaking the password at which point the sentry opened fire killing him. Billy did not believe it. Corporal Harris was a squared away Marine. They had seen heavy action all day and spent most of the night setting up camp. This had left them all tired and on the edge.

Private Jones was known to be a bit of a slacker in the execution of his assigned duties. Billy had heard other Marines talk about the possibility that Jones might get taken out by friendly fire to protect them from disasters due to his negligence. It was bad enough to have the enemy attacking you at every opportunity, but to have your brothers die because a fellow Marine was sloppy, was intolerable. Private Jones had made a terrible mistake. Billy had watched as his friend was covered with a poncho. Harris would join his dead brothers tomorrow on the way back to the world. Their families would mourn and question why their loved ones were being slaughtered in a country they had never heard of. Billy remembered his friend telling him he had no one to go back to, the streets of St. Louis had consumed them all. "Don't worry brother, I'll be there in spirit. I love you bro! These assholes will pay."

Billy hadn't slept that night he could see the eyes of the Vietcong watching them, waiting for them. The life sounds came to him, softening the blow of his brother as if Corporal Harris' spirit had been released and absorbed by the canopy of life. Billy saw the face of the young Vietnamese soldier and saw the look on his face as the round from the M-16 penetrated the top of his head. One minute you're here and in a flash you're gone. Watching his comrades and the enemy die was becoming common place. Billy wondered where the dead went. What was there when they got to the other side. He wondered how each of their lives were, who were they leaving their memories with? Did they have a girlfriend? Were they married? Did they have kids? Questions kept passing in front of him. He felt sad in his heart he knew them all, they were him and he was them. In the Marines they were all green and they were all killers.

They were back in the jungle. It felt comfortable in a strange way. As he cautiously moved forward, he was surrounded by the liquid glass. The ebb and the flow were alive! Everything was part of it. Billy stopped and motioned his platoon. He had been here before, was this ever going to end? Billy spotted 4 enemy soldiers in front of them who employed machine gun and small arms fire. After Billy's platoon received reinforcements, they received the order to move forward and investigate the action. As the platoon moved up a hill, they were hit extremely hard with rocket and mortar fire from three sides. The canyon they had been following had taken them right into an ambush.

Billy with complete disregard for his safety unhesitatingly maneuvered through the impact area, laying down a base of deadly counter fire at the hostile force to detain the enemy long enough for his platoon to establish a hasty defense and quickly tend to their wounded. Billy was not thinking about what he was doing. He had become someone else, someone who didn't want to see any more of his brothers die. Corporal Harris' death had a huge impact on him, as did his dreams of home and all the people he had let down. He would not let them down again. Billy stopped for a moment to catch his breath. "You want some, you gook eyed motherfucker, here comes some."

Billy was up and moving again. He could feel his movements as if he was floating in air. He could see, hear, and feel everything. He felt at home in the moment as if this was where he was meant to be, he was saving fellow Marines. He repeatedly exposed himself to ferocious enemy fire. As his platoon started to move downhill, he spotted one of his comrades who was wounded and bleeding into the jungle. "Don't worry brother, I've got you!" "Billy, you have go! Get out of here! I'm gone bro! Just do me a favor." "What is it?" Billy had a sense of urgency as he spoke. "Tell my family I love them!" Billy immediately started to administer badly needed first aid. After applying field dressings Billy gradually moved the wounded Marine down the hill, then it went white. Blinding light with red swirls had him in its grip. He fought it but the fire was consuming him like gasoline being poured into flames.

Billy was laying on his back, he felt the release from the blinding light. The rain had started and was cool against his skin. He was back in El Guache surrounded by his friends and family who were laughing as El Gordo lovingly threw him in the stinky mud and shoved mud at him with his snout. "Man, what a beautiful day that was." His life flashed in front of him. It was peaceful, the good was vivid in his life's flashback. Billy's sojourn back through time was different. As he looked up, he could see the blue through the jungles coat of green and the mist of the Asian rain. He could feel his spirit yearning, wanting to fly into that blue. From the blue into the black.

When he was done reliving his life, he knew that he needed to say goodbye to those that he loved the most. His spirit visited them one at a time and found himself with Santiago, his heart was breaking one last time. "Hey bro, it's nice to see you. You've grown up since I saw you last." Billy could see the joy of Santiago blended in with the beauty of the Sangre de Christo mountains, the Rio Grande Valley, and the jungles of Vietnam. "Don't worry about coming with me, your time has not come yet. I want you to focus on getting an education. I love you little brother. Thank you for always loving me. I have to go now." Billy knew and felt that his spirit had pulled apart from his body. His visit was spiritual. In an instant he was wrapped in white and didn't care when the figure of the Conductor broke through. He knew the Conductor would not get him; he had paid the price for all he had done. He looked down and saw the Conductor standing over his body with his dead heart in his hand. Billy smiled! He had escaped! Out of the corner of his spirit he saw Santiago looking at the Conductor with hate in his eyes. Then he smiled, "Run little brother, run!"

Billy was gone! He had returned to the spirit world from which he had come, the collective past. Santiago dreamt that night, the soothing voice comforted him. "Tomorrow your life will change, it will get more challenging. Learn from Billy, he paid and escaped. The Conductor has special plans for you. Pray for what you do, and for what you have done. The pieces of your legacy and that of your forefathers, rests on your shoulders. Life is a Continuum, and you are part of it. Humanity is but a small piece of it, the window through the liquid glass will reveal all, be careful Santiago." Santiago recognized the soft voice from his dreams. He walked into the living room and saw his mom and dad at the door talking to two Marines in Dress Blues. "We are sorry to have to inform you that your son, Private Billy Martinez is Missing in Action"

Chapter | 36

A PIECE OF 'MI VIDA'

Today I sat and talked to the ghosts from the past, brothers of brothers, fathers of sons, our mothers and sisters loving everyone. My life flashed before me, I tried to outlast, my spirit is hungry. I'm tired and empty of words across voids, littered with garbage and shadows that last, nobody listens their worlds hurry past. It dawned on me the load I have carried. I remember the love always tainted with pain. Cemeteries, jails and hospitals, the cross of love is heavy, laden with purpose unasked. I carried it with pain I carried it with love. Today I realize the weight of the load. I'm tired and I'm weary but I struggle ahead. The legacy of history I saw as it passed. I saw behind me a road strewn with the aftermath. A life given, not chosen, it came on like a blast, the continuum of my life moving fast. Out of a pistol fired in vain, it saw me in passing and gave me a name. A life as a witness, pain and agony fueled by love. Life made me grew into that name. El Guache born and El Guache raised, it flows through my veins. I still have the soul that they wore. American refined and honed, the anguish, horror, and pain. US Marines provided the frame, me, and my ghosts, are we truly the same? My brothers and I washed by the rain, the Asian Rain, the El Guache Rain, the cleansing of the pain, they knew not his name. He honored his enemy, he fought to his death embedded under the canopy. The National Cemetery in Santa

Fe, granite, silent and worn, silent sits, bearing witness to a Spaniard forgotten and forlorn. The voices of loved ones cried out in the night, some fueled by anger, some silenced by shame. The rain of sorrow, the rage in the cage, on a child not catered, left on his own, willing but lacking the skill to attain the promise given such a long time ago, his name. Be still until tomorrow, a new day will come, try to love it all as it follows the sun. It will touch us all yet waits for not a one. Tomorrow awaits, I will try to carry everyone that came before me, after all, they made me. Voices from the past cried out in agony and love today, one from below and one from above. Crying out in silence, my dad gave me his sin. Generational madness, child of a visitor dropped off and left to endure. Violence driven by fear, taught to our children, the need forgotten, with no replacement nearby. Turning on ourselves when there is no one left to fear. And yet I smile at my memories blowing through the trees and falling from the sky. In Santa Fe, the Cross of the Martyrs stands as a testimony to the Franciscan Friars long ago dead, a piece of 'mi vida'. The one truth I gathered is the stronger the pain, the stronger the love. I think I'll choose the one from above, silent and renewing. I lift my face in the rain as it washes away my pain.

In loving memory of A Piece of 'Mi Vida,' my brother.

About the Author

ERIC JAMES (SANTIAGO) MARTINEZ was born and raised in Santa Fe, New Mexico. The assimilation of his culture into mainstream America, both challenged him and inspired him to write about his experiences and challenges. The author has been writing his whole life; this is his first published work. James received his undergraduate degrees at the College of Santa Fe and the University of Albuquerque, and his master's degree from the University of New Mexico. His military service as a Non-Commissioned officer in the U.S. Marine Corps and as a Commissioned Officer in the U.S. Air Force has given him a unique perspective though which he came to understand the resiliency embedded in his culture and to understand the full spectrum of their contributions to his country.

www.ericsantiagomtz.com

Made in United States
Troutdale, OR
07/17/2023

11332899R00226